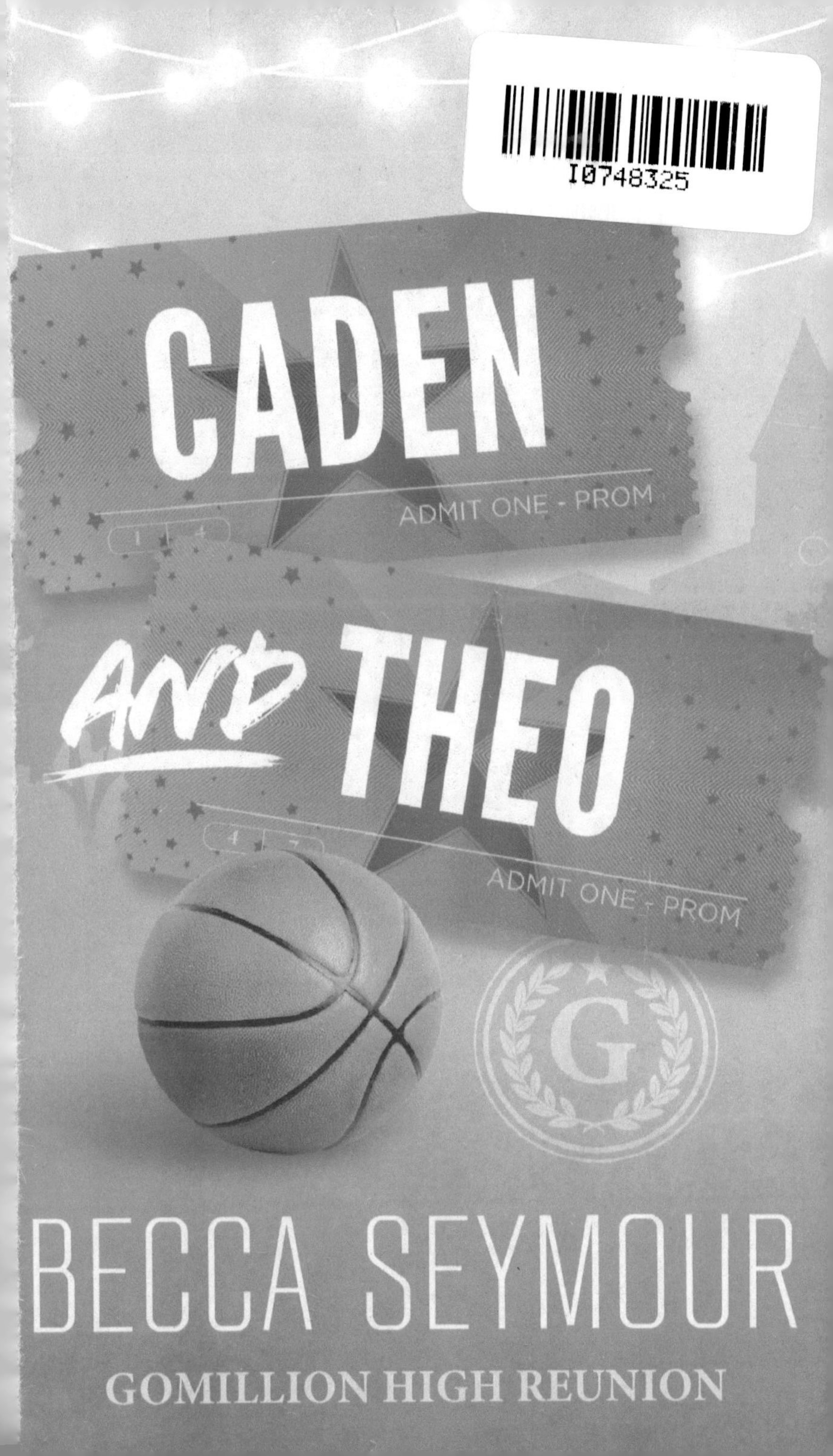
CADEN
ADMIT ONE - PROM
AND THEO
ADMIT ONE - PROM
G
BECCA SEYMOUR
GOMILLION HIGH REUNION

THEN

ONE

THEO

THE WORLD'S AGAINST ME, I SWEAR. I DON'T EVEN BOTHER rolling my eyes at the hyperbole this time. Me? Dramatic? Never. But this sucks.

It's the first official prom ever at Gomillion High, and unlike most other schools in South Carolina, ours decided to limit the event to seniors only. Meaning, as a junior, I'm left behind. Spectating. Watching my best friend get all dressed up for the night of his life while I sit here, sulking like a rejected promposal meme.

I'm on his bed, trying but epically failing to read *1984*. I'm pretending I'm chill, but I'm radiating "left-out little brother" energy, and I know it. Meanwhile, Caden's jabbering on about the event and Alice, his "date."

Did I mentally add air quotes around that word? Damn straight, I did.

Alice is fine. Nice, even. Friendly. But still—what the hell? Other people are going solo or rolling in squads, but Caden? No, he's gotta go with a date. And of course it had to be Alice, with her blemish-free Black skin, silky curls, giant eyes, and perfect teeth like she eats whitening strips for breakfast.

None of this is rational, I know. Jealousy never is.

I tell myself it's normal. I mean, I've known the guy since I was three. When his family moved in next door and our dads bonded over basketball, we became attached at the hip. Every day since has basically been one long Caden-and-Theo hangout. If friendship were a sport, we'd be championship-tier.

But if I'm being real—and I always am, even when I shouldn't be—I've been in love with him forever. Like, first-boner-during-a-water-fight kind of forever. My first wet dream? His garage gym. Him shirtless. Don't even get me started.

As for other firsts... if only.

"Theo, come help me with this tie. The damn thing keeps going crooked."

I close my book and swing my legs off the bed. Of course I'm going to help him. He's standing in front of his mirror, brow furrowed, mouth slightly open like he's concentrating extra hard. He's already dressed in a fitted black suit with gold-and-green accessories—our school colors—and I swear, the gold makes his dark brown skin glow like it's been kissed by literal sunbeams. He's so fine. Stupidly so.

"Geez, Cade, what did you do to this knot?" I mutter as I step close, fingers brushing against his collar.

"It looked right a minute ago," he says, grinning. "And now it looks like a sad pretzel."

I snort. "A pretzel that gave up on life halfway through the twist."

He grins wider. "You love me anyway."

Too much, probably.

"I tolerate you," I say instead, tightening the knot and smoothing it down. "There. Fixed. Try not to dance it crooked again."

"Only if my date can keep her hands off me," he says, turning back to the mirror.

I roll my eyes, flopping back onto the bed again.

He notices. Of course he notices.

Caden spins around, leaning against his dresser, arms crossed. "You're still mad I'm going, huh?"

I shrug. "It's whatever."

He frowns, and I hate that I made him frown. "You know if I could sneak you in, I would."

"I know," I mumble.

"I even tried to talk to Coach about it," he adds. "Told him my loner friend needed emotional support."

I laugh at that, despite the extra-hard thud of my heart that he cared enough to ask. "And Coach said?"

"He said, and I quote, 'Theo's too smart to risk suspension for some sparkly gym party.'"

"He's not wrong," I mutter, smiling despite myself.

There's a pause, and then Caden pushes off the dresser and grabs his blazer. "Look, you'll come to the after-party, though, right? Even if you can't be at prom, you're still part of the night. I want you there."

The words ease the tight knot of bitter jealousy in my chest just a little. "I dunno," I say, feigning nonchalance. "I might be too busy crying in my room. Alone. Watching *Love and Basketball* and eating marshmallow fluff straight from the tub."

"You'll ruin your pancreas," he says.

"You'll ruin prom if you don't stop checking yourself out in the mirror."

He flips me off, laughing. "You better be there."

"I'll think about it." Yeah, of course I'm full of shit, as I'll absolutely be there.

He grabs his cologne and sprays, making the room smell like citrus and warmth. Then he pauses and turns toward me. "Seriously, Theo. I hate that you can't come. You should be there. With me."

Something in the way he says it makes my heart stutter. I sit up a little straighter. "You'll survive," I say lightly because I can't afford to read too much into it. "Just don't let Alice drag you into one of those dance-offs. I swear, if I hear about you doing the Cha Cha Slide on the gym floor—"

"I'm a grown man," he says, puffing his chest out. "I don't slide. I glide."

I chuckle, tossing the mini basketball he keeps at the side of his bed at him. He catches it easily, then lobs it into the hoop mounted above his closet door. Swish. Because of course.

"You sure you don't want me to fake being your chauffeur? I could drive you and Alice, roll up the windows real slow, make everyone think you're rich and mysterious."

He laughs. "You offering to valet in your mom's Prius?"

"She's got seat warmers," I say. "Luxury."

There's a knock at the door, and then his mom's voice carries through, warm and lilting over the hum of gospel music drifting up from the kitchen. "Caden, sweetie! Alice is here—don't you keep that girl waiting now!"

He meets my eyes. "Guess that's my cue."

I stand. "Break a leg, superstar."

He heads toward the door, then hesitates before turning back. "You sure you're okay?"

Not even close.

"Yeah," I lie. "Go have fun."

He gives me one last look, then leaves.

When the door clicks shut behind him, the silence hits like a dunk to the chest. I flop backward on his bed, stare at the ceiling fan spinning lazily above, and let the jealousy simmer a little longer before I text him a simple message:

Me: Fine, I'll be there.

Because if I can't have the night of my dreams... at least I can still see him after.

And maybe—just maybe—that'll be enough.

THE AFTER-PARTY'S already in full swing by the time I pull up, and the bass is thumping like the heart of some mythical beast. Whoever's house this is—I think it's Shane Bailey's older cousin's place—has clearly made peace with the idea of their lawn being permanently wrecked. The driveway is packed with double-parked cars. Glowing string lights are draped over trees and balconies like a home décor magazine exploded.

Prom-goers in full glam are everywhere—satin dresses catching the breeze, bow ties hanging loose, glitter on cheeks, and the kind of electric energy only a "we survived high school" celebration can produce.

I'm not the only junior here. I clock a few familiar faces from my own class—Jonah, who's deep in a conversation with a girl who I think has actual rhinestones glued to her eyebrows, and Marissa and Lee sharing a plate of something suspiciously shaped like meatballs but somehow also glowing orange.

I wave at them, and a couple of people shout, "Theo! You made it!" at me in return as I make my way past the firepit and into the thick of the crowd.

I'm not really looking for anyone else, though. Not really. I'm looking for *him*. It doesn't take long.

Caden stands near the back patio, under a cluster of swaying string lights, laughing with the rest of the basketball team like they're in a *GQ* shoot disguised as a team reunion. They might as well be.

There's Cam, the quiet point guard, standing back and letting the others have the spotlight. Shane Bailey—the small forward—still rocking his prom tux jacket like it's a designer coat and not something from Men's Wearhouse. Ray Barker, our no-nonsense power forward with Mexican roots, is double-fisting soda and trying not to look impressed by anything. And towering over them all, Dale Rivers, the center, calm and imposing like always, with a deep voice that makes anything he says sound like it's coming from a wise mountain sage.

And in the middle of it all, there's *Caden*.

God, he looks… unfair.

The tailored black pants hugs him just right. That same gold-and-green tie I helped with is still perfectly knotted, and his jacket's tossed over one shoulder like he's a model who just finished a runway. His tight coils are shaped up clean, and the gold in his watch catches the light every time he lifts his hand to talk. He's laughing—bright and easy—and his smile does that thing where it spreads slow, like it's creeping across his whole face, until you can't help but smile too.

I look for Alice. She's not with him, thank God. I spot her a little ways off, perched on the arm of a patio couch, deep in conversation with a guy I don't recognize. He's got the kind of long hair that makes him look like he's either a poet or in a band—or both—and they look... cozy.

A stupid little grin pushes its way onto my face before I can stop it. I don't even feel bad about it. I just let myself have it.

I start toward the group, weaving through the crowd, and before I even say anything, Caden sees me.

His whole face lights up. "Theo!" he calls, sounding as if he wasn't sure I'd come, and the second I'm close enough, he loops his arm around my shoulders in a way that seems like instinct. Like it's where I'm supposed to be.

The rest of the team immediately shifts to make room, and just like that, I'm in. Doesn't matter that I'm a year younger. There's never been a space in Caden's life that I wasn't just... part of.

"Look who finally dragged himself out of his emo cave," Shane says, bumping my fist.

"Only took the promise of free pizza," I shoot back.

"Pizza and the chance to watch us recount the best night of our lives," Dale adds, grinning.

"Speak for yourself," Ray mutters. "My tux ripped during a slow dance. Full ass cheek out."

Cue a *lot* of laughter.

"No!" I say, choking on air. "Who saw?!"

"Everyone," Cameron intones, deadpan. "Everyone saw."

Caden's shaking with laughter beside me. "You should've heard the DJ. He just went 'Oops' and dropped the bass harder."

I'm laughing, too, even as that little pang stirs in my chest again. I missed this part—the inside jokes, the wild chaos, the buildup. The prom. But I'm here now. And Caden's arm is still around me, warm and firm, like I'm part of the story even if I skipped a chapter.

I glance up at him, and he's already looking down at me, eyes soft in the way that always makes my stomach flip. He gives my shoulder a gentle squeeze.

"You good?" he murmurs, low enough that only I can hear.

"Yeah," I lie. Then amend, "Mostly."

He nods like that's fair. Like he understands. And honestly, with him standing beside me, laughing with his team, tie still perfect... maybe that's enough for now. Maybe it has to be.

Caden shifts beside me and squeezes my shoulder once more before pulling his arm away. "I'm gonna get you a drink," he says, already stepping back. "You deserve at least one warm beer for showing up."

"Ooh, what a treat," I deadpan, but I follow him

anyway because where Caden goes, I go. That's just how it's always been.

We wind our way through the house, nodding and smiling at people as we pass. The party isn't wild—nobody swinging from chandeliers or anyone crying in a bathtub—just music pulsing through portable speakers, a low murmur of voices, and that undercurrent of end-of-an-era energy. The kind that makes everyone feel a little nostalgic and just drunk enough to believe they'll stay in touch after graduation.

There's a mix of people in every room—some seniors still dressed to impress, jackets off and heels abandoned, and plenty of juniors too. No one seems surprised to see me with Caden. If anything, a few offer friendly waves or shout, "Hey, Theo!" over the music.

Most of Gomillion is made up of good people. Sure, we've got our token jerks—your classic hallway terrors and lunchroom commentators—but we've learned how to steer clear. There's an unspoken rule: If someone's going to bring the drama, they don't get invited to the good stuff. So nights like this? Pretty chill.

We squeeze into the kitchen, where a folding table has been turned into a makeshift bar. It's stocked with half-empty bottles of soda, a bowl of questionable punch, and the holy grail of teen parties: a mountain of red Solo cups.

Caden grabs two and fills one from the keg tap with all the grace of someone who's watched other people do it often enough.

"Voilà," he says, handing it to me.

I sniff it. "Smells like regret."

He laughs. "Tastes like it too."

The beer's warm and vaguely metallic, like someone filtered it through a sock and left it on a windowsill for three hours. I drink it anyway. I'm not a drinker—neither of us really are. Caden's whole future depends on his body staying strong and clean. So no drinking, no smoking, no anything that could tank his game. By default, I follow his lead. Always have.

Still, it feels weirdly rebellious to be holding a drink tonight. Like I'm finally a part of something I usually watch from the sidelines.

We head back outside, where the air is cooler and easier to breathe. The backyard is dotted with groups of people, some clustered around the firepit, others lounging in conversation. Off to the side, there's a quiet corner with a couple of mismatched lawn chairs, slightly rusted but blessedly unoccupied.

Caden gestures toward them. "Our thrones."

We sink into them, the metal creaking a little under our weight. For a few minutes, we just sit there, side by side, sipping our drinks and watching the blur of movement around us. It's peaceful in that way parties sometimes are when you're not in the center of the chaos. When you get to be the observer instead of the event.

I turn to look at him. "So," I say, tilting my cup toward him, "how was it? Prom?"

He leans his head back, eyes closing for a second like he's pulling the night out of storage. "Honestly?" he says, cracking one eye open. "Pretty good."

"That's it? I've been salty all week for 'pretty good'?"

He laughs. "Okay, okay. The venue was actually nice. They had fairy lights and this weird indoor tree setup."

"I need more visuals," I say.

"There was a chocolate fountain."

"Ooh. That's five points already."

"Dirk danced with the librarian."

I nearly spit my beer. "Ms. Callahan? Of course it was Ms. Callahan—Dirk must have dog-eared too many paperbacks."

I know her way too well—I'm in the library so often she's practically memorized my reading habits. She slips me new releases before anyone else, but God help me if I return them late.

Caden grins. "Yup. He asked her as a joke, and she said yes very seriously. Then they waltzed. Like, full-on elegant twirls and everything. I think she might be in love with him now."

"I'm traumatized just hearing about it." And no doubt she'll tell me all about it next week when I pick up a book she special ordered for me.

"You're welcome."

I grin. "Was it weird without me there?"

He hesitates just a second too long before answering, "Yeah. It was."

Something fluttery and annoying flaps in my chest. I take another sip of beer just to give my hands something to do. "And Alice?" I ask, trying to sound casual.

He shrugs. "We danced once. Talked a bit. But she kinda paired off with this guy from the catering staff."

"Seriously?"

"Dead serious. He had one of those little bow ties and apparently plays acoustic guitar in his free time. She was gone like *that*." He snaps his fingers. "Honestly, I don't blame her. Guy had the whole 'tortured artist' vibe going on."

I smirk. "Glad to know I didn't miss your romantic prom arc."

"You were the highlight of the night anyway," he says simply.

I blink. "What?"

He doesn't repeat it. Just sips his drink and keeps his eyes on the firelight in the distance. Like he didn't just say something that made my brain short-circuit.

So I sit here, warm beer in hand, heart doing backflips, and try not to read into things.

I absolutely fail.

TWO
CADEN

Sitting here next to Theo, I feel relaxed for the first time tonight. Which says a lot, considering prom was supposed to be the big moment. The culmination of senior year. Fancy suits, twinkly lights, catered desserts that ended up tasting like sadness. None of the details really hit me until Theo showed up.

Now we're out here, parked in a pair of half-rusted lawn chairs on the edge of the yard, warm beers in hand, stars overhead, and Theo's voice rolling on about his summer job. I should be listening. I *want* to be listening. But my brain? Absolutely refusing to cooperate.

Because Theo's mouth is moving, and I'm too busy staring at it.

It's not even what he's saying. It's just... him.

That look he gave me earlier—when I told him he was the highlight of the night—I can't get it out of my head. I meant it as a joke. Sort of. Okay, maybe not really. But when he looked at me like that, all wide-eyed and quiet and hopeful, something in my chest flipped.

Now he's going on about some gig at the rec center, coaching kids through chaotic games of foam-ball dodgeball, and I swear, I haven't heard a word in the last two minutes.

Because I'm thinking about what it'd be like to kiss him.

And that's… new.

Like *really* new.

I've never thought of myself as anything but straight. Girls have always been the thing. Or at least I *thought* they were. I've had crushes, dated a couple here and there, nothing serious. But lately… lately it's like my brain's rewiring itself every time Theo walks into a room.

And I have *no* idea what to do about it.

Theo's always just been Theo. My best friend. My ride or die. Since we were barely out of diapers and my family moved next door, he's been the center of my orbit. Every birthday, every scraped knee, every game, every late-night shootaround—it's always been me and him.

Most of the street are white families, but the Brookses and the Norths had been side by side for over a decade. Cookouts, shared lawnmowers, backyard basketball—it made us a kind of island, but not a lonely one.

When he told me he liked boys, he was thirteen. We were in my room, playing video games, and he paused the match mid-battle and just… said it.

"I like guys," he blurted. No buildup, no explanation.

I remember turning to him, blinking. "Cool," I said. "You wanna switch to two-player?"

That was it. I didn't think twice. Why would I? Theo's my best friend. Him being gay didn't change anything.

Until, apparently, *now*, when I can't stop thinking about what it would be like to grab his jaw and pull him in just to *taste* him.

I don't even know if I *am* into guys. Maybe it's just him. Just Theo. The way he laughs, the way his curls bounce when he's excited, the way he always seems to *get* me in ways no one else ever has.

I haven't told anyone. Not even him. Especially not him.

People in town wouldn't get it. Gomillion's not a terrible place, but it's small. Small enough that everybody knows your business. Narrow enough that anything outside the usual gets side-eyed. Folks still whisper if they think somebody might be gay—and for two Black boys like us, people already watch harder, like we've got to walk softer just to keep the peace. And don't even get me started on what it would mean if what I'm feeling got out in the sports world.

I've heard the locker room jokes. The offhanded slurs. Coaches turning a blind eye. And if that's what Theo could face from classmates, I don't even want to imagine what a pro team—which is where I'm on a mission to land—would do with a player who doesn't "fit the mold."

Still... I *strongly* suspect he's into me.

It's in the way he looks at me when he thinks I'm not paying attention. The way he gets quiet when I mention dating. The way he lit up when I said he was the highlight of prom and then tried so hard to play it cool. He always brushes against me—his hand on my shoulder, knee bumping mine, his stupid little smirk when I tease him.

It's not nothing.

And yeah, maybe I should be careful. Maybe I *shouldn't* flirt back. I don't want to ever hurt him.

But God, I want to kiss him.

Even now, while he's animatedly describing being mobbed last year by foam ball-wielding eight-year-olds, I can't stop watching the curve of his mouth. I imagine leaning in, enough to catch him mid-sentence, shutting him up with a kiss and feeling what it's like.

But then come the what-ifs.

What if it ruins everything? What if I misread the signals? What if I'm not actually into guys and this is just some kind of best friend confusion? What if I *am* into him, and it makes everything harder?

"What if it ruins everything?" I say quietly and without thinking.

Theo frowns. "What?"

Shit.

"Nothing," I say quickly. "Just... thinking about the future."

He studies me for a second, and I know he knows I'm dodging. But he doesn't push. He never pushes.

"Yeah," he says quietly. "Me too."

We fall into this easy silence we've always been good at. Comfortable. Familiar. But under it, there's this crackling energy I can't explain. I feel it when our shoulders brush. In the way he shifts just slightly closer, like he's settling in. Like maybe he feels it too.

I stare at the stars for a while, trying not to think about kissing him again—and failing miserably. Because now that the thought is in my head, it's like it *won't* leave.

And maybe, if I'm being honest with myself, I don't want it to.

"—and Shane actually ate it," Theo's saying, pulling me back into the conversation with that mischievous glint in his eye. "Like, full-on chewed and swallowed. Thought it was a meatball. It was a dog treat. Shaped like a meatball, yeah, but *still*."

I blink. "Wait, what?"

Theo grins. "See? You miss *one* punch line and the whole story falls apart."

"I was paying attention," I lie.

"You so weren't." He nudges me with his knee. "Try to keep up, North."

"I'm trying," I say, smiling. "It's just—your face is really distracting."

He freezes.

My mouth goes dry.

"I meant, like, *you* make distracting faces," I scramble, waving a hand vaguely at him. "You're expressive. It's… uh… charming."

Smooth. Real smooth.

Theo lifts one brow slowly, eyes sharp with interest now. He sips from his cup like he's trying not to smirk. "Mm-hmm."

I can't tell if he's messing with me or filing that away for later. Probably both.

I drag a hand through my cropped curls and look out at the firepit, where someone's trying to toast a marshmallow with a sparkler. "So, uh… Shane swallowed dog food, huh?"

"Fully. Cam's got video. He's saving it for blackmail when Shane's rich and famous."

"Honestly? Smart."

"He's calling it the Pup-Peroni Incident."

I laugh, relieved to be back on safer ground. "You really have a gift for attracting chaos."

Theo leans back, arms spread on either side of his chair like he owns the lawn. "What can I say? Drama follows me."

"I think *you* follow *it*."

"Okay, that's fair."

A breeze stirs through the yard, lifting his curls. He looks over at me, relaxed and glowing under the string lights, and I get that same stupid urge again—to just lean over and kiss him.

I swallow it down like I have been.

He bumps my knee with his again. "You're not planning on working this summer, right, Mr. Scholarship?"

"Nope. Coach lined up that summer training program. Strength stuff. Film sessions. Basically they're gonna break me down and rebuild me with kale and protein powder."

He grins. "So, like, Athlete Frankenstein."

"Exactly. Biceps first, soul later."

"You'll be eating egg whites like breath mints by the time you start college."

"I already am."

Theo snorts. "Gross."

But then he smiles at me—really smiles—and I forget how to breathe for a second. It's stupid. It's dangerous. And it's getting harder to ignore.

I'm about to say something—anything—just to break the tension when a shriek splits through the night.

Not the horror movie kind. The "what the hell did you just throw at me" kind.

We both turn toward the house as a glowing cloud of *something* comes barreling through the side gate like a rogue weather system. A half-dozen people are fleeing from behind it, some covered in bright neon pink and green.

"What the hell is that?" I ask, half standing.

Theo cranes his neck. "Is that… foam?"

Then someone yells, "FOAM BLASTERS!" like it's the last thing they'll ever say, and a geyser of pastel bubbles explodes from the patio.

"Why is there always a foam machine?!" Theo groans, but he's already moving, grabbing his cup and abandoning the lawn chair.

"We should run," I say.

"Definitely."

And then *splat*—a foamy clump of something cold and lavender-smelling lands squarely on Theo's shoulder.

He freezes. Looks at me. "They *hit* me."

I try not to laugh. "It's barely a graze."

"*They. Hit. Me.*"

And then a second splat lands across my back, soaking through my shirt.

"Okay," I say, "now it's personal."

We both bolt.

Laughter and foam trail behind us as we take off across the yard, cutting around the house. There are shouts and more bubble grenades flying through the air.

Someone's got a water gun full of paint. It's full-on prom after-party warfare now.

Theo grabs my arm at one point to steer us around a kiddie pool (why is there a kiddie pool?), and my hand finds his without thinking, fingers interlacing.

We don't let go.

The property's bigger than I expected. We weave through a side gate, down a little dirt path that leads into the trees lining the edge of the backyard. After a few more turns and one close call with a low-hanging branch, we find a quiet patch behind a shed, just far enough from the house that the music and chaos sound like background noise.

We stop, finally, both of us panting and wheezing with laughter.

Theo doubles over, hands on his knees. "I'm too young to die like this: covered in off-brand bubble bath and glitter paint."

I lean against the shed, grinning. "If this is how we go out, at least we'll look fabulous."

He stands and wipes his face with the back of his arm, which only smears the pink foam worse. His cheek is streaked with something neon, a splash of blue across his jaw and temple. There's foam in his curls, sticking up like whipped cream.

I can't help it. I step forward and reach out. "Hold still."

His breath catches just a little as I touch his face, but I don't stop. I brush my fingers along his cheekbone, wiping away a streak of purple with slow, careful pressure. I move my hand down to his jaw, then gently run my thumb along the edge of his mouth, catching the last of the foam there.

The moment stretches.

He's three inches shorter than me, and he's so close now, we're nearly chest to chest. I can feel his breath. Hear it hitch.

He looks up at me with those hazel eyes, soft and golden and a little bit startled. His skin is warm under my touch, a golden brown that's a few shades lighter than mine thanks to his white Irish grandma on his mom's side. There's moonlight filtering through the trees above us, mixing with strands of leftover fairy lights someone's strung along the fence. It casts his face in a glow that makes him look unreal. Dreamlike.

His lips part like he's going to say something, but I don't let him. I move closer. One breath. Two. And then, without thinking—without planning—I close the distance.

I kiss him.

It's not long or practiced or perfect. It's soft. Hesitant. Testing.

His mouth is warm and still for a second, and my heart is a thunderstorm in my chest. I think he might pull away. I'm ready for it. But then—God—he kisses me back.

His fingers curl into the front of my damp shirt. My hand moves to cup his cheek, thumb brushing just below his eye. We fit. We *fit*, and I feel it in my bones, in the way his body leans into mine, in the way every nerve ending lights up with relief.

We pull back only a little, our foreheads almost touching.

Theo's eyes flutter open. "So… foam machine, huh?"

I laugh—soft, breathless. "Best prom after-party ever."

And in this quiet little pocket of the night, with the chaos behind us and Theo in front of me, I realize there's no more pretending.

I'm in deep. And I don't want to run.

THREE
THEO

Kissing Caden is hands down the best thing in the history of ever. For real. The time I won the school science fair with a Mentos and Coke volcano? Second place. The feeling of a perfect three-point swish on the court? Not even close. The night I finally beat him at *Mario Kart*? Okay, that's top five. But this? Kissing him? Undisputed gold medal.

Which is wild, because this time yesterday, I thought the only kiss I'd be getting anywhere near prom night was if someone spun the bottle wrong and panicked.

And now we're on my bed. Kissing.

It's still early afternoon the day after Caden's prom, and the sunlight coming through my window is warm and soft, like the world is giving us this moment on purpose. I've showered, thrown on clean clothes, and tried (but failed) not to replay every second of last night on a loop. Caden showed up half an hour ago, looking like a Rocawear model with his hoodie sleeves shoved up to his elbows and hair a little damp from the shower. He brought muffins, like we're a couple that brunches.

My little sister, Amelia, poked her head in when he first showed up, stealing one of the muffins out of the box before he could set it down. "Seriously? Do you live here now?" she teased, grinning at him like she always did. Caden just smirked, muttered something about freeloaders, and she rolled her eyes on her way out. It was barely thirty seconds, but it left me buzzing—because even she had no idea what he really was to me.

And then we somehow migrated from muffins to making out. As you do.

Out there, we're just teammates, just neighbors, just best friends who trash-talk over *Mario Kart*. That's the script everyone knows, the roles we play so well that no one thinks to question them. On the court, in the halls, even on the walk home, we're the version of ourselves that fits what everyone else expects.

But in here… in here, it's different. The walls hold our secrets. The blinds erase the outside world. I don't have to laugh too loud or keep my hands to myself. He doesn't have to pretend I'm only his buddy. Here, he's mine. And I'm his. And that truth is enough to make me greedy for every minute we get.

His hand is under my shirt, splayed warm and steady over my ribs, not moving—just there. I've got one hand in his short strands, the other resting on the side of his neck. Our kisses are soft and slow and a little sloppy because we keep smiling into them like idiots. Every time we pause to breathe, one of us says something stupid or sweet, and then we're back at it again, like we're magnetized.

I pull away for a second, breathless. "So, just checking… you're not under the influence of post-prom foam toxins, right?"

When I shift a little, my elbow knocks into the book on the nightstand, the bookmark jutting out like a reminder of what my Saturday afternoons usually look like. Reading, hiding in stories. Not this. Not him. The contrast is dizzying—in the best way.

Caden chuckles against my mouth. "Pretty sure I'm lucid. Unless I dreamed your grandma's floral body wash in the shower."

"That stuff *lingers*, man," I say, grinning.

He grins back. "I like it. You smell like lavender and sass."

I hum, tilting my head. "That sounds like a bad indie band."

"Would still headline Coachella," he murmurs, leaning back in.

The next kiss is deeper—more deliberate—and my chest goes tight in the best way. I don't know how to describe this feeling except that it's all-consuming. I've wanted him for so long, and now that I have this—him— it's like a thousand little fireworks going off behind my ribs.

We break apart again, just slightly, foreheads brushing. "I really like you," I say, voice quieter than I meant it to be.

Caden eases back to look at me. His eyes search mine. "Yeah?"

I nod, suddenly shy. "Like… it's not new. It's just been sitting in my chest for years, getting louder."

He's quiet for a second. Then his hand brushes my cheek, thumb tracing just below my eye.

"I think I started noticing stuff a couple of months ago," he says softly. "Like... weird stuff. The way I'd look for you in every room. Or how I'd zone out during practice because I'd be thinking about that dumb way you hum when you're focused. Or the way your hair curls behind your ears when it's wet. It wasn't... sudden. It was more like I looked up one day and you weren't just my best friend anymore."

My heart absolutely stutters. "Cade," I say, barely a whisper.

He smiles gently. "I still don't know what to call it. Like, labels. But I know I want *this*. I want *you*."

I bite my bottom lip, trying to keep it together. "I'm not asking you to call it anything. I just... I'm really happy right now."

He leans in again, nose brushing mine. "Yeah. Me too."

Another kiss, this one slower, and I slide my hand under the back of his hoodie, fingers tracing the curve of his spine. His weight shifts just slightly, enough for his thigh to press into mine, and my brain short-circuits again in the best way. It's not rushed or messy—just charged. Close. *Intimate*.

I pull back a little, grinning like a goofball. "This is such a weird flex, but I can't stop smiling. Like, my face might actually crack."

"Please don't crack," Caden says. "I really like your face."

I snort. "Smooooth."

"You love it."

"Unfortunately, yes."

He kisses me again. Quieter this time. Sweet. The kind of kiss that says, *I'm not going anywhere.* And yeah… maybe that's the best part.

We fall into silence, the kind that feels easy. My fingers trace lazy lines across the inside of his wrist where our hands are tangled between us. His thumb strokes the back of my hand. It's all stupidly perfect, the kind of moment I'd roll my eyes at in a movie if I weren't currently *in* it.

Still, there's this question buzzing at the back of my brain. Not because I need labels or anything. I really don't. But… well, I'm curious. And this—*we*—aren't exactly what either of us expected.

I shift a little, turning more onto my side to look at him. "So, like… do you think you're gay? Or bi? Or something?"

Caden shrugs, totally casual. "No clue."

Just like that. No flinch. No tension. Just honesty.

"I mean," he continues, brushing his fingers through my curls, "I liked girls. Still do, I think. My last girlfriend? I was into her. Physically, at least."

I raise an eyebrow. "Right. You got to second base with Ava."

His grin goes full smug. "You remember the base count?"

"You told *everyone*, Caden."

"I did not."

"You did. You told Cam, who told Shane, who told basically the entire basketball team *and* most of AP Chem."

"Okay, fine," he says, laughing. "I might've been proud."

I glare at him. "So what, it was good?"

"I mean, yeah," he says with a shrug, and for some reason, that sets something off in my chest.

It shouldn't. Really, it shouldn't. But it *does*.

He sees it instantly. "Wait—are you jealous?"

I try to cover it. "No."

He gives me the most obnoxious, knowing look.

I roll my eyes. "Shut up."

"*You're* jealous of second base?"

"You're *bragging* about second base!"

"I wasn't bragging!" He's laughing now, big and bright. "Oh my God, your face!"

"Caden," I groan, hiding under a pillow.

He tugs the pillow away and kisses me. Just plants one right on my mouth and shuts me up in the most effective way possible.

He pulls away to speak, lips still brushing mine. "I'm not into *her*, Theo. I'm here with *you*. This—" He gestures between us. "—is better than any base I ever got to with anyone else."

That stops the petty jealousy in its tracks. I blink. "Yeah?"

He nods. "I think... bi, maybe. That makes the most sense right now."

My chest goes warm.

Then he says, voice quieter, "But I've never thought about another guy like this before. Not even close."

I try not to let the ridiculous grin stretch across my face, but it's a losing battle. "That's.... I hella like that—a lot."

He laughs softly and leans in again, kissing the corner

of my mouth, then my jaw, then—just because he can—nuzzles his nose against my cheek until I'm laughing too.

We're quiet again, but the air feels different now. Charged. Curious.

I glance at him. "So, is this just... kissing? Or have you thought about more?"

His cheeks go pink. And considering he's got rich brown skin, it's super noticeable. Adorable, really.

"Definitely more," he says, voice just a little hoarse.

That fries my brain for a hot second. I should probably be embarrassed. I *should* feel awkward. But this is *Caden*. He's the person I've told everything to. The person I've loved, secretly and not-so-secretly, for years. If I can't talk about this stuff with him, who the hell else could I?

Still, I clear my throat. "Okay, so... not, like, *now* or anything. We don't have to—"

He nods quickly. "No, yeah, same. I mean, not that I don't want to. Obviously. I do. A lot."

"Yeah," I echo, trying to sound cool and chill and not like I've fantasized about seeing him naked since I was fifteen. "Definitely. But also... I'm good with just this right now."

He smiles. "Me too."

But then he adds, under his breath, "Although, if you *did* want to see my dick...."

"*Caden!*"

He dissolves into laughter, arms wrapping around me as I half push, half hug him in retaliation. And yeah, okay, *do* I want to see it? Hell yes. But we've got time.

And right now, the way his mouth finds mine again—gentle and sure that it's *his*—is more than enough.

Caden's mouth is still warm against mine, his hand splayed across my waist like he's memorizing the shape of me. My fingers are curled in the fabric of his hoodie, and every few seconds, we pull apart to breathe before diving back in like we're making up for lost time—for every day we didn't do this sooner.

We've kissed a dozen times now, but somehow each one feels like a surprise. A really, really good surprise. Like unwrapping your favorite candy only to find another piece hiding underneath.

Caden shifts, lips brushing the edge of my jaw. "You're really kissable," he murmurs.

"Yeah?" I ask, grinning. "I've been practicing."

He lifts his head and squints at me. "With who?"

I laugh. "My hand."

He snorts, burying his face in my shoulder to muffle the sound.

We're so wrapped up in our bubble of warm skin and soft laughter that I don't hear the front door until it slams shut. The sound jolts straight through me.

Then comes the unmistakable voice of my dad. "Theo? You home?"

Caden freezes. We both do. Like deer caught mid-make out.

I launch off the bed like I've been electrocuted, trying to smooth my tee and figure out how to make my flushed face look *less* like it's been suction-cupped to my best friend's for the last hour. Caden sits up, too, fixing his hoodie, raking a hand through his hair like that's going to help.

I mouth, "Oh my God," at him, and he mouths back, "Play it cool."

Cool. Right. Totally cool.

Meanwhile, I feel like I've got a giant neon sign blinking above my head: **MADE OUT WITH BEST FRIEND. WOULD DO IT AGAIN.**

My dad's voice travels up the stairs again. "Theo, can you come down for a second?"

Caden pats my back. "You got this," he whispers like we're heading onto a battlefield.

I glare at him. "You're enjoying this."

"A little," he admits, grinning way too smugly for someone who still has my lip balm on his mouth. Okay, technically it's not mine, but I stole it from my sister because it makes my lips feel really soft.

I stumble out of my room, trying to pull myself together. By the time I get to the bottom of the stairs, I'm pretty sure I still look like a mess, but it's the "best friend sleepover after prom" kind of mess, right? Not the "my tongue's been in my bestie's mouth" kind.

My dad's in the kitchen sorting through the mail he's ignored since Friday. "Hey, son," he says, looking up. "Can you take the recycling out? Your mom filled the bin again."

I blink. That's it?

"Uh—yeah. Totally."

I move toward the side door, my legs still jelly, when I hear footsteps behind me. Caden's followed me downstairs, the absolute picture of calm. His face is neutral, polite smile in place, like he didn't spend the last hour with his hand under my shirt.

"Hey, Mr. Brooks," he says, grabbing a bag of cans without being asked.

My dad smiles. "Hey, Caden. You survive prom?"

"Barely."

They laugh, and I want to crawl under the table and die.

We head out to the bins. Caden's chill. Like, "we just kissed for the first time, but now we're tossing recyclables" kind of chill. Meanwhile, my heart is breakdancing in my chest, and I'm positive I'm glowing like a radioactive peach.

We come back inside just in time for *her* to walk in. Amelia is fourteen, all attitude, and with a sixth sense for existing *exactly* when I want her not to.

She pauses at the bottom of the stairs and narrows her eyes at me. "What's with your face?"

I freeze. "What?"

"You look weird."

I fumble. "I don't—this is just my face!"

Caden snorts behind me, and I shoot him a murderous glare.

Amelia tilts her head, suspicious. "You're acting like you did something. Or *someone*."

"I—Amelia!" I practically screech. "Go. Away."

She smirks. "Oh my God, you're *so* weird right now."

My dad walks in. "Hey, Theo, have you finished your homework?"

"Uh-huh. Just working on it now. Gotta go!" I grab Caden's arm and drag him back upstairs. We slam the door behind us and stand in my room, trying not to laugh.

"You *are* being weird," Caden says, amusement all over his face.

"You don't understand," I say, pacing. "She has powers. She *knows things.*"

"She's your little sister, not a psychic spy."

"Same thing."

He laughs and flops back onto my bed. Papers and notebooks are scattered everywhere, corners bent and pages sliding half off the comforter—leftovers from when we'd started kissing before I was finished. He nudges a crushed worksheet out of the way with his elbow. "Pretty sure this is not how you get an A."

I groan and sink beside him. "Yeah, well, I need that A." I smooth the nearest page, like that'll undo the wrinkles. "It's not just about grades. If I want to get out of here—really get out and make a difference—I can't half-ass anything."

He tilts his head, studying me. His smile softens. "That's so you. Already thinking past this town, past high school. Most people can't see past Friday night."

I shrug, but there's a little fire in my chest anyway.

He reaches out, hooking a finger through mine. "Well, you're cute when you overthink."

And just like that, the panic dissolves. My pulse slows. The smile comes back.

So yeah. My sister's annoying, my dad's recycling bins are a battlefield, and my essays are probably glowing with post-kiss crinkles, but Caden's right here. Holding my hand like it's easy. Like we're already figuring this out.

And I wouldn't trade it for anything.

FOUR

CADEN

I KEEP WAITING FOR THE FREAK-OUT, BUT I'M TWO WEEKS into spending every spare second I have kissing Theo, and honestly? I'm good with it. Okay—*mostly* good. Not being able to hold his hand in the halls or sneak up behind him at his locker just to nuzzle his neck definitely sucks. But none of that really matters when I know that the second we're alone, I *can* do those things. I *do* do those things.

Sneaking around at home, though? Way harder. We've been caught in almost-compromising positions more times than I'm proud of. His little sister has developed a sixth sense for "Theo's acting weird," and my mom has officially stopped knocking before entering.

It's not even about Theo being out. That's been true for years, and both our families are supportive in that "open-minded but still slightly awkward suburban parent" kind of way. But as for me.... Well, I'm still building up to the full coming-out conversation. The "so, remember how I've always been straight? Surprise!" talk.

That, and I keep wondering if my parents will get

weird about *us*. Like, will they overreact? Stop leaving us alone in a room together? Start side-eyeing our sleepovers? Make it *a thing*?

I don't want it to be a thing. I just want to date my best friend without anyone watching us like we're fragile or temporary.

"What's up?"

My smile shows up before I even look. Theo's leaning against my bedroom doorframe like he belongs there—which, let's be real, he does. He's in soft jogging pants and a hoodie I'm 90 percent sure used to be mine but looks a hell of a lot better on him.

I spin on my desk chair to face him. "You're what's up."

"Lame," he says, coming in and flopping onto my bed like it's his. It basically is. "I ask a question and get pickup lines."

"You like my pickup lines."

"Unfortunately."

He's lying on his back now, curls spread out on my pillow, cheeks still flushed from the bike ride over from his grandparents' house. There's paint on his knuckles—he was helping them redo the porch railing this morning—and it's somehow just unfair how good he looks in natural light.

Theo's six months younger than me, not as tall or broad. His skin's lighter than mine—a soft golden-brown. His curls are looser than mine too—he's been growing them out into an afro, and it's adorable as hell. He claims he's aiming for "cool, vintage blaxploitation, but make it millennial." I tell him he already looks like the poster boy for "crush-worthy junior who knows more than you do."

Which is also accurate.

Theo's smarter than I am. Always has been. He's rocking a 3.6 GPA while I'm coasting at a 3.0, and I know that number would be lower if he hadn't spent the past few years forcing me to study, quizzing me, editing my essays, and making flash cards for history class like some kind of academic personal trainer.

And it's not like he doesn't know what he wants—he does. He says it plain: He wants to teach English. For all the time he spends on the court, he's just as much a book nerd. He gets this look in his eye when he's talking about Baldwin or Morrison, like the words are alive under his skin. Even when he's stuck writing about *The Scarlet Letter* or *The Great Gatsby*—the usual stuff teachers throw at us —he'll flip the whole assignment sideways, make it about power or injustice or resilience. Over the past few summers, he's been working at a kids' club over at the rec center, and every time he comes back with some story about the younger ones hanging on his every word. He laughs about it, but I can tell—he loves it. Loves the idea of opening up whole worlds for kids the way books opened them for him.

I just hope wherever he ends up isn't far from Lexington.

Because yeah, I had offers from other schools—some way flashier than UK—but the University of Kentucky was a sweet spot: still solid, respected, and close enough to come home when I want to. Six hours isn't a commute, but it's not a universe away either.

Even then, I think some part of me just knew I'd want to stay close to him.

"I gotta go car shopping tomorrow," I say, kicking my heel against the wheel of my chair.

Theo glances over. "Oh yeah? Big day."

"Dad's been looking at used stuff all week. He wants me to have a car for Lexington, says he doesn't want me 'riding with strangers.'"

Theo snorts. "Because college basketball players *never* carpool. I bet the car's gonna smell like protein powder within a week."

"Most likely."

He laughs, then sits up, legs crisscrossed at the end of my bed. "You excited?"

"Yeah," I say. "I mean, it's a car. Freedom. The ability to drive and visit someone cute on weekends...."

"Mm. Wonder who *that* could be."

"Some guy. Curly hair. Ridiculously pretty."

"Sounds annoying."

"Definitely is."

I lean forward to steal a kiss—quick, sweet, addictive. His fingers curl into my hoodie when I don't pull back fast enough, and for a minute, we're just there, breathing each other in. Kissing slowly and softly like it's muscle memory already.

When I do finally lean back, his eyes are hazy, but he's smiling. "Car shopping and secret kisses," he says. "You're living the dream, North."

"You're part of the dream," I murmur.

And I mean it. God, I mean it so much it scares me a little. Because yeah, we're sneaking around, and yeah, it's still new, and messy, and kind of terrifying, but it's also real.

And right now? It's mine. *He's* mine. And I wouldn't change a damn thing.

I run my thumb along the inside of his wrist again, then say it before I can talk myself out of it. "I've been thinking about telling my parents."

Theo's eyes go wide—like, cartoon-anvil-just-fell wide.

My stomach clenches. "What? Too much?"

He shakes his head quickly, blinking like I short-circuited his brain. "No. No, it's just—seriously?"

I nod, slower this time. "I mean... yeah. Not just about me, but about *us*."

He stares at me for a second longer, and I can see it— the shift from panic to something softer, something kind of stunned.

"That's what you want?" he asks.

I glance down, then back at him. "Yeah. I think so. I mean, I'm nervous—don't get me wrong—but not because I think they'll freak out or anything. My parents love me. They're super open. Dad literally works for an equity and inclusion nonprofit. He's the guy who leads workshops about bias and posts rainbow graphics on MySpace every Pride Month."

Theo snorts. "Okay, your dad might actually beat *my* dad in the progressive-parent Olympics."

"I know. It's annoying. He's going to be so chill about it I might end up feeling worse for keeping it from him this long."

"So why now?" he asks gently.

I lean back a little, propping myself up on one elbow. "I think it'd just... take the pressure off. This whole sneaking around thing—it's fine. Kind of exciting, honestly. But it's also exhausting. And if I can tell *them*, that's one less thing to carry."

Theo is quiet for a moment, nodding slowly. Then he smiles. "Okay. If that's what you want, I'm in."

I grin. "Yeah?"

"Yeah. You're not doing this solo."

God, I love him.

He taps his fingers on my knee. "What about telling other people? At school?"

I know he's not saying *out* out, as his sexuality is very much on the down-low. He only trusts a few people with it. I chew my bottom lip, the answer already clear. "I think we keep it quiet there. For now. Not forever. But I don't feel like fielding questions every time I hold your hand between classes, y'know?"

"Agreed," he says quickly. "Like, I love you—well—*not saying that yet—*"

I laugh. "Too late. I heard it."

"Shut up. I was saying, I love your face," he corrects, smirking. "But also, yeah. High school is full of gossip goblins and walking red flags. I don't want to deal with it either."

There's a pause, and then he shifts a little, his tone softening. "What about… you going pro? Like, one day."

I sigh, rubbing the back of my neck. "Yeah. That part? Still scares the crap out of me."

He nods, watching me.

"There's no one out in the league right now. Not a single guy," I say. "And maybe I'm being selfish, but… I don't want to be the first. I don't want that pressure. I just want to play."

"I get that," he says, and the way he says it—no hesitation, no judgment—grounds me.

"I want to be honest with you," I continue, "and maybe one day with the world. But right now? I just want to enjoy being yours without it becoming a statement."

"You *are* a statement," he says, grinning. "But no, I totally get it."

"Thanks."

"Besides," he adds, tilting his head, "I'm pretty amazing. Being with me is already an achievement. You don't need to carry *two* historic milestones."

I burst out laughing. "Wow. Humble much?"

He shrugs, playful. "Just being honest."

"Okay, honesty pact," I say, holding out my pinkie.

He links it with his. "We just be us. No pressure. No trying to be perfect."

"No trying to be anyone but… us."

We sit there for a moment, pinkies locked like dorks, smiling like idiots.

Then Theo grins. "Look at us. Having adult conversations. Emotional maturity and everything."

"We're basically icons of healthy communication."

He leans in, brushing his nose against mine. "And we're *so* hot while doing it."

I kiss him. Slowly. Sweetly.

Responsibly.

It hits me—like a "light bulb over the head" kind of moment—right after Theo pulls back from our kiss, smiling like he has any idea how in love with him I already am.

I sit up straighter. My chest is buzzing with nerves, but the feeling underneath is something solid. Unshakable. "You know what?" I say, voice low but sure. "Now's as good a time as any."

Theo turns to me, eyebrows raised. "For what? Another round of emotional maturity?"

I glance toward the window, where the lawnmower's finally gone quiet. "My mom just finished mowing. Dad's probably downstairs pretending his spice rack is a tactical mission. We could tell them. Today."

Theo sits up, too, his playful smirk fading into something wide-eyed and cautious. "Wait. *Now* now?"

"Yeah." My heart's thudding hard enough that I feel it in my throat, but the word tastes right in my mouth. "We've already talked through it. And I don't want to keep… hiding. Not from them. Not from anyone, ideally, but I know that's not possible. Not right now."

He nods slowly, like he's scrutinizing each emotion as it passes through him. "Okay… wow. That's big."

I nod back. But part of me is still trembling, somewhere behind my ribs. The part that's lived half in the shadows, even in the open. The part that's learned to stay smaller, quieter. Keep people guessing. Let them assume. Especially when you're a young Black kid with a basketball scholarship.

And hell, that's only been for a couple of weeks, and the months before when I've been stumbling over my confusion.

But this? This is mine.

I glance at Theo, then take a breath. "Actually… what if we did a two-for-one?"

He frowns. "A what now?"

"We tell your parents too." I shrug like it's no big deal, but it's everything. "We just… get it all out there. One sweep. Like ripping off the Band-Aid, but with more eye contact and potential awkward silence."

Theo's quiet for a second. "You're serious."

I nod again.

He runs a hand through his soft curls, shaking his head like he's trying to reboot. "Okay, but… just so I'm not hallucinating this—this is a yes about us, right? Like, we're *together* together?"

I blink, then huff a laugh. "I mean… yeah? Aren't we?"

He half smiles, like he wants to believe it but needs to hear it out loud. "I just don't want to be that idiot who assumes he's someone's boyfriend and ends up in a viral sad song called 'Mixed Signals and Missed Texts.'"

I let out a breath and look at him directly. "We're dating, Theo. For real. Officially."

He nods, and I offer him my pinkie—our stupid little ritual that suddenly means way more than it ever has.

He loops his around mine. "Boyfriends?"

"Boyfriends," I echo. "Even if we're kind of a disaster at timing."

He grins. "Speak for yourself. I'm excellent under pressure."

"Perfect," I say. "You can do all the talking."

He laughs. "Absolutely not."

We stand up together, and as we head toward the

stairs, our hands brush once, then again. On the third brush, we just… hold.

The house is quiet but not empty.

We walk through my home like something's humming in the walls. My heartbeat's a drumline in my ears, and I can tell Theo's nervous too—he keeps adjusting his sleeves like they're responsible for his entire emotional state.

But we don't let go.

When we reach the bottom of the stairs, I hear my dad in the kitchen, humming some old-school Marvin Gaye. My mom's probably cleaning up in the laundry room. Everything feels weirdly normal. Like the world doesn't know it's about to shift, just a little.

I glance at Theo. "You ready?" '

He doesn't answer right away, but then he squeezes my hand. "Yeah. Let's do this."

And we take the last few steps forward, together.

My parents are in the kitchen when we walk in—Mom's wiping her hands, and Dad's slicing limes like he's judging them. They both look up when we enter, and before they can even say anything, I blurt, "Can we talk to you guys for a sec?"

Mom blinks. "Sure, honey. Everything okay?"

I open my mouth, then look at Theo. He's doing his best not to bolt.

"I was thinking we could pop next door too," I say casually—too casually, like I'm suggesting snacks or a walk, not a dual-family reveal that might upend everything.

Dad looks up from where he's squeezing lime juice

into a pitcher and frowns. "Next door?"

"Just for a sec," I say, trying to keep my voice light and neutral. "I want to say something. To all of you."

Theo mutters, "Two-for-one," like a man walking to his doom.

Mom and Dad exchange a glance. Not alarmed, just… alert. But they nod.

A few minutes later, we're standing in Theo's kitchen, slightly damp from the walk across the sprayed grass, surrounded by the warm smells of lemon cleaner and left-over breakfast sausage. His parents look up from their Saturday paper and the half-finished jigsaw puzzle taking over the kitchen island. There's a blue-sky piece stuck to Theo's dad's elbow.

Amelia's perched on one of the stools, bonnet and pj's still on, fork in hand as she picks over the last of the sausage. She glances up when we walk in, gives her brother a once-over when he heads straight to the fridge and starts grabbing drinks, then smirks. "Look at you playing host. What's next, you fixing them a plate too?"

Theo shoots her a look, but she just laughs, shaking her head as if to say she's got the whole thing clocked.

He starts pouring Lori, his mom, a glass of pinot and hands his dad a beer like it's a backyard barbecue rather than the morning. Then he grabs a soda for my mom and a beer for my dad. He's got that grin on—charming, prac-ticed, nervous as hell.

I watch him set the cans and glasses down like sacred offerings. "If I'm gonna emotionally strip down," he says, "y'all may as well do it with a drink in hand."

His dad, James, chuckles, taking the beer. "This sounds serious, especially since it's not even midday yet."

Theo's mom squints. "This isn't some surprise 'we're expecting' announcement, is it? Because that would raise a *lot* of questions."

There's a beat of total, deafening silence. Then all four parents turn to *me*.

Amelia is the first to snort a laugh. I follow, saying, "That's… not even physically possible in this situation."

Theo coughs into his soda. "Nope. Not that kind of announcement."

I breathe in. And then again. My chest feels tight, like something's been living there for a long time and is finally ready to come out. Theo shifts closer, his shoulder brushing mine, and it helps.

"So," I start, voice trembling just slightly. "I wanted to tell you all… I'm bisexual."

The room quiets, but not in a bad way. It's the silence of gears turning, emotions settling. No gasps. No horror. Just stillness. Then my mom crosses the room and hugs me like she's been waiting years to do it.

"Okay," she whispers into my ear. "Thank you for telling us, sweetheart."

Dad steps up beside her. He doesn't hug me—he clasps my shoulder firmly, like an anchor. "We love you, son. You know that. Always."

My throat's tight now. I just nod.

Theo gives me a tiny, smug smile. *Told you so*, it says, without saying a word.

I clear my throat. "Also… I'm dating someone."

Four sets of eyebrows go up at once.

"Someone you know," I add, and glance at Theo, who lifts his soda in the world's most awkward toast.

"Hi," he says. "Someone you know here."

This time, the silence stretches longer. His mom's mouth falls open just a bit. His dad blinks three times, processing.

Amelia lets out a small laugh, her eyes wide. "Okay, wow. I didn't *know* know," she says, dragging the words out, "but I kinda suspected. You weren't exactly subtle about barricading your bedroom door." Her grin's sharp but warm. "For the record, I think it's awesome. About time you said it out loud."

"Oh," Lori finally says after shaking her head at Amelia. "Wow."

"We didn't want to keep it from you," Theo says quickly. "We've been figuring it out. But we're happy. Like, *really* happy."

His voice softens on that last part. And it's true. We are. I feel it in the quiet way his hand brushes against mine again, and I don't pull away.

There's a beat, and then my dad exhales through his nose and looks right at me. "Well," he says, "we love both of you. And we're glad you told us. But—" He pauses, brow furrowed. "I'd be lying if I said I wasn't… worried."

Theo's mom nods slowly, her wine forgotten. "It's not about you two. You know we love you. But you've only just turned eighteen," she says to me. "You've got your whole lives ahead of you. And this… this isn't small."

"People aren't always kind," my mom adds gently. "Especially to boys who look like you. And *especially* when they're breaking the mold."

Dad nods. "You've got a full ride to one of the top basketball programs in the country, Caden. And as of right now, there are no out players. Not in the league. Not even in D1."

I meet his eyes. "I know."

"Have you thought about what that means?" he asks, not accusing, just... bracing me.

"Yeah," I say. "We're not planning to tell the world. Not now. We'll tell a few close friends—people we *know* we can trust. Like Cam." I glance at Theo, and he nods, already on the same page. "But for college, for the team... we'll keep it quiet. At least for now."

Theo adds, "We're not trying to get a ton of attention, and I'm pretty sure Caden doesn't want to be anybody's poster boy. We just want to be honest with you. That's all."

James leans forward, arms crossed but face softer now. "And you're prepared for how *not* easy that'll be?"

"We'll figure it out," I say. "One day at a time."

Mom's hand tightens around my wrist. "I believe you. But I need you to be *ready*, Caden. Because loving someone in secret... that's hard. It's lonely, even when it's good."

"I'd rather be lonely with him than loud without him," I say. "We're not trying to prove anything. I just... I need to be real."

Theo squeezes my hand.

Lori smiles a little. "You boys are brave. And young. That's a dangerous combination."

"Hopeful too," Theo says. "Don't forget hopeful."

That gets a small laugh.

"We trust you," my dad says. "We just don't trust the

world. That's not a judgment on your relationship. That's a reality check from someone who's *seen* what the world does to Black boys who it decides don't fit."

I nod. "We're not being reckless. We're being careful. And honest. That's it."

There's another long pause, and then his dad leans back with a sigh. "All right. Then I guess we've got two new things to be proud of."

Theo's mom wipes her eyes discreetly, then clears her throat. "Well, now that you've ruined any chance I had of finishing this puzzle today...."

"We could always do one with less sky," I offer, smiling weakly.

Theo grins and knocks his hip against mine. "Or we could get cake and celebrate."

"Celebrate what?" I ask.

He shrugs. "Telling the truth. Surviving it."

Mom wraps an arm around me again. "I like that."

When we finally head out, my hand slips naturally into Theo's again. None of our parents say anything. They don't need to. They see us. And for now, that's enough.

FIVE

THEO

THERE'S SOMETHING ABOUT THE SOUND OF SUMMER THAT makes everything feel both slower and faster at once—kids hollering in the distance, the low drone of cicadas in the trees, the rhythmic *splshhh* of someone cannonballing into the pool. It's like time is lounging beside us in the heat, too lazy to move, even though I can feel it slipping past me like water through my fingers.

We're at Kurtis's place. He's one of the few white kids I hang with outside school or the basketball team. It's not that people don't mix in Gomillion—they do. Just... not often. Sports and class projects are one thing. Sitting on each other's decks in the summer, that's different. But Kurtis never made it weird. He'd just toss me a Coke and act like I'd always been here.

His parents are the kind who stock the fridge with SunnyD and never ask too many questions, and they've got a pool, which makes them practically royalty in July. There's a boom box by the diving board blasting Green Day's "Boulevard of Broken Dreams," and someone's tossed a bunch of those oversized neon pool noodles into the deep end like they're confetti.

I'm perched on a lounge chair under a striped umbrella, pretending to be invested in a bag of Cool Ranch Doritos while sneak-watching Caden from behind my sunglasses.

There's a paperback open on my lap, too, but I've been on the same page for twenty minutes. Every time I try to read a line, my eyes wander back across the pool. The book's basically camouflage at this point—a flimsy excuse for why I'm sitting off to the side instead of diving in.

He's across the pool, sitting on the edge with his feet in the water, laughing at something Shane said. His T-shirt's damp and clinging to him in all the worst (best) ways, and his basketball shorts temptingly ride up his thighs to make it impossible to focus on anything else. His skin glows, all sun-warmed and deep brown, and his tight curls are a little damp and a lot perfect.

And I—despite my best efforts—am trying very hard not to eye-fuck my boyfriend in front of a dozen people who only know us as best friends.

Caden's taking this whole "I'm about to leave for college" thing in total stride. He's been training all summer—early-morning runs, strength workouts, protein shakes that smell like sadness—and still somehow has time to hang out with me nearly every day. Like clockwork. Like nothing's changing.

Except everything is.

He leaves in less than a month.

Me? I start school next week—senior year. One last lap before the finish line. But it doesn't feel triumphant or exciting. It feels like we're living in the part of the movie where the sun starts to set and the music gets all wistful.

Cameron flops into the chair beside me, dripping water onto the towel I forgot to use. His brown skin gleams under the bright light, the kind of summer shine we all carry after hours on the court and in the sun. "You good?"

I pop a Dorito into my mouth. "Yeah. Just thinking."

"About Caden leaving?" he says, way too casually for someone who doesn't know. Or does he? Cam's sharp. If anyone's clocked us, it'd be him.

I lift a shoulder. "Sort of."

He nods but doesn't press. Instead, he grabs a soda and leans back with a sigh. "It's going to be weird without seeing everyone."

I nod again. "Yeah."

Truth is, it already feels weird. Every time I look at Caden, I feel that tug in my chest—that constant aware-ness that we're on a timer. Every kiss, every shared look, every time he brushes his hand against mine when no one's paying us any mind... it all feels loaded. Like we're soaking up as much as we can before the clock runs out.

A splash hits nearby, and I glance over just in time to see Shane belly flop into the shallow end with the grace of a brick.

"Dumbass," Cameron mutters, but he's smiling.

Caden stands and stretches, his muscles flexing, then jogs toward the group gathering by the diving board for some new game that involves a football and probably too much testosterone from the guys here. His grin is bright, his movements easy.

He fits here. With them. With me. With all of it. But soon, he won't be here at all.

I take another sip of flat root beer and pretend the ache in my chest is just sunburn.

About twenty minutes later, he wanders back over, damp and grinning. He drops down beside me on my lounge chair, taking up way too much space and knocking my knee with his.

"Hey," he says, a little breathless.

"Hey yourself." I glance around. Everyone's occupied—Cam's still by the snacks, Shane's mid-wrestle with Dale over a pool float, and the rest are too busy trying to outsplash each other to notice us.

"You okay?" Caden asks quietly.

"Yeah. Just thinking."

"You've been thinking a lot lately."

I shrug. "Maybe I'm just practicing for senior year."

He gives me that look—the one where his eyes soften and his lips twitch like he wants to smile but knows better. "Is this about me leaving?"

"No," I lie. "I mean, yes. Kind of."

He nods slowly. "I get it. I really do."

There's a pause. The kind that could be filled with something important if we were somewhere else. But we're not. So instead, I say, "You excited?"

Caden leans back on his elbows, gaze drifting toward the sky. "Yeah. Nervous, but excited. I've got to earn my spot on the team, y'know? Try for the starting five? Scholarship or not, they're not handing me anything."

"You will," I say, because it's true. "You're a beast."

He grins. "You say the sweetest things."

"I mean it," I say, more seriously this time. "You've been working your ass off. They'd be stupid not to notice."

He nudges my knee again, gentler this time. "Thanks."

I glance down at my drink. "We're still keeping it quiet, right?" My chest tightens. Gomillion's not the place to come out at seventeen—not if you want peace. But I get why it's different for Caden. Why it'll *keep* being different, maybe for a long time. He's got scouts, coaches, a whole future riding on how the world sees him. I love him enough to be okay with that. Still, part of me hopes college will be different. Bigger. Safer. Maybe even open.

At least for me and my secret boyfriend.

He nods. "Yeah. For now. Couple of close friends, maybe. But I don't want this—us—to get tied up in anything else. Not with scouts watching. Not with a thousand eyes in the locker room."

I nod, swallowing the lump in my throat. "I get it."

And I do. I really, really do.

"I've been thinking about telling Cam," he adds quietly. "He's solid. I trust him."

"I think he'd be cool," I say. "He's not one of the gossip types."

Caden hums in agreement. "Yeah. And he's chill around, y'know, stuff. He doesn't feed into Soren's 'pause' jokes."

I wince. "God, Soren's such a prick."

Caden snorts. "You think we can do this?"

"What, the long-distance thing?"

He nods.

I glance at him. At the strong lines of his cheekbones,

the rich, coppery glow of his skin in the sun, the way his lashes catch the light. I think about how I know every dip and drawl of his voice—even when he whispers.

"Yeah," I say. "I think we can."

He leans in slightly, his shoulder pressed to mine. Not much, but enough. And for now, that's all we can afford.

The next round of water volleyball starts with a war cry from Dale, who jumps into the pool holding a beach ball over his head like it's a sacred relic. "Let's go, losers!" he bellows.

"We literally beat you last time," Cameron mutters, grabbing one of the pool noodles and using it as a lance to jab at Dale's knees.

Caden's already sliding into the shallow end with that stupid grin of his—the one that makes my brain short-circuit and forget how to human. "You in, T?" he calls over, splashing water in my direction.

I shove my sunglasses into my stubborn curls—the ones that still spiral instead of fanning out like I want—and toss my towel aside. "You're going down, North."

"I'm already in the pool," he deadpans. "Technically, I've *been* down."

"Wow," someone mutters. "Was that flirting or dad humor?"

"Can't it be both?" I say, wading in.

Caden's eyes flick to mine just for a beat—quick, quiet, enough to make my heart hiccup—and then he's tossing the ball to Cameron and arranging people into teams.

The teams sort out fast. Me, Shane, Jess, and Kurtis on one side. Caden, Cam, Dale, and Kiara on the other. The pool's wide enough to split lengthwise with a rope and two empty floaties rigged like goalposts.

"House rules!" Kurtis calls out. "If the ball hits a noodle, it's a redo. If you hit someone in the face, you owe them a soda. If you catch someone cheating, you're legally allowed to dunk them."

"Wait, what if *I* get hit in the face?" Dale asks, rubbing his temple from the last round.

"Then we all owe you an apology and a better aim," Kiara says sweetly.

The first serve comes from Cam—a bullet straight toward Jess, who actually yelps but recovers quickly. The game is chaos in the best way: bodies splashing, arms flailing, water arcing into the air like it's part of the scoreboard. The ball bounces off the floatie-turned-net three times before Kurtis manages to spike it hard enough that Cameron misses.

We cheer. I steal a glance at Caden across the pool.

His hair is soaked, clinging to his forehead, and there's a drop sliding down the line of his neck, glinting in the sun. He smirks at me like he knows I'm staring—and he *does* know. He always knows.

He mouths, "You're going down," and I mouth back, "You wish."

Every time we bump shoulders or pass close, my skin sparks. Every time he laughs, it hits somewhere low in my chest. And every time he does that little half smile thing—like he's enjoying a joke only we get—it makes me want to pull him under the water and kiss him breathless.

But we keep it light and hidden behind splash fights and team trash talk.

"I swear he's cheating," Jess groans after Caden somehow volleys the ball one-handed while talking to Cam.

"I'm just talented," he replies, completely unbothered.

"He's slippery," I add, moving next to her. "We'll take him down together."

Caden throws water in my face. "You've *tried*."

I stick my tongue out. "Your ego's showing."

He shrugs. "It always does."

Everyone laughs, but beneath the noise, I feel the tug again—that low ache that won't quit. The clock's ticking. In a few weeks, this will all be *before*. These sunny days, the dumb jokes, the stolen glances. The version of him I get every day.

At least he's got his own car now. That helps. The old white Honda Civic runs loud but steady. Still, I know the truth—once he's in Kentucky, he'll have class and early practices, weight training, film study, and God knows what else. He'll be making new friends. Living in dorms. Being seen, admired, challenged.

He deserves it. I *want* him to have it—but that doesn't mean I won't miss him like hell.

We play until the sun slips low enough that Kurtis's mom yells from the kitchen window about "dinner or heatstroke." We all groan and clamber out of the water, dripping and exhausted, towels wrapped around our shoulders like victory flags.

Kurtis tosses me a soda and bumps my arm. "Y'all staying a while?"

"Probably," I say, glancing at Caden.

He lifts a brow, his signal. I nod, barely perceptible.

LATER THAT NIGHT, after the pizza boxes have been flattened and shoved in the recycling bin, after the rest of the crew crashes on couches or heads home with half-hearted goodbyes, Caden and I slip out the back door and around to the far side of the house. There's a strip of grass near the privacy fence, tucked behind the shed, where the moonlight hits just enough to see and not enough to be seen.

It's our spot. Or at least, it is now.

He leans against the side of the shed, arms folded, watching me approach with that quiet intensity that makes my skin hum.

"Took you long enough," he says, voice low.

"You're the one who had to say goodbye to everyone twice," I reply, stepping close.

He smirks. "I'm charming."

"You're slow."

We're toe to toe now. My heart's already racing.

Caden reaches for my hand, threading our fingers together. "You were good today. In the game."

"You're just saying that because I didn't throw the ball at your face."

"I mean… the bar is low," he teases, but his thumb brushes mine in a way that makes me forget how to breathe.

We're so close now I can feel the heat coming off his skin. I slide my free hand up his chest, fingers skimming the damp cotton of his T-shirt.

He leans down, just a little, and I meet him halfway.

The kiss is slow, deep, and unhurried—like we're making up for lost time even though we know we'll never have enough. His hands settle on my waist, mine on his shoulders, and everything else fades.

When we finally pull back, I keep my forehead pressed to his. "I'm gonna miss this."

His grip tightens just a little. "Me too."

"I hate how fast it's going."

"I know."

We stay this way, quiet in the dark, the sounds of summer a low background hum. A dog barks somewhere down the street. Crickets sing. My pulse refuses to slow.

I shift, pulling him a little closer. My mouth brushes just under his jaw. "You know... we've got a few more weeks."

"Yeah." His voice is rougher now. "But we're not doing *that* here."

I smirk against his skin. "Didn't say we would."

"You're thinking about it."

"I'm *always* thinking about it."

He groans. "Theo."

I look up. "Come on. It's not like I haven't earned it."

"You've earned a medal for self-control."

I grin. "You know my birthday's at the end of September, right?" Eighteen and I can't fucking wait.

"I'm aware."

"I've... been thinking," I say carefully. "Maybe I could visit. For the weekend. To celebrate. I'm already figuring out a way to make it happen."

His eyes widen slightly. "You'd come all the way to Kentucky?"

"I would if you wanted me to."

He nods, eyes dark. "I do."

Something about the way he says it makes my chest tighten all over again. "Good," I whisper. "Because I plan to celebrate properly."

He kisses me again—quick, hard, like he needs it.

Then he pulls back with a shaky breath. "We should head home before someone decides to come out this way."

"Let them," I say, but I know he's right.

We walk back slowly, hands brushing, eyes heavy. And even though it hurts knowing the countdown is real, I also know one thing for sure: We'll make it work. We *have* to.

SIX

CADEN

A HEAVY LUMP CLOGS MY THROAT. I KNEW IT WAS GOING TO be hard, but saying goodbye to Theo is something I've been quietly dreading all summer. I just didn't realize how much it would feel like pressing pause on the best part of my life.

Outside, I can hear the soft thud of a car door closing. Probably my dad rearranging bags for the third time. Mom's been fussing over snacks and maps since six thirty. We're supposed to hit the road by eight sharp. It's now seven thirty.

My room's pretty empty now—closet mostly bare, desk stripped, posters rolled and rubber-banded in a box in the back seat. There's a duffel near the door with the stuff I didn't want crushed under a printer or a crate of clothes. And then there's me, flat on my bed, wrapped around Theo.

It's quiet in here, but not the peaceful kind. It's that thick, weighted silence—like the world is holding its breath.

Theo's tucked into my side, one leg hitched over mine, his hand curled in the fabric of my T-shirt like he's afraid I'll float off without the anchor. His cheek's pressed against my chest, and I can feel his lashes flutter every few seconds. He's not crying. Neither of us are. But it's all there, just under the surface.

He shifts slightly. "You've got thirty minutes."

I nod, then tip my chin down until my lips brush the top of his soft curls—those stubborn, gentle ones that still won't grow into the afro he wants. "I know."

"They're gonna start calling for you any minute."

"I know."

He exhales through his nose. "Still not going."

"I wouldn't ask you to."

Because we already talked about it. No big dramatic goodbye in the driveway. No awkward hug in front of my parents. And definitely not in the dorm. I'm sharing a room with some guy named Bryce who already sent a three-paragraph intro email about his collection of vintage video game controllers. Not the place.

Honestly, if Theo came, I wouldn't know how to stay.

So here we are. On my old mattress. On the edge of everything.

He tilts his head back to look at me, and his eyes— God, those eyes—are glassy but steady. "You're excited."

"I am."

"I hate that I'm kind of mad about that."

I smile, even though it cracks something in me. "I get it."

"Because I want you to go. I want you to do every-thing—like, all of it. The classes and basketball and new friends and parties with weird dorm food and loud music."

"Sounds incredible."

"But I also want to hit pause right here," he says, curling tighter into me. "And just... keep you."

I bury my hand in the back of his fluffy strands. "If your mom had gotten frisky just five and a half months earlier, we'd be going together."

He snorts. "Or if yours had waited."

"Greedy woman," I mutter.

"Sloppy timing," he agrees, then quiets. "Do you think we'd be different if we were the same age?"

I hesitate. "I think we'd be dangerous."

He laughs at that. It's soft and sharp all at once. "We're already dangerous."

"True," I say, brushing his jaw with my thumb. "But then I'd get to do this every day."

His expression wobbles a little. "You think it's going to be hard? There?"

"Yeah," I admit. "Freshman with a scholarship? They're going to expect everything and then some. I have to show up early, prove I'm not just hype. I've already got training sessions scheduled before classes even start. And then there's Bryce."

"Bryce the enthusiastic gamer."

"With two lava lamps," I say flatly. "He mentioned them twice."

Theo laughs again, but it fades. "Do you think you'll have time? For me?"

My chest tightens. "Always."

"But like... really?"

I lean down and press my lips to his forehead. "Yeah. It'll look different. Might feel different sometimes. But this isn't something I want to lose."

He swallows. "Even if it gets hard?"

"Especially if it gets hard."

We fall quiet again, into the kind of silence that feels like both a hug and a punch.

My fingers trace along Theo's spine, memorizing the shape of him. I don't want to forget any of this. The way he smells faintly like pool chlorine and citrus body spray. The tiny scar above his eyebrow from when he tried to flip off the diving board in eighth grade. The way he exhales when I touch him like it's the only thing keeping him grounded.

I want to say it. It's right there, lodged behind my teeth, swelling behind my ribs.

I love you.

Not just in the shy, puppy-love way. Not in the flirty texts or the slow kisses. But real and raw. The kind that curls into your bones and takes root.

I shift slightly to look at him. His eyes meet mine—so open, so *there*—and I part my lips. "Theo, I—"

He pulls back suddenly, not far, but enough. His fingers tighten on my shirt.

"Don't," he says quickly, voice tight. "Not like this."

"What?"

He shakes his head, and his smile is trembling. "Not when you're about to leave. Not when I can't say it back the way I want to. I don't want it to be a goodbye thing. It shouldn't *start* with an ending."

I close my eyes, my heart thudding hard. "Okay."

"I mean it," he says, softer now. "I *feel* it. I just… not right now."

I nod. "Yeah. Okay."

We hold each other for a while longer, our legs tangled, our breaths synced like muscle memory.

There's a soft knock at the door. "Caden?" my mom calls. "We're ready when you are, sweetheart."

My heart drops. "I'll be out in a sec," I call back.

Theo rolls onto his back, staring at the ceiling like it might give him strength. I sit up slowly, rubbing at my eyes.

"Do I look like I've been crying?" I ask, my voice rough.

"You look hot, if that helps."

"It does, actually."

We both laugh, but it's tight around the edges.

I grab my hoodie off the chair and tug it on, stuffing my Nokia and wallet into the front pocket. Theo sits up, knees drawn against his chest. He doesn't say anything for a second, then reaches out, grabbing my hand.

"You promise?" he asks quietly. "About my birthday?"

"End of September," I say. "We'll make it happen."

"You better. I'm not turning eighteen without you."

I lean down and gently kiss him again, like we're exchanging maps that will lead us back to each other. "I'll see you soon," I whisper.

He nods, but his eyes are shimmering.

I open the door. The light spills in like it's another world entirely. And when I step into it, I carry him with me.

Mom's downstairs when I come out, sipping coffee

from the thermos she's been nursing all morning. She looks up the second she hears me, her eyes flicking over my face like she's doing a silent check-in. She doesn't ask if I've been crying, but she doesn't need to.

"Car's packed?" she asks, voice gentle.

I nod. "Just gotta do the goodbye part."

She puts the cup down and opens her arms. I go to her, and she hugs me tight, her cheek resting against my shoulder. "I'm so proud of you, Caden."

My throat squeezes, but I manage to get words out. "Thanks, Mom."

She pulls back and smiles up at me, but her eyes are glassy. "You're ready. You've been ready since you were ten and tried to organize your own basketball tryouts."

"That was a deeply flawed plan," I mutter.

Her smile grows, and for a second, we're just standing in the kitchen, not on the verge of this huge, life-changing thing.

She cups my cheek like she used to when I was little. "Are you okay?"

I glance toward the stairs, toward my bedroom. "Not totally. But I will be."

She nods, understanding what I'm saying—and what I'm not. "He's special."

"I know."

She pulls me in for one last squeeze, whispering, "He's gonna be okay, too, baby. You both will."

I let her hold me for a few seconds longer, then step back. "He'll let himself out. I, um… I left him something."

She arches an eyebrow.

"In his room. Just something small."

She smiles but doesn't press. "Well, we'll be waiting in the car."

Dad's already outside by the trunk, fiddling with the GPS that's stuck to the windshield like a barnacle. When I come out, he straightens, rubbing his hands on the front of his jeans.

"Got snacks, jumper cables, and your favorite water bottle," he says, like he's ticking items off a list.

"I'm not driving across a desert, Dad."

"Doesn't mean you shouldn't be prepared."

I grin. "Thanks."

He puts a hand on my shoulder. "You know, when I was your age—"

"Here we go," I mutter under my breath.

"—I didn't even *have* a car. I moved into a dorm with two bags and a secondhand alarm clock that broke on day one."

I smirk. "Is this supposed to inspire me or lower the bar?"

He chuckles. "Just reminding you that you're already ahead of the game. And that you've got this. You're smart, you're focused, and you've got a damn scholarship, which is more than I ever had."

"Thanks, Dad."

He gives my shoulder a quick squeeze. "We're proud of you. No matter what."

There's a pause. Then I take a breath and glance between them. "Actually... would it be okay if I drove by myself?"

They both blink.

"I just—I need a little time to clear my head," I add

quickly. "I'll follow you, but... I want to go alone. Is that okay?"

Mom, who'd planned to be my passenger, tilts her head, clearly warring between maternal instinct and understanding. Then she nods. "Of course."

Dad shrugs. "We'll be the car in front doing the speed limit."

"And I've got Theo's playlist," I add. "I'll be fine."

Mom presses a kiss to my forehead. "Flash your lights if you need to stop for gas."

"Will do."

Across the yard, the front door of the Brookses' house opens. Lori steps out first, apron still tied at her waist like she left something on the stove. James follows, slow and solid, and Amelia slips between them, barefoot on the porch.

"Lord, I can't believe today's the day," Lori says, coming straight for me with her arms wide. She hugs me tight, rocking me once like she used to when I was small. "Feels like I just watched you and Theo chasing fireflies out here last summer." Her voice catches, but she pulls back smiling. "You call your mama, but you better call me too. Don't make me have to track you down."

James clasps my hand in both of his, then pulls me in for a one-armed hug. "We're proud of you, Cade. Always have been. You put your mind to something, you do it. Now go prove us right." His voice is deep, even, the kind that settles in your chest.

Amelia hangs back until I glance her way. Then she comes down the steps, half grinning. "Guess this makes me the one stuck keeping Theo out of trouble." She bumps my shoulder. "Don't think you're off the hook, though. When you come back, I want my *Mario Kart* rematch. And don't be surprised if I've leveled up while you're gone."

I laugh, but it snags in my throat. Because she's right—I am leaving them with Theo. And after everything that just happened upstairs, that thought twists in me harder than anything else.

I say goodbye and round the car, keys in hand, but just before I slide into the driver's seat, something makes me pause. I look back. Back at the house. Our house. The one Mom and Dad worked their asses off to buy when I was four. I remember sitting on the floor in what would become my bedroom, drawing on a pizza box while movers tried to wedge a couch through the door. That memory hits me like a freight train now. The chipped paint on the porch. The creaky screen door. The patch of grass where Theo and I used to practice skate tricks until we both fell into a rosebush and declared the sport evil.

I blink hard, then look up at the second-story window —my room.

And there he is.

Theo.

He's lit by the morning sun, hair haloed and messy, hoodie zipped up halfway like he's trying to hold himself together with the strings. His hand is resting on the sill, and he's looking down at me like he doesn't want to blink in case I disappear.

Our eyes lock. And then he smiles.

It's small, soft. Not showy. Not brave.

Just real.

My breath hitches. And somehow, that smile is enough to push me forward.

I duck into the driver's seat, shut the door, and click the belt into place. The car smells like summer—old air freshener and pool towels—and the faintest trace of Theo's cologne from when he helped me load up last night.

I slide the CD into the stereo. The player whirs, clicks. Then music blares through the speakers: "Hot in Herre" by Nelly. I burst out laughing, loud and sudden and completely ridiculous.

Of *course* he started the playlist with this.

Three years ago, we got dared at a sleepover to learn the dance to it. Theo went *all in*. He tied a bandana around his head, grabbed a hairbrush as a mic, and spent the whole night yelling, *"Take off your clothes!"* until his mom made him shut it down.

It was the stupidest, funniest, most *us* moment—and I'd nearly forgotten it.

Until now.

I laugh so hard I tear up, wiping my eyes as I pull out of the driveway and onto the street.

The song changes a minute later to something mellow —"Just Friends" by Musiq Soulchild—and my laughter fades, but the warmth stays. The beat's smooth, easy, like a breeze through an open window. The lump in my throat's still there, but now it's wrapped in something gentler.

Gratitude.

I'm leaving my home, and I'm leaving *him*. But I'm also heading toward something big.

And we've got plans. He'll come for his birthday. I'll

find a way to visit when I can. We've carved out this space between us—something soft and strong—and I believe in it. In *us*.

The music plays on. The sun climbs higher. And the road unfurls in front of me like a promise.

I keep driving. Hope, curled like a secret, rides shotgun the whole way.

SEVEN

THEO

It was tucked under my pillow.

I didn't find it until later that night, after Caden left. After I waited too long in his room, staring at his dresser like he might come back just to grab one more thing. After his parents had driven off down the street, I descended the stairs back to my house like I'd aged twenty years, my body weighted down, each step carrying the ache of something I couldn't name.

Then I crashed onto my bed, flipped the pillow, and there it was.

A folded-up sheet of notebook paper. My name written in his all-caps, slightly slanted print. My throat closed up the second I saw it. I didn't even open it right away. Just held it for a while.

And yeah. I cried.

He'd drawn a little comic. Stick figures, obviously. It was us—him with a basketball, me with a book (okay, fine, it looked more like a square with legs, but I *got* it). In the first panel, we were lying on my trampoline from last spring, stargazing. In the second, I was snort laughing while he tried to kiss me with his mouth full of popcorn. In the third… we were kissing. Just us, no distractions. A word bubble from me said, *"Can I say it now?"* and his said, *"Not yet. Wait till Kentucky."*

I taped it inside my closet door.

It's been two weeks since he left, and every time I look at it, I feel everything all over again. The ache. The missing. The hope. It's also been the *longest* we've ever gone without seeing each other. I thought maybe I'd settle into it. You know—school starts, life gets busy, I'd get used to it.

I haven't.

Classes are full-on. Senior year isn't chill like I hoped. AP Lit is basically emotional warfare, and calculus just stares back at me like I'm the problem. Add that to basketball practice every afternoon, and I should be distracted.

But I'm not. Not really.

I've been playing phone tag with Caden all week. Between his training schedule and classes and God knows what else, we've mostly just swapped missed calls and slow-ass texts.

Seriously, texting should count as a sport. T9 predictive text is *not* a gift from heaven like people think. It's a punishment.

Case in point:

Me (2:47 p.m.): u good?

Caden (5:01 p.m.): yeh srry just done w practice. Dead

Me (5:03 p.m.): same. calc is trying to murder me

Caden (5:15 p.m.): u win. my legs hurt so bad i forgot my name

It's been like that for days. Bite-sized glimpses of each other.

But tonight, finally, he calls.

I'm stretched out on my bed with a paperback balanced on my chest, eyes skimming the same paragraph for the third time without taking it in. I keep pretending the words are enough to distract me, to make me forget how empty the room feels without him here. But they blur together, restless as I am.

Then the Nokia buzzes against the cover, startling me. Caden.

I snatch it up like it might disappear and hit the green button so fast I nearly drop it. "Hey."

His voice comes through a little staticky but warm and familiar. "Took you long enough."

I grin. "I answered on the first ring, don't even start."

"I know. I'm just talking crap."

My smile softens. "Hi."

He sighs. "God, I miss you."

I close my eyes, pressing the phone tighter to my ear. "Same."

There's a quiet beat between us. The kind that says everything we're not saying. Then he says, "So, I made it through week one of classes."

I sit up a little. "And?"

"And… it's wild, Theo. Like, the campus is huge, my

dorm smells like Axe and microwaved noodles, and I have a professor who legit swears in class."

"That's your dream professor."

"Right? She said *bullshit* today and no one even blinked. I nearly applauded."

I laugh. "Please don't get kicked out of class for clapping."

"No promises."

He tells me about his classes—Introduction to Business, a required history class about Southern politics ("Why do they hate us so much?"), and a writing seminar that's already making him rethink using contractions. Then there's basketball. That one makes his voice shift slightly—lower, a little heavier.

"Training's brutal," he says. "It's not even official season yet, and I'm already sore in muscles I didn't know I had."

"You're gonna kill it," I say, trying to sound more sure than I feel.

"I don't know. Everyone's good. Like, *really* good. I'm just hoping to make it past tryouts."

"You have a scholarship, Cam. You're already in."

"Yeah, but that just means they expect more."

He doesn't say it, but I know what he means. A Black freshman from a public high school in South Carolina—people expect him to prove he belongs every second of every day.

"You will," I say again, because I need him to believe it.

He doesn't answer right away. Then, quietly, he murmurs, "Thanks."

There's shuffling on his end, probably him lying back in bed. "I'm going to a party tonight," he says after a moment.

My stomach twists. "Oh?"

"It's just a team thing. Nothing crazy. But yeah. First party."

"Nice." My voice sounds a little too neutral. I clear my throat. "Wear deodorant. Don't fall for the Jungle Juice scam."

He laughs. "I've been warned. It's probably Gatorade and regret in a bucket."

"You know it."

We're quiet again, and I can tell he's about to say something, so I fill the space first. "I've got four weeks left," I say. "Until my birthday. I already asked my mom, and she said I can take the car."

"Yeah? That's amazing."

"I'm coming up Friday afternoon and staying till Sunday. Nonnegotiable."

He exhales slowly. "God, I can't wait to see you."

My heart pounds. "I want to kiss you so bad it hurts."

He groans softly. "Don't start."

"You started it."

"I said I was going to a party, not that I needed to hear about your thirst."

"Too late."

He laughs again, but I can hear the ache underneath it. "You still got the comic I made you?" he asks, voice low.

"Of course I do," I say, no hesitation. "It's taped inside my closet. I see it every day."

"Still holding up?"

"Couple of creases, but yeah. It's my favorite thing."

There's a pause—one of those soft ones that stretch and breathe. Then he says, "I really wish I could touch you right now."

My whole chest tightens. "Me too."

We don't say more. Not the big thing. Not yet. We don't have to. Not when it's folded into every breath, every word, every beat of the line between us. Still holding. Still strong.

When I finally put my phone down, I head downstairs. Amelia's sprawled on the couch, scrolling her phone. "Wow," she says without looking up, "you're actually leaving the house? What's the occasion—lonely hearts club meeting?"

"Shut up," I mutter, pulling on my sneakers.

She smirks. "Don't sulk just because your boyfriend's off at college and you've got no other friends."

My ears burn. "I so do," I correct, a little too quickly.

"Mm-hm," she says, clearly not buying it, then goes back to her screen. The worst part? She's not entirely wrong. Thankfully, I've got Kurtis, and I like some of the guys on the basketball team well enough, but it's not lost on me how much of my time—years of it—has been spent orbiting Caden.

I didn't really plan to go to the lake, but I can't stay in the house either. Not after that phone call. Not after hearing Caden's voice, full of noise and random people as students outside his room were gearing up for the party, knowing I can't be there. That I'm *not* there.

It's almost nine by the time I make it to the lake.

The lake's one of those unofficial spots. No signs, no security, just a patch of sandy shoreline off a gravel road where teenagers go to pretend they're in a music video. There's a firepit burning low near the rocks, a couple of old lawn chairs, and someone's Jeep parked too close to the water blasting Lil Jon through tinny speakers.

I park a little ways off and walk the rest.

A few people nod at me as I pass—kids from school, some upperclassmen, some juniors I recognize from gym or assemblies. There's drinking, low-level flirting, some folks paired off and sitting too close on someone's tailgate. It smells like cheap beer, bug spray, and humidity.

I find my friend Kurtis near the back, sitting on a log and nursing a Coke like it's something stronger. He's been my friend since middle school, when we both got cut from soccer and sat on the bleachers talking trash about gym class.

He sees me and lifts his drink. "Thought you bailed."

"Nah," I say, sliding down next to him. "Just got caught up."

He snorts. "Caught up with what? Practicing your dramatic stare into the distance again?"

"Maybe. It's my signature move."

"You need better hobbies."

"You need a better face."

"Touché."

He tosses a pebble at my sneaker. We sit in comfortable silence for a minute, watching the fire flicker and someone nearly fall off a cooler trying to impress a girl.

"Can't believe we're seniors," he says after a while.

"Feels like we were just freshmen getting shoved into lockers."

"I was *never* shoved into a locker."

Kurtis gives me a side-eye. "Dude, you're five-nine and delicate. You *absolutely* could've been."

I laugh, not even offended by his description. "Fair."

Kurtis sips his Coke. "You ever think about what you're doing next year? Like, after graduation?"

"All the time."

"Yeah?"

"Yeah. I mean… I don't have it all figured out, but I know I want to teach. English, probably."

His eyebrows shoot up. "Look at you, Mr. Hawkins. Inspiring the youth."

"Don't make fun," I say, though I'm smiling. "I like it. The idea of showing kids how words matter. How they can carry you places."

"I'm not making fun," he says, holding up his hands. "I think it fits. You already tutor half the team anyway."

I duck my head, tracing patterns in the dirt with my sneaker. "The hard part is where. What school. How far."

He smirks knowingly. "Where Caden goes, right?"

I force a laugh, like it's an obvious joke. "Yeah, something like that."

He chuckles and lets it go, attention drifting back to the fire.

But inside, my chest is tight. Because it isn't a joke. I do want to follow Caden to UK. Desperately. But I also want college to mean being out, living honestly, not hiding in shadows. And I don't know if those two things can coexist. Not with him. Not yet.

The uncertainty sits heavy in my gut as Kurtis takes another sip of his drink, oblivious.

I also want to be able to go wherever *he* is once he's finished college. Whatever city Caden ends up in, whatever team picks him up—if it happens, and I believe it will —I want to be able to follow. Not like a tagalong. Just… near enough that we don't have to do *this* again. The distance. The silence. The ache.

Teaching's been floating in the back of my head for a while. I'm good with people. I love stories. And schools always need teachers—everywhere. But I can't say that out loud. Not to Kurtis. Not yet. So I just sip my drink and say, "I'll figure it out."

And I will. Because I'm not letting this—*him*—slip away.

Kurtis nudges me with his shoulder. "You'll kill it, man. You'll have your pick of schools and courses."

"Thanks."

"What about a girl?"

I stiffen, just a bit. "What?"

He shrugs. "You know. You've been flying solo since like forever. Just wondering if there's anyone on your radar."

My throat dries up. He doesn't mean anything by it. Kurtis is chill. He's not the kind of guy who makes jokes at someone's expense. But still. I've never said the words *I'm gay* to anyone outside my family and Caden's. And especially not around here. Not in Gomillion.

I force a half shrug. "Not really."

He studies me for a second. "You sure? 'Cause you've had this whole mysterious thing going on lately. Like you're always texting someone but pretending you're not."

My face heats. "Maybe I've just got talented thumbs."

He laughs, but he doesn't press. I appreciate that.

He leans back on his hands, eyes on the water. "Sometimes I think I want to go to Atlanta. Just start fresh. Get outta here. I love my family, but this town… it's too small for my brain."

I nod. "Yeah. I know what you mean."

My phone buzzes in my pocket, and for a second, my heart jumps.

> Caden: Night good. u okay?

I smile and type back.

> Me: at lake. miss u.

Then I click the screen off and slide the phone away before I get too obvious.

Kurtis is watching me. Not nosy, just curious. "You good?"

"Yeah."

"You seem… I don't know. Different, lately."

I bite the inside of my cheek. "Maybe I am."

He nods like he gets it, even if he doesn't. "Well, whatever it is, I hope it's good."

We sit in silence for a bit longer. The fire pops. Someone yells from the water. A truck revs, then cuts off again.

I look around at the couples leaning into each other, at

the people stumbling around with red Solo cups, the silhouettes laughing like this is the best night of their lives. And I feel like I'm *here* but not really part of it, because the only person I want to be with is a little over three hundred miles away. Probably at some party with sweaty walls and sticky floors, surrounded by people I don't know—people who don't know him the way I do.

And maybe it's dumb, but I still feel him. Like some thread connects us, stretching thin but unbreakable.

"Four weeks," I murmur to myself. Kurtis doesn't hear me. He's distracted by someone trying to freestyle near the fire. I stand up, brushing dirt from my jeans. "I think I'm gonna head out."

"Already?"

"Yeah. Gotta help Dad out tomorrow with something."

Kurtis nods. "All right, man. Be good."

I snort and shake my head. "You too."

I walk back to Mom's car, air cool on my face, the lake behind me reflecting nothing I want to hold on to. And as I drive home with the windows down and Caden's CD in the stereo, I don't hit Skip when his voice comes through between tracks.

Because, yeah, I may have burned him a CD for his drive, but the asshole went all out and made me one too. It arrived in the mail a few days back. Of course he did. Caden's ridiculous like that—ridiculously romantic in a way that sneaks up on you. All low-key and casual until suddenly your heart's on fire and you're trying not to cry at a stop sign.

"Hey," he says. *"So, I picked this one for you to play when you miss me but don't want to say it out loud."*

A beat.

"It's okay to miss me, by the way. I miss you too."

My hands tighten on the wheel. Four more weeks. Just four. And then I'll get to see him again. Not through a screen via Skype. Not with delays and dropped calls. Just *him*. Real and close and mine.

I press Play on the next track and drive through the dark, the music holding me like a promise.

EIGHT

CADEN

I'VE CHECKED MY PHONE FIVE TIMES IN THE LAST THREE minutes. Which is ridiculous, because the screen is still blank. There are no new messages. No "almost there." No "parking now." No Theo. I know he wouldn't be able to text and drive, but still, it's driving me insane… the waiting.

I'm standing on the edge of the parking lot, pacing like I've got somewhere else to be. I don't. I've been here for twenty minutes already, bouncing between the grass and the curb like a damn wind-up toy with too much charge and nowhere to go.

I can't sit still. Won't.

Six weeks.

That's how long it's been since I last saw him. Since I hugged him in his bedroom with the door half closed, tried to be quiet about it, and left him something stupid and sweet to find later.

Now it's Friday, late September, and the day after his eighteenth birthday. The air's different—still warm, but gentler and less aggressive. The leaves around campus are starting to think about changing, a couple of brave ones going golden too early, like they want to be first. It smells like cut grass and cheap laundry detergent and fried food from the student center. My legs ache a little from this morning's drills, but I barely notice.

I got lucky this weekend. Bryce, my roommate, decided to go home. Something about his cousin's wedding and needing clean socks. I didn't ask questions. I just grinned and helped him pack, because it means I have the room to myself. Me and Theo.

God, just thinking it makes something knot tight in my stomach. He's on his way. I know it. But every second without him is another second too long.

I nod at a couple of people as they pass—Marisol from my writing seminar, clutching a giant reusable coffee cup like it's oxygen; Rashad from the team, earbuds in, hoodie up. He nods back but doesn't stop, which is fine by me.

The sky's that soft, early-evening blue where everything looks like it was shot through a vintage filter. I can see across the lot to the line of dorm buildings, red-brick and boxy, softened by the trees between them and the basketball courts in the distance. There's a low thud of a ball bouncing, followed by a shout. Someone's still putting in work. I should be too.

But I'm not.

Because then, finally, I see it.

A silver Prius turns the corner, creeping slowly through the narrow rows. I know it's his before I even see the driver. It's the same car I've been picturing in my head for days—his mom's, technically, but it suits him. Quiet. Practical. Undeniably reliable.

It parks halfway down the row, and then the door opens, and he steps out.

Theo.

His hair is a little longer and is just starting to fall into his eyes. He's wearing a faded navy hoodie and cutoff khaki shorts, and he's squinting into the sun like it personally offended him. He looks... tired. Like school's already been a lot. But also lit up from the inside, like this is the thing that's been keeping him going.

And he's here.

I move without thinking. Feet carrying me forward too fast, too eager.

He spots me just as I reach him, and his face breaks into that stupid, perfect grin. The one that gets me every single time.

We don't say anything. We just grab each other. His arms lock around my waist; mine wrap around his shoulders, and I bury my face in the crook of his neck. He smells like cinnamon gum and car air and him. I inhale like I've been holding my breath for a month.

"Hey," he murmurs.

"Hey," I say back, voice already thick.

We pull apart, but just barely. His hands are still on my sides, mine on his shoulders. If this were a movie, we'd kiss now. Right here, in front of the Prius and the half-empty parking lot and whoever's watching.

But this isn't a movie. It's Kentucky, and we're not out. Not here. Not yet. So instead, I give him a bro hug. A second round. This one tighter and fiercer.

"I missed you," I say into his shoulder.

"Same," he breathes. "So much."

When we finally step back again, I catch his eyes flicking up and down, like he's checking me over. "You look good," he says, voice a little too casual.

I grin. "You look tired."

"Drive was long," he says, stretching his back. "And I forgot how boring the radio is once you leave the state."

"You didn't listen to my playlist?"

"I did! I just… may have looped it three times and then needed a break from 50 Cent."

I laugh and reach for his duffel, slinging it over one shoulder. "Come on. Let's get you inside." I wrap my arm around his shoulder and steer us toward the dorm building.

We walk together across the lot. The sun slants low now, turning the pavement warm and the windows of the buildings gold. Some guys are tossing a football on the green. A group of girls sit on the front steps of another dorm, eating from foam take-out boxes and talking loud enough to echo. Campus is alive, but not overwhelming.

"This place is bigger than I imagined," Theo says, glancing around. "Everything feels… wide."

I nod. "Yeah. It does that. Took me a week to figure out where the laundry room is."

He laughs. "You? Mr. Campus Map himself?"

"Hey, I printed one. Just didn't *read* it." We pass the outdoor seating area, a couple of metal benches under a tree that's already started shedding leaves. I nudge him. "That's where I eat breakfast most days. Better light."

"Better light?"

"For my cereal. Gotta set the vibe."

He rolls his eyes, but I can tell he's filing it away, picturing me sitting out there in the morning sun.

The dorm entrance is ahead now. Brown-brick with a metal-framed glass door. It's not fancy, not by a long shot, but it's been home for six weeks. I reach for the handle, glancing back at him.

"You ready?"

He nods. But his eyes say everything. I squeeze his shoulder one last time and push the door open. He steps inside first, and I follow before leading him to my room.

My bedroom door clicks open, then shuts behind us, and everything shifts.

The sounds of campus dull to a murmur. It's just us now—Theo and me, finally behind closed doors.

For a second, we just stand here, breathing. Staring. Six weeks is a long time.

He drops his duffel to the floor. I let his backpack slide off my shoulder. Neither of us says a word.

I'm not sure who moves first. It might be him. Might be me.

But the second our arms are around each other again, something in my chest loosens, then tightens all at once. My hands find the back of his neck, his waist, his spine— anywhere I can hold on. His mouth crashes against mine like it's been aching. Like it's starving.

And I get it. Because I'm starving too.

We kiss like we're trying to make up for every second we lost. His lips are soft but urgent. His fingers fist the back of my shirt, and I groan into his mouth when he shifts closer. Every part of him presses into every part of me—heat to heat, need to need.

"God," I gasp against his jaw. "I missed your mouth."

"You missed *me*," he breathes, hands skimming under my shirt. "All of me."

"Damn right I did."

I walk him back toward the bed, barely looking, just going by memory with the sound of his breath in my ear. We tumble onto the mattress in a tangle of limbs and a shared laugh that cuts too close to a moan. My twin bed creaks.

He's beneath me, curls sprawled on my pillow, grinning up like I never left.

I hover over him, chest brushing his. "You're here."

"I'm here," he whispers, tugging me down again.

We kiss slower this time. Still hot. Still hungry. But full of something else too. Like we're remembering who we are together. Relearning skin, pace, and rhythm.

I shift my weight, groaning softly when our hips align. He's hard. So am I. But it's not frantic. Not yet. Because all I can think about is how much I missed him. His mouth, his lips, the way he wraps around me like he belongs there.

He adjusts his legs around my waist and pulls me in, locking his ankles behind me. The movement draws a gasp from both of us as we grind, clothes in the way but friction thick and full.

I break the kiss and glance down at him. I brush his cheek with my hand. His eyes are glassy and warm.

"Happy birthday," I murmur, thumb brushing the corner of his mouth.

Theo grins, breath catching. "I turned eighteen."

"I'm sorry I missed it."

"I'm not," he says, voice rough. "Because I'm here now. And we can celebrate."

My breath hitches as I dip back down, kissing the edge of his grin.

We slowly rock together, aching, the grinding of our hips turning into something that feels dangerously close to too much. His fingers are in my hair, tugging enough to make me bite my lip. My hands roam his ribs, his back, tugging up the hem of his hoodie to get to skin.

"Caden," he gasps.

"Yeah?"

"You're—God—you're gonna make me—"

I push my hips down again, just once, and he arches beneath me, trembling. I can feel the tension in every part of him, the way he's holding back just like I am.

But we don't rush.

I kiss his collarbone, his neck, that spot just under his ear that makes him squirm. "You're so hot like this," I whisper. "You don't even know."

"I *do* know," he says breathlessly. "You tell me every time we kiss."

We laugh softly into each other's mouths, still grinding, still clothed.

I pull back to see his face. His hair is a mess, cheeks flushed, lips red and wet. He's the most beautiful thing I've ever seen.

And he's *mine*.

We're tangled in each other, breathless, pressed so close, there's no space left between us. His legs around my waist, his hands in my hair, my mouth moving against his like I've been desperate for it—because I have.

Six weeks is a long time when every part of you wants someone. And I want him. God, I want him.

His hoodie's off, and his tee's shoved up around his ribs. My sweats are hanging low on my hips, and all I feel is heat—his skin, his mouth, his breathy moans in my ear every time we grind together. We've done this before, touched and kissed and gotten each other off more times than I can count. But this? This feels different. This is six weeks of missing and texting and *not touching*. Of late-night calls with hands shoved under blankets while whispering, *"I wish you were here."*

Now he *is* here. And I'm not wasting a second.

He's hard against me, shifting his hips in just the right way. I press down, and he gasps, throwing his head back as his back arches off the bed.

"Caden—God—don't stop," he pants.

"I wasn't planning to."

We're not going to go all the way tonight—not yet. We talked about it, agreed we'd know when it was right. But that doesn't mean we're holding back. Not when we're both this desperate. Not when every kiss feels like catching fire.

I push my hand down between us, palming him through his boxers. He lets out this needy, broken sound that makes my pulse spike. I love making him come apart like this—love knowing exactly how to touch him to get him there.

He bucks up into my hand, grinding back hard. "You're the worst," he mutters, voice wrecked.

"You like it," I say, nipping his jaw.

"Shut up and—ahh—keep going."

I do.

My hand slides beneath the fabric, fingers curving around the heat of him. He's already throbbing in my palm, impossibly hard and twitching with anticipation. I stroke him slow at first—lazy, teasing—just to feel the way his breath catches. His hips jerk up involuntarily, a sharp gasp punching from his chest, and then he lets out a sound that's more moan than breath, raw and aching.

His eyes flutter shut, lashes trembling. His lips part, full and kiss-bitten, and when I tighten my grip slightly, he groans loudly. I don't care. Let the whole building hear him. Let the walls hold that sound forever.

No one's here. No one matters but him.

"You're so hot like this," I whisper again, leaning closer, pressing a kiss just under his jaw. His fast pulse thrums erratically there. "I missed watching you fall apart."

His laughter is short and breathless, breaking on a gasp when I drag my thumb across the head of his cock. He bucks into my hand, his muscles pulling tight like a bowstring.

"You're—mmh—unbelievable," he grits out, one hand fisting the sheets, the other gripping my shoulder so hard it's almost bruising.

I grin against his throat, teeth grazing skin. "You started it. Turning eighteen and showing up looking like *that*? What'd you expect me to do?"

He gasps out a shaky laugh, then moans as I quicken the rhythm. "Self-control?"

"Wrong guy," I mutter, breath hot against his neck.

His body is trembling now, a sheen of sweat shimmering on his chest, catching the dim light of the dorm. His thighs tense on either side of mine, and I can feel the shudder working its way up his spine. The way he moves—desperate and instinctive—sets fire to my blood. I know this body. I know every gasp, every twitch, every tell.

"Caden—shit—don't stop, don't—"

"I've got you," I promise, kissing the hollow of his throat. "Let go for me."

He does.

With a low, fractured cry, he arches up, head thrown back, mouth open in a silent gasp as he unravels in my hand. His whole body tightens, then shakes as he comes, warmth spilling over my fingers. I keep stroking him through it—gentle now, coaxing, comforting—while watching every flicker of feeling race across his face like a storm breaking over open sky.

He's beautiful like this. *Wrecked*, undone, but still soft around the edges. Vulnerable in a way only I get to see.

As his breathing slows and his body goes slack, he opens his eyes, blinking up at me like he's not sure what planet we're on. And I swear, nothing has ever made me feel more *right* than that look.

When he finally slumps back into the sheets, chest heaving, I grin and kiss his temple. "Welcome to Kentucky."

He groans. "You're so smug."

I press my non-sticky hand to my heart. "With reason."

Theo rolls onto his side, breath still hitching, skin flushed and warm while I grab some tissues and wipe my palm. His eyes are hazy but locked on me, and the soft, lopsided smile he gives me sends heat spiraling through my chest.

"Your turn," he says, voice rough with satisfaction and something tenderer underneath.

I blink, my throat suddenly dry. "You don't have to—"

"I want to." His voice leaves no room for argument. He's already shifting closer, warm fingers finding the waistband of my sweats with steady certainty. "I *need* to."

And the second his hand slips beneath the fabric and wraps around me, all the teasing, all the posturing I might've thrown in, it disappears. Gone. Blown clean away by the feel of him, of Theo, touching me like he knows exactly how I fall apart. Because he does.

Because it's *him*.

My whole body jerks, hips rising instinctively into his palm, and I bury my forehead against his shoulder, trying to catch my breath. My hand curls at the base of his spine as he starts to move—slow at first, maddeningly slow, dragging every drop of pleasure out like he's savoring it.

"You okay?" he murmurs.

I can't even speak. I just nod, eyes squeezed shut, my entire nervous system tuned to his hand, his breath, his warmth against me.

His other hand trails up my back, fingers splaying out between my shoulder blades to hold me steady as he finds a rhythm. My body arches into his, chasing every motion. I'm panting now, every breath a ragged prayer, every nerve lit up like a live wire.

Theo leans in, presses his lips to my jaw, whispering, "You feel so good like this."

I release a deep, raw moan into his neck, my hand fisting in the sheets beside him.

He keeps going, steady and unrelenting. I feel the shift as he tightens his grip, the slick slide of skin, the unbearable heat building inside me. We don't say much—just gasps, broken moans, and whispered curses. His name is on my lips like it belongs there, over and over, tangled with *please* and *God* and *don't stop.*

My whole body tenses. "Theo—" I manage, voice cracking.

"I've got you," he breathes, mouth close to my ear. He throws my words back me. "Let go."

And I do.

I come hard, my body jolting with each wave, his name the only thing I know how to say. He strokes me through it, soft and slow, until the shaking stops and all I can do is cling to him like he's the only solid thing in the world.

And right now, he is.

Afterward, we lie here tangled up, sticky and half dressed, grinning like idiots. We don't untangle for a while. Eventually, we clean up—quick wipes, fumbling grins, kisses in between—and collapse back into bed under the blanket, limbs a mess of heat and skin.

I tuck my chin over his shoulder, my fingers tracing lazy patterns on his stomach. "I'm never letting you go six weeks again," I murmur.

"Next time," he says, yawning, "I'm kidnapping you."

I smile against his skin. "Deal."

We lie here a while longer, curled together on my narrow twin bed. The window's cracked, the breeze carrying in the sound of people outside—shouts, laughter, someone playing music too loud.

But in here, it's just us. Warm, close, steady.

Theo traces lazy circles on my back. "I've been dreaming about this," he says, voice barely above a whisper.

"Me too."

There's a beat, and then he shifts under me to look at me properly. "I don't want to go home on Sunday."

I kiss the tip of his nose. "Then let's not think about it yet."

He closes his eyes and breathes deep, like he's trying to soak this all in.

"Happy birthday, Theo," I whisper again.

"Best one yet." His smile is slow, sleepy, and everything.

NINE

THEO

Waking up with Caden's mouth on my dick probably ruined me for regular mornings. I don't know how I'm supposed to go back to alarm clocks and cereal after that kind of sunrise.

I'd barely opened my eyes, still heavy with sleep and travel aches, when I felt him—warm breath, hot mouth, soft hum against my skin, like he was trying to wake me up slowly and sweetly. Like a gift.

It worked.

We didn't talk much. We didn't need to. We'd simply touched and moved and let it happen again, the way it's always going to happen when it's just us in a room and we've got enough hours to get tangled up without time running out. Later, we laughed about it while brushing our teeth, naked except for boxers, bumping hips like we weren't both fully addicted.

Best. Morning. Ever.

We spent the whole day together—Caden showing me around campus, pointing out weird student traditions, claiming a corner of the library as "his," telling me about classes and professors and how tough Coach has been on him even though his scholarship pretty much guaranteed him a spot. "Tryouts were hard," he said, "and the pressure's real. If I want to start, I've gotta earn it."

I believed him.

He's got the kind of drive that burns through everything. It scares me a little, if I'm honest. Not because I think it'll pull us apart, but because it makes me wonder how I'll coexist next to that kind of fire when I'm not even sure what I want yet—besides *him*. I know I'll follow him here in a heartbeat if I can, but I also don't want to mess up what he's building by hovering too close.

Still.

Today made it harder not to imagine that future— lunch at the campus café, making out in the stairwell of a dorm I'll probably never live in, holding his hand under the table at a hole-in-the-wall diner in town where no one looked twice at us. If I went to school here, we could have that *all the time*. Well, some of it. The whole together-in-public thing would have to continue to remain on the down-low.

By the time we get back to his dorm, the sun's barely begun to set, spilling a warm gold across the floorboards like a movie scene that doesn't know how to end. Caden shrugs off his hoodie and tosses his keys into the ceramic bowl by the door—some half-assed attempt at adulthood he swears keeps him organized.

He stretches, arms over his head, shirt lifting to expose a sliver of warm brown skin and the curve of his waist. I catch myself staring, and he catches me looking.

"Hungry?" he asks, eyebrows raised, teasing already curling at the edge of his voice. "I've got leftover spaghetti that may or may not be a health hazard."

I laugh, because of course he does. "You planning to poison me before the party?"

He shrugs. "There are worse ways to go."

"I'll pass," I say, dropping onto the couch. "I think I'd rather starve."

He snorts and walks over to me with a small bag he drops dramatically on the bed.

I raise an eyebrow. "What's that?"

He grins. "Part of your birthday gift."

I lean forward and pull it open. Two mini LEGO kits. One is a tiny street food cart with a hot dog vendor. The other looks like a firefighter with a dalmatian.

"We're building these?" I ask, bemused.

"You're damn right we are," he says, already tearing into the box. "We've got time, and I need a pre-party wind-down."

I snort. "Is this a thing now? LEGO dates?"

Caden shrugs. "Could be. You trying to judge me or fall more in love with me?"

"Dangerous question," I say, and open the second box.

We work in silence for a while, soft music playing from his stereo. He's got a little furrow between his brows as he clicks pieces together, biting his lip in concentration like he's assembling a space shuttle and not a four-inch plastic hot dog cart.

I finish mine first. It's crooked, but charming. "Mine's got personality," I declare.

He leans over, inspecting it critically. "Yours looks like it survived an earthquake."

"Still standing."

He laughs, that deep, warm kind that settles behind my ribs. Then he holds up his finished figure—a proud firefighter with a red helmet and blocky shoulders. He even gave it a tiny mustache. "Behold: me, in another life."

"Heroic," I say, handing him my own figure. "Mine owns the hot dog stand across the street. Secretly feeds your dog when you're not looking."

"Illegal," he replies. "But hot."

We swap the minifigures without ceremony. Just a quiet trade, his fingers brushing mine in the handoff. I look down at the firefighter now in my palm—my Caden.

He clears his throat. "So now you've got me. Miniature edition. Travel-sized for convenience."

I smile, throat tight. "I'll keep him safe."

His eyes meet mine for a second too long. The air shifts—thickens. Not in a bad way. Just… full. Like everything we're not saying is pressing up between us, quiet but loud as hell.

He nudges my foot with his. "You've got that look."

"What look?"

"The one that makes me feel like you want to undress me and stay in for the night."

I want to tell him I do want that. That any time alone I can get with him, I'm here for. But instead, I just say, "That obvious, huh?"

He grins, and for a moment, we snuggle—bare feet tangled as we rest on the bed talking shit, spare LEGO pieces scattered like confetti, sunlight skimming through the blinds.

The light outside starts to shift, the gold of late afternoon sliding toward the cooler blue of evening. It's the kind of shift you can't ignore, no matter how good it feels to stay still.

Eventually, we get up. The spell breaks gently, without drama.

We shower, then dress. He looks too good in low-slung jeans and a snug black T-shirt, the sleeves hugging his biceps in a way that's downright disrespectful. I watch him in the mirror, barely bothering to pretend I'm not staring. He catches me once, smirks, and throws a balled-up sock at my chest.

We laugh.

And then we don't.

Because this part—the next part—requires masks. We both know it.

By the time we're out the door and heading toward the party, the shift is complete. I slide my hands into my pockets. He walks with too much space between us, posture loose but shoulders tight. We could be room-mates. Just friends. Just two guys heading out for a fun night.

And that's the story we'll tell tonight. This is the version of us the world gets.

I know how important this is to Caden. Bonding with the guys—especially the upperclassmen—matters. Even if his talent is a given, respect isn't. Chemistry isn't. And no matter how much I want to take his hand in mine, I won't be the reason he loses ground before the season even starts.

So I nod and grin and keep my damn hands to myself.

Just a couple of friends, heading out.

But my LEGO version of him is already in my back pocket. He doesn't know it, but I'm bringing him with me anyway.

The house is already loud when we show up—music pulsing through the walls, red plastic cups clutched in almost every hand. There's a grill going in the backyard, a few people dancing in the living room, and the unmistakable smell of cheap beer, cologne, and charcoal hanging in the air like a frat-boy fog.

Caden gives me a look—half apology, half warning—and I squeeze his shoulder once before we step inside.

"Let's just do the rounds," he says quietly. "Won't be long."

"I'm good," I say, and I mean it. "Just don't ditch me with someone who only talks about protein powder."

Caden laughs, and the tension in his jaw eases a little.

We work the room, shaking hands and nodding at people I'll probably never see again. Some guys recognize me from pictures in his room. One of the freshmen nudges Caden with a smirk and whispers something, and Caden rolls his eyes but takes it in stride.

And for a while, it's fine.

The music thumps low under our feet. I sip a Sprite and listen to stories about preseason drills and how brutal Coach can be when he's "in a mood." I catch Caden watching me a few times, subtle and soft-eyed like he's still surprised I'm here. I give him a grin and bump his arm, and for a second, it feels almost normal.

Until it doesn't.

We're outside near the grill when one of the juniors, a wiry guy with a chipped tooth and too much swagger for someone wearing flip-flops, tosses a joke into the conversation like it's nothing.

He's talking about another guy on the team, some freshman who wears a bandana and always sings along to Destiny's Child in the locker room.

"Dude's probably got a *boyfriend* in his sock drawer," he says with a laugh around a sneer. "Real secret garden type."

There's a pause. A few guys laugh—tight and awkward, like they don't want to but can't quite help themselves. Someone coughs. The air shifts.

Caden and I go absolutely still. My stomach twists. I glance at him, but he's staring straight ahead, jaw clenched, eyes unreadable.

I feel a flicker of heat rise in my chest, but before I can say anything, Jamari, one of the seniors, steps forward, holding a plate of wings and looking not at all amused. "Yo," he says calmly, but loud enough to cut the noise around him. "Nah. We don't do that here."

The guy blinks. "What?"

Jamari's eyes narrow. "I said, we don't do that. Ain't nobody here tryna hear you act like being queer's a punch line."

The air goes taut, a rubber band pulled too tight. To his credit—or maybe just because he's smart enough to know when to back down—the guy mutters something and backs off, heading inside.

Caden lets out a breath so slow it's nearly silent.

Jamari glances at us, eyes sharp, and nods once. "Glad y'all came tonight," he says, voice easy again, before turning back to the grill like he didn't just cut tension with a single sentence.

Caden nudges me lightly, barely touching. "Let's go find some place quiet."

I follow him, heart pounding—not from fear exactly, but from the way one careless sentence can unravel so much. Still, I catch myself smiling just a little.

Because Jamari had our backs, even though he doesn't know it.

Because Caden is surrounded by at least a few good players, should he ever want to share his sexuality with them.

Because I'm here with him.

We step around the side of the house and keep on going to the street, the distant thump of bass fading behind us. It's quieter now, the kind that hums with the buzz of everything left unsaid. Caden walks close, not touching, but his shoulder brushes mine now and then, like he can't help it. Or maybe I can't. I don't even know anymore.

He exhales, long and slow. "So, that guy—the one who made that comment...."

I glance over, jaw already tight. "Yeah?"

Caden frowns, eyes forward. "Name's Alan. Total dickhead. He's not on the team, just some guy who hangs around because he thinks being near athletes makes him one."

I scoff. "Well, he's doing a great job repping the worst kind."

"But Jamari—our captain—he's not like that," he says, more serious now. "He's actually a good guy. Called Alan out once before, quiet but firm. He doesn't put up with that crap."

I nod, letting that sit for a second. "Anyone out? On the team?"

Caden shakes his head. "Not that I know of."

My heart sinks, just a little. Even after everything, after all the texts, the phone calls, the whispered wishes across hundreds of miles, reality always cuts sharp.

But then he adds, quieter, like he's trying not to make a big deal of it, "But there's an LGBT group on campus. They do events, have meetings. Safe spaces and all that. And… I've seen couples, same sex, just walking across the quad, holding hands like it's nothing."

I stop breathing. My chest flutters with something warm and wild and way too hopeful. "Really?"

He nods, glancing sideways at me, like he's gauging how much he should say. "Yeah. More than once."

Something inside me expands, like a balloon inflating in my ribs. It's ridiculous—how just a small thing, like seeing someone *else* living a little freer, can make me feel like the whole world might crack open for us someday. That maybe, somehow, it won't always be this complicated.

But the feeling crumbles almost as fast as it comes,

because it can't be us. Not here. Not yet. Not when the price for being visible is *everything* for him—scholarship, future, pro career. One whisper could undo everything he's built.

Unless… unless someone else does it first. Unless a trail gets blazed that makes it even a little bit safer for someone like him. Like us.

Caden stops walking and turns to face me. His expression's unreadable for a second, but his eyes—God, his eyes are so *familiar*. They tell me everything. "Wanna head to my room?" His voice is low, rough in a way that scrapes across my skin and curls under my ribs.

And just like that, the air shifts. Thickens.

There's a gravity between us that snaps into place, taut and magnetic, like the whole world went still and the only thing pulling us forward is *this*. I can feel him. The warmth of his body, the tension under his skin. His breath brushing the space between us.

And I *know* what he means. I know it without him saying another word.

And my body answers before I do—heat pooling low, my pants tightening, pulse skipping like I just hit a free fall. It's been weeks. Six long weeks of distance and discipline, of holding back, of pretending that words in texts and pixelated smiles on grainy video calls were enough.

But it hasn't been enough. Not even close.

It's been building, quiet and steady and unstoppable— every lingering glance, every brush of his fingers across mine, every slow kiss that ended with me half out of my mind and aching.

And tonight… I can feel it down to my bones. Tonight is the night.

There's no question in my mind. No fear. Just this fierce, overwhelming need to be close. To *feel* him in the only way we haven't yet. Something sacred and new and inevitable.

I step in. Just a few inches, but it's enough. I feel the way his breath stutters, the way his eyes drop to my lips. I lean forward, close enough that my voice barely has to cross the space between us. "Cade," I whisper, and his name tastes like lightning on my tongue, "I want you inside me."

His eyes widen before going half-lidded. Lips parting just a little.

I don't look away. Can't. "I want it more than anything," I say again, softer now. A confession. A promise. A truth I've known for weeks but couldn't say until now.

His fingers find mine and curl tight around them. They're warm and trembling and solid, grounding me when I feel like I might float right out of my skin.

He squeezes once, breathes in deep, then nods before releasing his hold on me. "Let's go."

We walk in silence, the space between us charged, humming with anticipation. His fingers brush mine once, twice, until finally they stay, linked loosely as we move down the dark sidewalk, away from the party and into something quieter. Something just ours.

By the time we climb the stairs to his building, my pulse is racing. I don't know if it's the climb itself or what's coming.

Caden's room is dim and quiet, the door clicking shut behind us like a seal on something sacred. It smells faintly of laundry detergent and his cologne—warm, familiar. My heart is thudding too fast. My hands won't stay still. But he looks at me with this soft, open gaze like he's just as rattled, just as sure.

We kiss first. It's slow and deep. Every second of it's charged. His hands find my waist, my neck, my back—like he's mapping me. And I let him.

Sometimes it feels like this bed is the only square of the world that belongs to us. Everything outside is borrowed, performative. But here—here I get all of him. But after a while, I pull back and clear my throat. "I, uh… I should freshen up."

Caden tilts his head, curious.

"I just… I want to be ready. Properly," I mumble, cheeks hot. "I read stuff. Online. You know. Prep."

Understanding flashes in his eyes, and he nods. "Okay. Yeah. Um… take your time."

I duck into the tiny bathroom. My hands shake a little as I go through the motions, doing what I've read about, trying to remember tips from LiveJournal threads and blog posts. It's awkward. It feels clinical. But it also feels right, like I'm making space for him. For us.

When I return, Caden's sitting on the edge of the bed, legs apart, elbows on his knees. He looks up and shoots me a nervous smile full of warmth.

I cross to him and kneel beside the bed to dig into my bag. "I brought… lube. And condoms. If you want."

He exhales a laugh that's mostly relief. "God, thank

you. I was hoping you'd know what to bring. I had nothing."

We both laugh softly, and it cracks something open—a release of tension we didn't know we'd been holding. Caden pulls me in again, arms warm and certain, and we kiss—this time deeper, hungrier, like we've both decided to stop pretending we're not already halfway gone.

Clothes come off in uneven bursts: a sock here, my shirt over my head, his hoodie tugged with a shared grin. Clumsy. Beautiful. Our fingers keep brushing, catching, like we're drunk on permission.

And when his shirt lifts, and I see him, *really* see him, I forget how to breathe.

He's changed since he left for college. I *knew* he had, saw it for myself last night and this morning, plus he'd mentioned that the coach said he's grown an inch and that he's been lifting harder since training, but seeing him now, bare skinned, it hits me like gravity.

Caden's chest is cut, lean muscle carved in sharp, clean lines down his torso. His abs catch the soft light from the window—not gym-rat ripped, but athlete strong, all fluid strength and purpose. His shoulders are broader, arms thicker with power he wears without trying. Everything about him feels refined, sharpened. Like the boy who first caught my eye has quietly grown into the man I can't stop looking at.

His skin glows dark brown in the low light, warm and velvet smooth. I reach without thinking, running a hand along his side, just under his ribs. He shivers. "I could stare at you all the damn time," I murmur, almost without meaning to.

He laughs, low and shy, ducking his head. "Yeah? I thought I was imagining that."

I shake my head, smile tugging at my lips. "Nope. You're just… unfair."

His hand skims the waistband of my boxers, thumb brushing just beneath. "Still okay?"

"Yes," I whisper.

We trade pieces of ourselves in touches and half sentences. My fingers skim the inside of his wrist, and Caden stills. His pulse jumps beneath my thumb.

"You're shaking," I murmur.

He huffs out a laugh, breathless. "So are you."

I lean in and brush my mouth along his jaw. His eyes flutter half-closed, lips parting as though he's already waiting for me. "You're beautiful" slips out before I can stop it.

He turns toward me, smile quick and shy, and then it's gone when our mouths meet. His lips are soft, hesitant, tasting of peppermint gum. I cradle the back of his neck, holding him there, and he exhales against me like the air's been punched from his chest.

"God, Theo," he whispers into the kiss, pulling me closer.

The kiss shifts, grows deeper. I take his bottom lip between my teeth and his breath stutters—then he presses back, hungrier, desperate. My hand slides down, over the curve of his hip, and I feel the muscles twitch beneath my palm. He gasps, sharp, and bites his lip to swallow the sound.

"Don't hide from me," I whisper, kissing down the line

of his throat until I find his collarbone. My words spill against his skin. "I want to hear you."

His fingers cling to my back. "You're going to ruin me," he says, but it's a laugh, too, trembling and soft.

I press my lips harder to his collarbone, tongue tracing the ridge there. He tilts his head back, offering me more. His breath comes faster, uneven.

"I like when you do that," I tell him, and he groans, a sound I feel more than hear.

"Is this okay?" he asks again, softer now, voice threaded with awe.

I nod, heart full. "Yes. Every part of it."

"God," he murmurs as he grazes his fingertips over my chest. "You're perfect."

I laugh, a little breathless. "I think your standards are broken." But my voice hitches when his palms skim my ribs. I run my hands down his back, feeling the slope of muscle, the ridges of his spine. He's solid and warm and right here. The realness of him undoes me.

When our mouths meet again, it's slower. More deliberate. A different kind of hunger, one that's deeper and aching. My whole body feels lit from within, like someone struck a match inside me and the flames are licking through my veins.

Caden pauses as he unpacks the lube and condoms, awkward as hell, and then glances at me with a sheepish look that's too endearing for words. "You know I haven't done this before," he says, voice low.

"I know," I say. I'm trying to stay calm, to not let nerves override the way I'm shaking with need. "Me neither."

He hesitates again, then reaches out like he's afraid of

rushing, of hurting. I lie back on the bed, trying to still my breathing. Every nerve in my body is tingling and wide open.

"You okay?" he whispers.

I nod, pulse pounding in my ears. "Yeah. Just… ready."

His fingers are cautious at first, slick and slow, tracing circles like he's learning me by touch alone, memorizing every small shift in my breath. When I tense at the first brush around my opening, he goes still, patient, his eyes on mine as if he's asking without words. I force myself to exhale, nodding, and only then does he ease forward, pushing one finger inside.

The stretch burns, a raw pressure I didn't expect, sharp enough to make me wince. My chest tightens, but his voice is there immediately, soft and steady, grounding me when he says, "You're so good. I've got you. Just breathe, Theo." He strokes his thumb along the back of my hand, holding it tight enough to anchor me but gentle enough to let me pull away if I need to.

It hurts, yes, but beneath the pain, there's something I've wanted for longer than I can admit. The ache is almost holy—proof of what it means to open myself to him, to let him in. It isn't about enduring; it's about surrender. Trusting him to walk me through it, step by step, until the pain blurs into something I can hold.

"Don't stop, Cade," I whisper, my voice hoarse, trembling with more than just nerves. "Please don't."

His answer isn't just words—it's a kiss, soft against the inside of my knee, then another pressed to my hip bone. His breath is warm on my skin. His hand never leaves mine.

My body is flushed, damp with sweat, every nerve sharp and electric. I feel exposed, raw, but not alone. Every movement, every touch says the same thing: *I've got you. I've got you.* And I believe him.

He watches me the whole time—not with ego or assumption, but with a kind of reverence that makes my chest twist. Like he can't believe this is happening. Like he can't believe *I'm* happening.

When he finally removes his fingers and slides over me, breath shaky, body trembling with restraint, our eyes meet. "You sure?" he asks again, voice wrecked.

I nod once, throat tight. "Yeah. I want this. I want *you.*" I pass him a condom with shaky hands.

And when he enters me, slow, careful, my hands curl tight into the sheets. The stretch is sharp, and I bite my lip hard to keep from crying out.

He freezes instantly. "Do you want me to stop?" His voice breaks on the last word.

"No," I manage, eyes squeezed shut. "Just... give me a second."

He doesn't move. His forehead rests against mine. His breath is shallow. We stay this way—caught in the space between discomfort and something incredible—until my body adjusts, until the fire dulls to heat.

And then something shifts. I breathe. Let go. And suddenly it feels like falling into a rhythm I didn't know my body was waiting for.

When I open my eyes, Caden's staring down at me. And his face—Jesus—it's undone. Full of awe, like I'm the most beautiful thing he's ever seen.

I nod, and he moves again—slowly and carefully at

first. Each thrust is deliberate, like he's committing to memory how I feel around him, how I gasp when he hits just right.

We move together, hips and hands and mouths in a kind of silent sync. There's nothing frantic about it. It's tender and intimate, the kind of closeness that makes me want to cry.

His hand cups the side of my face. His thumb strokes just beneath my eye. "I missed you so much," he whispers.

"I missed you too," I breathe, my hands curling around his shoulders, holding on like I might fall apart otherwise.

He kisses me again, and this time, it's more than heat. It's love, even if we haven't said the words yet. It's all there —in the pressure of his mouth, in the way his hips move against mine, in the way he looks at me like I'm something precious.

I feel it building, low and hot, coiling tighter with every push and pull, every brush that makes my body jolt. My legs lock around his waist, pulling him closer, needing him deeper. Our skin is slick, every movement a slide of heat against heat, and our breath tangles, broken, desperate.

"I'm close," he gasps, his voice raw.

"Me too," I manage, though my throat feels tight with the force of it, the inevitability.

The pressure crests, unbearable, and then it breaks— my whole body tightening, trembling, giving in. His voice fractures into mine, the sound of both of us unraveling together, and in that instant, it isn't just release. It's everything we've poured into this—the trust, the longing, the love we've been carrying in silence until now.

When it's over, he doesn't move. Just stays there, heavy and warm, his forehead pressed to mine. His fingers trace slow lines down my arm, trembling like he's afraid I'll vanish if he lets go.

"I hope that was okay," he murmurs, almost too quiet to hear.

I tilt my head, pressing my lips to his damp temple. "Cade," I whisper, "it was more than okay. It was everything."

He kisses me with a lingering slide of his lips, then gently begins to ease out. I wince, a sharp ache blooming low in my spine, and he pauses immediately. "Sorry," he whispers.

"It's okay," I breathe. "I'm okay."

Carefully, he detaches, then shifts and removes the condom, tying it off and reaching for a tissue from the nightstand. I watch him in the dim light—his skin still flushed, hair mussed, movements quiet and thoughtful.

I'm sore. There's no way around it. My thighs ache, and I can feel the slick mess between them—lube smeared and drying tacky on my skin. But I don't want to move. Not yet. The bed is warm, and his body is still close enough to chase away the chill creeping into my limbs.

He slides back beside me, still naked, and tugs the sheet halfway over both of us. His arm wraps around my waist, and I sink into him instinctively, even though every part of me feels stretched and spent.

We stay like this a while—sweat-damp, tangled in a mess of limbs and sheets, breaths calming bit by bit. My chest rises against his, and I can feel his heartbeat begin to settle, like a song winding down.

"I should probably clean up," I mumble, though I make no move.

"You don't have to," he says softly, thumb brushing lazily over my hip. "Just stay a little longer."

And I do. The room smells like us now—like skin and heat and nerves and something far bigger than either of us can name. My body feels wrecked in the best way—stretched, tender, sore in places I didn't even know I could be sore. But also held. Warm. Safe.

I run my thumb absently along the dip of his hip. It's stupid how much I love that part of him. Like, it's a hip. But it's *his* hip. That makes it art.

Eventually, Caden rolls onto his side, pulling me into his chest with one strong arm. Our legs stay hopelessly tangled, like they don't know how to let go yet. His palm rests flat between my shoulder blades, big and steady, like he's still trying to hold me together.

We don't talk. We don't have to. There's a certain kind of quiet that only comes after something seismic.

After a few minutes, his voice finds me. "Are you... okay?" he asks softly. "I mean, really. Afterward. Was it... was it what you thought it'd be?"

I let the question settle for a second, because it deserves more than a knee-jerk reaction. My body gives an instinctive "ouch," but my heart answers louder. "It hurt," I admit, honest as ever. "More than I expected."

His arm tenses a little, but I tighten my fingers at his side.

"But," I continue quickly, "I don't regret a single second of it. Not with you." I bury my face into the curve of his neck, breathing in his scent—faint shampoo and skin and the same cologne he's worn since he was fifteen. "It felt like… everything we've been building toward. I wanted that. Even the hard parts."

He exhales against my hair, his arm curling tighter around me. "God," he whispers, voice a little shaky. "Being inside you… I've never felt anything like that. Not just the physical part." He pauses like he's not sure if he can keep going, then presses his forehead to mine. "It felt like you were giving me something I didn't know I'd been missing. Something… I don't know. Sacred."

My heart clenches. *Sacred*. He said it like it meant everything. Because it did. "It was sacred," I murmur, so quietly I'm not sure if he hears me until he kisses the side of my head.

"You were beautiful," he says, like he's still a little dazed. "The way you let me in. The way you looked at me like… like I was more than just a guy with a dick and a plea-like prayer."

I snort against his chest, which makes him laugh too.

"There it is," Caden says, grinning sleepily. "I was wondering when the afterglow sass would kick in."

"You were nervous," I say, teasing just a little, my smile pressed against his skin.

"Terrified," he admits. "I was so scared I was gonna screw it up and make it… I don't know. Awkward. Or painful. Or accidentally elbow you in the face."

"That was a real risk," I murmur. "Your arms are lethal weapons."

"You're lucky I love you."

I freeze for just a second, the words hanging in the air like they're trying to decide if they're real.

His eyes widen. "I mean—not like—" he babbles. "I didn't mean to say it like that. Or maybe I did. I don't know. I just—"

I laugh. Not to deflect, not to dodge, but because I *get it*. Because that's exactly how it sneaks up on you. Because I've been holding the same thing inside.

"Careful," I tease, kissing the edge of his jaw. "That sounded dangerously like a post-sex confession."

"Yeah, well," he mutters, rubbing the back of his neck, "I hear it's a classic mistake."

"Guess we're both screwed, then," I whisper, softer now.

"I was going to say it before I left. And you stopped me." He meets my eyes, something flickering there—something raw and wide open.

"I just didn't want you to say it when we were saying goodbye." I sweep my thumb over his cheek. "It didn't feel fair. It didn't feel like enough."

"But this does," he murmurs. "Right now. You. Me."

My nod is slow and sure. I nudge our foreheads together. "So… I love you too. Just in case that wasn't obvious."

His grin is instant, boyish and wrecked and *everything*. "Yeah," he whispers. "It was. But hearing you say it? Kinda makes me wanna float through the ceiling."

"Don't," I say, tugging him closer. "I just want to keep you in this bed."

With that, the tension between us dissolves into something weightless. Like finally saying the words made space for the next part of us.

Together.

For real.

We snuggle close, arms wrapped around each other, our legs tangled beneath the sheets. The silence between us doesn't feel empty. It's rich and full—weighted with everything we've shared, everything we've just said. For the first time in weeks, maybe longer, I feel like I can fully breathe.

Caden gently, aimlessly traces soft lines along my spine with his fingers, like he's trying to catalog every inch of me. My own hand rests beneath his ribs, feeling the steady rise and fall of his breath. Each inhale is deep and even, like he's finally relaxed. Like we both are.

But even as I sink into the warmth of him, there's a quiet pressure building in my chest. I don't want to think about what comes next, but I can't stop it from creeping in.

Tomorrow, I have to leave.

And it's not fair. We just found our way back to each other. We said what we've been holding back for months. We crossed a line that changes everything. It felt easy—natural. Everything between me and Caden does.

Now I'm supposed to say goodbye all over again?

The thought hurts. It settles low in my gut, making everything feel heavier. Still, I don't let it show. I won't let it ruin this. Not tonight. Because tonight is ours.

We've worked so hard to get here—to trust each other, to love each other in the way we both needed. We made space for something real, and I'm not going to let dread steal that away.

I shift and press a kiss to Caden's shoulder. My lips linger there, soft against his skin, and I close my eyes.

We'll figure it out. I believe that. The distance won't undo what we've built together. It won't erase the way he looks at me, the way his touch makes me feel grounded and wanted and known.

Tomorrow will come, and I'll get in that car and drive away. But that's not what matters right now. Right now, we're here. Together. And I am holding on to this moment with everything I've got.

TEN

CADEN

Mid-October went in a quiet blur. I traveled home during fall break since there were no games on the schedule and barely any team obligations. I spent most of those few days glued to Theo—metaphorically and, when we could swing it, literally. Thanksgiving wasn't much different. Sure, I did the family dinners and made an appearance for all the important photo ops, but any time I wasn't stuffing my face or being grilled by my aunts about how college life's treating me, I was right next to Theo.

Long-distance sucks, but somehow, we're making it work. Between long phone calls, mixed CDs we mail back and forth, AIM chats that stretch past midnight, and the occasional questionable photo sent via email (blurry and low-res, but still effective), we're holding it together. It's not perfect. But neither of us expected perfect—we just wanted honest. And we've got that, in spades.

And now he's *here.*

Theo drove up yesterday, fresh out of school for Christmas break, looking way too good to be legal in those damn black jeans and his favorite hoodie—the one that rides up when he stretches. And because my roommate dipped for the holidays, we had the dorm room to ourselves. Let's just say... we made the most of that privacy.

But now? Now I have to focus. Because today, for the first time, I'm starting.

Home game. Packed stadium. Bellarmine University across the court. And I'm in the starting five.

I bounce a little on the balls of my feet as we line up in the tunnel, the thud of bass-heavy hype music rumbling through the floorboards, fans chanting above us like a wall of noise. My jersey feels tighter today. Not in a bad way. In a "this is real" way. Like the cotton's holding in something more than just adrenaline—maybe every dream I've had since I was eight and pretending a garbage can was a hoop in the driveway.

Coach has been slowly giving me more minutes this season, testing me in tougher matchups, pushing me past my comfort zone. And I've earned this spot. He didn't say that out loud, but I could tell by the way he clapped my shoulder during practice yesterday and said, "You ready to show them what you're made of?"

Hell yes, I am.

I take a deep breath and glance up into the stands. My eyes find him immediately. Theo's in a UK hoodie—*my* hoodie—and his curls are soft and loose again. After months of trying to grow it out into an afro, he finally gave up. His hair's too soft to hold the shape, and honestly? I'm not mad about it. I like it like this. It's easier to run my fingers through. Not that I'd ever do that in public.

He's sitting in the student section near the front, flanked by two of my teammates' girlfriends. To everyone else, he's just my best friend, here to support me like always. That's the story, and we're sticking to it. But I know better. I know that half smile on his face, the way his eyes track my every movement like I'm the only thing in the gym. He's trying to play it cool. He's failing.

Our eyes meet, and he gives me the smallest nod. Like *I see you. I'm here. You've got this.*

It hits me harder than I expect.

"Yo, North," someone calls from my left—Jamari, who's taken me under his wing from day one. "You gonna float off, or you sticking with us for tip-off?"

I grin, snapping back to the now. "I'm good, man."

"You better be," Leroy says, grinning as he adjusts his headband. He's our point guard and a walking highlight reel. "We've been waiting for this day. Don't make me look bad."

"I'd never," I say, bumping shoulders with him.

Price, our center, leans in with a low chuckle. "Just don't trip on your way out. Cameras are rolling."

"Gee, thanks."

Dirk, our power forward, slaps the ball against his palm and offers a smirk. "You got this, rook. You've been putting in the work."

And I have. Hours in the gym. Film sessions. Running drills until I couldn't feel my legs. All leading to this moment.

The lights flicker in a pregame strobe, and the

announcer's voice booms through the arena. "Starting at shooting guard… number 11… *Caden North!*"

The roar that hits me as I jog out of the tunnel is overwhelming. Blinding. Euphoric. But it's nothing compared to the way I feel when I glance up again and catch Theo jumping to his feet, clapping like a maniac, smiling so wide I can practically hear it.

I swear I feel lighter. Faster. Like I could fly.

As we huddle at half-court before the jump ball, Leroy throws an arm around my shoulders. "Let's eat, boys."

Price smirks. "Starters, baby. Time to remind them why we bleed blue."

Jamari slaps my back. "Just breathe, North. Run your game. You're not here by luck."

I nod, pulse racing, heart pounding.

And when the buzzer sounds, it's go time.

I'm ready. Because he's watching. And because I've got something to prove—to myself, to the team, to everyone who thought a Black kid from a small town no one's heard of couldn't make it. But most of all, I want Theo to be proud. I want him to know I see him up there. That every minute I've worked for this, I've done it with him in mind.

And today, I get to play the game I love with him in the crowd, wearing my hoodie, smiling like I'm already winning—because honestly? I kind of am.

The tip goes up.

We lose it—barely—but my body is already electric with focus. The guy I'm marking is quick and twitchy— the kind of guard who keeps you guessing with sudden bursts of speed. Bellarmine's players always bring that edge, but I stay close, shadowing him like my sneakers are stitched to his. My feet stay light, my stance low. I've got my arms out, reading his hips, anticipating every shift in direction before it happens.

On the first possession, he tries to drive baseline. I'm ready, cut him off and force him back toward the help defense. Leroy claps once—sharp, precise—and it's the signal. Our trap comes hard and fast. Jamari slides in, cutting off his passing lane, and the ball's ours. Leroy's already in motion, darting up the sideline with the speed of a bullet, and I follow instinctively.

He tosses a no-look behind-the-back pass—bold, but clean—and it finds me like it was magnetized to my hands.

One bounce. Up off the glass.

Layup.

The crowd erupts behind me in a wall of sound, thunderous and immediate, but I don't break focus. I don't pump my fist or shout. Not yet. My eyes scan, almost automatically, and they find Theo. He's already standing, arms half raised like he wants to cheer but doesn't want to be obvious.

It's quick, that glance, but it fuels me and warms my chest. I look away and keep moving.

This game? It's fast and chippy. The first ten minutes are a full-on grind. Bellarmine runs a tight system—constant motion, high pick-and-rolls, staggered screens. They're trying to wear us out, confuse our switches, force mismatches. But we studied them all week. Coach drilled every angle, every cut, and every fake. We know their rhythm, and we disrupt it like we were built for this.

Still, it's tied 9–9 when I find my next opening. Leroy swings it out to me on the wing, and I don't think—I just move. One dribble, hard left. My defender hesitates. I pull up.

The ball leaves my fingertips in a clean, perfect arc.

Swish.

The net snaps with that pure, satisfying sound that makes every hour in the gym worth it.

Twelve to nine.

I jog back on defense, adrenaline humming in my veins, every nerve lit up with energy. I've never felt more locked in. Every movement is crisp. Every rotation smooth. I see the court like it's slowed down, every screen and shift unfolding like choreography.

I belong here.

This isn't just a dream anymore. It's real. It's mine.

Coach doesn't say much when I get subbed out for the first time, but the hard slap to my shoulder and the nod of approval tells me everything I need to know. I sink onto the bench, my jersey clinging to my sweat, chest heaving. I suck in a deep breath, heart pounding like it's trying to break through my ribs.

I glance into the crowd once more. There he is.

Theo hasn't moved from his seat. He's leaning forward now, elbows on his knees, watching me like I'm the only player on the court. My hoodie swamps his frame, sleeves bunched up, his curls soft and loose. He's all big eyes and hidden smiles, doing his best to look casual while failing spectacularly.

No one around him knows he's watching his boyfriend.

But I do.

And it makes my heart thud even harder.

When I get back in, I find another gear.

I push through off-ball screens, reading plays before they form. I pick off a lazy pass at the top of the key and launch a break. I don't take it all the way—I dish it to Jamari, who drains the corner three. We slap hands on the way back up court, and he grins like a proud older brother.

A few possessions later, I drive hard, drawing contact. I hit the floor, but the foul is called, and I grin up at the ref through the sting in my elbow. This is what I trained for. This is what I love.

At the line, I take a second to focus.

One bounce. Breathe. Shoot.

The first free throw is smooth. The second follows it with ease.

By the time the halftime buzzer sounds, we're up by six.

My stat line isn't jaw-dropping—eight points, three assists, one steal, two boards—but I've made an impact. I've kept the tempo up. I've held my ground. I've played smart. And above all, I've earned every second I've spent on that court.

As I jog toward the bench, I feel that ache in my legs, that tight pull of muscle across my back, and it feels *right*. Like proof of effort. Proof that I'm exactly where I'm supposed to be.

Leroy slaps my hand with a laugh. "You've got juice today, North."

"Trying not to let you carry us for once."

"Too late," Jamari mutters, throwing a towel at me. "You owe me an assist."

"I got you in the second."

Coach gathers us, running through adjustments while we sip water and towel off. He's calm but direct. Bellarmine's not going to back down. They'll tighten their defense, test our second looks, try to force us into jump shots.

We nod, listen, commit.

And even as I'm taking in every word, there's still a flicker of warmth in the back of my mind—one I don't try to shake. Because Theo's up there, watching me from the stands, wearing my clothes and my smile, and I swear I can still feel his fingers in my hair from last night.

Basketball has always been mine. But today, it's ours too.

Coach claps once to break the huddle, snapping us back into motion. The buzz of the crowd rises again, echoing off the gym rafters. I jog onto the court, refocusing, adrenaline already coiled tight in my chest.

The second half tips off, and Bellarmine wastes no time showing their hand. Whatever their coach said to them clearly lit a fire. They come out pressing hard, aggressive on every possession. Every pass we make is contested. Every cut, crowded. We lose the ball twice in the first three minutes, and just like that, our lead shrinks to one.

Coach is barking from the sideline. Jamari calls us into a quick huddle midcourt during a free throw.

"Settle," he says, his voice low and steady. "We play our game. Let them rush. Not us."

We nod. Refocus. Adjust.

I tighten my laces during the time-out. My jersey is soaked. My legs are burning, but it's the good kind. The kind that says you're pushing your limits. That you're *in* this.

We get back into rhythm. Leroy draws a foul on a fake. Price finishes a tough bucket through contact. Dirk makes a block that's going on every highlight reel this week.

Me? I fight for every inch. I keep my hands active on defense, chase rebounds like they're personal insults, and hit one more midrange jumper that keeps the score tight. I don't light up the court, but I hold my own, and I make my minutes count.

The final two minutes are chaos. We're up three, but they close the gap with a corner three that swishes so clean it silences our crowd. One possession later, Leroy gets fouled. He drains one of two. We're up by one with thirty seconds left.

Defense decides it.

We switch on every screen, talking loud, hands up. My guy tries to slip past me again on a fake, but I recover, body low, and force him into a tough floater. It rims out. Dirk skies for the board, pulls it down like a beast, and draws a foul as the clock winds down.

He hits one. Misses the second.

Bellarmine gets off a prayer with two seconds left, but it clanks off the back iron.

Buzzer.

We win. 66–64.

The gym erupts.

The bench clears. Arms wrap around shoulders, we

slap backs, and someone grabs me by the neck and shakes me like a rag doll.

"You did it, Frosh!" Leroy yells into my ear.

"I *contributed*," I yell back, grinning.

"Same thing." Jamari laughs, mussing my hair.

The moment's a blur of sweat, noise, and high fives. My heart's still pounding as we huddle with Coach, who's all smiles now. This was our last nonconference game before SEC play in January, and we finished strong. It's not just a win—it's momentum.

Coach gives us a short rundown on winter break training plans, reminders to check in with our strength coaches, and one last "don't do anything stupid over break" speech.

As we start to split, Leroy claps me on the shoulder. "You heading home tonight?"

"Nah, tomorrow morning. Gonna chill with Theo tonight."

He raises an eyebrow but just grins. "Cool. Tell your homie I said hey."

I manage not to roll my eyes too hard. Barely.

I stick around long enough to shake hands, joke around, listen to Dirk talk about his plans to eat a twelve-piece bucket solo from KFC "as a reward for being a *goddamn wall* tonight." Then I duck out to find Theo.

He's waiting in the hallway just outside the locker rooms, leaning against the wall, hands in his hoodie pocket, that crooked smile already playing on his lips.

"Hey, superstar," he says, voice low and teasing.

"Hey yourself." I close the distance, drop my duffel by his feet, and lean in so that only he hears the next part.

"Wanna come back to my room and let me be really inappropriate in ways that would make my Catholic grandma cry?"

He snorts, grinning. "Jesus, Caden."

"What? She's not alive to be offended."

"Wow."

"What?" I say, mock-innocent. "You coming or not?"

"Oh, I'm coming," he says, eyes glinting. "But I'm not letting you talk about your grandma again while we're making out. That's officially banned."

"Fair."

We walk together back through campus. It's quiet tonight. Most of the student body's already left for the holidays. The air's crisp and the sky's clear. It smells like pine and cold asphalt, and Theo's shoulder keeps brushing mine as we walk.

I feel bigger next to him, like I always do. I'm still holding out hope for at least another growth spurt. Gotta hit that six-four mark, just to be safe. Maybe I'll start sleeping upside down or chugging calcium by the gallon.

When we get back to my dorm, I unlock the door with a little too much urgency.

Theo laughs behind me. "Subtle, North."

"Whatever. It's our last shot at real privacy. My parents are going to be up my ass all break."

He steps inside, drops his bag, and kicks the door shut behind him. "Well, then," he says, his voice low and playful as he walks toward me, "better make it count."

I catch him around the waist, and in the quiet of the room, I kiss him hard.

It tastes like victory. Like sweat and Gatorade and

something more—something that grounds me after the rush of the game. His hands find the hem of my shirt, and mine tangle in his hair, which is soft and easy to thread my fingers through.

I plan to make good on the promise to wear him out and make him hoarse from yelling my name.

But just as I lean in to kiss the corner of his mouth, Theo lets out a small breath. "My mom called," he says.

Not exactly the sexy phrase I was hoping would come out of his mouth. Still, I blink. "Yeah?"

He tugs my hand and leads me to my bed, where we sprawl out. "She said two envelopes came in the mail this morning."

That gets my attention immediately. "The colleges?"

He nods, and something flickers in his eyes—excited, maybe a little stunned. "I told her she and Dad could open them if they came. I didn't want to wait."

"And?" My stomach tightens, but I try to keep it light. "Tell me one of them was UK."

"Yep." He smiles, soft and fond. "Got into both."

My breath catches for a second. "So, what's the verdict?"

He doesn't answer right away. Instead, he curls one of his fingers in mine, eyes on the ceiling like he's thinking of the right words. That alone makes me nervous.

"I'm going to accept the offer from Louisville," he says finally.

I blink. My heart sort of stumbles, like it missed a step. "Oh." It's all I manage. Just one tiny, empty syllable, because what the hell else can I say?

Theo sits up a little, tugging me with him. "Hey—don't do that."

"Do what?"

"Act like I just told you I'm moving to another country."

I stare at him, caught between logic and disappointment. "I just… I thought maybe you'd pick here. You applied here. You got in. We wouldn't have to do long-distance again. It'd be—" I stop myself before I say *perfect*.

Theo shifts closer. "It's only an hour away. I can come to home games. We can do weekends. We can text, and call, and write dumb love emails."

I try to smile. I do.

He takes my hand again, squeezing gently. "You know I've been going back and forth on this for months. And yeah, UK's got a great undergrad program. But Louisville's BA English track is better. Plus, they've got a sport admin minor, and the post-grad education certification is top tier."

"UK has that too," I mumble, even though I already know his reasons are solid.

"I know," he says. "But it's not just that." He draws in a breath, exhaling unsteadily. "Being here with you every day—don't get me wrong, that sounds amazing. It's my dream. But it's also scary. Because I know me, Cade. And if I saw you every day—walked by you on campus, ran into you at the rec center, watched you stretch before practice—" His voice drops, low and teasing. "I wouldn't be able to not touch you."

That hits me. Hard.

"I could handle the hiding," he goes on, "but being that

close and having to pretend I'm just your best friend or your study buddy? I don't think I could. And worse—I'd mess up. I'd forget we're not supposed to be anything. I'd grab your hand or kiss your cheek without thinking."

I feel that in my gut, because... damn it, he's right.

"We barely made it through Thanksgiving without giving something away," he reminds me.

I flash back to the night we hit the ice cream shop back home. It was cold. He looked adorable in my hoodie, licking a cone like it was a challenge. And I—being the idiot I am—reached for his hand while we were walking back to my car. Out in public. Without thinking.

We let go fast—snapped apart like someone'd shocked us—but not before Mrs. Hightower spotted us from across the street. Town gossip number one. We spent the next ten minutes nervously laughing and fake arguing about who owed who ice cream, just to sell our "just horsing around" cover.

I remember the way Theo looked at me afterward. A little hurt. A little scared. Like he already knew this was the part that would suck most.

"I'm not mad," he says softly. "I get why you're not out. I do. But I've told you since I was fifteen that once I'm out of Gomillion, I'm not hiding anymore. Not at school. Not with friends. I've done the quiet thing for years. I'm tired."

I nod. I want to tell him I'm proud of him. That I love how brave he is. That I wish I was too. But instead, I say, "I hate that I'm not brave enough to be that with you."

Theo cups the side of my neck, thumb brushing under my jaw. "You're brave in a hundred ways I'm not. You play in front of thousands of people. You train like your life depends on it. You let the whole world expect greatness from you, and you carry it like it's nothing."

"That's not the same."

"It's not. But don't act like it doesn't count."

I close my eyes for a second. "I just wish I could tell people you're mine."

He kisses me softly, but it's deep enough to make my chest ache. "You can," he whispers against my lips. "Just not the world. Not yet."

I wrap my arms around him, holding tight. "You're still mine, though. That doesn't change."

"Not even a little," he says.

For a long time, we don't talk. We just hold on. Breathing. Letting the weight of it settle without crashing through us.

It's not the life I imagined. I wish I could give him everything he wants without hiding. Without waiting for someone else to go first. Without worrying that I'll lose everything if I'm honest.

But I *do* love him. That part, at least, is crystal clear.

And I'm his.

Even if hardly anyone else knows it yet.

ELEVEN

THEO

Spring hits Lexington like it's making up for lost time.

The air smells like grass and warm pavement, and every tree on campus is showing off, bursting into pinks and whites and those fuzzy green buds that make everything look like a painting. It's the kind of day that feels like it's holding its breath, like it knows something good's about to happen.

I step out of my car and immediately regret wearing a hoodie. It's too warm. The sun's already baking the sidewalk, while the breeze is just shy of sticky. But it's *Caden's* hoodie, so obviously, I'm not taking it off.

His building looks exactly like it did the last time I was here a week ago—still part of campus, but cleaner, newer, and less chaotic than the freshman dorms he was in last year. The suite-style setup means fewer people crammed into one space, and it's a lot quieter. A guy in flip-flops lumbers past, earbuds in, muttering like he's trying to psych himself up for a final. I text Caden that I'm outside, and it takes less than a minute before the door swings open.

And there he is.

Six-foot-four now, his lineup is crisp, and his hair is tapered low on the sides and in the back with longer tight coils on top that I love twisting with my fingers when we cuddle. They appear damp like he just got back from the gym or maybe just showered, wearing shorts like it's July, and grinning like I've just made his whole damn week.

"You wore the hoodie," he says, voice already half laughing, stepping out onto the cracked cement and pulling me in before I can even drop my bag.

"You say that like I don't wear it every other day," I mumble into his shoulder. It's one of my favorites. Though, it's not something I can get away with wearing on campus at Louisville.

He presses his face into the side of my neck for half a second. I feel the breath he lets out. His fingers curl just slightly tighter around my waist. "Still smells like me," he says softly.

"Gross," I reply, not stepping back.

"Shut up," he mutters.

We stand there too long. Hugging like this on a public sidewalk like we don't know better. Like this campus doesn't have eyes. Like someone won't make a comment. Like we're not trying to keep this just ours.

And right on cue, a second-story window creaks open and someone yells, "Y'all need a room or what?"

Caden doesn't even flinch. He lifts a hand, middle

finger high in the air, not even looking up. "Kick rocks, Mason," he calls, casual as breathing.

I force a laugh that doesn't quite feel right and untangle myself like it's nothing. Just a bro hug. Just friends being dumb.

No one knows. We've continued to keep it that way. Shared emails, texts, late-night Skype calls that end with silence and stubble against the screen. Another year of pretending we're just close. Of playing it cool while texting like we're dying. But since I moved to Louisville last year, it's been a hell of a lot easier.

Caden grabs my duffel like it weighs nothing and nudges open the door with his shoulder. Inside, the hallway smells like Axe body spray. Nothing's changed. It's familiar, and what's better is this year, Cade has his own room. And the other guys here—most of the basketball team—they don't even raise a brow that I'm here so often.

Once we're inside his room and the door clicks shut, it's like a switch flips. My back hits the wood with a quiet *thud* and he's there, hands on my jaw, mouth already on mine like he's starved for it. He fists the hoodie between his fingers like he's reminding himself I'm real.

God, I missed him.

Two years in, and I still can't believe this is real.

When he finally pulls out of the kiss, forehead pressed to mine, both of us breathless, he whispers, "Happy anniversary."

I blink. "Wait—today?"

"You absolute asshole."

"No, no, I knew it was close—like, I *knew* it was this week."

"It's *literally* today," he says, pointing at his wall calendar with an inked heart. "Marked and everything."

I exhale, grinning despite myself. "You made a calendar event?"

He shrugs, and I want to kiss him again, but he steps back. He's practically vibrating. "Okay. Get ready. I have plans."

"Plans?"

He tosses me a water bottle from his mini fridge. "Yes. Plans. Blanket, food, music, and one absolutely perfect hill. Don't make fun of me."

"Wouldn't dream of it. Well, maybe a little." My heart stumbles at how sweet he is. Since his second season ended—Final Four heartbreak and all—we've been stealing these pockets of time before finals hit. Then it's home to Gomillion, where, if we get our way, we'll be wrapped up in each other every night. Thankfully, our parents don't even do a double blink anymore.

We grab stuff—he pulls a blanket from under his bed, a cooler bag from his closet—and we head out the back entrance. It's quieter this way. He keeps brushing my knuckles with his when we walk, like he can't help it, and I pretend not to notice even as I lean into it.

We don't talk much as we walk across campus. It's warm enough that the air feels heavy, but not hot. Just humid spring. The scent of magnolia clings to everything. We cut around the library and up a side path to the hill behind the art building—the one spot on campus no one seems to care about. Which is probably why it's ours.

We settle near the top, under one of the big trees that hasn't quite bloomed yet. He spreads out the blanket and collapses backward like he's already exhausted.

"This is your plan?" I tease. "Lying here and doing nothing?"

"No," he says, pulling out a container of strawberries. "Also, feeding you fruit."

I smirk. "Very romantic."

He shrugs. "It's low-key. We're low-key."

Right. *Low-key.*

He hands me a strawberry, fingers brushing mine. Our knees touch. His foot nudges mine under the blanket like it means nothing.

I eat the strawberry and lie back, closing my eyes.

"So," he says after a few minutes. "Two years."

"Two years."

"That's wild."

"Yeah," I say. "It kind of is."

I open my eyes. He's watching me. He has that soft kind of look he only ever gives me when no one else is around. The kind that makes my stomach do something complicated.

We lie here in silence, wind moving through the grass, music playing soft and low from his small boom box— some sleepy R&B song I don't know the name of, but it fits the mood too perfectly.

"I love you," he says quietly, like it's the first time, even though it's not.

I glance around—no one's close enough to hear—and say it back. It still hits me like it's new.

There's a pause, and the world exhales around us.

Somewhere down the hill, someone's playing Frisbee. Laughter floats up on the wind. A bird dives into the branches overhead. But right here, where our arms brush and his pinkie keeps nudging mine, it's like nothing else matters.

And still, I don't move. Not to take his hand. Not to lean in. Not to kiss him even though I want to. Because we don't get to have those moments in public. Not here. Not yet.

I tilt my head to look at him—really look—and for a second, I think he might be fighting the same urge. His mouth twitches like he's about to say something, but then he just sighs and settles onto his back, one arm bent behind his head.

We stay this way for a long minute. Not touching, not *not* touching.

"I wish I could," I say quietly.

He turns to me. "What?"

I swallow. "Hold your hand. Out here. Just… be normal."

His face shifts, softens in that way that makes it worse. "You are normal," he says.

"You know what I mean."

He nods. "Yeah. I do."

I push my sleeve up higher and let the warmth settle into my skin. "At Louisville, I don't really think about it anymore. I'm just… out. I don't have to come out every time I talk to someone, you know? People don't make it weird. It's not perfect, but… it's mine. My space."

Caden nods, looking somewhere past the trees. "That sounds nice."

"It *is* nice," I say. "I didn't realize how much I was shrinking before until I stopped."

His jaw ticks. Just barely. "You think I'm shrinking?"

"No," I say quickly. "That's not—" I pause and try again. "I think you're doing what you need to. To survive here. To play. To stay safe."

He's quiet for a long beat. Then he practically whispers, "Sometimes it feels like I'm holding my breath."

My chest tugs. "I know."

"And then you show up," he says, voice lower, "and suddenly it's easier. But harder too."

I nod. Because yeah. *Exactly that.*

"Every time I see you at a game or in the distance, I want to call out. I want to pull you into me and not care who's watching. But then I think about who *is* watching, and I can't." His voice is raw around the edges now. "It's not that I don't want to. I just—"

"Cade." I sit up a little, shift closer. "I know. I never doubted that."

He finally meets my eyes, and it guts me. There's too much in them. Love, frustration, fear, hope. A whole damn storm.

"You're worth it," I say.

He exhales. "You shouldn't have to say that."

"Maybe not. But I mean it."

And I do. Even if I hate that we have to hide. Even if it stings every time he looks at me like this—full of everything we can't show. I'd still do this a hundred times over.

His hand brushes mine again, and this time he lets it linger. His fingers wrap around mine, light and loose and secret behind the bag near our feet.

I could cry from something that small. Instead, I ask, "Have you thought about what happens next?"

He glances at me, confused. "Next?"

"After next season."

A flicker of recognition. "Oh. Yeah." He rubs the back of his neck with his free hand. "I've been talking to Coach about the draft. Like, actually having those conversations now."

I sit up straighter. "Seriously?"

"Yeah. I mean, I'm not declaring yet. That wouldn't be 'til after next season. But Coach thinks I've got a real shot at going pro next year."

My heart kicks in my chest. This is what he's been working so hard for. I know his parents want him to complete all four years first, but they also won't stand in his way. Neither will I. "Caden, that's amazing."

He shrugs, but he's trying not to smile. "It's just talk for now. But he said if I keep up the numbers, keep working on my off-ball movement, and improve my shooting consistency, I could be looking at second-round projections."

I blink. "That's huge."

"I know." He looks out over the grass, where the sun's dipping just slightly behind the trees. "I've got to meet with an adviser this summer about getting registered with the NCAA's eligibility center, maybe start thinking about agents. Thought I'd talk to Cameron."

I nod in understanding. While Cameron, one of our high school basketball friends, is also in his sophomore year out west, his dream is to become a sports agent.

Knowing the guy, and how dedicated he was, I suspect he's already got connections and internships set up.

"Coach said I can test the waters next year—go to the Combine, get feedback, and still come back if I don't like where I land."

"Right. That's the new rule now, huh?"

"Yeah. I can declare for the draft and still retain eligibility if I don't sign with an agent. As long as I withdraw in time."

I squeeze his hand. "I'm proud of you."

He laughs under his breath. "You say that like I've already made it."

"No," I say, shaking my head. "I say it like someone who sees how hard you're working. Who knows how much you've given up for this."

His smile fades a little, and something more vulnerable settles there. "What if I get everything I want and still can't be myself?"

I pause. That one hits deep.

"You'll get there," I say. "When *you're* ready. Not when other people want you to be."

He nods slowly. "I just—I don't want to get to the league and still be hiding after years of playing, you know? I want to walk out of a tunnel and know that I don't have to lie about who I'm going home to after the game."

I slide my hand out of his and press my palm against his cheek, just for a second. Just long enough to ground us. "Then we'll get there together."

His eyes flutter shut.

When he opens them again, he leans forward and kisses me. Soft. Barely there. Like a secret passed from his mouth to mine.

And that's all we need. Not because it's enough, but because, right now, it's what we *can* have.

And honestly? For him? It's worth everything.

TWELVE

CADEN

Draft Day.

There are a dozen things I thought I'd feel when I woke up this morning—hype, nerves, maybe full-body nausea—but not this floaty, out-of-body feeling like I'm a background extra in my own life. My clothes are sharp, I've got my hair trimmed, and I'm parked on a couch in a downtown hotel suite with my parents on one side and Theo on the other. But my brain? My brain's still back at the practice court, shooting free throws until my shoulders ache.

Theo leans in so no one else hears him. "Breathe."

My eyes slide to his, and I do. His pinkie rests against mine on the cushion, barely touching, but enough to remind me I'm not alone. Not now. Not ever.

"You okay?" Mom asks softly, adjusting the edge of her navy dress like she's smoothing the fabric's nerves along with her own.

"Yeah," I say, trying to pass off the tightness in my chest as excitement. "Just staying cool."

Dad lets out a low chuckle. "You've been cool since you were twelve, boy. Don't let it go to your head."

I crack a smile. It helps. A little.

The TV screen is massive, muted for now, but the ESPN logo pulses in the bottom corner like a heartbeat. Highlight reels flash. Stats scroll. Analysts dissect my game like I'm already somebody. Shooting averages. Rebounding. Wingspan. Interview answers. Everything but blood type and whether I put ketchup on my eggs (I don't).

I glance again at Theo, and for a second, he's just my person. No titles. No hiding. His button-down's slightly wrinkled, his foot tucked under him on the couch, and his curls are freshly trimmed. He looks casual, like he belongs here—which he does. He's played just as much of a role in getting me to this point as my coaches have. But right now, to everyone else in the room, he's just my best friend.

And I hate that part. I hate pretending.

Still, pretending is better than not having him here at all.

We'd gotten here an hour ago, threading our way through a sea of press badges, media crews, and jittery players with suit jackets lying stiff over their nerves. Everyone had a smile they practiced in the mirror this morning, and an agent somewhere lurking like a hawk.

Mine, Marcus—thanks to Cameron hooking me up with the agency he interned for and plans to work for when he graduates next year—had briefed me with a grin and a bottle of water, saying, "Eyes bright, smile clean, hands off everything except the mic and your career. Got it?"

Now he's perched by the minibar, phone in one hand, sparkling cider in the other, just in case the moment strikes and he needs to pop a cork without actually breaking NCAA image rules.

"Second round is the sweet spot," he told me on the drive over. "You've got teams looking. Stay calm."

Right. Stay calm. Easier said than done when your entire future is crawling across the bottom of a screen next to college stats and the words "projected pick."

The first round begins. The room stills, the volume clicks up, and suddenly it's real.

Names get called. Families scream and sob. Players in pristine suits hug their moms and dab at their eyes as cameras zoom in. I smile at the right moments, clap when I'm supposed to, but my knee won't stop bouncing and my palms are starting to sweat.

"You're vibrating," Theo murmurs. "Knock it off."

"Trying," I mutter, not even pretending to deny it.

He leans over just slightly, so no one else can hear. "Whatever happens, I'm proud of you. And I'm yours."

God, I want to kiss him. Instead, I just breathe through it and nod.

The first round ends and my name hasn't been called. Nobody says anything right away. Mom grabs a snack from the table like she's totally chill. Dad focuses on the newspaper. Theo shifts his foot again, brushing my leg.

"You holding up?" Dad finally asks, glancing at me over the top of his glasses.

"Yeah."

"You're here. That's already more than most ever get."

I nod, appreciating it even if it doesn't quite make the disappointment loosen its grip on my chest.

Marcus checks his phone every two minutes like the screen might change the game. He doesn't say much. But his eyebrows twitch upward every so often, and I know he's waiting on something.

Theo's chatting with my mom now about his summer course. She's asking if he's still planning to TA this fall. He says maybe. She laughs, soft and warm, and I watch the way she looks at him—like she loves him almost as much as she loves me.

The second-round picks start to roll. 37. 41. 47.

Still nothing.

My pulse is thudding now. I stop watching the screen. Instead, I stare at my hands.

"Atlanta's eyeing you for 52," Marcus finally says from the window. "If that doesn't land, we go into free agency prep."

Free agency prep. That means scrambling. That means proving myself without a draft spot beside my name. And Atlanta would be too perfect. Just six hours or so away from Theo while he finishes his last two years of college.

Pick 52 blinks onto the screen. The name they call isn't mine. It's like a punch to the ribs. Not sharp, just dull and heavy.

Theo doesn't say anything. He just squeezes my knee.

Marcus doesn't waste time. "Okay. We work now. Don't lose focus."

I nod, because I know he's right. There's still a chance.

Still a way in. But the draft was supposed to be the moment.

Ten minutes pass. Then Marcus's phone buzzes on the arm of the couch. He all but dives for it, grabs it, reads, and turns toward me like a coach calling the final play. "Don't move," he says. Then he walks away, phone pressed to his ear.

Every breath I take feels like it might shake my whole chest loose.

Theo's pinkie finds mine again. "You're doing great," he whispers. "No matter what."

The call is short. Marcus returns with a look I've never seen before—sharp and bright, like lightning and sunrise all at once. His phone's still in his hand, and his other pushes through his hair like he's letting himself feel it for half a second.

"Detroit," he says. "Undrafted free agent. Two-way contract. You're invited to training camp."

The silence in the room cracks like ice.

I blink, trying to catch up with the words. *Detroit. Two-way. Training camp.*

Detroit.

My stomach flips—then steadies. Because holy shit, Detroit is closer to Louisville. Like way closer. Barely five hours if traffic behaves. And that small detail lands harder than everything else.

My knees give a little under the weight of all of it—the disappointment of not being drafted, the surge of *still making it*, and this unreal twist of fate that places me even closer to Theo than I dared to hope.

Hope slams into my chest like a fast break. And this time, it blooms.

My mom's the first to move. She's up and around the coffee table before I can stand, wrapping her arms tight around my shoulders and kissing my cheek like I'm still seventeen and just nailed a game-winner at districts.

"Oh, baby," she breathes. "I knew it. I knew it would happen."

I don't have words yet. Not ones that make sense. I just squeeze her and nod.

My dad's next, pulling us both into his arms. His clap on my back lands solid, grounding. He doesn't say much. He never does in moments like this. He simply holds on and lets me know he's proud.

And Theo... Theo just watches, beaming like the sun cracked right down the center of his chest.

I reach for him, without even thinking, and tug him into the huddle of bodies. For a second, I forget who's watching, who *might* put two and two together.

He leans in, sliding his arm around my waist, soft and familiar and absolutely necessary. "I am so fucking proud of you," he murmurs, right against my jaw where only I can hear.

I squeeze his hand behind my back and whisper, "Love you."

"Always."

My heart swells so fast and so big it might actually explode.

And just like that, I'm a pro.

Not the way I imagined—no ESPN cameras zooming

in on a teary-eyed Caden North as his name blares from the stage. No confetti. No Draft Day snapback from a glittering first-round table.

But it's real. It's honest. It's mine.

And ours.

Marcus clears his throat, breaking the moment like a coach refocusing a huddle. "Okay, fam, emotions are good, we love emotions—but I need you focused again for a sec. You've got ten pages of contract paperwork to sign and a quick Skype call with Detroit's media rep. Let's keep it tight, twenty minutes max."

Theo lets go of me, hands in his pockets, as I nod and follow Marcus to the dining table, where the laptop's already set up. The contract slides open on the screen. My mom grabs reading glasses from her purse like she's been preparing for this moment her whole life.

Theo stays close but quiet, leaning on the back of a chair, watching as I scroll through paragraphs of legalese about terms, expectations, and conditional clauses. He doesn't say anything, but every time I glance up, his eyes meet mine like he's checking in on my heart as much as my head.

The Skype call is short. Just a welcome, a nod from a media manager, and a few "We're excited to see what you bring to the table" lines. I smile, I thank them, I say all the right things—even though the real victory is standing quietly behind me, wearing a smile I'd give anything to kiss.

By the time we've wrapped, Marcus is already lining up training camp details, dates, travel logistics. He tosses a folder onto the couch along with the hotel list. "You've got two days to breathe. Then we start work."

I nod along, but my mind's somewhere else. My hands are still shaking slightly from adrenaline, but my eyes keep flicking to Theo—who looks like he's barely resisting the urge to grab my hand and pull me into the next room.

Which… honestly, sounds perfect.

He catches my eye, tilts his head just slightly, and smiles.

Marcus claps me on the back. "You earned this, kid. You really did."

"Thanks," I say. And I mean it. But I'm also suddenly so aware of how badly I want to get out of here. Not forever. Just long enough to feel what today means. Just long enough to have Theo—without pretending, without hiding, without even speaking.

I spin toward Theo as casually as I can and say, "You cool to help me grab my bag?"

He straightens immediately. "Absolutely."

We duck out of the room with a few quick nods and fake mentions of packing or organizing, and I catch my mom smirking faintly, like she knows exactly what's happening and is choosing not to ruin it.

Theo doesn't say anything until the suite door closes behind us.

Then we're moving fast—down the hall to where my room is. The second the door is locked, I press him back against it and kiss him like the biggest moment of my life didn't happen an hour ago.

His hands slide up under my shirt, fingers pressing

into my sides like he's trying to memorize every inch of me. "You okay?" he breathes between kisses.

"No," I say, and laugh softly. "But I will be."

He pulls back to meet my eyes. "Detroit."

I nod. "It's closer to you. Closer than Atlanta, than home. We'll make this work."

He grins that same grin from my senior high school year when we first kissed covered in foam. "You're really doing it."

"*We're* really doing it," I correct. "You've been there every step."

His hand cups the back of my neck. "I'll be there for all the rest."

And then we stop talking. Because some things—like celebration, like hope, like love—don't need words. Not when they're pressed into skin and whispered in the dark.

Not when they already feel like forever.

But we don't have much time. Not right now.

Instead, we're all hands and mouths, breathless laughter against skin, a tangle of limbs and need. My hoodie hits the floor. Theo's fingers are in my hair like he's trying to ground us both, but the urgency between us decides otherwise. It's not slow. It's not sweet. Not this time.

Theo pushes me backward onto the bed, eyes dark with heat, mouth swollen from kissing like we forgot how to stop. The world outside—the sunset, laughter—dissolves beyond the door we locked. Here, it's just us.

His hands are everywhere. Sliding under my shirt, curling around my ribs, greedy in a way that makes my chest tighten with something bigger than just want. My pulse stutters when he pulls the shirt over my head and tosses it aside like it offends him.

"God, Caden," he mutters, leaning down to kiss just below my collarbone, lips dragging heat across skin. "Do you have any idea what you do to me?"

I don't answer. I can't. His mouth finds that spot just under my jaw and I shiver, fingers tightening in the sheets. It's like every part of him is tuned to mine. He knows exactly where to touch, where to bite. And I'm burning for him.

I tug at his shirt until he lifts his arms and lets me strip it away, revealing the lines of muscle I've memorized from too many nights of doing exactly this. I run my hands down his chest, over his stomach, and he exhales like I knocked the wind out of him.

"Come here," I whisper, and he does.

He kisses me again, rough and perfect, but then he breaks away just long enough to press his forehead against mine, our breaths mingling, sweat already clinging to our skin. "This feels like a dream," he says, voice low and wrecked.

"Then don't wake up," I say breathily.

He grins—and then he's moving again, trailing heated kisses down my body like he's starving for it, like touching me is the only way he remembers how to breathe. His hands hook into the waistband of my shorts, unhurried just for a second, like he's giving me the chance to stop him.

I don't.

He drags them down, and then he's there—between

my thighs, looking up at me like I'm something sacred, even now, even with nothing left to hide between us.

"Cade," he murmurs, voice rough with want, "you're gonna ruin me."

And then his mouth is on me. It's hot, measured, devastating. I bite down hard on the inside of my cheek to keep from making a sound that would definitely get us caught.

Theo's always been good at this. Focused. Intent. Like he's proving how well he knows me by feel, pressure, and rhythm. His eyes flick up once, and the sight almost undoes me.

The room is dim, quiet but for my harsh breathing, the faint whisper of his lips moving up and down my dick, and the wet pull of sweet suction. My fingers tangle in his hair, not pushing, not guiding—just needing to hold on. His tongue drags over me like he's savoring it. Like he wants this just as much as I do. Like maybe he needs it.

My limbs shake, and I brace myself with one hand, the other still buried in his hair. My chest tightens with something more than lust. It's him. It's always him.

He cups my balls gently, fingers firm but tender, like he's not just trying to bring me pleasure—he's trying to tell me something. Like he loves me without needing to say the words out loud again. It's all in the way he touches me, the way he lets me tremble, lets cade hold back the sounds I can't afford to make.

My heart pounds against my ribs the deeper he sucks. My breath comes out in short, shallow gasps. And still, he moves with calm precision, like he knows my body better than I do.

My stomach coils. My thighs tense. I'm so close, and the only thing I want is to come whispering his name like a prayer. But I grit my teeth, trying to hold back, the fire of it building behind my eyes.

"Theo," I rasp. Just his name. Nothing else. My voice is wrecked.

He hums around me, and that's it. I fall. Not loudly. Not dramatically. But inside, it's a crash. A beautiful, blinding collapse.

When I finally open my eyes again, Theo is resting his cheek against my hip, looking up at me with a small, smug smile.

"Happy Draft Day," he says, soft and cocky at the same time.

I huff out a shaky laugh. "You're gonna kill me."

He moves leisurely, kissing my stomach, my chest, then my lips, like he's putting me back together. "I hope not," he says, brushing his thumb across my cheek. "We've still got years to go."

I pull him close and press a kiss to the corner of his mouth. My hands slide down his back, fitting over the curve of his hips. "Come here," I murmur, voice rough. "Climb up. Let me take care of you."

Theo's eyes turn molten. He hesitates for half a second —just long enough to confirm he heard me right—then moves, smooth and sure. He straddles my waist with a confidence that makes my breath catch. His knees press into the mattress on either side of me, and he shuffles forward and lowers himself slowly, settling across my chest.

The weight of him grounds me. His skin is warm

against mine, and I let my hands roam against his skin, dragging my palms up his thighs before palming his ass. He shudders.

I tilt my head up, urging him forward, then dragging my mouth across his balls until he's squirming. I love how responsive he is—always have. Every sigh, every twitch of his body, every subtle shift of his hips tells me exactly what he needs.

"You look so good like this," I whisper. "Always do."

Theo leans down, catching my eyes. His lips are red, eyes glazed. "Then don't stop," he says softly.

"Wasn't planning on it."

His breath catches as he dips his hips forward and I mouth his cock, urging him deeper. I adjust his angle and mine, giving him more access, letting him move the way he needs.

We don't rush it.

It's messy, and hot, and good—better than good—and all the while, I keep my eyes on him. Every flicker of emotion, every soft curse, every whispered, "Caden," makes something twist sweet and sharp in my chest.

I love him.

God, I love him.

And when he falls apart, his cum spurting deep in my throat, gasping against the bedhead, shaking with the force of it, I hold his thighs, cradling him through it, drinking him down.

He pulls out and collapses on top of me. We're both slumped against the mattress, breathing like we just ran drills. We don't say anything for a minute. We just lie here, pressed together, my hand on his back, his thumb brushing lazy circles over my hip like he's afraid I'll vanish if he stops.

Eventually, he huffs a soft laugh. "Well. That was… celebratory."

"Understatement of the year," I say, grinning into his shoulder. "It kinda sucks we need to get moving."

True. I nod in response and press a kiss to his lips. "We really do."

We clean up in the bathroom, trading towel swipes and teasing smirks. My legs are still half Jell-O, and Theo's hair is a mess—completely my fault. He tries to tame it with water, but I stop him. "Leave it," I murmur. "It's perfect."

He rolls his eyes, but he doesn't touch it again. We both know we've pushed our luck timewise. So we straighten our clothes, check for signs of anything obvious, and head for the door.

I glance back once as I open it. Theo does too. There's something in his eyes—satisfaction, affection, disbelief. He leans in before either of us can overthink it, catching my mouth in a kiss that's supposed to be quick but lingers anyway.

It's instinct, not strategy. Just a tiny, helpless moment between us.

And of course, that's when we hear someone clear their throat.

We both freeze.

Standing just a few feet down the hall, dressed in business-casual exasperation and holding a phone like it's part of his arm, is Marcus.

Theo stiffens beside me.

"Sorry," I start. "We were just—"

Marcus lifts a hand. "Don't."

I shut my mouth.

There's a long beat where none of us move. Then Marcus sighs, scrubs a hand over his face, and gives us a look that lands somewhere between exhausted and bemused.

"Listen, I don't care if you two are writing love letters on each other's Gatorade labels," Marcus says, arms crossed but not unkind. "But if you're gonna be kissing in hotel hallways on the night you sign your first pro contract? Try not to do it where a PR rep or scout might see it. All right?"

We both straighten like we're back in high school and just got caught making out behind the bleachers. Theo clears his throat and looks away. I rub the back of my neck.

"Sorry," I say, sheepish.

Marcus exhales and waves it off. "I get it. You're young. It's a big night. Emotions are high, and your guy is hot. But I've got to ask..." His eyes flick between us, serious now. "Are you planning to come out?"

The weight of that question sinks into my gut. Theo glances at me, letting me lead again. I shake my head. "Not yet."

Marcus nods slowly. "And this—" He gestures between us again, less flippant this time. "—is serious?"

"Yes," I say.

"Very," Theo adds.

Marcus gives us a long, assessing look. Then something softer settles over his features. "All right. I'm glad you're keeping it quiet. I know it sucks, but the truth is, the first openly gay—"

"Bisexual," I correct quietly.

He nods. "Right. Queer. The first openly queer guy to play in the league? That's going to be huge. And it's not going to be easy."

He doesn't say what I already know: I'm not a guaranteed success story. I wasn't drafted. I'm coming in as an undrafted free agent, trying to earn a spot in a league that chews people up. My contract might say "two-way," but that just means a split between the big team and the G League. No promises. No guarantees.

Marcus doesn't have to say it. I feel it in the silence between us.

"I know," I murmur.

"Then keep your head down. Focus on training camp. Make them want you so bad, they forget to blink."

I nod.

"And if you need help navigating any of this, I'm your guy. Not the coaches, not the front office. Me."

I nod again, more firmly. "Thanks."

Marcus gives Theo a long, thoughtful look. "And you —if you're in this, be ready for the long haul. This world? It's not always kind."

Theo lifts his chin. "I know. I've known that a long time."

"Good," Marcus says. "Because from what I've seen, you're both in deep."

"We are," I say without hesitation.

He stares at us a moment longer, then claps a hand on

my shoulder. "Then congratulations, North. You're officially in the league. Don't screw it up."

And just like that, he turns and walks off, leaving the two of us standing alone in the hallway.

Theo lets out a breath. "Well. That wasn't as bad as it could've been."

I glance over at him, still feeling the echo of Marcus's words in my chest. "No," I say. "It wasn't."

THIRTEEN

THEO

It's loud. Like, body-vibrating, floor-thumping, bass-in-your-rib-cage loud.

It's the kind of loud that drowns out thoughts and pushes everything else—stress, exams, deadlines, guilt—to the back of my skull until all that's left is the heat of too many bodies and the neon pulse of the strobe lights above the dance floor. I needed this. A break. My English lit course is kicking my ass, but in the best way. I've been buried in Baldwin essays and Chaucer translations for weeks, my dorm desk a graveyard of coffee cups and highlighters running dry. I love it, I really do—but if I didn't come up for air, I was going to start dreaming in MLA format.

So I let Jordan drag me out here.

It's not a gay club, but it's queer-friendly, with rainbow stickers on the entrance and unisex bathrooms that don't make anyone flinch. The air smells like sweat, vodka, and bad decisions. It's perfect.

I'm wearing a slim-fit tee that clings to my chest and

jeans that ride a little lower than I usually go for. My curls are pushed back off my forehead, and I've had just enough vodka to stop worrying about whether they're frizzing from the humidity.

"Didn't think we'd see you tonight," Jordan shouts over the beat, leaning close.

I glance at them, eyes adjusting to the strobing lights that paint their brown skin blue, then red, then purple. Jordan's wearing glitter eyeliner and an oversized button-down shirt that somehow works as clubwear. They grin, tipsy and warm.

"Thought you'd be off playing house with your mysterious baller boy," they add, smirking behind their drink.

"He's not mysterious," I say, dodging the question more than answering. "Just… busy. Game on Sunday."

"And you're not going?"

I shake my head, trying to play casual. "Midterms are coming. I needed a weekend off."

Jordan gives me a knowing look, but they don't press. That's one of the things I love about the group I've found here. Nobody pushes. Nobody assumes. They know how complicated it can be—being out, being closeted, being somewhere in between. They've all lived it. They get that sometimes, you can't say everything.

Still, a flicker of guilt dances in my chest. I know where Caden is right now—at his apartment having an early night after spending all day with the team and reviewing film. That or he's running drills in his head. It's his first season, and yeah, he made it through training camp, and yeah, he's had some decent minutes, but nothing's guaranteed.

His contract is a two-way deal, which means he's splitting time between the league squad and the G League affiliate. One minute, he's flying across the country with pros. The next, he's taking a bus to bumfuck nowhere to play in half-full gyms with barely functional scoreboards. He's grinding every day, trying to prove he belongs.

And I'm here.

Dancing. Drinking. Laughing.

Living.

Which makes me feel like shit.

But I also know I need this. My junior year is kicking my ass. The course load is brutal, my GPA's hovering around a 3.6, and I'm finally locking in my focus—secondary education with an English major and a sport admin minor. That means even more internship hours, observation reports, and fieldwork.

I love Caden. I do.

But he's not my whole life.

He's part of it—an incredible, heart-racing, curl-your-toes part—but I've built something else here too. A group of friends who know me as me. Theo. Not Caden's best friend. Not the quiet kid from Gomillion. Just... Theo.

I deserve to be here. Even if part of me misses him like crazy.

Jordan nudges my arm again. "You good?"

"Yeah," I say. Then, because it's true, I smile. "I'm really good."

They tilt their head, studying me. "You ever gonna bring this basketball 'bestie' around?"

I roll my eyes. "He's got games pretty much all the time. Even if I wanted to, which I don't, he's swamped."

Jordan arches a brow. "Uh-huh. Just checking. You talk about him like he's a second major."

"I've told you," I say, trying to keep it light, "we've been friends forever. That's all."

They hold my gaze a beat longer, but thankfully they let it go. "Sure, Theo. You know you don't have to play it cool with us, right? If you were into someone—"

"I'm not," I cut in gently. "I've got school, field hours, barely enough time to breathe. Dating's not exactly high on the priority list right now."

Jordan sips their drink, then shrugs. "Fair enough. Just don't forget to make space for fun."

"Fun I can do," I say, raising my glass.

They tap theirs against mine. "To fun, distractions, and dancing like nobody's filming."

The DJ shifts into a remix of Beyoncé, and the dance floor pulses like a heartbeat. I let myself get pulled toward it, laughter bubbling up before I can stop it. Because tonight, I'm Theo. Just Theo.

The floor is packed. Sweat-slick bodies sway under the strobes, and the bass rumbles through the soles of my shoes. Someone's blowing bubbles from a wand near the DJ booth—tiny, glimmering orbs catching in the lights before they pop midair. It's all so ridiculously joyful, and for the first time in weeks, I let my muscles relax. I let go of the weight I've been carrying. Spring midterms, my field hours, the constant ache of wanting more time with Caden.

Jordan loops their arm through mine, pulling me into the middle of our group. There's Tiff, their partner, Jules, and Kiera—whose boyfriend, Caleb, is already spinning her in lazy, half-drunken circles like they're in a club scene from a teen movie. It's messy and affectionate and pure serotonin. I grin, my head light, the vodka still warm in my blood.

We dance, laugh, shout lyrics to songs we only half know. When the beat shifts to something with a filthy synth line and a driving tempo, I throw my arms up and let my hips follow the music. For a second, I'm not a student or a boyfriend or the guy keeping a secret. I'm just a body in motion. Happy.

And then I feel someone slide into the space beside me.

"Hey." The word's said close to my ear but low enough to not feel invasive.

I glance sideways and find Elias there.

Of course.

Tall, confident, and handsome in that "absolutely knows it" kind of way. His cheekbones catch the blue light like glass, and his shirt is unbuttoned just enough to be suggestive. I've met him twice before—once at Jordan's birthday and another time at a game night they hosted. He's always been flirty. Last time, after a few drinks, he asked if I wanted to grab dinner sometime. I'd said no, gently. He'd taken it with a shrug and a smile, no pressure. Still, I didn't expect to see him again so soon. Definitely didn't expect him to move into my orbit tonight.

"Elias," I say, raising my voice to be heard. "Didn't know you were coming."

"Jordan mentioned everyone was here," he replies, his smile easy and not overplayed. "Figured I'd come dance."

His eyes flick over my face, checking in, not pressing. I

appreciate that more than I can say. Some people flirt like they're owed something. Elias? He flirts like it's a conversation you can step into—or out of—without consequence.

"Looks like you needed this," he adds, nodding toward the floor.

"Yeah," I say, breathless. "Kinda did."

We keep dancing. He doesn't push closer. Doesn't grab my waist or try to steer my hips. He just dances next to me, his smile bright and his energy infectious. It's… nice. Nice enough that I don't realize how long we've been out here until my shirt is sticking to my chest and I'm blinking sweat from my eyes.

I lean in, raising my voice again. "I need water."

Elias nods. "I'll come with. Hydration solidarity."

We head off the floor, weaving through the crowd until we reach the bar. The air is slightly cooler here, the fans overhead doing their best.

He leans on the bar while I flag down the bartender. I glance over at him, and he's looking at me again—not in that casual way people do when they're just making conversation.

"You know," he says slowly, "I still think dinner would be fun."

I pause. And yeah, it's tempting—for a fraction of a second. Someone this attractive wanting my attention? It's flattering as hell. Especially with how quiet things have been with Caden lately. Busy schedules. Missed calls. Me, jacking off to the sound of his voicemail. It's not exactly glamorous.

But I know where my heart is.

I smile, a little apologetic, but honest. "Thanks, but I'm not really looking for anything."

Elias nods. "Still not dating, huh?"

I exhale a small laugh. "Told you. Complicated."

"Fair," he says, backing off with a casual smile. "Still think whoever eventually gets you is lucky. Even if you're terrible at making time for a social life."

I chuckle. "Tell me about it."

He lifts his glass. "To complicated hearts."

"To simple exits," I reply, tapping my water bottle to Elias's glass. The music behind us thumps with another remix, but I take a long sip and let the cool water wash down the heat lingering in my throat.

The dance floor is still packed, the beat insistent, but my legs are starting to ache and my shirt clings to me like regret.

I motion toward the tables on the far side of the club, where a couple from our group are already reclaiming their seats. "Mind if we sit for a bit?" I ask.

Elias nods. "Honestly, I was about to suggest it."

We weave through bodies and low tables, finding the half-empty booth near the back wall. Marcy and Kahlil are there, deep in a tipsy debate about the ethics of grading curves, and barely glance up when we slide in across from them.

Elias settles beside me—not too close, not touching, but still comfortably present. It's nice, easy even. We fall into conversation about school, swapping stories about professors, finals prep, and the chaotic mess that is registering for electives.

"I still can't believe you're taking two 300-level lit

classes this semester," Elias says. "Do you hate yourself or something?"

"I think I might," I admit, laughing. "But I want to finish with options. And both of them cover periods I love. Victorian realism and queer theory in twentieth-century American fiction? It's like academic catnip."

He chuckles, tipping his chin toward me. "You're kind of a nerd. It's hot."

I roll my eyes, grinning. "You're drunk."

"Only a little."

We keep talking, low and easy, and for a moment, I forget how tightly wound I've been lately. School, the distance, trying to pretend like I'm not already counting the days until I can see Caden again. It's been weeks. Our last weekend together felt like a lifetime ago.

And then, I feel it.

A shift in the air. Like a string pulled taut behind my rib cage. I straighten, glance toward the entrance, then over to the bar. I don't know what I'm expecting—maybe nothing. Maybe everything.

But I see him.

He's standing just off to the side of the bar, half obscured by a huddle of people laughing and waiting on drinks. His cap is low, shadowing his face, and his hood is up like he's trying not to be noticed, but I'd know him anywhere.

Caden.

My breath stalls. It catches mid-chest and refuses to come back down. The club noise blurs, my pulse kicking up like someone grabbed a volume dial and cranked it all the way.

He's here.

He's actually here.

The fuck?

My brain short-circuits for a beat, trying to make sense of it. The last text I got from him was six hours ago.

Caden: Early night. Crash hard. Love you.

It was like he was settling in for sleep, not making a five-hour drive to Louisville. But now he's standing in this club that smells like sweat and citrus vodka, looking at me like I'm the center of his universe.

He hasn't moved. He doesn't need to. Hope punches into my chest, hot and bright. I slide to the edge of the booth, grabbing hold of my jacket as I do, already moving to stand.

Elias touches my arm. "Hey—where're you going?"

"I just—I need a sec," I say, not even trying to cover the way I'm staring.

Elias follows my gaze, eyes narrowing slightly. "That your friend?"

The question is gentle, but it makes my skin prickle. "Yeah," I answer. "That's him."

Understanding flickers across his face. Not judgment. Not disappointment. Just something calm and measured. "He came all this way?"

"Apparently."

Elias nods. "Go, then."

There's no edge to it, no bitterness. Just quiet honesty.

Still, I feel like I owe him more. "Elias—"

He cuts me off with a smile. "Theo, it's okay. I know

you said you weren't seeing anyone, and I'm not trying to push. But… you talk about him like you don't mean to. That says enough."

My throat tightens. "I didn't lie."

"I know," he says, kind. "Go."

I squeeze his shoulder once before slipping from the booth. My legs feel loose and jittery, like the adrenaline's hitting all at once. The crowd barely registers as I cut through it, my eyes on the one person who never stops pulling my focus.

Caden hasn't moved. He's still watching me, and there's something wild and open in his expression. "Hey," he says softly.

Just one word. Just that stupid, simple word—and it hits me in the chest like a freight train.

"Hi," I reply, and somehow manage not to touch him, even though every nerve in my body is screaming to throw myself into his arms, wrap myself around him like my lifeline, and never let go.

He glances around, like he's checking the space, maybe instinct, maybe nerves, then shifts his weight and nods toward the door. "My car's outside. Wanna go?"

I don't even answer. I just nod, move, and follow him through the crowd. The music keeps pounding behind me, the strobe lights still slicing through the air, but it already feels like we left that version of the night behind. The drinks, the dancing, the occasionally forced laughter with friends who don't know half of what's going on inside me. All of it slips away as we step into the cold.

Outside, it's one of those winter nights where everything's wet but it's not quite raining. Misty and gray and heavy, like the sky is holding something back. Streetlights buzz faintly overhead, but they don't do much. It's too late. Or too early.

The parking lot is quiet. We don't speak.

When he clicks the lock, his car chirps softly in the dark. Before we even get there, I'm on him.

I catch his sleeve, spin him by the wrist, and press my mouth to his like I've got something to prove. His back hits the passenger door with a soft *thunk*, and he lets out a surprised laugh that turns into a groan against my lips.

My fingers fist in the front of his hoodie—*his* hoodie, God, I've missed this stupid hoodie—and I kiss him like the world might stop if I don't. Fast and hungry and open-mouthed… the kind of kiss that tastes like frustration and relief and weeks of missing him.

"You're here," I murmur against his mouth, breath catching. "You're really here."

His hand slides under my coat, fingers splaying wide against my lower back. "Been a while since I've seen you tipsy."

"I'm not drunk," I lie, and he grins because we both know I've had enough to be bold. "Okay, maybe a bit. But mostly I'm just—God, I missed you."

"I missed you too," he says, brushing my curls back from my forehead. His touch is so familiar it nearly brings me to my knees. "Get in the car, Theo."

He doesn't have to ask twice. Once I'm in the passenger seat, I twist toward him immediately. He's still got one hand on the wheel, but the other reaches for me like it can't help itself.

"How long can you stay?" I ask, not hiding the hope in my voice.

"Not long," he says, pulling out of the lot. His eyes flick toward me. "I've gotta be back in my own bed by tomorrow night. Game's early Sunday."

Disappointment hits hard, but I nod. "Still... I can't believe you came."

"Yeah, well." He slips his fingers between mine over the center console. "Phone tag sucks. And I needed to see you. Thought I'd surprise you."

"You did," I say, voice soft. "Best surprise ever."

We drive in silence for a few minutes. The city thins around us, turning from clamor to hush. The windows are cracked an inch, and the February air curls around us, clean and cold. The buzz in my head from the club, from the drinks, from the ache of missing him, it all starts to ease. I can breathe again.

"I'm alone tonight," I tell him. "Housemates are all out. You've got me for the whole night."

"Perfect," he says, voice low and thick, like that means more than I can even begin to process. "I plan to take full advantage."

I laugh. I can't help it. Then I glance at him, sobering. "Hey, so... how's everything going? With the team?"

He's quiet for a beat, then exhales, like he's been holding that question in his chest too long. "Good," he says finally. "Better than expected. I've been getting more minutes lately. Couple of guys got banged up, so Coach pulled me into rotation. He told me today."

"That's huge," I say, heart swelling. "That's *so* huge, Cade."

"I mean, I'm not starting. And it's not guaranteed. But it's something. They're saying if I stay consistent, there's a shot they keep me up through the end of the season."

"I knew it," I whisper. "You've worked your ass off for this."

He shoots me a quick look—something soft, like pride edged with disbelief. "Coming from you, that means everything."

We pull into my building's lot. He cuts the engine and just sits there for a second, eyes trained on the wheel. I watch him in the glow of the streetlamp—his jaw tight, shoulders tense under the hoodie.

"You okay?" I ask.

He nods. "Yeah. Just… tired. The travel. The uncertainty. I don't want to get sent back down, Theo. I want to stay. I want to *belong*."

I reach for him and let my hand rest on the side of his face, thumb brushing his cheekbone. "You *do* belong."

He turns into the touch, eyes fluttering closed. "Say that again."

"You belong, Caden."

He leans across the console, and this time when he kisses me, it's different. It's not rushed. Not hungry. Just… real. Full of everything we don't say face-to-face often enough.

Once we're upstairs, the door barely shuts behind us before we're on each other again. My jacket and his hoodie hit the floor. Shoes get kicked off. Our mouths crash together in the low light of my bedroom. There's laughter in it, the kind that comes from relief. From finally being in the same place again.

Caden backs me toward my bed, his hands slipping beneath the hem of my shirt, rough palms against skin. "You feel so good," he murmurs, kissing down the side of my throat. "You always do."

"I didn't know I could miss someone like this," I breathe. "I thought it would get easier."

He pulls back to meet my eyes. "Me too. I thought I'd get used to it."

And then we're kissing again—open-mouthed, deep, messy in a way that makes my knees weak. His tongue slides confidently, slowly against mine. He knows what I like. What makes me gasp. What makes me melt. My fingers curl into the hem of his tee, dragging it upward, revealing warm skin and the curve of his waist. He helps me strip it off, and then we're chest to chest.

When he pushes me gently down onto the bed, he follows, bracing himself above me with a smile that's all trouble. "I've got you," he says, voice thick with promise. "All night."

"Prove it," I challenge, grinning up at him, even as my chest tightens around something deeper—need, trust, the ache of weeks apart.

His eyes darken, but it's not just lust. It's that quiet, serious focus he only ever gives to the things that matter most. "You think I came all this way not to?" He kisses me again—longer this time. Slower. His hand cups my jaw, thumb brushing along my cheekbone.

"I missed you," he murmurs into my skin as his lips move lower, trailing across my jaw, down the line of my throat. "God, I missed you."

I close my eyes and tilt my head to give him more. "It's been too long."

"Every time I closed my eyes, it was you," he says, voice rough. "At practice, on the bench, alone in hotel rooms—*you.*"

My breath hitches as he peels off my shirt, and then we're skin to skin, warmth sinking deep between us.

He unhurriedly kisses down my chest, like he's redis-covering everything. My body arches beneath him, desperate for more, but I don't rush him. I *can't.* There's something sacred in the way he touches me. Like I'm not just a body, but something he's *choosing*—over the game, over the grind, over the walls we've had to build.

"Tell me what you need," he whispers against my ribs.

"You," I say without hesitation. "I just need *you.*"

He looks up at me then—really looks—and his eyes go soft in that way that undoes me. "I love you," he says, like it's stitched into his breath.

I reach for him, pull him up until we're face-to-face again, and kiss him. "I love you too," I whisper back.

The way he holds me—gentle, sure, like I'm breakable but also made of fire—makes me feel both cherished and wanted in a way that has nothing to do with sex and everything to do with love.

Our bodies move together like they remember everything.

It's not rushed this time. Not desperate.

It's slow.

It's deep.

It's the kind of intimacy that feels like confession. Like every press of skin is a vow. Every gasp a promise.

He whispers to me the entire time—soft, hot words that make my heart race faster than my pulse. "You're beautiful," he says as his mouth finds my chest again. "I dream about you. About this. About touching you again."

I wrap my arms around his shoulders, dragging my fingers down his spine. "You're mine," I whisper back. "Every inch of you."

"You've *always* had me," he says. "Since that first night we got hot and heavy on your couch."

I laugh at the memory. "You were wearing mismatched socks and fell asleep on my thigh."

"Best nap of my life."

His mouth finds mine again, and the kiss deepens, hands tangling, bodies moving in a rhythm we haven't forgotten, even after all these weeks. Every sound I make, he answers with a kiss or a gentle word. Every touch he gives, I echo back in kind. And when he finally settles over me, pressing into me with a kind of reverence that makes my eyes sting, I don't hold anything back.

I let him see me. All of me. Because I trust him.

Because it's *him*.

"Caden," I whisper, voice cracking just slightly.

"I know," he breathes, pressing his forehead to mine. "I've got you. I *always* have you."

It's the kind of connection that makes the world fall away. There's nothing else—just his body, his breath, the way we move together like we were built for this. For each other.

I don't know how long it lasts. Time becomes meaningless. We lose ourselves in each other, in the sound of our breathing, the slide of skin, the whispered *I love yous* and *missed yous* and *stay with me.*

And when it's over, when we're tangled up in the sheets and each other, limbs heavy, hearts pounding, I feel more full than I have in weeks. Not just physically but emotionally. Like something empty inside me finally filled.

Caden runs his fingers through my hair in a gentle and soothing gesture. "You okay?" he asks softly.

I nod against his chest. "Better than okay."

He kisses the top of my head. "You were amazing."

"You weren't so bad yourself," I tease, even though my throat's still tight.

We lie together for a long while in silence, his heartbeat thudding steady beneath my ear. Then, quietly, I say, "I hate that we can't have this all the time."

His arms tighten around me. "I know."

"I hate that you have to hide it."

"I hate it too," he says. "But I'm not hiding *you*. Just… protecting what we have."

I nod. Because I know it's true. Still, it aches.

"You're worth it," I say into the quiet. "Even if it hurts sometimes."

"I don't deserve you," he murmurs.

"Shut up," I say, lifting my head. "Don't even go there."

His smile is tired, but real. "I'm trying. For us. For a future where I don't have to compartmentalize the best part of my life."

"I'll wait for that future," I whisper.

And he kisses me again. This time soft and slow, like

maybe that future is already starting to take shape right here in this bed. Where it's just us: real and raw and unafraid.

FOURTEEN

CADEN

THE WORLD OUTSIDE THE WINDSHIELD IS SILVER-BLUE AND endless. Snow frosts the edges of the road, clinging to low fences and naked tree limbs like sugar. The Michigan winter doesn't do subtle. It's all sharp edges and breath you can see, and tonight, it's showing off under a sky that's gone full cotton candy—soft pink and pale gold bleeding into each other as the sun dips low behind us.

We're winding through M-22, about forty miles out from Glen Arbor. The road curves like someone traced it with a lazy finger, bending around frozen vineyards and quiet lakes that shimmer through the trees. I should be soaking it in, memorizing every peaceful stretch, every snow-dusted roofline and rusting mailbox.

Instead, I'm busy trying not to fall asleep again. I jerk upright in the passenger seat, blinking hard. "Shit. I did it again."

Theo doesn't take his eyes off the road. "Third time, actually."

"Why didn't you wake me?"

He shrugs, smirking. "You looked too peaceful drooling on yourself."

I wipe my chin automatically, scowling. "I wasn't drooling."

"Oh, my bad. I meant snoring."

"You're the worst," I mutter, but my voice has zero heat. Because really, this—this right here—is everything.

Theo's hands are tight on the wheel, fingers bare because he swore it wasn't cold enough for gloves. He's got a stubborn streak about things like that, and I gave up trying to change his mind years ago. The heater's blasting at our feet, the only sound besides the low hum of tires on pavement and whatever lo-fi playlist he's got running through the speakers.

"Pull over soon," I say, stretching my arms above my head. "You're looking tired."

"I'm fine," he answers, but it's followed by a yawn that nearly unhinges his jaw.

I raise a brow. "Uh-huh."

"I'll stop if my vision starts swimming."

"Jesus. Comforting."

Theo chuckles and glances my way. "We've only got, like, forty miles left. I want to get there before the snow starts back up."

I nod, shifting in my seat to better face him. "Still can't believe you drove three hundred and sixty miles for the game."

His eyes soften. "Would've driven double."

God. He says stuff like that, and I swear it never gets old. Not even after all these years.

Tonight's game had me flying. I dropped ten points, snagged six boards, and even Coach said my defense was tighter than it's been all season. I'm finally in the rotation now—really in it—and the difference is showing. Minutes mean everything when you're a second-year guy on a two-way deal. Every possession is a chance to prove you belong.

But the real high? Theo, in the stands. Eyes shining, grinning like I'd already won just by being on the court.

"I'm proud of you," he says, like he read my mind.

I smile and tilt my head against the seat. "I'm earning minutes. Coach said he wants me dressing for every game this month. And if things stay strong, they might offer me a standard contract by summer."

Theo whistles low. "That's huge."

"Yeah. Doesn't mean I'm safe. I've seen guys get dropped mid-season like nothing."

"You won't."

"I might." I shrug. "This league doesn't owe me anything. I'm just trying to stay sharp, stay healthy. Make the most of it."

"You've already made the most of it," he says. "You went from undrafted to standing your ground on a league court. That's huge, Cade."

I nod, letting that settle.

I know I'm lucky. And I've done everything right with the money so far—invested half with a guy my dad trusts, socked away enough for a rainy decade. But even now, with a steady salary and some buzz building, I can't pretend this dream doesn't come with an expiry date.

If I get ten good years, I'll be one of the lucky ones.

I glance at Theo again, taking him in. His profile in the dusk. The little crease between his brows when he's concentrating. The way the corner of his mouth kicks up when he catches me looking.

"You sure you're okay driving?" I ask.

"I'm running on adrenaline and two Red Bulls. I'm golden."

"Yeah, and the second we get to the cabin, you'll crash face-first into a pillow."

"Maybe," he says. "Or maybe I'll get a second wind." He winks, and the temperature in the car spikes about twenty degrees.

"Not fair," I mutter, trying not to laugh. "Teasing me when I'm too tired to retaliate."

Theo grins. "I like you defenseless."

I lean back, smiling out at the icy landscape zipping by. "We're really doing this, huh?"

He nods. "Two whole days. No training, no class, no phone calls. Just us and nature."

"And a fireplace."

"And a kitchen."

"And hopefully a bed that doesn't squeak like a haunted swing set."

Theo laughs. "I made sure it's a real mattress, not some fold-out nightmare. I want you well rested."

"I thought the plan was the opposite."

"Touché."

I glance at his hand on the wheel. "Can't believe you'll be living with me soon."

Theo's smile is quieter now. "Me neither. It still feels far off."

"You graduate in four months."

"Three, if I ace everything."

"You will."

He hums. "Gotta start job hunting soon."

"You're gonna be an amazing teacher."

He pauses. "You think so?"

"I know so. The way you explain stuff, the patience, the dorky jokes… it's a package deal."

"You think my jokes are dorky?"

"I think they're perfect."

The road narrows a bit, the pines closing in. Snowbanks climb higher the farther we go. The sky has turned lavender now, the sun almost gone. I reach out and brush his thigh, just lightly. "Thanks for doing this."

Theo glances over. "Thanks for needing me."

We don't say anything for a while after that. We just drive. The scenery becomes more remote, quieter, until it feels like we're the only two people left in the world. And honestly? I wouldn't want it any other way.

The last thing I remember is the low sound of Theo humming along to the radio and the gentle bump of the road beneath us. Then sleep pulls at me again—unhurriedly, heavily, like hands dragging me underwater.

When I blink awake, the world is wrong.

The tires screech.

A squeal penetrates my ears, loud and sharp, and the headlights flicker as we veer hard to the right. I lurch sideways in my seat, my chest clenching.

"Theo—" My voice is a rasp.

But Theo's not answering.

He's slumped forward. His head jerks up in the next

second, eyes wide, frantic, hands snapping to the wheel, but it's already too late.

We hit the shoulder.

Snow explodes in the beams of the headlights, a wall of white swallowing us whole.

Theo screams my name.

Then it all goes to hell.

The world flips. A crunch of metal, the terrible groan of the car folding in on itself. My head slams into the side window. A blinding burst of light erupts behind my eyes, and I feel weightless—shredded from the seat, from gravity, from sense. We spin, and spin, and then something hits us hard enough to snap the breath from my lungs.

We stop moving, but the world doesn't.

Everything tilts.

Everything aches.

The windshield's smashed. Glass sparkles like snowflakes in the air. The roof is bowed, pressing down. The dashboard's pushed in, swallowing my legs. I taste blood, thick and metallic on my tongue.

There's a ringing in my ears that won't stop.

Then—

"Caden!" Theo's voice is hoarse, breaking. "Caden, baby, answer me—please—"

I try to move. Pain slices up my leg like fire.

"Don't move," Theo chokes out. He's crouched next to me, somehow out of his seat. His face is smeared with red. Blood runs down his cheek and drips from his jaw. His hoodie—my hoodie—is torn at the shoulder, the fabric stained. His hands are shaking. "Shit, you're bleeding. You're bleeding so much."

I try to say his name, but it gets stuck in my throat. It feels like trying to speak through gravel.

"The ambulance is coming," he says quickly, almost too fast. "You're going to be okay, I swear. You've just got to stay awake, all right?"

I nod—or I think I do.

My leg is screaming.

"I need—" I start, then cough. It tears through my chest, a deep, broken sound.

"Hey, hey, I got you." Theo presses a hand to my cheek. It's warm. It's everything. "I'm here. I'm right here."

His breath fogs in the cold. The wind's rushing in through what's left of the passenger side, and snow is whipping across the dashboard. I can't stop shaking. I don't know if it's the cold or the pain or both.

I try to lift my hand to his, but my arm won't cooperate.

"Theo." My voice is so faint, I barely hear it.

"Yeah, yeah, I'm here." His hand is around mine now, gripping tight. "Just keep talking to me, okay? You've got this, Cade."

Everything inside me is throbbing. My ribs, my shoulder, my neck. But the worst is my leg. I can't feel my foot. Or maybe I can feel it too much. The pain is hot, sharp, alive. My stomach churns.

I blink again, and the world tilts sideways.

Darkness crowds the edges of my vision.

"Caden!" Theo's voice spikes with panic. "No, no, no. Eyes on me. Please."

I force them open. I try.

Theo's face blurs.

"Can't lose you," he whispers, voice wrecked. "I swear to God—don't you fucking dare."

My head tips back against the seat. There's blood dripping somewhere—mine or his, I don't know.

And then I really notice it. The blood on his temple. The jagged gash on his forehead I missed the first time. It's deep. He's bleeding. A lot.

My stomach lurches. "You—you're hurt," I rasp.

Theo laughs, but it's wet and raw. "You're in a mangled car, probably concussed, and you're worried about me?"

"Always," I whisper.

His eyes shine, and for a second, I see the tears he's trying so hard to blink away. He swallows hard. "It's just a cut. I'm okay. It's not deep. You're the one I'm scared for."

I don't know how to say I'm scared too. Not of the pain, or the blood, or whatever's happening inside my leg. I'm scared of this ending. Of not seeing him again. Of not making it out of this car.

Time slips again.

I fade.

Come back.

It's darker now. Or my eyes are worse.

Theo's voice is quieter, like it's coming from the end of a tunnel. "They're on their way," he says. "I saw the lights. Almost here."

He's still holding my hand. I squeeze back—or maybe I just imagine it.

"Keep talking," he pleads. "Say something."

I try. But my mouth won't work.

His hand tightens. "Please."

I close my eyes. Not because I want to. Because I can't keep them open anymore.

Theo sobs—loud and broken. But he doesn't let go.

Not once.

Not ever.

Red flashing lights bleed through the dark, pulsing like a heartbeat gone haywire. I can't tell if the sirens are still far or already screaming over us. It's hard to think, harder to breathe. Every sound comes in waves—too loud, then muffled like I'm underwater.

The cold hits me next. Sharp and merciless, cutting through the broken windows, curling into every inch of me. I try to shift, but pain claws through my chest and leg, white-hot and blinding.

"Theo—" I choke the name out, but it's barely a breath, my throat sandpaper and blood.

"I'm here." His voice. Theo's voice. Shaky and broken and right next to me. "I'm right here, baby. You're okay—you're gonna be okay. Help is coming, I swear."

I want to see him. I need to see him. I force my eyes to open, blinking through tears and something warm trickling into them. He's leaning over me, face pale and panicked and streaked with blood.

Then a louder voice cuts in. Someone shouting. Doors slamming. Feet stomping the ground.

"We need the cutters. Passenger's pinned. Driver's responsive."

I feel Theo flinch beside me. Someone tugs at him. "Sir, you need to step away. Let us in."

"No! No, I'm not leaving him. He needs—he needs to know I'm here."

A stronger voice, sterner. "Sir. We've got it. You need to step back now."

I feel him slipping away from me—his hand ripped from mine—and panic tears through my ribs like broken glass. I try to shout, but it's just a groan, and that's when the shrieking starts.

Metal grinding. Ripping.

The Jaws of Life tear into the car like a beast, vibrating through my bones. I clench my jaw to keep from screaming. My leg—it's wrong. Twisted. Trapped. Pain pulses through me in waves, every one worse than the last. My vision whites out.

A face appears above me. Mask. Helmet. "Hey there, buddy. Stay with me. We've got you, okay?"

I try to nod, but it's useless. My head won't lift. My chest won't move right.

Where's Theo?

I blink hard. The lights blur and smear. Shapes move around me, shouting things I don't understand. I'm being touched—stabilized, lifted. The car creaks and groans like it might give out beneath me.

The pain spikes so high it steals the breath from my lungs.

And then there, just through the shattered window, I see him. Theo. Being held back. Struggling. Crying.

Blood's still on his face, but he's alive. He's alive. Thank God. He's screaming my name. I can't hear it, but I know it. I know the shape of his mouth when he says my name. When he pleads.

I try to reach for him. Try to say something. Anything.

But it's too much. My body's not mine anymore. It's fire and ice and shrapnel.

I feel them lift me—the sudden motion, the sky spinning. And the last thing I hear before everything goes black... is Theo.

Still calling me back.

Still holding on.

FIFTEEN

THEO

The sound of the rotor blades is deafening, slicing through the air like knives. We're crammed into the back of the medevac helicopter that arrived shortly after the ambulance, the scent of antiseptic mixing with the metallic tang of blood—his blood. Caden's.

I can't stop looking at him.

He's strapped down next to me, unconscious, pale, and far too still. There's a bandage over his forehead, but the worst is lower—his leg is a mess of twisted bone, torn flesh, and blood that keeps soaking the gauze they've packed around it. It doesn't even look like a leg anymore. Not really. I can't look at it for long, but I can't look away either.

I'm holding on to the edge of the stretcher so tightly my knuckles are white. And even though my right arm is useless, cradled against my chest and screaming with pain, I grip the bloodstained LEGO fireman Caden made years ago like a lifeline. I took it out of my pocket because I thought holding it would stop me losing my shit. The medics keep asking me questions, their words muffled under the roar of the blades and the thudding in my skull. My head's bleeding. My ribs are a mess—I can't breathe without sharp pain stabbing through me—but I keep saying I'm fine.

Because none of that matters.

Only Caden matters.

"Please," I rasp when one of the paramedics checks my vitals again. "His parents. Call his parents. I know the number. I know it."

I tell them the number I memorized when I was eight, the one written on slips of paper for sleepovers and basketball camps and just in case. My throat tightens around it like it's made of glass. The medic nods and radios it in, but I don't know if they'll be able to reach them right away.

I can't tell if I'm crying or if it's just the wind and pain and shock. All I know is I feel like I'm outside my body, watching everything from someplace far away. Caden doesn't move. Not once. I watch the machines strapped around him, his chest rise and fall. I count every breath like it might be his last.

The lights of Traverse City bloom beneath us, bright and blurry. Munson Medical Center comes into view, and something like relief starts to flutter in my chest.

We're going to make it. *He's* going to make it. He has to.

The helicopter banks and begins its descent, the sudden shift pressing me sideways, jarring my ribs. I groan but bite it down. My vision's swimming. I keep my eyes on Caden until the second the doors open and we're swallowed into the chaos of voices and lights and fast-moving figures.

I try to follow his stretcher as they roll him out.

"Wait—hey, wait, I'm with him!"

A nurse catches me as I stumble, her face grim and calm all at once. "You need to be seen immediately. You've got a head injury. You've lost a lot of blood."

"I don't care about that!" I shout, or try to. It comes out wet and weak. "Please. Just let me stay—" But my legs give out. Blackness creeps in at the edges of my vision, and the last thing I see is a smear of blood on the white sheet covering Caden's body.

And then—nothing.

***

I WAKE up in a bright room with a pulse monitor beeping beside me and a pounding headache that feels like a battering ram. My left arm is strapped in place, heavy and sore. My ribs burn with every breath.

Caden.

I bolt upright, then scream as my ribs explode in pain. A nurse rushes to my side, her face a practiced mix of concern and calm. "You need to stay still, Theo."

"No—where is he? Caden. Where's Caden?"

"You were in a serious accident," she says gently, adjusting the mask over my face. "You've got two broken ribs, a fractured ulna that'll need surgery, and a concussion. You passed out before we could finish your intake."

"I don't care," I croak. "Tell me about Caden."

She hesitates. That hesitation sends an icy stab through my chest.

"He's being stabilized," she says. "He arrived in critical condition. I can't say more."

"I'm his boyfriend," I tell her. "Please. I need to know."

Her lips press together in a tight line. "I'm sorry. Due to privacy regulations, unless you're listed as next of kin—"

"Call his parents," I snap again. "Please. They'll tell you. I gave the number." Fuck, it'll take them hours to get here.

She sighs. "I believe they were contacted. But until we verify—"

I close my eyes, hating everything about this moment. Hating that I'm here and he's there. That we were five minutes from somewhere beautiful. That I fell asleep behind the wheel. That I—

I can't finish that thought.

"Am I going to surgery?" I ask when I can finally open my eyes again.

"Yes," she says. "They'll be here shortly to prep you."

I nod, but it feels distant. Everything does.

All I can think about is the last look I had of Caden's leg. The way it bent the wrong way. The blood. The glass. The mangled door pressed against him. The way he never spoke again after they pulled him from the wreckage. He never opened his eyes.

Not even once.

He always opens his eyes when I say his name.

The nurse squeezes my shoulder gently. "We'll let you know the moment we're able to, okay?"

I don't answer, because the truth is, I already know.

Something's broken that can't be fixed. And I'm the reason it happened.

The ache in my chest isn't just from broken ribs or guilt. It's from the fear that the person I love most in this world might never open his eyes again. And if he does, it might be to a world where our lives are forever changed.

Iᴛ's late morning by the time my parents arrive. The hospital staff have been keeping me up-to-date about when to expect them.

The sterile light in my hospital room is too bright, making everything feel surreal and too real all at once. The quiet hum of machines and the faint murmur of nurses moving outside my door fills the silence as I lie here, heavy with drugs and heavier with dread. My head feels like it's stuffed with cotton, but my thoughts are jagged and sharp, refusing to dull.

I blink blearily toward the doorway just as it opens. My mom rushes in first, her face blotchy and streaked with worry, followed closely by my dad—his jaw set tight, his eyes already shining. Amelia trails behind them, moving slower, her hoodie sleeves tugged down over her hands like she's trying to make herself small. Her braids are frizzed at the edges, the way they get when she's been pulling at them.

They look like they haven't slept. I doubt they have. It must have been hell for them to have to wait until this morning for a flight to get to us.

My mom is crying before she even gets to my bed.

"Oh, baby," she says, her voice cracking, and she carefully leans in to kiss my forehead. "Are you okay? Are you in pain?"

"I'm fine," I whisper. "They've got me on meds." I glance down at my casted arm, the bruises blooming beneath the hospital gown, but none of it matters.

"Is Caden okay?" I rasp, before they can ask me anything else. My throat burns with the question I've been carrying since I woke up. "No one will tell me anything. What's going on?"

My mother opens her mouth—but nothing comes out. She turns away, covering her mouth with her hand as fresh tears fall. And just like that, I know. I know it's bad. Something inside me cracks.

"Dad," I say, hoarse and urgent. "Please. What happened? Tell me. Tell me now."

My father steps forward, taking a steadying breath. His voice is rough when it comes. "Theo... he's alive. He's stable now, but... it's serious."

I nod, bracing.

"His left leg," he says slowly, gently, like the words might break me if he's not careful. "They had to amputate. Below the knee."

Amelia makes a sharp, choked sound. She presses her sleeve to her face, shaking her head like she can't take in the words. Then she crosses the room quickly, climbing onto the edge of the bed the way she's done since we were kids, slipping her arm through my uninjured one like she's holding me together.

The room tilts.

I hear myself making a sound—something low and broken—and I try to sit up too fast. Pain screams through my ribs, and my head spins.

"No. No. No." I shake my head, desperate to reject the truth. "That can't—he can't—"

"Theo," my dad says, firm but kind, placing a steady hand on my good shoulder. "You need to breathe."

But I can't. I can't breathe. I can't think. My heart is trying to claw its way out of my chest.

"I did this." The words fall from my mouth before I can stop them. "I fell asleep. I was driving and I fell asleep and now he—" My voice shatters, just like everything else inside me. "He's never going to play again. I ruined his life."

Amelia stands and Mom's arms wrap around me gently as I sob, broken and full of guilt. I feel her trying to soothe me, whispering things like "It was an accident" and "You didn't mean for this to happen" and "You love him so much."

But none of that matters.

Love doesn't give him his leg back.

Love doesn't give him basketball.

Love doesn't erase the sound of metal crunching or the image of blood and flesh and twisted bone or the weight of his hand in mine as he drifted in and out of consciousness, scared and hurting and trying to stay awake.

"I can't ever look at him again," I whisper into her shoulder. "How can I? How can he?"

My dad crouches down beside the bed. "Because he's

alive. And he's still here, Theo. And he loves you. That hasn't changed."

"You don't know that," I whisper.

"Yes, I do." His voice is unwavering. "He loves you."

From the corner of the room, Amelia's voice wavers. "Of course he does." I turn my head, and she's standing there stiff, her arms wrapped tight around herself like she's holding something in. "You think he's gonna let go of you just because of this? No way." She swipes at her cheek with the heel of her hand, sniffling hard. "You're stuck with each other. Everybody knows that."

Her words are shaky but fierce, and they punch through the fog for a second, like only a younger sister's could.

I wipe at my eyes with my good hand, blinking through the tears. "Can I see him?"

They don't answer right away. My mom glances at my dad. He looks toward the closed door. There's hesitation. Too much of it.

"Not yet," my mom says softly. "They're keeping him in intensive care. They're monitoring everything closely. You need to rest and heal too."

"No," I say, but the word is weak, barely a protest. "Please."

My mom takes my hand gently, her thumb stroking over my knuckles. "We know you want to see him, baby. But they're not letting anyone in yet. Not even us."

"Caden's parents went straight to him," my dad adds, voice low. "They were taken to the ICU as soon as they landed. He's still being monitored. It's serious."

That knowledge shatters something deep inside me.

The fact that they're with him—where I should be— makes the emptiness in my chest crack wider. They're at his side while I'm stuck here. We might as well be separated by miles even though we're in the same building.

I nod, or I think I do. My body feels too heavy to be sure.

The pain in my ribs pulses with each breath. My broken arm lies useless at my side, the cast a dull, throbbing reminder. My numb fingers, though, still manage to keep a tight grip on the LEGO figure, which I found on the small table by my bed. My head pounds with every heartbeat, but none of it compares to the ache in my chest.

The weight of knowing the person I love more than anything in this world is lying in a hospital bed just like me—only worse, so much worse—is almost too much. And there's nothing I can do.

Not yet. Not until they let me.

Not until he's ready. Not until someone says it's okay.

And even then... even then, I don't know how I'll face him. What I'll say.

How I'll ever stop blaming myself.

There's a beat of silence that stretches like pulled skin. My dad clears his throat gently, and I can tell it's taking everything in him to keep it together. "The police are here, Theo," he says carefully. "They'd like to speak to you. Just a statement."

I blink at him. "Now?"

He nods. "They've been waiting a while, but your doctors asked them to give you some time."

I nod absently, my throat dry and thick with guilt. "Okay."

"We'll stay with you," he says quickly, and I feel my mom's fingers lace through mine again.

I turn to her. "Do they know?" My voice is rough. "Caden's coach—his team. Do they know?"

My dad leaves quietly to get the officer. My mom shifts to sit closer to me, brushing a hand over my hair like she did when I was a kid too feverish to sleep.

"Yes," she says. "They were notified not long after the accident. I think his coach is flying out this morning with his agent. They'll be at the hospital soon."

Her voice tightens just a little. "They've been calling constantly. Checking on him. On you."

I nod again, my eyes blurring. The Detroit Devils. I still can't believe he made it there, even after everything. And now... now he's lying in an ICU bed, missing part of his leg.

He wasn't a starter, not yet. He was working his way in, part of a two-way contract—half in the league, half in the G League—but making waves. Getting minutes. Gaining traction. His coach said he was a grinder, someone who could get under the skin of bigger players and force turnovers. He was fast, explosive, smart.

Now? Now it's all over. At least professionally. And that's if—*if*—he makes it through recovery. No one has said as much, but until I see him for myself, I can't believe otherwise.

Some teams would offer support, I know. Medical care. Counseling. A chance to transition into another role.

But I also know that contracts don't mean guarantees. Especially not for undrafted players. It's all too easy for someone like Caden to be quietly let go.

He's not just injured.

He's vulnerable.

He's broken in a way that could define the rest of his life.

And I—

I was behind the wheel.

My stomach turns again. I was driving.

My arm curls tighter around my middle, cradling the pain in my ribs like I deserve it.

There's a knock on the doorframe, and I look up to see a man in uniform step in, followed by my dad. The officer is tall, maybe mid-forties, with dark eyes and a kind, professional face. He holds a notepad in one hand but doesn't open it right away.

"Theodore Brooks?"

I nod, my throat thick. "Theo."

He glances toward my parents. "It's up to you if you want them to stay."

"They can stay," I say, and I clear my throat. "It's okay."

He steps closer, pulling over a chair. "I'm Officer Keller. I understand you've just had surgery. This won't take long. I'm just looking to clarify a few details about last night's accident."

I nod, suddenly lightheaded. "Okay."

He gives me a small, reassuring smile. "Take your time answering."

As he begins, my mom squeezes my hand again, and I

try to breathe. Maybe—just maybe—once I say it out loud, I'll start to feel something other than this endless, crushing guilt.

Maybe after this, I'll be allowed to see him.

I'M NOT. I haven't even seen his parents.

He's awake and communicating, that much I know, but getting more information is like trying to dig through concrete with a spoon. It's been three days since the accident. Three days since I destroyed his life. Three days since my heart shattered into something sharp and unrecoverable. I don't know how it'll ever repair itself. Not if I can't see Caden for myself. Not until I can check with my own eyes that he's out of ICU and truly okay.

Okay.

The word sticks in my throat, too bitter and wrong. There's nothing okay about this. Not even close.

What's worse is I'm being discharged today. My parents are finalizing the paperwork, organizing aftercare at home, and making sure I have the pain meds and follow-up appointments lined up like good, responsible parents do. They've already contacted the university, filed for medical leave on my behalf. Everything's lined up so neatly.

But I don't care.

None of it matters if I leave this hospital without seeing Caden.

Fuck it.

I slip away while they're distracted, ignoring the stabbing ache in my ribs and the heavy fog behind my eyes. The pain is a good thing—it keeps me grounded, reminds me why I'm doing this. I deserve every twinge, every throb, every bruised breath. I almost killed the person I love most.

I creep down the corridor, one hand pressed lightly to the wall for balance. Nurses pass by, a few glancing my way, but no one stops me. I don't know exactly where I'm going, but I find a staff board listing patients by wing, and I scan it, eyes locking on his last name like it's screaming at me.

Room 417.

Private.

Of course it is. He's a professional athlete. Or… was.

The thought makes my stomach cramp. I swallow hard and move, dragging my battered body to the elevator. Every second feels like it takes a minute. Every footstep adds another brick to the weight pressing down on my chest.

When I finally reach his floor, I pause. The hallway is quiet. My breath rattles in my chest as I inch toward his door. It's cracked open just slightly. No nurses are in sight. There's no noise but the soft beep of machines from inside.

I rest my hand against the door, fingers trembling. Then I push it open.

Caden's in the bed, propped slightly on pillows. His hair is flattened on one side, his jaw dark with a few days of scruff. There's a thick bandage on his forehead. The moment I see it, a vivid flash of memory hits me like a sucker punch to the chest—blood streaking down his face, the way his eyes fluttered in and out of consciousness, the helplessness in his expression as the world went sideways.

My knees nearly buckle. But I'm here now. And he's breathing.

I let my gaze drift down, seeing past the blanket draped over his body. I take in the curve of his chest, the rise and fall that confirms he's alive. That he's really here.

And then I see it.

The dip in the blanket.

The place where half of his leg used to be.

Reality slams into me, and my chest squeezes so tightly it feels like my ribs might crack all over again. My vision blurs, and I can't look away.

Then his voice slices through the silence like a blade. Low. Tired. Sharp. "You shouldn't be here."

My gaze snaps up. His eyes are open, bloodshot and heavy-lidded, but focused on me. "I—" My voice is sandpaper. "I just needed to see you."

He doesn't smile. Doesn't even blink. "Well, now you've seen me."

I flinch. "Caden...."

"Don't," he says, his tone flat. "Don't pretend this doesn't change everything."

"What does that even mean?"

He shifts, and the slight movement pulls a groan from him. But he doesn't stop. He's pushing himself up a little straighter, grimacing through the pain like he's daring me to challenge him. "It means I don't need your pity, Theo."

I stumble back a step like he's struck me. "Pity?" My voice breaks. "Jesus, Cade, that's not what this is."

His eyes flash. "Then what is it? Guilt? Responsibility?"

"No!" I close the distance, stopping just short of the bed. "It's love, you idiot. I love you."

His jaw works, but he doesn't speak.

"I love you," I repeat. "And I'm so sorry. I know that doesn't change anything. I know what I did—what I didn't do—cost you everything."

A muscle ticks in his jaw. His eyes flick away from mine, toward the window. "I don't want you here," he says quietly.

The words tear through me like glass. I nod, swallowing past the lump forming in my throat. "Okay," I whisper. "I get it."

He still won't look at me.

I back up a step, blinking fast, heart thudding like a war drum in my ears. "I'm heading home. With my parents."

He nods, barely.

"I'll give you space," I say, fingers squeezing closed over the yellow firefighter I keep in my grip. "However much you need. But… I still love you."

He's silent for a beat. Then, bitterly, he says, "Lucky you. You get to leave."

My breath hitches. "I'd stay," I offer desperately. "If you wanted me to. I'd stay and be here for you. Help you through this. Anything, Caden. Anything."

His eyes meet mine, finally. But there's no warmth, just exhaustion and pain. So much pain. "I don't want you here."

The finality in his voice cuts deeper than anything else has. I nod once, then turn. The door closes softly behind me. As soon as it does, I collapse against the wall. My legs give out, and I slide to the floor. My cast bumps the linoleum. My ribs scream. But none of that matters.

Because nothing will ever be the same again.

Not for him.

Not for me.

Not for us.

NOW

SIXTEEN

THEO

TWO DAYS UNTIL GOMILLION HIGH'S INAUGURAL CLASS reunion, and already, ghosts from the past are showing up in town like clockwork.

I saw Greg Tullman outside the gas station this morning—still wearing camo, still talking like every sentence deserves a punch line. He didn't recognize me at first—not all that surprising since I was in the year below him. But when he did, his eyes lit up, and he clapped me on the back like the last twenty years since he graduated from high school had been a week and we were still teenagers and invincible.

I smiled, made polite noises, and left with my coffee.

Now it's early evening, and I'm back home, sitting on the porch of the house I grew up in, nursing a beer and trying not to think too hard about what the next few days will bring. The wind's turned crisp, just sharp enough to sneak under the hem of my hoodie. Somewhere a dog's barking, and the high school stadium lights have just flicked off for the night, signaling the end of whatever summer program ran late.

The porch creaks beneath my foot, and I stretch it out, resting it against the peeling rail. The same rail I once leaned over while counting down the days until graduation. Back when I thought the whole world was mine.

Back when Caden was still mine.

I rake a hand through my hair and exhale breathily.

I bought this place ten years ago, right around the time my parents started eyeing retirement somewhere "blue"—someplace with good healthcare, walkable neighborhoods, and fewer Confederate flags. Not that there were many in our small town, but the state as a whole still clung to its symbols like armor.

Gomillion's always been complicated for us. It's the kind of place where your neighbors wave and bring over casseroles when someone passes, but also where you never stop noticing which families get the side-eye at the grocery store, or who has to "prove" they belong on the sidelines at Friday night football. Growing up here meant we knew every crack in the sidewalk, every shortcut between the pines—and also every unspoken rule about which roads you didn't drive after dark.

For me, it's equal parts nostalgia and unease. There's comfort in the church picnics I occasionally attend—usually when my parents are visiting—and the sound of cicadas rolling in with the summer heat, but under it all, there's the quiet weight of history, the knowledge that this place held us but never fully embraced us.

Coming back as an adult, I've had to learn how to carry that duality. To love the pieces of Gomillion that raised me while refusing to excuse the parts that cut deep. To make space for myself here anyway.

My sister didn't stay. Amelia left after college, chasing a boyfriend to Charlotte. They married, had Connor, and then divorced before he turned ten. She's doing fine now—single mom, fierce as ever—but she only comes back occasionally. When she does, she brings her son, and for a little while, this porch feels like it did when we were kids, crowded and loud, before all of us scattered.

My parents considered Maryland, even parts of North Carolina, but nothing ever felt quite like home. They didn't want to sell this house to strangers. Too many memories in the walls. And honestly? I didn't either. This place meant something. It still does.

Maybe that makes me pathetic. A guy encroaching on forty, living in the same house he used to sneak back to after heated kisses in parked cars and nights spent pretending his heart wasn't already spoken for. The same house he came home to at twenty-one, shattered and hollow, after the only man he ever loved ended things with a look he's never been able to forget.

But the thing is, I didn't want new walls. I wanted ones that remembered. Ones that creaked in the same places, that smelled like lemon oil and Sunday roast—and something deeper too. Like simmered collards laced with vinegar and ham hock. Like cornbread crisping in a cast-iron pan. Like warm peach cobbler cooling on the counter, the sugar still crackling on top.

And okay, maybe there was a part of me that still wanted to be close to him. Not that that had ever worked. A week after the accident just over fifteen years ago,

Caden's parents put their house on the market and left town. They were gone overnight, like ghosts who didn't want to haunt.

My parents were heartbroken. They tried reaching out, even after Caden's parents stopped calling. They respected the space, but I think it broke them a little too. Two families who'd once vacationed together, spent holidays wrapped up like one giant crew—gone with one midnight sale and a quiet, permanent goodbye.

As for Caden…

I saw him once. Or tried to. A few months after his rehab started. I'd finally healed enough to drive and built up the nerve to find him. I ended up on some quiet street hundreds of miles away in Detroit where all the houses looked like new money. I knocked. His mom answered.

She looked older than I remembered. Sad, not angry. She told me gently but firmly that Caden didn't want to see me. Said it wasn't personal, that he was going through a lot. That he needed time. That she hoped I was healing too.

And then she shut the door.

That was the last time I saw anyone from the North family in person. Until now. Because this week, Caden's name sits on the reunion RSVP list, a checkmark beside it. No additional notes. Just a ghost I can't stop thinking about.

He's coming back.

I've known for weeks. I've helped with some of the planning—one of the perks of teaching at Gomillion High. I'm the assistant basketball coach, too, though these days my knees groan more than they used to. Still, I love it. The kids, the game, the smell of the court. All of it.

And if I'm being honest, this place saved me. When I didn't get to be with Caden, I poured everything into trying to be the version of me he used to believe in. The one who cared about stories, about truth, about kids who needed someone in their corner.

But now, with the reunion looming, I can't help but feel like the loser who never left. The guy still carrying a torch for someone who walked away without looking back.

I tip the bottle of beer to my lips and let the cold sting my throat.

From inside, my phone buzzes.

I don't move right away, letting it buzz again. It's probably Vanessa texting me about the sound equipment for Friday night's "Millipede Memories" mixer. God help us all with that theme.

Eventually, I drag myself up, bones protesting, and grab the phone from the kitchen counter.

It's not Vanessa.

Miles: I'm ten minutes out. Try not to fall asleep before I get there.

I shake my head with a tired laugh and text back.

Me: I'm not that bad. Bring snacks.

Miles: They're already in the back seat, and I picked up dinner from the diner too. You know how you get when you skip meals.

I snort, because he's not wrong. Miles might be the town's quietest handyman, but he's also uncannily observant. We're not the type of friends who sit around having deep talks about life and trauma, but we get along. We always have, ever since I moved back.

We weren't close in high school—he was a year older, on the football and swim teams, and kept mostly to himself —but we shared a few classes and nodded at each other in the hallways. Since I came back and started teaching, he's helped fix everything from the gym bleachers to my leaky sink. And somewhere in the middle of tool kits and quiet companionship, we became something like friends.

I head back to the porch and settle into my chair just as a car pulls into the driveway next door. The headlights wash over the faded siding of the Norths' old place, casting it in that eerie soft glow that makes it feel alive for a split second. Like the past is reaching out just enough to say hello.

Two days.

Two days until I see Caden again.

If he shows.

I grip the neck of the beer bottle a little tighter and whisper to the quiet night, "Please show."

Because I don't know what I'll do if he doesn't.

The sound of gravel crunching under tires reaches me, and I glance down the driveway to see the boxy silhouette of Miles's pickup trundling into place. The porch light glints off the hood, highlighting the dull paint and a smear of dirt across the side panel.

He climbs out slowly, like he always does, with a

Tupperware container tucked under one arm and a paper sack swinging from the other. He doesn't say anything until he's on the first step, then grunts, "I hope you're hungry."

"You know I am," I say, reaching for the bag like a kid on Christmas morning.

"Rose packed extra hush puppies," he mutters as he drops into the chair beside me. "She said you looked 'thin and stressed' last time she saw you."

"She's not wrong."

He shrugs, cracks open a beer from the sack, and hands me one too. I must look seriously sad if he's passing me a beer despite the half-full one in my hand.

We sit in silence for a moment, both of us digging into the fried chicken and sides like men who've earned their keep. The food's greasy and glorious and makes the weight of the day soften a little around the edges.

The sun's set now, leaving the yard steeped in navy shadows. The air smells like damp pine and fried batter. Miles is halfway through his thigh when he speaks again. "You know I'm not one to spread rumors," he says, wiping his mouth with an already messy napkin. "But I think it might cheer you up."

I glance over at him. "What?"

He leans back in his chair, arms crossed. "I heard someone talking down at Stanley's Hardware this morning. They said Caden was calling around last week asking about rental cars."

My chest goes tight. "Really?"

"It could just be gossip. You know how people are."

"Yeah," I say, trying not to let too much hope rise too fast. "Still… thanks for telling me."

Miles shrugs again. "Of course, man. I didn't want you to be blindsided."

We go quiet again, the night humming gently around us. Miles doesn't talk just to fill space. That's something I've come to appreciate. The world is full of people who talk too much and say too little. Miles is the opposite. He says what he means, when it matters.

I look over at him. "You ever think about leaving this place?"

He lets out a slow breath. "Not really, which probably means there's something wrong with me." He smiles "I guess I like being needed, even if it's just to unclog the elementary school toilets or patch drywall at Jeb's Landscaping."

"You ever… I don't know. Regret never leaving?"

He takes his time answering before settling on "Sometimes, but every time I have to go to Atlanta and drive in that traffic, I get over it really quick."

I laugh, the sound surprised and full. "That's fair."

He takes a swig of his beer, squinting out at the tree line. "Did your parents call today?"

"Yeah." I nod. "They're good. Still living the dream up in Asheville. Mom's taking pottery classes. Dad's golfing too much."

Miles grunts. "I bet your dad's driving the instructor nuts."

"He's probably corrected her form ten times already."

He chuckles under his breath. "What about your sister?"

"She invited me out this summer. Wants me to spend some time with Connor."

He bobs his head in understanding. "Is he still struggling?"

"Yeah. The divorce hit him hard. She says he's been acting out. I think she's hoping Uncle Theo can swoop in and work some magic."

"Are you going?"

"I think so. It's hard to say no to him. Plus, it's been a while since I got away for longer than a weekend."

Miles nods again. No judgment. Just quiet understanding.

"Town's been weird lately," I add. "Gearing up for this reunion has everyone acting like it's senior year all over again."

"It's bad, right?"

"Yup. Let's just say I've heard more fake-nice this week than I have in the past five years combined."

He huffs. "People think they can outgrow high school. Most of the time, they're wrong."

"Tell me about it."

He finishes off the rest of his chicken, wipes his hands on a napkin, and leans back in the chair with another sigh. "I'm guessing you'll see him this weekend. Caden, I mean."

I don't answer right away. I just stare at the house next door, which was once full of life and laughter and love with Caden at the heart of it. Now it belongs to a young white couple expecting their first kid. They're friendly enough—always waving from the porch, stopping to chat about renovations or the weather—but it still feels strange, almost disorienting, to know that every echo of the North family has been replaced by someone else's story.

"Maybe. I want to."

Miles doesn't press. He just nods, grabs another hush puppy, and settles into the silence with me like he's got all the time in the world. And maybe, just maybe, that's what makes him a good friend. Not the big speeches. Not the reassurances. Just the quiet company of someone who's still here.

The cicadas have joined the evening chorus, buzzing from somewhere deep in the trees behind the house. The porch light above us flickers once, like even it's curious about what comes next.

I look out over the yard, watching the porch light spill across the overgrown grass. "You know what's weird?" I ask, breaking the silence, my mind whirring with all things Caden.

"What?"

"I still sometimes expect to look out that window and see Caden's parents walking up the drive, arms full of takeout and wine, like nothing happened. Like it's just any old night."

Miles doesn't respond right away. He finally says, "Have you ever thought about just calling him up and talking to him?"

I chew the inside of my cheek. "All the time. And then I think about what I'd even say."

"Do you know what you're going to do if he shows?"

"No clue," I answer. "Somehow I don't think 'Hi, sorry

I destroyed your life. Want some punch and to sign the alumni guestbook?' is going to cut it."

"Fuck, man," Miles says, shaking his head. "You didn't destroy anything. It was an accident."

"Yeah," I say quietly. "But it wasn't just anyone behind the wheel, was it?"

He opens his mouth to respond, then closes it again. There's nothing he can say that'll change what I still carry.

"Anyway," I mutter, pushing up from the chair and heading toward the railing, "he probably won't even come to the actual reunion. Maybe the fundraiser, maybe a photo op, but that's it."

Miles stretches, his beer dangling from his fingers. "I don't know. If he RSVP'd, he's probably at least curious."

"Maybe."

I don't say the rest—that I've been wondering if that curiosity has anything to do with me. That some desperate part of me hopes he wants answers too. That he might show up and see me across a crowded gym, look into my eyes, and find something still worth forgiving.

"Anyway," I say again, more firmly this time. "We'll see what happens. If he's here, he's here. If not...."

Miles finishes the sentence for me, voice soft. "Then that's on him."

I nod, staring out at the dark. "Right."

But in my gut, I know better. If Caden shows up, it won't just be about nostalgia or old friends. It'll be a reckoning.

And God help me, I don't know if I'm ready for it.

SEVENTEEN
CADEN

"Last one," I call out, standing just behind the squat rack. "You've got this, Mendoza. Dig deep. Pretend that barbell is your ex's new boyfriend."

Julian Mendoza lets out a snort that's half laughter, half groan. His face is flushed, and sweat trickles down the side of his jaw like it's racing to escape his body faster than his self-control. He grits his teeth and drops low, quads trembling, his knee joint locked as he pushes back up with a guttural sound that could easily be mistaken for a roar.

I clap once. "Hell yes."

He racks the bar and stumbles back, catching himself on the padded bench behind him. "You're an evil man," he gasps. "Seriously. Sadistic."

I toss him a towel. "And yet, you keep coming back."

Julian, a former wide receiver and current rehab patient, has been training with me for eight weeks now. ACL reconstruction, plus some serious scar tissue buildup from trying to "push through the pain" like every stubborn pro athlete I've ever known. He's tough as hell, which makes him one of my favorite clients—and a bit of a cautionary tale to the rookies.

"Remind me why I let Cameron talk me into this," he mutters, slumping forward and rubbing his towel over his face.

"Because he's smarter than you?" I offer. "And he knew your ego couldn't handle being shown up by a one-legged trainer."

He laughs, full-bodied this time, and tosses the towel back at me. "Touché."

I grin and catch it easily, walking over to wipe down the equipment. The gym's quiet now, late-morning light pouring through the floor-to-ceiling windows and casting long strips of sun across the rubber flooring. My shadow stretches as I move—tall, lean, and distinct. You can see the difference in my gait if you know what to look for, but these days I barely notice the slight tilt of my left leg or the sound the carbon fiber foot makes when I pivot on it.

Fifteen years ago, I thought my life had ended.

Today, I make a living helping people rebuild theirs.

"You're getting stronger," I say over my shoulder. "Week nine's gonna feel like a breeze compared to this."

Julian groans again. "You keep saying that. I'm beginning to think you're just here to torture me for your own amusement."

"Only partially true," I reply. "You'd cry without me."

"Lies. I'd cry with joy."

I laugh again and finish wiping down the rack before tossing the rag into the bin. I glance at the clock. 11:42. I've got forty-five minutes before my next session, which gives me time to answer some emails and, maybe, drink something that isn't water or protein sludge.

Julian stands, rolling his shoulder. "Seriously, though. Thanks, man. You're the first person who didn't treat me like I was broken."

I meet his gaze. "That's because you're not."

Something flickers across his face—something raw and real—and he nods, brushing a knuckle under one eye like it's just sweat. He grabs his gym bag, shooting me a grin. "Same time next week?"

"You bet."

I watch him go, shoulders squared, stride even. Still a little stiff, but he's getting there. Every time someone like Julian walks out of my gym standing taller than when they came in, I feel it in my chest. Like maybe, just maybe, this life I didn't ask for has turned into something worthwhile.

The door swings shut behind him, and I let out an unhurried breath.

I limp slightly as I head back to my office—not because I'm in pain, but because my socket's been bugging me today. It's nothing major, just a reminder that no matter how many times I upgrade my leg, there are always going to be days that don't go down smoothly. I've got a blade for running, a waterproof model for swimming, and the one I'm wearing now—my everyday athletic model, black carbon, with a polished shock-absorbing pylon that glints faintly in the sun.

I named it Nelly.

Because she's hot, high-performance, and a little temperamental.

The desk chair squeaks as I drop into it, spinning gently in place as I reach for my water bottle. The walls around me are covered with photos—clients I've worked with, some famous, most not. There's a shelf of trophies in one corner, and yeah, a couple from my playing days are up there too. Not for vanity, but to remind myself of where I came from.

Most people think I stayed in Detroit after the accident. Or maybe went back to South Carolina. But after the surgeries, the rehab, the insurance hell, the media circus, and a year of barely holding myself together, I packed two bags and moved west.

San Francisco offered something I hadn't had since the crash—anonymity at first, and eventually, possibility.

Cameron, my old high school teammate, hadn't been my actual agent. But after college, he started working under Marcus—my former agent—and eventually became my main point of contact. He showed up at the hospital. Sat by my bed when I was too angry to speak. Tried to help with the calls, the chaos, the plans. But I shut him out —just like I shut out everyone. My parents ran interference. I convinced myself I didn't need anyone. Especially not people who reminded me of who I used to be.

We didn't speak for years.

It wasn't until I'd clawed my way through physio training, opened my own studio, and finally stopped flinching every time someone mentioned my name in the past tense that I reached out.

He didn't hesitate.

Since then, he's been one of my biggest supporters. He sends athletes my way—clients in the thick of recovery who need someone who's been through the fire and lived to talk about it. He trusts me. And I never forget that.

It took a few years. Trial and error. Certification programs. Licensing. Building a business from the ground up. But now, I have a waitlist that stretches six months, a full-time assistant trainer, and a roster of clients who trust me with their bodies and their stories.

I love it. I really, really do.

But sometimes… sometimes I still wake up and expect to feel both legs under the covers. And some nights, when the fog rolls in off the Bay and the whole city feels ghosted over, I dream about him.

Theo.

It's been fifteen years, and I can still see his face like it's burned into the inside of my eyelids. He doesn't know where I live. Doesn't know what I do. I never responded to the emails from my old account or the texts or the voicemails. After that first shut door, he stopped knocking. I made sure of it.

I had to.

At the time, it was the only way I knew how to deal.

The door to my office opens, accompanied by a belated knock. My assistant, Lacey, who also works at the front desk, pops her head in, holding her tablet. "Quick heads-up. You've got a media inquiry in your inbox. Some podcast wants you to talk about injury recovery in athletes."

I grimace. "Send it to my PR guy. And remind me to thank Cameron again."

"He's helping," Lacey singsongs, rolling her eyes. "He loves you. We all do."

"Yeah, yeah. Tell him not to start charging a finder's fee."

She waves me off and disappears into the back again.

I lean back in the chair, letting the hum of the gym I can see out of the overlarge window in my office and the sound of weights clinking drift around me. This life is good. It's hard-won and mine. But there are still parts of me Theo never got to see grow back, and parts I never figured out how to show him.

With time before I see my next client, instead of grabbing a protein shake or stretching out, I wiggle my mouse, waking up my Mac, and sigh. I don't need to check the reunion page again. I've already RSVP'd. The flight's booked, B&B confirmed. But still, my hand grips my mouse like it's a nervous tic, this constant rechecking.

One more glance, just to be sure.

It's not nerves, exactly, but something close. Maybe *compulsion* is the better word. I mean to look at client files —Cameron sent a new referral this morning—but instead, my fingers hesitate for only a second before I open a new tab and type: *Gomillion High School.*

The site loads, the school's logo stretched at the top in tired reds and golds. The Millipede's still the mascot, bless its little segmented soul. I chuckle under my breath, dry and fond.

"Go Millions," I murmur, shaking my head. That phrase still makes no sense.

And there it is. Front and center, beneath a grainy banner of the high school: *Gomillion High: 20-Year Reunion Weekend!*

My heart flips strangely. It's the same information I

was forwarded in December, but seeing it here—on the school's actual site—makes it feel official. Concrete.

Two days to go.

I swallow and scroll through the schedule, the font a little too bright against the dark background.

The reunion spans the whole weekend—cocktails and mingling on Friday night, a tour and alumni basketball game Saturday, and some kind of wild throwback prom, complete with speeches, dinner, and dancing. It's ambitious for a town as small as Gomillion, but that's just how folks there are—small town, big energy.

And I'd bet good money Kirkwood had a hand in the flair. That guy always did love a legacy moment.

My eyes catch on "Alumni Game."

Yeah. Not this time.

Well, maybe.

I scroll faster, a little too fast, then slow down and click into the Staff page before I can change my mind.

There he is.

Theo.

English teacher. Gomillion High's all-around smart kid turned homegrown legacy.

His staff photo is casual but professional. A navy button-up, sleeves rolled to the elbow, paired with bright yellow suspenders that shouldn't be as charming as they are. His smile tugs slightly to the left, modest but warm. His hair's in a low fade now—with brush waves on top and clipped extremely short at the sides and back, neat with crisp line up, no curls in sight.

My breath catches.

He looks older. Stronger. Grounded in a way that's

new. Still lean, but not fragile. He looks like a man who's done the hard work of becoming himself. And hell, he's still beautiful.

I lean back and let my eyes close for a second. Something deep and dull aches in my chest. Nostalgia twisted with regret. I can still smell lake water and sweat from the gym, still hear the slam of a locker door and his laugh echoing off cement walls.

I open my eyes again and click into the Sports page and then the basketball schedule. His name's there again—assistant coach.

It wasn't even a surprise the first time I looked.

He always remembered the plays, read the scouting reports. I just showed up and improvised. He made the game matter.

I stare at his picture for a long time. The lines at the corners of his eyes are new. But the eyes themselves—still sharp. Still thoughtful. Still full of the things he never quite said out loud.

And I miss him.

Damn it, I didn't expect that part to hit this hard.

I close the tab.

I don't need reminders of everything I left behind. Even if I had reasons. Even if I've spent the last fifteen years convincing myself it was the only way he could move forward.

With someone else. Somewhere else.

He deserved that.

I just never expected he'd go back home, though, to Gomillion.

That thought knocks into me like a cheap shot to the ribs.

Cameron mentioned it once, years ago. I'd just opened the gym. My business was still barely standing upright.

"Yeah, Theo's back in Gomillion. Teaching now. Can you believe that?"

Teaching, yes. But heading back to our hometown? No. I couldn't believe that.

He used to talk about leaving constantly. City lights. A school where he could really make a difference. His dream was never small. And the unspoken part—the part we both knew—was that he'd be wherever I was. Wherever my contract took me. That was always the plan.

I rub my eyes and let my hand drop to my leg. I adjust the athletic sleeve over my prosthesis. It's sleek and dark, the carbon fiber catching the soft light from my desk lamp.

There's no shame in this anymore. Not in the leg. Not in the way I've built my life from the wreckage. I'm proud of what I've done. Of who I've become.

But vulnerability? That still sticks to me like sweat on skin.

No one back home's seen me in person since the accident—other than Cameron. They've heard, of course. The whole town probably heard. But hearing about a below-the-knee amputation is different from seeing one.

My phone screen lights up with "Dad" just as I put my Mac into Sleep mode. I hesitate only a second before answering. "Hey, Pops," I say, pushing back in my chair and stretching my leg out. The prosthesis clinks gently against the tile. "What's up?"

"Hey, son." His voice is warm and easy, like always. "Just doing my fatherly duty of checking in before you jet off to your past life."

I chuckle. "Still got today to ignore it all, but thanks for the reminder."

"You packed yet?"

I glance toward the gym bag by the filing cabinet, half zipped, still empty. "Of course not."

He sighs dramatically. "You're your mother's child."

I grin and lean forward, rubbing at the back of my neck. "She'd say I'm yours."

"She'd be right."

There's a pause. It's not awkward, just familiar. Dad's not big on filling silence unless it needs it.

"You, uh, taking anyone?" he finally asks, casually enough that I know it's not casual at all. "To the reunion, I mean."

I snort. "Yeah, I'm bringing the ghost of my emotional stability. Should make for great small talk."

Dad laughs, then sobers a bit. "Caden...."

"I know, I know." I rake a hand through my hair. "But no, I'm not taking anyone. You know that. It's been years."

"You dated that woman for a while."

"Almost a year," I say, sighing. "She said I was emotionally unavailable, if you remember. She wasn't wrong."

"And the guys?"

I give a half laugh, bitter around the edges. "You know about all of the disasters of my nonexistent love life." Well, obviously not the dirty details, but still. A few casual dates. Hookups, mostly. Nothing worth putting on a name tag.

Dad's quiet again. When he speaks, his voice is lower, gentler. "You ever think that maybe it's time?"

"For what?" I ask, even though I know exactly what he means.

"To stop living like a shadow."

The words hit harder than I expect. "I'm not—" I start, then stop. A breath shudders out of me. "I've built a good life. A full one."

"I know," he says softly. "You've worked damn hard for everything you've got. But a full life doesn't mean there's no space for more."

His voice is steady and knowing. He doesn't say Theo's name, but he doesn't have to. That shadow he's talking about? It has a counterpart. And that counterpart has a name. A laugh. A set of eyes I've never been able to forget.

And no matter how many miles or years have passed, he's always been there—in the back of my mind, lodged stubbornly in my chest.

I'm quiet. I trace the seam of my prosthetic sleeve. The carbon fiber is cool under my touch.

"Are you worried about seeing him?" Dad asks so softly, it almost doesn't register.

I swallow, throat suddenly dry. "Yeah," I admit. "I guess I am."

"He's still in Gomillion, right? Still teaching?"

I nod, forgetting for a second that he can't see me. "Saw his photo on the site." I don't tell him I've been staring at it for weeks.

There's a pause. I can hear the clink of Dad's mug against a countertop. "He still look like trouble?"

I huff out a breath, something between a scoff and a

laugh. "He never looked like trouble," I say softly. "He looked like… all the reasons I ever wanted to be good." I sigh. "He still looks like home."

That silence stretches again. This one hurts.

"I ruined everything, Dad."

"No," he says firmly. "It was a goddamn accident, Cade. It could've been any one of us in that car."

"I suggested we take a break," I whisper, "but I didn't push. I knew he was tired. He'd driven six hours after a full day of classes to be at that game, and I let him think he could push through."

"You were twenty-two," Dad says.

"But I blamed him. For a long time."

"You were grieving. You were angry. You lost so much."

"I lost everything," I say, voice rough. "And so did he. And I walked away. Pushed him away. I let Mom answer the door. I let that be the last memory."

"Son," he says, and there's something shaky in it now. "I get it. I do. But Theo wasn't the only one who lost something that night. We all did. Just… your mom and I managed to get you back. It took a while, but you're the same Caden we've always known and loved. We're so damn proud of you."

Guilt and gratitude tangle in my gut. "I know. Thank you, and I'm sorry." Those first two years had been hell for all of us.

"Don't be sorry to me," he says. "Just… if you see him, talk to him."

I let the words sit for a moment, my chest tight. "I don't even know if he'll be there."

"You said you saw his name on the committee list."

"Yeah," I mutter. "But that doesn't mean he'll show."

"Well," Dad says, "you're still going. That counts for something."

I nod again, uselessly.

"We really are proud of you, son," he repeats, softer this time, like he needs me to feel it. "You've built something incredible out of the ashes."

I blink against the sudden sting in my eyes. "Thanks, Dad."

"And hey," he adds, "if you bring me back one of those yearbooks, I won't have to pretend to remember what your prom date looked like."

I snort. "That was a disaster."

"I recall. She ditched you, right?"

I snort, remembering how I'd been so relieved when she had—especially because that night changed who I was to my core. It was the night I kissed Theo. "Yeah, yeah," I say.

"Still got the photos in the attic," he teases. "Your mother loves that one where you're blinking and look terrified."

"I *was* terrified."

We both laugh.

"I'll see you when you get back," he says. "Want us to drive you to the airport?"

"Nah, I'll grab a car. But maybe dinner when I get home?"

"Sounds good."

We hang up, and I sit for a long moment in the quiet

that follows. The hum of the gym's HVAC returns, low and steady. Outside, the city moves on without me.

I look back toward my Mac. *"Theo."* I let myself whisper it once, just to hear it aloud. His name settles in the air like dust in a beam of light—soft, weightless, and somehow impossible to ignore.

My chest tightens. I press the heels of my hands against my eyes and breathe in deeply, hoping to ground myself in the present, but all I feel is the stretch of time folding in on itself.

The boy I loved. The man I lost.

Tomorrow, I go back.

Back to the town I haven't set foot in since everything changed.

Back to the place where I learned how to jump—and where I learned how far you can fall.

And maybe... maybe back to the one person I never stopped missing.

I reach for my phone, set it to charge before I head out to see my final client, and murmur into my quiet office, "Please be there."

Because ready or not, I'm going home.

EIGHTEEN
THEO

By the time I finally lock up my classroom for the day, my shoulders ache, and I'm half convinced my planning skills have staged a walkout. School officially ended two days ago, but I've been coming in to tie up loose ends—sorting lesson plans, organizing a couple things for next year so I can get ahead. Somehow it's more exhausting than a regular day with students. Instead of grading freshman essays on *The Outsiders* or steering seniors through college application panic, it's me versus a mountain of binders and a copier that jams if you look at it wrong.

When I step out into the parking lot, the sun's dipping low over Gomillion, throwing a syrupy, golden haze over everything. It smells like crepe myrtle and someone grilling three streets over. A warm breeze rustles the faded American flag in front of city hall, and it flutters like a lazy wave hello.

The school's smack in the center of town, which honestly has a classic small-town South Carolina vibe, the kind of charm developers try to fake in cities but never quite get right. We've got one blinking red light, a diner with peach cobbler so good, it ought to be illegal, and storefronts that haven't changed since I was a kid. Even the font on the hardware store sign is the same.

The bunting's already up outside the small gym. Red and gold ribbons flutter under the banner that reads *Welcome Back, Millions! Class of 2005 Reunion Weekend.* Someone even added a big foam millipede cutout near the steps. It's ridiculous, nostalgic, and weirdly touching.

I smile, but it's tight.

I've spent the past week helping fine-tune the last-minute details of this thing—meetings during lunch, phone calls after work, spreadsheets and sign-up sheets that keep multiplying like rabbits. But now, the real part's starting.

The people are coming.

He is coming.

I'm just about to cut across the road to pick up bread from the store when a voice calls out from behind me.

"Hey, Theo."

I turn and spot Emmett Pearce leaning against his gray Toyota Tacoma, looking like he's on his way somewhere but in no particular rush. His smirk is as familiar as the dusty welcome mat outside the bakery.

"Emmett," I say with a chuckle. "Didn't I just see you arguing with Martha over shipping rates last week?"

He lifts a hand in a lazy wave. "Probably. You know how I feel about paying twelve bucks to mail a registered letter two towns over."

We exchange a quick clap on the back, nothing out of

the ordinary. Emmett was a year ahead of me in school, and like a few of us, he never really left Gomillion. We run into each other often enough—at the store, on Main, grabbing coffee at Mo's. It's all just part of the rhythm of small-town life.

"You heading home?" I ask, adjusting the tote bag slung over my shoulder.

"Yeah, I just swung out to pick up a few things for a couple of picky guests. B&B's filling up fast. Full-on reunion rush." He shifts his keys in his palm. "Guess who's on my check-in list?"

I pause. My stomach tightens in anticipation even though I already know.

"Caden."

I try not to flinch, but I feel it. My pulse kicks up, and something in my lungs forgets how to inflate. "Oh," I manage. "Right. Figured he'd be staying somewhere nearby."

Emmett eyes me for a beat—too casually not to mean something. "He's due any minute. I figured I'd give you the heads-up, just in case."

I nod like it's no big deal, like I don't suddenly feel like the sidewalk's tilted sideways. "Appreciate it."

"Sure. I didn't know if you'd want to… I don't know, avoid or ambush."

I snort. Like almost everyone else, he doesn't know the truth about Cade's and my romantic relationship. "I'm not ambushing anyone."

He grins. "I didn't think so. But I've seen you at the grocery store, Theo. You ambush the last box of oat granola like your life depends on it."

"You know I'm not right without fiber," I say dryly.

He laughs and gives my shoulder a squeeze. "Well, I'll let you get back to it. See you tomorrow?"

"Yeah," I say. "Wouldn't miss it."

And with a final wave, he heads off down Main Street, and I stand here for a beat too long, letting the weight of Caden's name settle on my chest like dust on a picture frame not touched in years.

Caden. In town. This evening.

For a minute, I consider walking to the B&B. Just... being there when he arrives. Like ripping off a Band-Aid with questionable impulse control.

But that idea really does feel like an ambush. Like something I used to do when I was seventeen and had zero chill. I have no idea what he wants, if he even wants to see me. It's been fifteen years. Fifteen years of silence so loud, it echoed in my bones. Fifteen years of living with his ghost even though he wasn't dead.

I blow out a breath and pivot on my heel, heading toward Timbers & Tallboys instead. If there was ever a day that called for a drink, it's this one.

The bar sits close by, tucked between the pharmacy and a thrift store that smells aggressively of mothballs. The neon sign flickers as I approach, buzzing faintly like it's on the verge of giving up.

Inside, it's exactly the same as it's been since we were teens sneaking in with fake IDs—and getting caught every time. Low ceilings, pine paneling, darts that are always slightly crooked, and the best damn wings south of Charleston.

Moses is behind the bar, polishing a glass like it

personally insulted his mother. It's not a face I've seen in a while. He looks up, his face creasing into a wry grin. "Well, if it isn't Professor Ball Game himself."

I slide onto a stool. "Hey, Moses. Good to see you, man." I reach out and we shake hands.

"Back at you. You look like a man who needs something stronger than sweet tea."

"Preach."

He sets down the glass and pours me a local IPA without asking. Impressive really since the last time I came in here when Moses was in town was probably four months ago. "You organizing all that reunion mess?"

"Some of it."

"God help you."

We clink glasses, and I take a long sip. Cold. Hoppy. Blessedly distracting.

Moses leans in, elbows on the counter. "You nervous about him?"

I pause. "Who?"

He just lifts a brow.

I huff out a laugh. "Word travels."

"Gomillion's the kind of town where you can't fart without someone's aunt posting about it on Facebook."

I shake my head, but the laugh that slips out is real. It catches me off guard—like a pressure valve cracking open.

"I don't know what to expect," I admit, voice quieter now. "I haven't seen him since…."

"I know," Moses says gently, his tone shifting.

"And yeah, I'm nervous. I'd be an idiot not to be."

Moses gives a slow nod, one of those bartender

expressions that somehow makes you feel both seen and unjudged. "Understandable."

He tops off my glass and leans on the bar. "Look, I'm not gonna pretend to know the whole story—only what people whisper when they think no one's listening. But I know what it's like to carry something for a long time and not say it out loud."

"Yeah?"

"Yeah," he says, wiping the counter absently. "So whatever it is between you two—whatever it used to be, whatever it is now—don't waste the moment. Talk to him. Don't dance around it."

I exhale through my nose. "That's your professional opinion, huh?"

"You want closure, ask for it. You want answers, go get 'em. You want to bolt, at least wait until you've finished your beer."

I snort. "You really missed your calling as a therapist."

"Nah," he says, grinning. "Shit pays less, and they don't let you wear flannel."

I finish my drink. Just one. Enough to settle the static inside my ribs.

Outside, the early-evening light spills golden over Main Street, casting long, gentle shadows that stretch lazily across the pavement. The air's warm but not heavy, threaded with the scent of honeysuckle and cut grass—quintessential May. Somewhere down the block, a lawnmower buzzes, underscored by the hum of cicadas starting to tune up for the evening.

I pause before getting into my car, one hand on the door, the other still in my pocket. Main Street looks the same as it always has—brick-front shops, the barber pole spinning slowly like it's got all the time in the world. I stare down the road like it might give me some kind of answer. Like maybe the asphalt remembers more than I do.

Caden's here. Or about to be.

And every nerve in my body is starting to wake up.

He's probably already checked into the B&B. Maybe he's unpacking. Maybe he's pacing, just like me. We've gone more than a decade without seeing each other, but somehow the thought of him being less than ten blocks away has my heart doing cartwheels and tying itself in knots at the same time.

I consider swinging by.

But showing up unannounced? If he didn't want to see me....

I take a long breath. Whatever happens tomorrow, the silence we've been living in is over.

One way or another.

The car's interior is warm from the spring sun, and my hand lingers on the wheel longer than it should. I sit for a second before pressing the ignition, the engine growling to life with a soft rumble. Just as the dash lights up, my phone rings through the Bluetooth system.

Mom.

I sigh and tap Answer on the steering wheel. "Hey, Ma."

"You sound distracted," she says, not missing a beat.

"Been a long day."

"Reunion chaos?"

"Something like that." I pause. "Caden's in town."

The silence on the other end stretches. It's not awkward, but it's layered. She knows *everything*. Not just that Caden and I were best friends, but that we were each other's *firsts*. First love, first everything. She knows how we mapped out our lives around each other. She knows I was behind the wheel that night. That I was the one who walked away while he nearly didn't. And she knows how completely I fell apart when he told me not to come back.

"You thinking about seeing him?" she asks softly. There's no judgment in her tone. It's more like she's just gently peeling back the lid on a box we both know is full of sharp fragments.

"I don't know," I say, turning onto Silvester Street. "Part of me thinks it might be easier to just... rip the Band-Aid off." I echo my earlier thoughts, hoping she'll tell me what I need to do.

"To protect your heart or to punish yourself?" she asks. It's gentle, but it cuts clean.

I flinch. "Ma...."

She exhales. "I know, baby. I know this is hard. But after everything that happened and how long you've carried this, don't you think it's okay to *wait*? See what he wants first?"

"I could just swing by the B&B, say hi. Pretend it's not a big deal."

"But it *is* a big deal," she says. "You don't have to pretend with me. Not after all this time."

I swallow. "It's just... fifteen years, Ma. I haven't seen him since that hospital room. Since he told me to go and not come back."

"I remember," she says, her voice tight with memory.

"You came home and didn't speak for three days. You looked like someone had pulled the sun out of the sky."

I blink hard, the road blurring for a second.

"Theo, listen to me. If he's here, it means something. He knew you'd be at the reunion. He's not showing up by accident."

"You think?" My voice cracks more than I want it to.

"I *know*," she says. "And I know you. You've lived fifteen years like you were waiting for a door to open that never did. Maybe this is it. But not tonight. Let tomorrow be what it's going to be."

I nod, even though she can't see it. "You're right."

"I'm *always* right," she teases gently. Then her tone softens. "But seriously, baby... don't let this shake you so hard, you forget how far you've come. You've built a life. A good one. You deserve to live in it fully."

I smile, a tired curl of my mouth. "You're not supposed to be this wise, you know."

"I've had thirty-seven years to practice. And I got front row seats to your heartbreak. I've earned a little wisdom."

We talk for a few more minutes—about nothing important. Her baking. My dad refusing to take vitamins. A new stray cat she's named Socks despite it being jet-black and thoroughly sockless.

But as I pull onto my street, her voice fades into the background. Because a car I don't recognize is parked in front of my house.

I glance at the plate. It's a rental.

My breath stutters.

I say goodbye, hit End Call, and then pull into my

driveway, the sound of gravel crunching under my tires loud in the stillness.

I barely get the truck into Park before the other car door opens.

And time halts.

Caden steps out at the same time I do.

And the past barrels into the present so hard, I nearly forget how to breathe.

The years collapse.

He looks older… a given. But thirty-eight suits him in a way that feels unfair. Like time gave him angles and grace, definition and quiet strength. His shirt is unbuttoned at the collar, sleeves pushed up to show the forearms I used to fall asleep within. Dark jeans, a slight five-o'clock shadow, casual and devastatingly composed.

He's still beautiful.

But this is the man version of the boy I loved. The one I planned my whole damn future with. The one I thought I'd follow anywhere, until "anywhere" became a hospital room with too much white and too many machines, and him saying, *"Don't come back."*

That was fifteen years ago.

Fifteen years since the accident.

Fifteen years since I stood by his bed, hands shaking, thinking love was enough to fix what had broken.

He told me to leave.

And I did.

And I've hated myself for it every day since.

But now—here he is.

Standing on the street we spent years playing together on, looking at me like I'm still someone he recognizes.

The world blurs a little at the edges just from how hard my heart starts to beat.

He doesn't speak. Neither do I. We just stare across the gravel and air and fifteen years of silence.

I take a step forward, unsure if I'll keep going, unsure if he'll run.

But he doesn't move. He just watches me, expression unreadable, but his eyes—his eyes still look like they did when we were teenagers and dreaming about apartments with too much light and cities that didn't know our names.

My mouth goes dry.

And then, finally, softly, he says my name. "Theo."

It lands somewhere between a prayer and a regret. I feel it all the way in my bones.

"Hey," I whisper.

And just like that, everything changes. It's not fixed, not forgiven. But started.

Again.

NINETEEN
CADEN

I don't know what the hell I'm doing here.

I didn't even enter the B&B. I just kept driving past it. Past the grocery store that has an updated sign. Past the field we used to cut through on the way to the gym, now fenced off and "under development" if the cheap banner signs are to be believed.

My hands did the driving, but my heart had steered.

And now I'm here. On the street I haven't dared to think about in nearly sixteen years. Parked in front of a house I once knew like the back of my hand. Except now the front door is the wrong color—dark teal instead of white—and there's a different car in the driveway. Not his old Jeep. Not his mom's sedan. But I know it's still home.

Theo's home.

I stare through the windshield, heart racing like I'm about to walk into a playoff game, only worse—because I have no idea what play I'm supposed to run. I've got no game plan. Just this knot in my chest and the way my hands won't stop trembling on the wheel.

He could slam the door in my face. Hell, he should.

But then the car door opens—so does mine—and time skips a beat.

Theo steps out.

And just like that, I can't breathe.

God, he looks good. Not just *handsome*—he's always been that—but solid in a way that speaks of stability and presence. There's a weight to him now that wasn't there at twenty-two. He was beautiful then, sure. Lean. Quick to smile. A little too serious about everything. But now? Now he's the kind of man people slow down to look at. A full-grown heartbreaker.

His brown skin is darker than I remember—May sun already starting to claim him for the season. His curls are gone, hair trimmed short and tight at the sides. He's wearing a faded Gomillion training T-shirt and jeans, and he's staring at me like this is just any other afternoon.

But it's not.

His gaze sweeps the street and lands on me. My feet hit the pavement unevenly, the weight of the prosthesis always more noticeable when I'm tired. I wince. My knee doesn't lock quite right, and I have to catch myself on the car door.

Theo freezes.

His eyes drop—right there, to my leg.

Denim covers it, but the outline's obvious. The awkward angle of my stance. The way I hesitate, shifting my balance.

And there it is. That flicker of guilt on his face. The wet glass of unshed tears in his eyes. His mouth parts like he's about to speak, but the words don't make it past whatever wall he's put up since the last time we saw each other.

The hospital.

The moment I told him to leave.

The last time I saw him standing in a doorway, expression cracked wide open with grief and fear and love I couldn't take.

A thousand memories crash into me all at once.

Theo holding my face in his hands in the back seat of his mom's car after my first big win.

Theo barefoot in my kitchen, wearing my hoodie and holding a spoon like a mic while making pancakes.

Theo whispering *forever* against my neck in the dark.

The boy who knew every scar, every dream. The man I left behind.

I take a breath. It's not enough. Another. Still not enough.

But somehow, his whispered name still escapes my lips.

His simple "Hey" follows, and then finally, after too many awkward, breathless heartbeats, he says, "You coming in, or do you want to keep standing there like a horror movie extra?"

His voice is soft. Familiar. Rougher than I remember, but God, it wraps around me like a thread pulling me forward.

I bark out a laugh, something strangled and surprised. "You always were dramatic."

He shrugs, but his lips twitch. "Yeah, well. You've got a flair for entrances."

A pause stretches between us.

"I didn't know you still live here," I say finally.

"Yet you came anyway."

I step closer. Not too close, but enough to cross the space between the sidewalk and the porch. I can feel my limp with every step, like a flare of heat under my skin.

"You're not gonna tell me I look like shit?"

"You don't." He looks me over, eyes lingering maybe a second too long. "You look… older. Tired."

I smile crookedly. "Accurate."

"You hungry?" he asks, like we're two guys catching up after a game, not two men standing on the wreckage of what they once were.

"I'm always hungry," I say.

He nods once and opens the door. "Come in, then. I've got beer and leftover spaghetti if you're brave."

The house smells like pine cleaner and something faintly citrus. It's tidy. Not overly neat, but lived-in. There's a framed photo of his parents by the door, a pair of running shoes kicked to one side. I follow him down the hall to the kitchen, watching the way his shoulders move, how he rubs the back of his neck like he always did when he's thinking too much.

He grabs two beers from the fridge, pops the tops, and hands me one without looking. I take it. The cold bottle sweats against my palm.

We stand there in silence for a beat. Maybe two.

"You don't have to explain anything," Theo says quietly, his eyes not quite meeting mine.

I open my mouth, then close it again. The instinct is there—to spill everything, apologize, rewind the years. But it's too soon. The silence between us isn't an empty thing—it's dense, packed tight with memories and regrets and the ache of too much time lost. So I just nod and let the words die in my throat.

We move into the living room with our beers, the space familiar, but Theo's clearly made it his own. We sit on opposite ends of the couch like polite strangers with a shared past neither of us knows how to address.

He doesn't ask why I'm really here. I don't ask how he's really been.

Instead, we talk around it, skimming along the surface of safer topics.

"You're coaching the team?" I ask, lifting my beer to my lips.

"Yeah. Well, assistant coaching," he says. "Varsity boys. We made district finals this year."

"That's great." I glance at him. "You always were patient with kids."

He chuckles lightly. "You're the only one who'd say that."

I smile. "Because I once saw you try to teach a four-year-old how to tie his shoes."

"That kid had it out for me," he says, and this time, the smile sticks longer.

We fall into an uneasy rhythm after that. Talking about town politics, the way Main Street's finally getting repaved, the new stores. I nod along even though I already saw it when I drove past it all. Still, I like hearing it from him. Like I'm borrowing his version of Gomillion to layer over my own memories.

Theo's body is relaxed, one arm slung over the back of the couch, but there's a tightness in his shoulders that doesn't ease. Like he's braced for something. Like he's waiting for me to break open the past while he's still trying to figure out if he even wants me to.

I don't. Not yet.

It's enough just to be here, even if I can feel the weight of the years pressing down like a hand on the back of my neck.

I clear my throat. "How's Amelia doing? I haven't seen her since…." I let the sentence trail off, because finishing it would mean saying *since before the accident*.

His expression softens. "She's good. Living in Charlotte now. Got her degree, went into social work. She's tough as nails—exactly the kind of person you want fighting for you."

"Yeah?" I smile into my beer. "Sounds about right."

"She and John divorced last year, but she's holding it down. Connor's eleven now." His voice. "Smart kid. Loves basketball, but he's really into robotics too. Joined a STEM league last year and won his first competition. You'd like him."

"Man." I shake my head, grinning. "We're old enough to have middle-schoolers running around calling us 'sir.' That's wild."

Theo laughs quietly. "Yeah. Makes you feel it."

He gets up at one point to grab us more drinks and a bowl of chips, and I watch him move—fluid and sure. Confident. It hits me all over again how much he's grown into himself. Not just older, but… more grounded. Like someone who built something after everything fell apart.

He hands me a bottle, and our fingers brush. Just for a second. But my chest tightens in response, heat rising up the back of my neck. I cover my reaction with a sip and glance around the room again, looking quickly away when I spot a photo of the two of us taken when I was thirteen and he was twelve. We'd survived whitewater rafting and were both wearing shit-eating grins like we were badasses.

We weren't. We'd screamed and hung on for dear life over the rapids.

"I almost didn't come," I admit, voice rough.

He doesn't turn to me, but I see the flicker of something in his expression. "I figured."

Another silence.

"I didn't know if you'd be attending the reunion at all," I add. "Or if you'd want to see me."

His jaw ticks, but he keeps his gaze forward, saying lightly, "But you're still here."

And that's the most honest thing either of us has said all night.

We linger in the quiet. The kind that used to be easy between us, filled with shoulder bumps and knowing glances and shared CDs. Now it's taut and cautious, full of all the unsaid things neither of us is ready to grapple with.

After a while, Theo leans back and stretches his legs out, one ankle propped on the other. His fingers still cradle the neck of his beer, and he rotates it absently like he's not ready to let go just yet.

"You still in San Francisco?" he asks casually.

I blink. "Yeah." I take a small sip, buying time. "Running my studio."

He nods once, like that tracks. "I figured," he says.

I narrow my eyes, curious. "You figured?"

He doesn't look at me. He shrugs one shoulder, eyes on some vague spot near the TV. "You never really struck me as the 'move back home' type. Not after... everything."

"Still," I murmur, "bit of a shot in the dark. You keeping tabs on me?"

He huffs a quiet laugh and finally glances my way, eyes glinting with mischief. "You think it's hard to find you online? Please. You're not exactly subtle, Caden. The studio's website basically treats your face like a branding strategy. I counted nine photos of you on the home page alone."

There's a smirk tugging at the corner of his mouth now, and for a split second, I see him—the Theo I used to know. The one who used to tease me out of bad moods, who knew exactly how to press a button and then soften the blow with a smile. It's like muscle memory: affection wrapped in sarcasm.

And damn if it doesn't knock the breath out of me.

"I didn't design the website."

"Sure." He smirks faintly again, but it fades quickly. A beat passes. Then he adds, quieter, "I saw an article a few years back. About a para-athlete you helped get back into competition condition. It mentioned you lived in Bernal Heights. That stuck."

I stare at him. "You read an article about me?"

He shrugs again, but his ears flush a little. "I read a lot of things."

I try to hide how much that gets to me. How much it means. Theo's never really been one for idle curiosity. If he looked, he wanted to know. And not because someone like Cameron handed him updates, but because he went looking himself.

That knowledge hits somewhere tender.

The light outside has dimmed, the sky folding itself into that indigo softness that May evenings always bring in the South. A dog barks in the distance, sharp and brief. The scent of cut grass lingers, mingling with the faint sandalwood from Theo's cologne.

I look at him again. At the strong lines of his jaw, the quiet confidence in how he sits, even with the weight of everything unspoken between us. His profile's sharper now. Still him, but more… settled. Like someone who built a life around the pieces he couldn't fix.

And here I am, still holding the ones I broke.

"You staying long?" he asks, interrupting the spiral I feel coming on.

"Just the weekend. I head back on Sunday."

He nods again with quiet acceptance.

The pause that follows hangs heavy. It's thick with everything unsaid. It presses into the space between us until I can feel it in my chest, a thudding kind of ache.

"Guess I'll see you tomorrow night, then," he says, his voice soft but steady.

"Yeah," I say, my throat a little tight. "Guess you will."

He stands, and I follow. The weight of the moment pulls me up slower than I mean to rise. I adjust out of habit, trying to make the shift smooth. But I catch it—his eyes flicking to my leg, just for a second. A tiny shift in his expression. Not pity. Not disgust. Just… awareness.

And this time, he doesn't flinch. He doesn't look away.

He meets my eyes, and in them, I see the same unspoken storm we're carrying.

There's a beat. Then, casual as anything, he says, "I was about to throw something together—nothing fancy, but definitely better than leftover spaghetti. You want to stay?"

I almost say yes.

Almost.

The words hover behind my teeth, and I can feel how easy it would be to let them fall. To sit down at his table like we haven't lost fifteen years. But I don't. Because I'm here, and he's here, but *we're not here*—not really. Not yet. The past is still sitting between us like a third presence, thick and sharp-edged and unnamed.

"I appreciate it," I say, forcing a small smile, "but I should get back. Still gotta check in and pretend I'm organized."

His eyes search mine for half a second longer than necessary, and then he gives a single, understanding nod. "Fair enough."

"Thanks for the beer," I add.

He nods again, gentler this time. "Drive safe."

I make it to the door, ignoring his wince when he spoke. I make it to the car, but I don't start the engine right away.

Instead, I sit here, the steering wheel cool under my hands, watching the porch light dim and the living room fade to dark behind the blinds. Somewhere inside that house, Theo's moving through his evening like it's just another day.

But it's not.

That was the first time we've shared space in years.

And though we haven't talked about any of it—not the hospital, not the accident, not the way I shoved him out of my life like he didn't anchor me through the best and worst years I've ever known—I feel it, still breathing.

Some part of us is still here.

Still alive.

Still waiting.

TWENTY

THEO

I've been in this gym a thousand times.

As a student, an athlete, a teacher, and now, for the past six years, assistant basketball coach. The floors have been polished since then, the paint freshened. New banners line the rafters. But the air still smells like waxed hardwood and too much adolescent ambition.

And tonight? It's packed with nostalgia. And hairspray. And the soft rustle of name tags being awkwardly pressed against button-downs and dresses.

Welcome Back, Millions! reads the glitter-strewn banner hanging above the check-in tables. It's still early—just after six—and the gym's filling up. Laughter rings out in waves. Hugs. Back slaps. People snapping selfies beside their old lockers. I help with some light crowd wrangling after a brief stint of manning the registration desks.

I recognize most of the faces. Some more than others. That's what happens when you're the teacher who stayed. You end up straddling two worlds—the guy who was one of them and the one they now call "Coach Brooks."

It's disorienting.

I glance toward the folding table near the bleachers. Maddie Coyle, two years below me in school and now the PTA president, is handing out name tags. Her toddler's already face-planted in a tray of glitter markers. I offer her a smile, and she throws me a look of deep maternal despair.

"Beer later?" she mouths.

I nod. "Count on it."

I do my rounds, slipping easily into small talk. I'm good at this. Familiar. Friendly. Safe. I float through conversations like someone who isn't half cracked beneath the surface.

It's 7:23 p.m. when it happens.

He walks in through the side doors.

He's not even trying to be dramatic, but everything slows. The music. The buzz of conversation. The quickening in my chest.

Caden.

I haven't seen him since he left my porch last night. I didn't sleep much after he left either—too wired, too raw, and too aware of how close his scent had clung to my sofa cushions.

He's wearing dark jeans and a soft gray Henley that fits just snug enough across his chest and forearms to punch the breath out of me. His hair is shorter than it was back then, his jawline more defined. But the shape of him, the weight of him in this space? It's unchanged.

He still draws attention like gravity.

A few heads turn. I hear a few murmured greetings—people recognizing the old basketball star, connecting dots. Someone claps him on the back. He smiles, polite but guarded.

Then his gaze finds mine across the room.

It holds, and for a second, I forget how to breathe.

He doesn't move toward me, and I don't move toward him. There's too much air between us, thick and humming. Instead, I turn away like I'm needed some-where—which, technically, I am. A mic isn't working. Another teacher from the art department needs help hauling a projector. I move through it all automatically.

By nine thirty, I've had two conversations about booster funding, one about my dating life (shout-out to Martha Brewer for that invasive line of questioning), and barely any sightings of the man who set my entire nervous system on fire just twenty-four hours earlier.

"Hey, Coach Brooks!"

I turn to see Trina Jennings waving me over near the bleachers, a sparkly reunion cup in one hand and a crooked smile on her face.

"Come do the yearbook photo trivia!" she calls out. "There's a prize!"

I give her a thumbs-up but don't move. Instead, I check the time again and let out a breath.

"I'm gonna head to Timbers," I tell Justin as I pass him. "See who's migrated over."

I grin as I back away, giving Vanessa a half-hearted salute and promising to swing by later to help clean up, though we both know I probably won't. My volunteer duties are technically done, and the weight in my chest has only grown heavier the longer I've stayed. Smiles are starting to feel a little too fixed. Every shadow at the edge of the gym has me turning my head, hoping—stupidly—that he'll still be here and I can talk to him.

But he's nowhere to be seen, so I make my exit.

Outside, the warm May air hits like a balm. The streetlights cast long shadows across the parking lot as I head to my truck. My name badge is stuffed in my pocket, and my pulse thrums somewhere in my throat.

I take the long way to Timbers, past our old route from the school to the court, past the convenience store that still stocks those awful green apple slushies Caden used to swear were "hydrating." I'm not particularly keen to stay out any longer, but I go anyway.

Because if he's going to be anywhere, it'll be here.

The after-party is already in full swing at Timbers & Tallboys. It seems like a lot of folks ducked out early. The bar's louder, darker, more relaxed than the school gym. String lights crisscross the ceiling. The old wooden floors creak under the weight of alumni reclaiming their youth.

I spot Moses behind the bar, already deep in orders. He clocks me and lifts a brow. I hold up two fingers and mouth, "Beer."

When I turn, Caden's leaning against the far end of the bar.

Of course he is.

He's nursing a bottle of something that's definitely not local. His stance is relaxed, but I know him. I see the tension in his jaw, the way his thumb circles the lip of the bottle like he's counting beats.

Swallowing my nerves, I slide in beside him, leaving just enough space between us to keep things plausible.

"So, how many 'remember whens' have you been hit with so far?"

He smiles into his drink. "Twelve, I think. Thirteen if you count the guy who swore I threw a game senior year because I wanted to impress a girl."

I laugh. "Let me guess. Max?"

"Bingo."

A pseudo-comfortable silence opens between us. Not the same one as last night. This one has edges. The kind you don't lean into unless you're ready to bleed.

"I forgot how loud this place can get," I say, nursing my beer. Sure, I come here fairly regularly, but it's never as packed as right now.

"Feels smaller," he replies. "Or maybe I'm just bigger."

I glance sideways. "You were always big."

That earns me a soft chuckle. "I don't know if that's a compliment or—"

"It is."

The music shifts to something older—Bon Jovi or Bryan Adams, nostalgia for some of the room. For others, it's just background noise while they wait for something with a little more soul. Couples dance near the jukebox. A group of former cheerleaders commandeer the photo booth. There's a flash as someone captures a moment that, after three whiskey shots, probably shouldn't exist.

"You didn't stay long at the school," I say.

"Didn't want to linger," he admits. "Felt too… staged."

I nod, sipping leisurely. "That's how it always feels now. Like I'm standing still while everyone else cycles through."

He looks at me then—really looks. "You ever think about leaving?"

"Sometimes," I admit. "But I like it here. I like the kids. The job."

He watches me for a beat longer than necessary. "You seem like you're good at it."

I lift a shoulder. "I try." Truth is, I love it. Teaching. Coaching. Staying rooted in this place in ways I never expected. But I don't say that. Not out loud. Not to him.

There's a pause. It's not awkward—it's charged. Like the moment before a storm when everything holds its breath.

"I was surprised to see you last night," I say finally, voice lower than before.

"I wasn't sure what I was doing or even if you still lived there," he admits, watching the condensation roll down the side of his beer bottle.

I nod, letting the silence stretch. I could ask him why he came. Why now. Why after all this time. But the questions feel too sharp for the space we've made tonight. So instead, I give him a softer out.

"How're your folks?"

He doesn't answer right away. His jaw ticks, eyes skimming over the bar like maybe there's a safer place to look. "They're in San Francisco, fairly close by to me," he says finally. "They wanted me to say hi for them."

I blink, caught off guard. "Yeah?"

He nods. "They always liked you. Missed you and your family after… everything."

There's something in his voice—a flicker of guilt, fast and sharp—and I know exactly what he's thinking because I've thought it too. He was the one who told me to leave. The one who shut the door on all of it.

And in doing so, he cut the lines between all of us.

"Mine ask about you sometimes," I say quietly, "wondering if I've heard from you. They know what happened and respected your choice to stay away."

Caden doesn't say anything, but the guilt deepens in his eyes like a tide rolling in. I don't push. He already showed up unannounced on my doorstep after fifteen years—maybe this is enough for tonight.

We do the only thing we can: pivot.

Caden glances around the bar like he's seeing it for the first time. "Did Moses always hang those ugly-ass antlers up there, or is that new?"

I follow his gaze. "They've been there since the second Bush administration. You're just finally noticing because they're now next to a framed photo of someone riding a mechanical bull in a prom dress."

He snorts. "God, please tell me that's not someone we know."

"Oh, it is," I say with a wicked grin. "Cassie Benson. Junior year prom. She wore the dress over her uniform because she was working first thing in the morning and was worried about oversleeping, and Brad dared her. You don't forget things like that."

"I think I just fell back in love with this town," Caden says dryly, raising his beer. "And I'm also still kind of terrified of it."

It's easy, this back-and-forth. Like the years haven't calcified between us.

"So," he says, after another sip, "the pizza place. Still as criminally bad as I remember?"

"Worse," I reply. "New owners last year. They tried to go fancy. 'Gourmet wood-fired crust' that tastes like its main ingredient is regret."

He chuckles, head tipping back, and for a second, he looks so much like the boy I used to know that it stings. "We used to eat similar crap after every game."

"Yup. Usually with you bitching about Coach and me pretending I didn't want to kiss you even with your mouth full of pepperoni."

He chokes on his beer, and I win that round.

"I can't believe you just said that." He laughs, dabbing at his shirt.

I shrug, trying not to grin too hard. "You started it with the antlers."

We keep going, trading stories like playing cards tossed onto the table.

"Remember when the gym lights used to flicker every time it rained?"

He groans. "Don't remind me. That buzzer beater in the regional semis? I couldn't see shit. I hit the shot blind."

"Which makes it sound way cooler than the truth," I say. "You were aiming for the other side of the rim."

"I'll never confirm or deny that," he says, smirking.

I roll my bottle between my palms, stealing a glance at him. "They finally fixed the lights in the east wing last year. Whole place smells the same, though. Bleach, rubber, and teenage angst."

His expression softens. "I miss it sometimes. The gym. The game. All of it."

"Yeah," I say quietly. "Me too."

A beat passes. He doesn't flinch. I don't either.

We talk about the seniors on the current team—my kids now. About how I inherited Coach Sanders's whistle and his overuse of the phrase *"Run it again."*

Caden smiles. "And that right there is how I know for certainty that you *are* good at it."

I snort and shake my head.

He's quiet for a second and then gently says, "I mean it. You always had a way of making people feel like they mattered."

I glance down, suddenly too warm in the face. "Well, at least someone still listens to me. I told Jeremiah not to wear mismatched sneakers to practice, and he said, 'It's fashion, Coach.'"

Caden chuckles. "He's not wrong. That's peak Gen Z defiance."

"And Coach nearly had a coronary. Thought the kid was concussed."

We laugh again. It's the kind of laughter you forget your body needs until it fills you up. The brimming tension is still there and pressed between us. But we're making space around it. Light is cracking through.

"So...." Caden leans an elbow on the table. "Moses still isn't here full-time, huh?"

"Nope. I rarely see him these days."

"Still because of all that shit that went on years back?"

I nod. "Yeah. I think so. But if you're drunk enough, he'll show you the shelf of people's secrets."

Caden lifts a brow. "Wait, what?"

I sip my beer. "You'll see. Just don't piss him off. He still remembers who broke the foosball table in 2004."

"That was definitely Finn."

"Tell him that," I say, laughing. "Moses has a memory like an elephant. A bitter, bourbon-soaked elephant."

The conversation meanders.

We talk about dumb pranks from senior year. About how Kirkwood's hair hasn't changed and how Vanessa still makes cookies for teachers. About Clara, who probably knows more than the NSA and has no shame about eavesdropping.

"It's wild," Caden murmurs, looking around. "Feels like the whole town just... paused. Like I could walk outside tomorrow, and it'd be senior year again."

I hum in agreement. "Except we're not those guys anymore."

"No," he says. "We're not."

But he doesn't sound sad about it. Just... aware.

And neither of us points out that despite the years, despite the scar tissue, we still fit like puzzle pieces with slightly softened edges.

At midnight, the bar starts to thin out. The jukebox plays something older than either of us. Moses yells good night to a group staggering toward the exit. I watch Caden finish his beer, the curve of his fingers around the bottle as familiar as the ache it triggers.

"You checked in okay at Emmett's?" I ask.

"Yeah."

"You good to get back tonight?"

He nods. "It's close enough."

I hesitate. "Tomorrow's the alumni game."

"I saw," he says. "You coaching?"

"Reffing," I say with a grin. "But yeah. I'll be there."

He holds my gaze. "Good. I'll come."

It's not a promise. But it's something.

We walk out into the warm, humid night. The scent of honeysuckle is thick in the air, crickets chirping like a soundtrack to something inevitable—like they know we're circling closer to what neither of us has dared to say.

At the curb, he pauses. "Good night, Theo."

"Night, Caden."

He turns and starts down the sidewalk. I watch him go, some part of me aching in a way that's both old and unbearably new.

And just before I climb into my truck, I see him glance back. Like maybe he's thinking the same thing I am. That this—whatever it is—still matters, even after all this time.

TWENTY-ONE

CADEN

Sleep took its time last night, the way it always does when my leg won't quite settle and every shift in bed feels like I'm dragging someone else's limb around with me.

By seven thirty, I give up and get moving. The shower sputters like it's clearing its throat. I wash fast, towel off, and seat myself on the edge of the bed to put on my liner and socket. The motions are automatic—liner rolled smooth, limb guided down, the quiet click and seal as the carbon fiber shell seats into place. I flex. It's solid with no hotspots. The day will be cold-start stiff until I warm up, but that's normal. I reach for my athletic cover—the matte black one that disappears under shorts when I'm training —and snap it into place. It feels like suiting up and coming home at the same time.

I text Cameron.

Me: The Roll in 15?

He texts back as I lace my sneakers.

Cam: Definitely. Bring your appetite and
your terrible taste in coffee.

It's not my taste that's terrible. It's The Roll's coffee. That's half the charm.

I cut through town on foot. Gomillion wears Saturday mornings well. Sunlight unspools across Main Street, making the shop windows glow like they're holding their breath. The bell above The Roll's door jingles when I push in. The scent hits like a hug: butter, cinnamon, sugar, and a hint of burnt drip coffee.

There's a banner behind the counter that's probably older than some of the kids Theo trains, reading *Voted Best Cinnamon Roll in the State for Over Twenty Years!* Someone added, in Sharpie: *They gave us the title for life and retired the category.* I barely hold back my laugh.

Cameron already has a table by the window, all elbows and easy charm in a soft gray jacket and a T-shirt that probably cost more than my first month's rent after college. His hair is immaculate. His grin isn't.

"You look like a man who fought a mattress and lost," he says as I drop into the chair across from him.

"I slept in a bed that had the springs of my youth," I say. "It was nostalgic. And crunchy."

He slides a plate toward me. Eight inches of spiraled sin glistens under a sheet of frosting, steam curling off the top like it's performing for the camera. There are two forks and two paper cups of coffee that smell like they were brewed yesterday.

"I bought the wheel," he says proudly. "And the state-sanctioned bad coffee."

"Bless you," I say, and pull the plate closer. The first bite is indecent. Sweet. Warm. A little yeasty, a little crispy at the edges. Joy in carb form. The coffee tastes like deadlines and determination. I drink it anyway.

Cameron watches me like he's timing a split. "Scale of one to sacred?"

"Somewhere near baptism," I say around another bite.

He laughs, then leans back and studies me. This is the part where he stops being my high school buddy and becomes the guy who negotiates with billionaires for breakfast. His eyes get a little sharper. He knocks softly on the table with his knuckles. "So. Eleven o'clock."

"The alumni game." I wipe my mouth with a napkin. "I saw it on the schedule."

"Come on," he says lightly. "Play. Ten, fifteen minutes. We'll check with whoever's wrangling team rosters. You start, you smile, you get out before your knee and residual throw a fit."

I snort. "Oh, so you're my trainer now?"

"God, no," he says. "I like my body too much to put it through whatever you put your clients through."

We share a grin. My chest loosens a little. It's always easy with Cam: old rhythms and new respect. He helped thread my life back together when I let him back in. He also knows when to push.

I cut another forkful of roll, stall with a sip of terrible coffee. "It's not about the leg," I say. "It's the... theater of it."

"Then control the script," he counters. "Wear shorts. Walk in like yourself. No hiding. No explanations. You'll be on your terms."

I know he's right. I also know the difference between a San Francisco gym full of clients who know me and a small-town high school where the bleachers are stacked with the past. No one here has seen me on a court since I was a different person with two natural legs and a future that felt like it couldn't break.

He sees it on my face and softens. "Listen," he says. "You love the game. You always will. Today doesn't have to be a referendum on anything. It's five-on-five in a small gym with a whistle and a scoreboard that might still buzz wrong on odd-numbered days. You'll run, you'll pass, you'll shoot once or twice. You'll wave at people who once painted your name on poster board. And then you'll go heckle AJ for clapping off-beat."

His usual joking tone doesn't quite land, but I don't push him on it.

"You say that like he's not going to turn this place into a minor celebrity sighting," I say.

"Please," he says. "He's pretending to be my date. We plan to be aggressively boring." He glances down at his phone as something shifts in his gaze, then back up at me. "You in?"

I look down at my plate. The roll's half gone. The frosting's found a home on my fingers. The coffee is cooling into something fearless folks might use to strip paint. I take a breath and let it out.

"Yeah," I say. "I'm in."

Cam doesn't fist-pump. He just nods, satisfied, like he knew he could land this before he ordered. "Good. I'll text the coordinator. You're starting."

I blink. "We're just giving me the ball right away?"

"You were born with it," he says. "The alumni will survive the insult." His grin slants. "And let's be honest, you like starting."

I do. The nerves lace into something else—a steadier hum. The part of me that lives in the rhythm of the game finds the beat again. Warm up. Check the floor. Feel the bounce. Read the angles. No pressure. No stakes. Just the thing I love, in the place that made me love it.

We eat in companionable silence for a minute. Outside, Main Street collects itself—shopkeepers flipping signs, a mom jogging behind a double stroller, a pair of teens gawking into the formalwear window at a wedding dress that looks like a chandelier.

Cam breaks the quiet with a fond groan. "I forgot how this town smells like grass and sugar at the same time," he says.

"It's the butter," I say. "And the humidity."

"And the ghosts of our bad decisions," he adds.

"Oh, those," I say. "They're loud."

He tips his chin at my leg. "Shorts today?"

I hesitate for half a heartbeat, then nod. "Shorts," I say. "No use pretending. The kids should see it. The old crowd too."

"You'll handle it," he says simply. "You always do."

I wipe my hands, stand, and feel the familiar tug of the socket as I shift my weight. The first steps out of a chair are always the most honest ones: a quick inventory, a private negotiation. Today, everything answers yes.

We leave cash under the sugar shaker and step into the light.

"Meet you at the gym," he says, slipping on sunglasses. "I'm going to collect AJ."

"Say hi to your fake boyfriend."

A frown dips his brows low for a beat before he replies, deadpan, "We prefer the term 'temporary decoy.'"

I snort and wave him off as he slides into his car, windows down, some smooth R&B rolling out as he pulls away. I stand there a second longer, let the town line up around me: the brick, the awnings, the dog tied to the bike rack, tail thumping like it's part of the percussion. I roll my shoulders back, turn toward the school, and start walking.

———

THE "SMALL" gym looks half the size I remember, which feels impossible. Light spills through the high windows in diagonal bars, dust floating like static. Bleachers line both sides. The scuffed varnish shines like a memory that got a fresh coat. Banners climb the walls, a few new ones tucked in among the old. The locker room still smells like damp cotton and detergent that gave up too soon.

A few alumni are already there, pulling on jerseys with the faded lettering spelling out FORMER on the back, talking about knees, kids, and early bedtime. Half the current varsity team has bounced in early, all long limbs and quick grins, their nervous energy snapping the air like rubber bands.

I nod hellos and a few how-you-beens, then duck into the locker room to change. The shorts feel familiar in my hands, but unfamiliar against the back of my thighs when

I pull them on. I sit to tug my sock smooth on my intact side, then stand and look at myself in the mirror.

This is me. Not the before. Not the almost. Just me.

I step back into the gym with my warm-up tee in one hand and my bottle in the other. Conversations dip a fraction. Not silence—just a soft recalibration as eyes flick down, clock the hardware, and come back up. There's surprise on a few faces. Curiosity on most. Pity on none that I choose to see.

Then someone whistles.

"North!" It's one of the older guys—Ray Barker, power forward from our day, with the same broad shoulders and a dad bod that wears its history with pride. He grins. "Look at you. Still built like trouble."

"High-fiber trouble," I call back. "Powered by cinnamon rolls."

Laughter bubbles out across the baseline. The tension diffuses another degree. I bounce the ball someone passes to me, feel the give of the floor, the return of the rubber. The first dribble is a handshake. The second, a promise.

I stretch along the sideline. Hamstrings. Quads. Calf. Hip flexors. The residual limb doesn't stretch the same way, so I work the muscles around it, take my time, feel the heat build. The team manager rolls out a rack of balls, and I take my first shot from the right elbow. Swish. The second hits back iron and drops. The third misses left. I adjust my feet, lift through the core, and the next five sing.

There's a whistle, and I turn.

Theo is there.

His assistant coach polo is stretched across his chest. There's a clipboard tucked under one arm and a whistle lanyard wound around his fingers like it belongs there—which, of course, it does. He stops when he sees me in shorts. His eyes fall to my leg for the briefest split second, then come back up. Awareness. Not shock. Not sympathy.

"Hey," he says, close enough that I catch the clean, warm scent of his laundry soap and something citrus that I remember from forever ago.

"Hey," I answer.

"You're playing," he says, and it's not a question.

"Yeah." I clear my throat. "Starting, apparently. Cameron bribed someone with baked goods."

"That tracks," he says, a tiny smile tipping one corner of his mouth. "How's the floor feel?"

I bounce once, look down the painted lane toward the rim that watched me grow up. "Like it remembers me," I say.

His eyes soften. "Good," he says quietly. "That's good."

A squad of current players wheels by, all elbows and confidence, and one of them gives me a look that's equal parts awe and appraisal. "You suiting up, Coach?" he asks Theo.

"In your dreams," Theo says. "I like my knees functional."

They peel off, laughing.

Theo's gaze returns to me. "You need anything, you tell me," he says. It's exactly what a coach would tell any player on his floor. It still lands like more.

"Water and a time machine," I say.

He huffs a breath that's almost a laugh. "I can get you the first one. The second's above my pay grade."

We stand there a moment, the past humming softly

under the present. He nods toward the rack. "You'll run the two?"

"Then and always," I say.

He tips his chin, and for a heartbeat, it's high school again: his eyes reading a defense before anyone else sees it, my body already moving toward the space he pointed to. We built a thousand games on that look.

"Okay," he says, business side surfacing. "Old guys versus varsity. Two twelves, running clock. We'll keep it light."

"You afraid we'll embarrass your kids?" I tease.

"I'm afraid you'll impress them, and I'll never hear the end of it," he shoots back.

"Fair."

Another whistle. People drift toward their benches. The crowd is bigger than I expected—alumni, curious locals, a few kids who only know me because their dads won't shut up about a season that happened before they were born. I follow the flow to the former players' side and drop onto the end of the bench to retie my shoe. When the PA crackles to life with someone's dad announcing names, I catch more than a few double takes as mine is called. It's fine. It's expected.

It's time.

I rise when the others do, huddle for a joking, loose game plan, and then we're breaking to the floor. I walk past the scorer's table, set my foot on the hardwood inside the sideline, and feel the whole world go quieter.

I do not look up to find Theo in that instant. I don't need to. I already know exactly where he is. Where he has always been.

Whistle hanging loose from his mouth, his shirt doing absolutely nothing to hide how good he looks, he's planted just off the baseline. Focused. Watching everything. Watching me.

The alumni game tips off, and for the first few plays, I'm all instinct. The kids are quick—fresh legs, light on their feet, darting in and out of passing lanes like minnows—but I've got strength and experience on my side. I muscle into position under the basket, feeling the slight give of the hardwood through my sneaker, the balanced weight of the prosthetic holding steady as I pivot. It's different than before—always is—but it's not a disadvantage. Just a different way of moving.

The leg hums with each push-off, a quiet reminder that it's both part of me and something else entirely. The strain in my quads, the solid slam of the ball into my palms, the heat building under the socket—it's all familiar in the best way.

Ten minutes in, my lungs are working harder, sweat slicking the back of my neck. My teammates are grinning at me like we've been running plays together for years. When I sink a short jumper over one of the varsity forwards, the crowd cheers.

It's enough. I know my limit. I slap hands on the way to the bench, chest still heaving, prosthesis ticking faintly as I slow down. Applause follows me—louder than I expect—and for just a second, I let myself feel it. That I'm not just the guy who lost his career. Not just the accident.

When I finally look toward the baseline, Theo's there, one hand resting on his hip, whistle spinning lazily from the cord. His eyes find mine.

It's not a smile exactly. But it's warm. Steady. The kind of look that makes it very, very easy to remember every single reason I came back here.

And for today, at least, he's on my side of the line.

I take a seat on the bench, towel over my shoulders, water bottle cold in my hand, and watch the rest of the half play out. The kids are quick, relentless. I can already tell their coaches have them drilled on speed over brute strength. They slice through open space like they're made of nothing but reflex and confidence. I find myself grinning, almost itching to get back out there, but knowing better than to push it.

Halftime hits. The scoreboard blares, and the gym fills with that restless chatter people fall into when they've got a few minutes to kill. I'm leaning back, catching my breath, when a shadow falls over me.

Soren Hayes.

I knew he was here—small towns never lose their ghosts—but seeing him up close, I'm reminded that time hasn't softened him. He's filled out, sure, but the smirk is the same. That smug, I'm-untouchable curve to his mouth. The mayor's son, wrapped in privilege like it's body armor. He always did know how to hide behind his dad when shit got real.

"Well, well," he says, eyes flicking down my leg and back up with deliberate slowness. "Didn't think you'd have the balls to play again after... you know."

My fingers tighten around my water bottle. "After what?"

He shrugs, all mock innocence. "The accident. Figured you'd stick to, I don't know, coaching the pity league or something. But hey, nice to see you proving me wrong." His grin sharpens. "Kinda. Guess the new hardware doesn't slow you down too much, huh?"

There's a ripple in the noise around us—people close enough to hear, pretending not to. My pulse jumps, not from embarrassment, but from the pure, clean edge of anger.

I stand. Not quickly, not threatening, but I'm looking down at him now. "You really wanna do this here, Soren?"

He blinks, but that smirk doesn't move. "Just making conversation."

"Yeah?" I take a step closer, letting my voice drop low enough that only the nearby gawkers get the full effect. "Then here's some for you—don't ever mistake me playing through something for me being less than I was. I'm still stronger than you on my worst day. And that's saying something."

That finally cracks his expression. His jaw ticks. "You think you—"

"Is there a problem?"

Theo's voice cuts clean through the air, sharper than the whistle hanging from his neck. He's there at my side, eyes locked on Soren with a kind of controlled fury that makes me almost sorry for the guy. Almost.

"No problem," Soren says, too fast.

"Good," Theo says, stepping just close enough that Soren has to shift back. "Then you can take your mouth and your half-baked insults somewhere else. Unless you're signing up for the alumni game, you've got no business talking about someone else's performance. Especially not his."

Heat curls in my chest. God, he's changed. Not in the way people mean when they talk about aging—though, yeah, he's thicker now, stronger through the shoulders, every inch of him built from years of staying active. No, it's in the way he holds himself, the absolute certainty in his voice.

And all I can think is, what would it feel like to taste him now? Does he still kiss like he means it—all heat and focus? Would it undo me the way it used to?

Soren mutters something under his breath and turns away, cutting through the crowd with his shoulders tight.

Theo watches him go, then glances at me. Not the quick once-over of a ref checking a player. This is slower, deliberate. His eyes lock on mine, holding just long enough for the noise of the gym to blur into the background. There's no smile, but the message is clear as day.

I've got you.

It hits harder than I expect, settling deep in my chest. I give the smallest nod in return, the kind that says, *I know.*

A hand claps my back—a teammate, I think, though I don't turn to check—as Theo stares at me, backing away, holding the whistle in his mouth for a beat before he blows it, signaling the second half.

I don't watch the court. The game.

I watch Theo.

Every movement, every pivot, every time the whistle hits his mouth. I track him like he's the only thing worth paying attention to in this gym. Because right now, he is.

I'm so full of shit. He always has been.

TWENTY-TWO
THEO

Whistles are supposed to make you heard. Mine barely cuts through the noise in my head.

I'm moving up and down the sideline, tracking feet and hands, counting three seconds in the lane, but all I really see is Caden's gaze every time he glances my way. It sits under my skin like heat, steady and unblinking, and it makes the court feel two sizes too small. I keep my calls clean, my voice even, but Soren's bullshit is still humming in my bones, and I can't shake the image of Caden's jaw tightening when he swallowed his temper.

By the time the final horn sounds, my smile is on autopilot. I blow the whistle once, give the players a quick "Good run" and a nod to the bleachers, and then I'm moving—off the floor, through the side door, past the trophy case with our dust-fogged faces trapped behind glass. I need air. My whole body feels buzzy and wrong, like a radio between stations.

I want to reach for him. That urge is so strong, it's almost a pain. I want to find him in the crowd, touch his wrist, say something stupid like "You were beautiful out there," because he was. I want to say I'm sorry again, as if repetition could sand down the edges of what happened. But I can't. Fifteen years is a canyon you don't jump because you feel brave for five minutes.

So I walk.

The corridor to the lot is quiet, dimmer than the gym, smelling like floor wax and old paper. My sneakers scuff the tile. My heart does this uneven stutter-step that has nothing to do with running the baseline and everything to do with the man who just played ten of the most breath-taking minutes I've ever watched.

He was strong. Not in a trying-to-prove-it way, but in the way a tree looks strong after a storm—roots deep, trunk scarred, still standing. The first time he planted on the prosthetic and rose for that elbow jumper, the whole gym inhaled at once. When the ball dropped through the net clean, the sound that followed wasn't just cheering. It was relief. It was pride. It was awe.

Mine most of all.

And I still saw it—the exact second he reached his limit. The tiny change in his footwork, the half beat he needed to reset. The small protective shift in his shoulders when he came down from a rebound. Ten minutes. I should have been savoring them like everyone else. Instead, guilt hooked into me because I knew that threshold like my own heartbeat. I'm the one who put it there. I can call it an accident until I run out of breath, and it will still be the single worst choice I've ever made: believing I could keep us safe on a road I was already losing to fatigue.

He's lived with it every day since. Learning to stand, to walk, to run again. The phantom pain he likely pretends isn't bad when weather rolls in. The way people stare, or don't, as if looking might be a verdict. What I felt in the gym wasn't pity. It was awe and love and the kind of pride that makes your chest hurt. It was also the same old gnawing guilt with new teeth.

No wonder he cut me out. No wonder he had to. I wouldn't forgive me either.

Sun hits me square in the face when I push through the doors at the end of the hall. The parking lot is a flicker of chrome and white gravel glare. I walk until I hit the thin shadow thrown by the flagpole and stop there, dragging air in and out until my pulse stops punching.

I should go home. Shower. Pretend I'm excited about volunteering at a "Totally '80s" prom. I should find the box of neon headbands Maddie dropped in my room and practice not dying of secondhand embarrassment when I hand them out tonight. Mostly, I need to get my head straight enough not to say something catastrophic the second I see him again.

I make it three steps toward my truck before Justin Kirkwood comes striding across the lot like a man with a plan alongside three backup plans in his pocket.

"Theo!" he calls, that deep voice of his carrying without effort. He looks like every spreadsheet ever made decided to become a person: neat, capable, built like a brick wall in a button-down he somehow hasn't sweated through. He breaks into a jog for the last few feet. "Hey, hey—hold up."

"Hey, Kirkwood." I force a grin. "If this is about the icebreaker supplies I 'lost' last night, I have no comment."

He huffs a laugh and studies my face. "I'm actually checking on you."

"I'm good," I lie, then soften. "I'm… upright."

His eyes flick toward the gym doors, then back. "You were somewhere else for half that game. Not a complaint. Just an observation."

"I was reffing," I say. "Not performing magic tricks."

"You were reffing while boring a hole through one particular alum with your eyes," he says, tone gentle, not teasing. He lifts his hands when I look away. "I'm not prying. I just wanted to make sure everything's okay."

"It's… complicated."

"Isn't it always?" He tips his head. "You two have history. Even people who don't know know."

I squint at him. "What does that mean?"

He shrugs, mouth tilting. "It means senior spring, you and North weren't as subtle as you thought you were. I was student body president, not blind."

Heat climbs up my neck before I can stop it. I glance away at the empty baseball field, the sun throwing diamonds across the outfield. "We were careful."

"You were careful," Justin says kindly. "And you were seventeen. Seventeen-year-olds leak feelings out of their pores. It was… sweet, actually." He pauses. "And later… I knew something bad happened, and then he was gone. Most of us never got the details. You know how small towns work. Too much noise, not enough truth."

I swallow. He doesn't push. He just stands there and lets the silence be a place I can put something down in.

"Soren being an asshole didn't help," I say finally.

Justin's expression ices over for a beat. "Did he say something to Caden?"

"Yeah," I say. "He made a comment. About the accident. About his leg. I shut it down. Caden did too. But still." My jaw aches. I unclench it. "I wanted to throw him into the bleachers."

"Get in line," Justin mutters. He drags a hand over his beard. "I'll talk to Vanessa. If he stirs up more trouble tonight, we'll have him escorted out. This is a fundraiser, not a reenactment of his worst impulses."

A laugh surfaces, quick and grateful. "Thanks."

Justin watches me for another moment. "How are things… between you and Caden?"

"Strained," I say, because I am tired of lying by omission. "But we both seem to be trying. Or… willing to be in the same room without bolting for the exits."

"That's not nothing," he says. "Is he here with anyone?"

I shake my head, my gut bottoming out at just the thought of it. "Not that I've seen."

He nods. The early-afternoon heat warms the top of my head. A group of alumni meanders toward the lot, laughing. Student volunteers wheel a cart of paper cups back inside. The ordinary life of the day presses around us and makes everything feel both too big and mercifully small.

"You know," Justin says, almost offhandedly, "tonight could be a chance. The prom you never had."

I freeze.

He lifts a palm. "I'm not saying make a scene. I'm not even saying dance if you don't want to. I'm saying… the theme's cheesy, but the night's yours if you take it. You were a junior when our class had prom. You weren't allowed. He went because he had to. Maybe tonight is the one you give yourselves. Whatever that looks like."

The idea hits me like a floodlight. Bright. Blinding. It is so tempting, I almost sway toward it.

But then the other thing rushes in—the memory of Caden in a hospital bed, telling me to leave. The way I watched his parents' taillights disappear down our street a short time later. Years of birthdays where my phone stayed dark because I had no right to text him. All the almosts I filled with people who were kind and fine but not him.

"I don't know if I deserve that," I say softly.

Justin studies me for a long second. When he speaks, his voice is gentler than I've ever heard it. "I can't answer that. I can only say… he came back. That has to mean something."

My eyes sting. I blink hard and breathe, steady and deep, like I tell my players to do when they miss an easy layup and want to hurl the ball at the ceiling.

"I have to help set up tonight," I say, because facts are safer. "Vanessa's got me on centerpiece duty and 'general vibes,' which I'm pretty sure is code for 'move chairs until Justin is satisfied.'"

He cracks a smile. "Absolutely code for that." He claps my shoulder once, solid and warm. "Go home. Shower. Eat something that isn't a granola bar. Then show up and let the night be the night. If it's awkward, we'll blame the decade-specific playlist."

"Please do," I say. "If 'Take On Me' starts and I cry, tell people I stubbed my toe."

He snorts. "I'll say you're allergic to synthesizers." He takes a step back. "You're not alone, Theo. Even when it feels like you are."

I nod, because anything else will turn my voice to gravel.

He heads back toward the school with the long, purposeful stride of a man who lives for a plan, and I stand there in the thin slice of shade until the sweat cools on my neck. The guilt is still there, but it's shapeshifted. It lives alongside the other thing now—the feeling from the court when I watched Caden plant and rise and release like the game was still in his bones and would be until the end of everything.

No one has ever touched me like he did. Not even close. I tried. Made a couple of semi-serious attempts over the years. Good men, most of them. Careful. Patient. We did the dinners and the trips and the polite fights about whether throw pillows are a scam. I even thought, once or twice, that I could be happy enough if I just kept moving forward and forgot the shape of his laugh.

But my heart is a stubborn bastard. It kept a ledger I could never throw away.

I walk to my car and sit with the door open for a minute, letting the air move over me. My hands find the steering wheel and hold on.

He came back. Cameron told him it would be fine. His old teammates were there for him. The gym didn't fall in on itself when Caden went up on one foot and made the shot. The alum who talks too much got told to shut up. I survived reffing with my veins full of static.

I can survive tonight.

I pull out of the lot and drive home, past the diner where I learned the names of every pie, past the park where we trained when the gym was locked, past the house that isn't his anymore and into the drive that's now mine because my parents trusted me with it when they wanted a smaller place and fewer stairs. I shower until the heat wrings me out. I eat eggs on toast and a peach so ripe, it drips down my wrist. I find the box of neon headbands and laugh until I choke at the sunglasses Vanessa picked for the photo booth.

And when I'm dressed, I stand in front of the mirror and look at myself like I'd look at one of my kids before a big game.

You're okay. You're allowed to want things. You're allowed to try.

I grab my keys and step back into the day.

Tonight might be the prom we didn't get. Or it might just be another night in a small-town gym with too many balloons and not enough AC.

Either way, I will see him again.

And when I do, I will not run.

———

By the time I pull into the lot behind the school, the sun's just starting to dip, staining the edges of the sky in pink and orange. The gym's already buzzing—Vanessa's outside, issuing orders like a general in a sequin blazer, and the scent of hairspray, perfume, and whatever's on the hors d'oeuvres table hangs in the humid air.

I'm dressed up. Suspenders and all.

They're obnoxiously shiny—black suspenders with little neon splatters that look like an art teacher's paint drop cloth—and I love them. When I came out in college, I made a quiet deal with myself: no more hiding the parts of me that didn't fit someone else's mold. Suspenders were one of those things. I'd always liked them in secret—dorky as hell, sure, but they made me feel... like me. When I moved back to Gomillion to take the job at the high school, I promised myself I wouldn't put any part of me back in the closet, suspenders included. So here I am, in black trousers, a fitted white shirt rolled at the sleeves, my ridiculous suspenders, and a tie so thin, it's practically a ribbon.

The large gym is transformed. Round tables draped in shimmery cloth crowd the floor. The DJ booth—already softly cranking through a mix of Wham and Cyndi Lauper—sits where the scorer's table usually is. Streamers hang in diagonals overhead, catching the glow from a disco ball that spins lazily, scattering light across the hardwood.

I'm here early, helping with the final touches—straightening chairs, checking water pitchers, making sure the dessert trays are within arm's reach for Maddie so she doesn't have to wade through the crowd later.

People start filtering in around six. The cocktail hour hum builds, laughter spilling into the air as groups cluster, comparing outfits and half-sincere gasps over who looks "exactly the same" or "totally unrecognizable."

And then—

Caden.

Earlier than I expected.

He's at the far entrance, tall and unmistakable, pausing just long enough to scan the room. For a moment, I think he's just taking it in, but then his gaze moves. Sweeps. Searching.

And when it lands on me—direct, unflinching—I realize I was right. He wasn't looking at the room at all. He was looking for me.

The hit is instant and sharp, like my chest's both caving in and filling up at once. He starts moving, weaving through the clusters of people, and I'm caught between standing my ground and suddenly needing to straighten every single water glass on this table.

It's impossible not to compare him to the last time I saw him at a prom.

Not *actual* prom, obviously. His was the year before mine. I remember adjusting his tie for him in the mirror. I remember watching his hands—steady even then— smooth over the front of his jacket. He looked stupidly handsome, and I felt both proud of him and bitter that I couldn't be his date. That I had to stand on the edges, waiting at home until the after-party.

And then?

That was the night everything changed for the first time. Before the accident. Before the distance. Before the years when silence replaced every word we'd ever said. That night, in the soft chaos of foam and the starry night and whispered secrets, Caden kissed me. Not a friendly brush, not a quick dare—but *kissed me.* Certain and slow and deep enough to rearrange my bones. I remember the smell of his cologne, the taste of soda and mint gum, the way my hands locked at the back of his neck like I was afraid he'd vanish if I let go.

And now he's crossing the gym toward me like no time has passed at all.

Only it has. Fifteen years. A lifetime. And still—*still*—he looks at me like I'm the point he's been aiming for since he walked in.

He stops in front of me, close enough that the noise of the room fades into a background hum. His gaze drops, just briefly, before rising again.

"Nice suspenders," he says, and the corner of his mouth tilts up.

I glance down at them, then back at him. "You mocking me, North?"

He lifts his hand, hesitates a second, then hooks a finger under one strap and gives it a soft snap against my chest. My skin prickles.

"Not mocking," he says. "Just… they're so you. I like them."

There's something in his tone that makes me fight not to look away.

Before I can think of a reply, he says, "You left after the basketball game."

I swallow and force a half shrug. "Yeah. Had stuff to do before tonight."

One eyebrow arches. "Stuff like… running in the opposite direction?"

I glare at him, but there's no real heat in it. "Stuff like…

minding my own business." I pause. "How are you feeling after the game?"

His eyes narrow slightly. "Why? Because of my leg?"

Fuck. My stomach tightens. This is the conversation we've never had, and it feels like walking barefoot across glass.

"Partly," I admit. And because I need to breathe, I add, "Also, you're pushing forty, old man. Thought you might need an ice bath."

That earns me the smallest smile, a flicker of the Caden I used to know. "Cute. Real cute."

My heart's pounding now, but I press on. "So… your prosthesis. I've… uh… read up on them. Over the years." I glance away for a beat, then back at him. "And a little more today when I saw what you were wearing on the court."

He studies me like he's trying to decide if I'm messing with him. "You… researched prostheses?"

I nod, heat crawling up the back of my neck. "Yeah."

Something softens in his expression—surprise, maybe, or something heavier.

Before either of us can say more, someone across the gym calls my name. It's almost time for the dinner seating.

"I should—" I start.

"I get it. Let's talk after the meal," he says, stepping in just close enough that my pulse jumps. "Somewhere quiet."

I want to say yes so badly, it scares me. But fear sits heavily in my chest—fear of opening that door and finding out nothing's changed, or worse, that everything has. He broke me once. I don't think I ever healed.

I hesitate long enough that he clearly notices.

His gaze flicks over my face, and then he says, "Here. Give it back after the meal."

Something small and solid presses into my palm. His fingers linger for the briefest moment before he turns and walks away.

I stand there, staring after him—at the broad shoulders, the easy, confident gait, the way his jeans fit far too well—and my fingers tighten instinctively around the object.

Hard plastic.

My stomach somersaults.

It can't be.

I look down, and my throat closes. Sitting in my palm is a LEGO man. The hot dog vendor.

The one I made.

He kept it. All these years. He kept "me" close.

My vision blurs, and I have to blink hard before anyone sees.

How the hell am I supposed to sit through the next hour—smiling, chatting, acting normal—when all I want to do is grab him, demand answers, and maybe—God help me—kiss him until I remember exactly what he tastes like?

I slide the LEGO man into my pocket like it's contraband, fingers curling around it until my knuckles ache. It's the only thing keeping me grounded right now.

Or maybe it's the opposite—maybe it's the thing unmooring me entirely.

By the time I make it to my assigned table for volunteers, I've got the reunion smile plastered on—polished, polite, just a shade too bright. The gym's been transformed into something vaguely resembling a wedding reception: round tables with white tablecloths, centerpieces of dyed carnations in retro glass vases, flickering LED candles. The catering staff is already making the rounds with plates of something that smells faintly of garlic and nostalgia.

But all I can think about is Caden.

He's across the room, laughing at something AJ said. Cameron's at his side, radiating easy charm. The three of them look like they were airlifted in from a cooler, better-dressed world.

Caden hasn't looked over at me again—not yet—but I feel the connection like a live wire.

Someone asks me about the alumni game—how hard the kids played, whether, as the ref, I was biased—and I manage to shake my head and throw in a joke about "generously ignoring a few traveling calls." They laugh. I smile. My hand stays in my pocket.

The first course comes out. I take a bite of salad that has a sharp kick of goat's cheese, nodding at the conversation around me without hearing a word. Across the gym, Caden tips his head back to drink his water, the line of his throat catching the light. I remember kissing that skin. I remember the exact sound he made when I did.

I press my fingers harder into the LEGO man.

By the time the main course arrives—ribs with red wine sauce—I've caught him looking twice. Quick glances, both times, but enough to make my stomach twist. The second time, his gaze drops to my pocket.

He knows.

I spend the rest of the meal trying to act normal while mentally cataloging every possible thing I could say when we finally talk. All the questions. All the apologies. All the things I never said because there wasn't time, or because I was too much of a coward, or because the moment had already passed.

The speeches start—former teachers sharing memories, a few classmates hamming it up with exaggerated stories from senior year. Laughter ripples around the room, but it feels far away. My eyes keep drifting to him. He's not laughing. Not really. He's watching me.

When the "fun awards" kick in—Most Changed, Still Hasn't Changed, High School Sweethearts Who Lasted—I'm clapping along automatically. My heart's not in it. The air between us is stretched so tight, I swear it might snap.

Finally, *finally*, the dinner portion wraps. Chairs scrape back. Music hums through the speakers. People drift toward the dance floor.

And across the room, Caden stands.

He doesn't smile. Doesn't wave. Just tips his chin the barest bit toward the side door, then starts walking.

My pulse hammers.

I know I should give it a minute. I know I should play it cool.

I also know I'm going to follow him right the hell now.

TWENTY-THREE
CADEN

THE IMPRINT OF THE LEGO STILL LINGERS IN MY PALM even though it isn't there anymore. When I handed it to Theo before dinner, I might as well have been cutting out my own heart and putting it in his hands. It was stupid, reckless—and the truest thing I've done in fifteen years.

Because it isn't just a toy. It never was. It's him. It's us. It's the reminder of a night when we thought we had the whole world ahead of us, when everything still felt possible.

And I've carried it everywhere. Every move, every new start, every time I tried to convince myself I was over him. It's been in my pocket, in the top drawer of a nightstand, sometimes in a shoebox shoved under a bed, but always close. Always safe. Even when I didn't feel safe in my own skin.

Now Theo has it. And the hollow ache in my chest tells me he understands exactly what it means.

We step outside together after the dinner and the speeches, away from the laughter and the music and the clinking of glasses. The night air is thick and humid, carrying the sweet sharpness of cut grass and the echo of cicadas. The gym doors shut behind us, muffling the sounds of the reunion until it feels like the world's holding its breath.

Theo's beside me, his suspenders catching the street-light. He looks a little ridiculous—no, not ridiculous. Brave. Free. The kind of brave I've never been. And it guts me how much I want him.

We stop at the edge of the parking lot. He stuffs his hands deep into his pockets, shoulders hunched like he's holding himself together. For a second, I think he's about to run again.

I can't let him. Not this time.

"You still had it," he says quietly, his voice shaking so that I hear the crack beneath. "All this time?"

"I always had it," I answer. My voice is low, rough with honesty. "Everywhere I went, Theo, that little guy came with me. Through every move, every camp, every hospital room, every game I had to watch from the sidelines. Sometimes it was in my pocket, sometimes on the dresser. But it was always there."

His throat works, and he looks away, like the truth is almost too much to look at head-on. "Why?" he whispers.

"Because it was you," I say simply. "Because even when I hated what happened, I couldn't hate you. That night, when we swapped them—you knew what it meant. I was in your pocket, and you were in mine. And when I left, when I couldn't face you anymore, I kept mine. I guess it was the only way I knew how to keep carrying you."

Theo's lips part, but no words come. His eyes shine in

the low light, and I don't know if it's anger, grief, or something else breaking through. Maybe all of it.

"You don't understand," he says finally, his voice hoarse. "When you cut me off, I thought I'd lost you. Not just your leg, not just the future we thought we had—I thought I'd lost *you*. That night…. Caden, I can't forgive myself."

I step closer. My chest feels tight, like every word costs me air. "Theo, don't you get it? I never needed you to forgive yourself. I needed you to be there. And I know I was the one who stopped you and pushed you away. But I get it now. Have made peace with it. We were barely adults. Scared. I was angry at the world, and you… you respected my choice. Even if it killed you."

His jaw trembles. "It did."

The silence that falls is heavy, but not empty. It's filled with every word we never said, every night we missed, every ache we carried alone.

I lift my hand, hesitating only a fraction before brushing my thumb along his jaw. His stubble scrapes against my skin, grounding me in the here and now.

Theo's breath catches, sharp and fragile. "Caden…."

My name, his voice—it's enough to undo me.

I lean in, drawn to him like gravity, and before I can stop myself, I close the distance. For the second time in my life, I'm the one to kiss him first.

It isn't cautious. It isn't gentle. It's everything—fifteen years of longing, regret, grief, and love bursting through the seams. His lips are warm, achingly familiar, and when he makes a soft, helpless sound against mine, something deep in my chest finally breaks open.

It feels like coming home.

The kiss lands like a door swinging fully open. Theo presses back with that small sound I haven't allowed myself to imagine in fifteen years, and the heat of it pours through me—sure and startling, like sunlight after a storm. His mouth tastes faintly of the sweet tea the caterer served at dinner and something that's only him. I angle closer, careful with the line of my body, careful with the prosthesis and the unevenness I still feel on hot nights like this, when the socket rubs and my balance shifts. His hands leave his pockets and find my sides, then curl into the fabric of my shirt as if he needs proof that I'm not a dream he'll wake from.

I force myself to ease off first. We're outside the gym. There are reunion name tags and committee clipboards on the other side of the door. If I don't calm down, I'll forget the rest of the world exists. I rest my forehead against his for a breath and count to three. Our chests lift and fall together. The cicadas burn the air with their endless electric hum.

"I missed you," he says. It's not eloquent, but it's honest enough to make my grip on his waist tighten.

"I know," I answer, because anything else would be dishonest. "Me too."

We stay this way for another long inhale. He's the first to lean back. His dark eyes shine in the streetlight and carry a thousand questions. He doesn't let any of them out. I understand that choice. If we let them all out now, they'll flood the parking lot, the gym, the town, and maybe the state.

"How is it?" he asks. His gaze dips, almost apologetically, toward my leg and then back up. "After the game. Are you in pain?"

"I'm okay," I say, and I mean it. "It was a good ten minutes. Fast, and I felt it at the end, but it was good." I study him. "You saw the moment."

"I did," he admits. "I'll always be able to read you."

There's no triumph in his voice. There's only the assertion of a skill he's had since we were boys playing one-on-one in his driveway. He could read my body like a book; I could trust him to tell me the truth when it lied. The fact that this is still true shouldn't matter so much, shouldn't squeeze my throat tight after everything that's happened. But it does anyway.

He looks down at his pocket and taps it lightly with two fingers. "Thank you for this," he says. "I'm trying not to cry over two inches of plastic, but I'm not making any promises if you keep being... you."

"Don't," I say, trying to make my tone light, "slander the hot dog vendor. He held a program together single-handedly. But I'll also be needing it back."

Theo's laugh comes out half choked and wholly beautiful. He wipes at his eyes with the heel of his hand and takes a step back after passing me the LEGO man, as if he needs to put a breath of space between us to stay upright. I let him. I don't want him to feel cornered by his own heart.

"I watched you leave after the alumni game," I say. "I wanted to follow. The guys stopped me, and I let them because it felt easier than pushing through. And then it was too late. I hated myself for that."

"I didn't leave to hurt you," he says quickly. "I left

because I felt like my skin didn't fit. I was angry at Soren and at myself, and honestly, I didn't trust my mouth not to make everything worse. You have a game face when you play. I had to put on my teacher face and keep my shit together."

"That tracks," I say, and it pulls another laugh from him—a small one that unspools my shoulders.

A pair of alumni come outside with their phones lit up like fireflies, talking loudly about who won "Most Changed." We step a few paces deeper into the shadow beyond the outside lights. I can still see him clearly enough: the line of his jaw, the clean cut of his hair, the suspenders that should be ridiculous and instead make me ache with a complicated kind of tenderness.

"You look good," I tell him, and I say it like a fact. "The suspenders are criminal."

He glances down at them, then up again with a sheepish tilt of his mouth. "They're dorky. I love them. I promised myself I wouldn't shove parts of me back into the dark when I came home, no matter who didn't get it."

"I get it," I say. "I always did."

His eyes soften. "You did."

We let the quiet expand again, and it's not empty, but full of the kinds of things people only understand when they've lived long enough to know what they almost lost. I hear a faint run of synth and drum machine from inside the gym, a beat that would have made us laugh in high school and is somehow perfect now.

Theo rocks once on his heels and then looks at me like he's decided to risk something.

"Tell me about the leg," he says. His voice is steady. "Not the medical chart. Your chart."

I breathe out. "It's carbon and silicone that fits me well enough that I can take stairs without thinking. It grips better than most shoes, even if I have to choose function over style. Some days I barely notice it. Some days I feel a phantom itch in an ankle that's not there, and I want to argue with my own body." I pause. "But it's solid. It carries me."

Theo listens the way he always did when it mattered. He doesn't rush to fill the silence. He doesn't pull the spotlight onto his own guilt. He lets the last sentence sit between us until it finds a place to land.

"I read about sockets and liners and suspension systems," he eventually says, and his blush is immediate and unhidden. "That sounds creepy when I say it out loud. I'm not a creep. I—"

"You're a man who wanted to understand," I say. "I'm not surprised. If roles were reversed, I would've made a spreadsheet with footnotes, which I'd have asked you to help me with."

"You would," he says, and the fondness in his voice nearly undoes me.

I shift my weight and check the fit out of habit. The socket is still comfortable, but the residual limb is a little warm from the day. "After tonight, I'll ice," I say lightly. "I'd rather hurt a little than not have played."

"I'm proud of you," he says. He holds my gaze when he says it. "Not for playing, though that was beautiful. For all of it. For building a life that helps people. For being here. For letting yourself be seen."

The words lodge in my chest with a kind of clean pain. I didn't realize how much I needed to hear them from him. I don't look away.

"I didn't come to hide," I say. "I came to see what was left."

"What do you see?" he asks.

"You," I say. "And a chance."

Something passes over his face then—a mix of relief and fear and the smaller, wilder hope I recognize from another night beyond another set of doors, when he stood in someone else's backyard at an after-party and looked at me like he didn't know who would move first. Back then, I reached for him and kissed him because hoping hurt more than acting. I understand now that this is the same moment, just twenty years later, dressed in different clothes and lit by different lights.

He clears his throat. "What happens next?" The question is careful. It's also honest.

"We don't try to fix fifteen years on a gym lawn," I say. "We don't bleed out every memory until there's nothing left to hold. We dance tonight if you can stand it. We talk after the weekend when the noise is down. You come to San Francisco."

His breath comes out in a single shaken rush. "You want me to come?"

"I've wanted you to come for years," I say. "I was a coward. I'm trying not to be one now."

"I can come," he says quietly. "School's out. I have flexibility in the first weeks of summer vacation."

The relief that floods me is so sudden, it almost makes me dizzy. "Good."

A swell of sound rises from the gym. The DJ leans into an anthem, the kind that runs on muscle memory. Someone shouts a lyric. Laughter scatters out the doors and down the steps.

Theo glances back, then toward me again. Sweat shines at his temple. I want to touch him there just to prove I can.

"I'm terrified," he admits. "I keep thinking of the last time I saw you in a bed, and the words you said, and I'm afraid this will be that again, just… slower."

"I know," I say. "I'm afraid too. But I'm not that man. And I don't want us to be boys trying to survive a fire by standing in separate rooms. We'll do this face-to-face or not at all."

He nods. The movement is small but decisive. "Okay."

We let the word settle.

Another couple steps out into the night, passing us with the distracted focus of people hunting for a quiet corner. We give them the space and drift another few steps toward the practice field until the noise thins again. A breeze lifts—warm and damp and full of honeysuckle from the hedges that line the far side of the lot. Theo tilts his face into it. I watch the line of his throat and remember a thousand things I don't want to pack into the span of a single chapter of my life.

"What did you think when you saw me walk in tonight?" I ask. "The truth."

He lets out a breath that's almost a laugh. "First, I thought the suspenders were a mistake because my heart started pounding like I'd sprinted stairs. Then I thought you looked… like a man. Not a memory. Solid. Taller somehow, even though you were always tall. I thought about how I wanted to touch your face and hated that I had no right to. Then I saw the way you were scanning the room and realized you weren't looking for the bar or taking in the space. You were looking for me." He swallows. "And I thought I should run before I did something that would make the night more complicated for both of us."

"And you stayed," I say.

"I stayed," he responds.

We stand in that simple triumph for a few seconds. I can feel the dance floor revving up behind us, signaling the way reunions loosen into something sweeter once the speeches are over. The idea comes into my head intact, as if it's been waiting for this exact type of air.

"Theo."

He looks at me, and even in the shadows, I can see the amber flecks in his eyes that always made him impossible to forget.

"Be my prom date," I say. "We lost the night we should've had. The party's already happening. Come inside with me and claim the dance we were supposed to share twenty years ago."

He goes still. His lips part. For a heartbeat, I am twenty again, braced for no because I don't know how to carry yes.

He doesn't give either. Not yet. He takes one step toward me until his suspenders brush my shirt, and he holds my gaze so long, I can hear my own pulse in my ears.

"No word of a lie, I really am scared," he whispers. The honesty is the kind of courage I've always loved in him.

"I'll lead," I say. "And if it feels wrong, we stop."

He nods once, slowly, like a man placing his feet on stones in a river, testing each one before trusting the weight of himself to it.

"Okay," he says. His voice is rough. "Okay, Caden. Take me to prom."

TWENTY-FOUR
THEO

The gym swallows us whole. It buzzes with nostalgia and noise—sequined dresses catching the gym lights, jackets shrugged on over bellies that weren't there twenty years ago, voices pitched just a little too high as everyone tries to convince themselves this is fun and not surreal.

But none of it really touches me. The only thing I feel, the only thing anchoring me, is Caden's hand wrapped around mine. His grip is steady, sure. It makes me feel like he's decided something and there's no going back. My own pulse is so frantic, I know he has to feel it thundering through my skin.

There are glances, of course. A few double takes. I brace for the worst, but most people only let their gazes linger a second before being drawn to some other spectacle across the gym. This room is full of distractions. Still, my stomach knots, the teenager in me bracing for the sting of whispers.

And then—just once—his thumb brushes across the

back of my hand. That's all. Barely any pressure, barely any motion. But it's enough to tell me I'm not doing this alone.

"You good?" he murmurs, low enough that no one else could possibly hear.

I clear my throat. "Define good."

He huffs a quiet sound, and it's not quite a laugh. The corner of his mouth tips up, not into a full smile—he saves those like they're precious—but enough to warm something in me that has been cold for years.

"Better question," he says. "You gonna let go of my hand?"

I glance down, then back up. My voice scrapes out rough, like it's caught on everything I've swallowed for the past decade and a half. "Not if you don't make me."

His gaze holds mine steady—so steady, I almost can't stand it. I look away first, pretending to scan the crowd, but the truth is, I'm reeling. From his kiss outside. From his words. From the fact that I agreed—like a fool or like a man who's been starving—to be his prom date tonight.

I should be careful. I should be shoring up walls. Instead, all I can do is still taste him faintly on my lips and wonder how I'm supposed to survive this night.

And then there's the LEGO.

I pressed it back into his hand earlier. The hot dog vendor, the one he'd kept all these years. It belonged to him, always had. The way he looked at me—God, it nearly cracked me open.

What I didn't tell him was that his isn't the only one.

Mine is a firefighter. Red helmet, blocky shoulders,

and a dalmatian at his side. I can still see us on the night we made them, as clear as if it were yesterday.

We'd sprawled out together in his room, two unopened boxes between us. I'd leaned forward and tugged one open, tiny bricks cascading out across the table.

We'd worked in companionable silence for a while, music spilling from his stereo, the world narrowed to the scatter of bricks and the furrow between his brows as he clicked pieces together with the focus of a surgeon.

I'd finished mine first—a crooked little hot dog cart with a lopsided awning. And without any fanfare, we'd swapped. A simple, quiet trade. His fingers brushed mine in the handoff, a spark I still remember. Suddenly I was staring down at the firefighter in my palm—at him, in miniature, travel-sized for convenience.

I'd promised to keep him safe.

And I kept that promise only halfway. The firefighter has survived nineteen years, four apartments, and every move I've made. He's sat on my nightstand more times than I'd ever admit out loud. He's whole. Untouched. Safe.

But Caden? I wasn't just not there for him in the aftermath—I was *there*, behind the wheel, when everything went wrong. I was the one who nodded off, the one who let exhaustion blur into recklessness. I was the one who should have been paying attention. The world can call it an accident all it wants, but when I look at him, I know the truth: I failed him in the most devastating way a person can fail someone they love.

Every time I hold that little red-helmeted man, I feel

the sharp edge of the contradiction. I protected the plastic version of him, tucked him carefully away, never lost him. But the real Caden—the living, breathing man who trusted me with everything—I couldn't keep safe. I shattered that promise the moment my eyes closed behind the wheel.

I kept a toy safe. But not him. And now, he's standing beside me anyway. It's enough to make me stumble inside. The guilt is stitched into me. It makes my grip on his hand falter and my chest tighten. How do you stand beside someone when you're the reason they had to learn how to walk all over again?

And yet, when he looked at me tonight while handing me back the hot dog vendor he'd carried all these years, it wasn't anger in his eyes. Not accusation either. Just something that cracked me wide open: The echo of the boy who once laughed with me over crooked LEGO while rap played through his speakers, and the man who somehow still carries me with him.

"Stop thinking so loud," Caden mutters beside me. His voice is low, threaded with something that isn't quite amusement but isn't unkind either.

I blink at him. "What?"

"You get this look," he says, tilting his head just slightly toward me. "Like you're trying to solve the world's hardest math problem. Don't."

A startled laugh escapes me. "That obvious?"

"Yeah," he says. Then softer—almost like he regrets letting it slip—he murmurs, "Always has been."

That lands sharp in my chest. Because it's true. He

always could read me, strip me down to the wire. Apparently he still can.

I swallow hard. "You sure about this?" I gesture faintly to our hands. To him. To everything.

His gaze sharpens. "I asked you to be my prom date, Theo. Didn't think I'd have to ask twice."

And there it is again. That steadiness. That unshakable confidence I used to lean on and resent in equal measure. It hasn't dulled with time. If anything, it's stronger now.

I draw a breath, but the air feels too thick in my lungs. The truth is, I don't know if I'm sure. I don't know if I'll ever feel sure again. But my hand is still in his. My heart is still racing. And maybe that's the only answer that matters right now.

Across the gym, someone calls my name. I glance toward the voice, but my eyes are drawn back to Caden instantly, unwilling to lose him even for a second.

He smirks faintly, like he can read my hesitation. "Go. Do your thing." Then, before I can argue, his fingers tighten around mine just once. He leans close enough that I can feel the heat of his breath at my temple. "But come back to me after. I'm not letting the night end with this."

I nod, throat too tight for words.

He releases my hand, and for the first time tonight, I feel the absence like a physical ache. My palm tingles, empty.

As I start to move away, I almost tell him. About the firefighter LEGO tucked into my life like the molded plastic deity of a secret shrine. About the way I've never stopped carrying him. But the words catch, and all I can do is look back once to see him standing there so solid, so sure, and promise myself maybe—*maybe*—I'll find the courage before the night is over.

———————————

BY THE TIME I finish wrangling the final detail for the reunion committee, my head's buzzing with more than logistics. The gym feels brighter now—maybe because I know he's waiting. And sure enough, when I weave back through the crowd, I spot him where I left him. He's leaning against the wall, arms folded like patience itself, but his eyes track me the second I step into view.

The world fades down to that gaze.

"Back," I murmur, almost apologetic.

"Took you long enough," he says, but the corner of his mouth lifts.

I stop in front of him, suddenly tongue-tied. There are words I should say, things I've carried too long, but they jam in my throat. So instead, I ask, "You happy?"

It startles him, just a little. His brows draw together. "Happy?"

"Yeah." I clear my throat, fighting to sound casual. "Like... not just tonight. In general. Life."

For a second, he looks at me like he's checking if it's a trick question. Then his gaze softens. "Yeah. I am. Took me a long time to get here, but... yeah. I'm good."

I sink into the words as if into warm water. He deserves that peace. That harmony.

He tilts his head. "You?"

My laugh is thin, almost swallowed. "Yeah. Content. My job's steady. I've got my routines. I'm good."

But the tension in the air between us says otherwise. We both know it. I can be content and still ache. Still miss. Still want. Because what I haven't gotten over—what I'll never get over—is him.

The silence stretches, heavy with everything unsaid. I force myself to breathe, to remember this moment is a gift. Twenty years ago, I wanted this so badly, it hurt—to come to prom with him, to have him look at me the way he's looking now. I never got it then. But maybe tonight is the second chance I never deserved.

The reunion committee's overzealous playlist switches tracks. A slow ballad from the Lionel Richie hums through the gym, tinny but familiar. It's the kind of song made for leaning close, for swaying on creaky gym floors under paper streamers.

I swallow, pulse hammering. "Dance with me."

His brow arches, like he wants to test if I'm serious. But then he nods, simple as a promise. "Yeah. Let's."

We step out onto the floor. Couples are scattered across the gym—some clinging too close, some laughing, some moving awkwardly in circles that don't quite sync to the beat. The disco ball throws fractured light across everyone's faces.

And then there's us.

I reach for him. My hand finds his shoulder, tentative at first. His palm slides against mine, warm and solid, pulling me closer until our chests almost brush. The air between us is electric, thick with memory and longing.

We start to sway a little unevenly, but it doesn't matter. The music threads in around us, but it's not the song that anchors me—it's him. The heat of his hand at my waist. The steady pressure of his palm against mine.

I can't help staring. His face is inches from mine, softened by the spinning lights. There's a crease between his brows, like he's trying to read me as carefully as I'm reading him.

"Never thought I'd get this," I admit, voice low. "Back then… all I wanted was to dance with you. Just once."

His throat works, and his grip tightens slightly. "Could've fooled me," he murmurs. "You always looked so damn sure of yourself."

I shake my head, almost laughing. "I was never sure of anything. Except you."

The words hang there, too raw to take back. His breath catches, and suddenly his forehead dips, just barely brushing mine. The closeness is dizzying. Every nerve ending in me screams to close the distance, to take what I've wanted for so long.

I tilt my head, eyes flicking to his mouth. He mirrors me, lips parting just slightly. The world narrows, heat rising like a tide, until I'm certain this is it—

Then he stops.

Not pulling away—just holding. Hovering in that fragile space where *almost* is its own kind of torment. His eyes lock with mine, darkened, burning.

"Theo," he breathes, the word so soft, I almost miss it. "You wanna get out of here?"

For a second, I can't think. The gym, the people, the music—they all blur into nothing. There's only him and the sharp pulse of possibility.

"Yes," I say, immediate and certain. "God, yes."

We break apart only enough to move. He threads his fingers through mine, and I don't care who sees that we're in a hurry to leave. The exit feels impossibly far, the floorboards creaking under every step like they want to mark our escape. My chest is tight with anticipation, nerves, hunger—everything I've kept caged for years pressing to the surface.

The cool air hits as soon as we push through the doors. Outside, the night is quiet, moonlight spilling across the parking lot. I exhale like I've been holding my breath since we stepped onto that floor.

He doesn't let go of my hand. Not once.

For a moment, we just stand there under the night sky, suspended between what was and what comes next. His thumb strokes my knuckles, tender and thoughtful over a scar I got when attempting some home renos a few years back. My body hums with the echo of his nearness, with the promise in his eyes.

I think of the boy I was—jealous and hopeful and so sure I'd never get this chance. I think of every mistake, every year of silence, every lonely night, a plastic firefighter on my nightstand my only company. And now, impossibly, I'm here. With him. Walking out of prom hand in hand, like we should have twenty years ago.

We head for Caden's rental, our footsteps echoing in the cool dark of the parking lot. His hand is still in mine, warm and steady, and I keep waiting for him to loosen his grip, to remember himself, to put that space back between us. He doesn't. Not once.

At the car, he pauses, then presses the keys into my palm. For a second, I can only stare at them, metal biting into my skin. My chest goes tight. The last time I was behind the wheel with him in the passenger seat, everything went wrong. One blink too long, one slip into exhaustion, and his entire life changed. Mine too. The accident is stitched into me so deep, it feels like my blood remembers it. I don't know if I'll ever forget the sound of crumpling metal, the silence after, the devastation of knowing it was my fault.

And now—he's handing me the keys.

It feels like something inside me is splitting open. He trusts me enough to climb in beside me again, to let me carry him forward when all I did back then was fail him. Forgiveness. Faith. Maybe even love. I don't know how to deserve it, but my fingers curl tightly around the keys anyway, trembling.

Without a word, he moves to the passenger side, opens the door, and slides in like it's the most natural thing in the world. Like he's already decided this isn't a night for ghosts.

I open the door and sink behind the wheel. My breath shudders in and out, the engine hums to life, and the headlights spill across the asphalt. The sound steadies me, but my hands ache from how hard I'm gripping the wheel with one and his fingers with the other.

The silence settles around us like new skin. We've shared quiet before—after games, after time apart, after long drives with music too loud to talk over. But this is different. This silence is sharper, fuller. It isn't bad. It's just... heavier. Weighted with trust and forgiveness, shaped by the men we've become, by everything we've survived separately and everything we might still risk together.

My chest tightens as his thumb strokes idly over the back of my hand, back and forth, like he's cataloging me.

I drive slowly, yes for the speed limit, but also because I want the minutes to stretch. The streets are empty, familiar in that bone-deep way only those in a hometown can be. Each intersection is a breadcrumb trail back to the boy I was, but the man beside me makes them feel new.

I sneak a glance at him, his profile lit up in fragments by passing streetlamps. He looks calm. Too calm. Like he isn't leaving tomorrow. Like he hasn't built a whole life three thousand miles away. And the questions stack up inside me until they're choking me: Does he mean it, what he said about San Francisco? Does "see me" mean next week? Next month? For a weekend, or for as long as it takes? Do I even deserve to ask?

My dick is throbbing like it has its own agenda, voting hard for reckless, for fuck it, for take him inside and let fifteen years collapse into this one night. But under that insistence, there's the smaller, crueler whisper: Is this a mistake? He's flying out tomorrow. He's lived a life without me. And I've learned, painfully, how quickly promises can vanish.

The silence keeps stretching. I grip the wheel tighter with my free hand, afraid if I let go, I'll say something that cracks the night in half. But then his thumb brushes that same scar again, one he's never touched before tonight, and I swear the world rights itself.

When I pull into the driveway, my chest is tight enough that I can barely breathe. The porch light is on—

automatic timer—but it still feels like a welcome. The house looks the same from the outside, but it isn't. Not anymore. It's mine. My parents' old room is mine now, the walls painted in colors I chose, the furniture carrying my stamp, not theirs. I've made it a place I love.

But the love I feel for my home is nothing compared to how I feel about the man sitting next to me.

I kill the engine. For a long beat, we don't move. The cooling tick of the car fills the air. He doesn't let go of my hand.

Finally, he turns to me, eyes shadowed but steady. He doesn't speak. He doesn't have to. Whatever this is— whatever happens next—whatever he might have said is already written across his face.

I swallow hard. "Come in with me?" A given, I suppose, since I drove him here and not to the B&B, but I still ask.

His answer is immediate, soft, almost a relief. "Yeah."

We climb out, palms reconnecting as we walk to the front door. The key shakes a little in my hand from the nerves connected to everything pressing down on me— the years lost, the hours left, the impossible luck of tonight. I get the door open, and we step inside.

The familiar scent wraps around me—coffee grounds, the pine polish I use on weekends, the faint trace of old carpet that never quite leaves. Normally, it steadies me. Tonight, it barely registers. Because he's here. Because the moment we cross the threshold, the questions that strangled me in the car all melt away.

It doesn't matter if this ends in whispered conversation, in kisses until our mouths are raw, or in something harder, faster, hotter. It doesn't matter if tomorrow he boards a plane, and I'm left with an ache I can't name. It doesn't matter if the only guarantee is this night.

What matters is that for the first time in fifteen years, I get to walk into my home with him at my side.

I'm not giving that up.

The door clicks shut behind us. The sound feels louder than it should, echoing through the house like a declaration. My house. My parents' once, now mine. I've spent a long time filling it with my choices, my routines, my attempts at permanence. But with him standing here, hand still twined with mine, it feels suddenly alive in a way it hasn't in years.

I kick my shoes off at the mat out of habit, then realize he doesn't remember the rules here anymore. The first time when he showed up unannounced doesn't count. He hesitates only a beat before bending down, slipping off his dress shoes one at a time. The motion isn't as quick as it used to be—his left leg moves differently now, the prosthesis stiff under the fabric of his pants—but he doesn't make a production of it. Just sets both shoes neatly by mine like he's been here a hundred times and knows how I live.

The small gesture lands harder than it should. My chest clenches stupidly at the sight of his shoes beside mine, like he's already marking space here, like he belongs.

The entryway light glows warm. Familiar. Safe. I should offer him a drink, ask if he wants water, beer, coffee. Something normal, polite, grounding. But my throat won't work. His fingers return to mine, warm and certain, and it feels like if I break the chain—even to do something as simple as open the fridge—the night will slip away from me.

He looks around, taking in the framed photos on the wall, the books stacked too high on the shelf, the small scuff in the baseboard I never got around to fixing. His gaze lingers on everything with quiet curiosity, but it keeps circling back to me, like he's tracing where I've been and what I've built but never forgetting that I'm what he came here for.

I clear my throat. "It's different, huh?" Sure, he was here a couple of days ago, but it had been different. Tense and more uncertain in a whole other way.

He hums low, glancing up toward the hallway that leads to my bedroom. "It's yours."

Something about the way he says it—like that simple fact is enough, like the claim itself carries weight—sends a jolt through me. I've lived here for years. Paid the bills, painted the walls, made the bed. But hearing him acknowledge it with that quiet certainty makes me feel like I actually own more than just the mortgage. Like I own this life too.

The silence stretches again, thicker now, charged with something that makes my pulse spike. My mouth is dry. Every question that haunted me in the car begins to claw at the back of my skull—what does he want? What happens tomorrow? How long until I lose him again?—but none of them fit the moment. None of them seem to matter when his hand tightens just slightly around mine.

I draw a breath. "Come upstairs?"

His answer is immediate. "Yeah."

My heart lurches hard against my ribs. I turn toward the staircase, and he follows without hesitation, his steps a half beat behind mine. The old wood creaks under us, the same creak that woke my parents up when I was seventeen and trying to sneak out. Tonight, I don't care who hears. Tonight, the creak feels like permission.

When we reach the landing, I push my bedroom door open. The space is familiar and mine, decorated in muted blues and grays, shelves lined with books, a lamp casting a soft golden circle across the bedspread. It isn't the room he once knew. It isn't even the room I grew up in. But it's where I sleep, where I dream, where I imagine futures I don't often let myself believe in. And now, impossibly, he's here.

We stop just inside the doorway. My hand finally slips free of his, not because I want it to, but because I suddenly don't know what to do with it. My fingers twitch at my side, restless, unsure. He looks at me with that steady gaze that always unraveled me, like he's waiting for me to decide which version of tonight we're stepping into.

"Caden—" My voice catches. I try again. "I don't know what this is supposed to be."

His mouth curves, soft but sure. "Maybe there's no 'supposed to be' about it?"

The question loosens something in me, but it also makes my stomach twist. Because no, it doesn't. But yes, it does. Everything with him always has.

I take a step closer, not trusting my words. His chest rises, then stills, like he's bracing himself. The space between us shrinks until I can feel the heat radiating off his dark skin. My hand hovers, then lands lightly on his chest. His heart pounds under my palm, fast, insistent, and the sound in my ears might as well be its echo.

We stand like that for a long moment—my hand over his heart, his eyes locked to mine—until he moves. He lifts his hand and cups the side of my jaw. His thumb brushes the corner of my mouth with just barely enough pressure for me to feel it. My knees nearly buckle at the touch.

And then he leans in.

The kiss is gentle, almost reverent. No rush, no demand. Just the quiet press of his lips against mine, fifteen years of absence collapsing in the span of a heart-beat. I clutch at his shirt, dragging him closer, afraid he'll slip away if I don't anchor him. He groans low in his throat, and the sound sends heat racing through me.

The hunger builds fast, urgent, like it's been waiting under my skin all this time. The kiss deepens, our mouths parting, tongues meeting, and suddenly there's nothing quiet about it. His hand slides through my hair. My body shudders, my cock straining painfully against my jeans.

I break the kiss just long enough to rasp, "God, Caden," before his mouth claims mine again, harder.

We stumble toward the bed, our hands roaming now—his across my back, mine gripping his waist, pulling, tugging, desperate. The air between us snaps and sizzles with every brush of fabric, every gasp. I don't know if we're about to talk, to make out until the sun rises, or to strip the years from our skin and fuck until we can't stand. And the truth is, I don't care. Any of it. All of it. As long as it's with him.

When the backs of my legs hit the mattress, I sink down, pulling him with me. He lands half on top of me, bracing his weight on one arm, and the kiss doesn't stop, doesn't falter. His hips press into mine, the hard line of his cock grinding against me through denim, and my groan breaks open against his mouth.

"This—" I choke out between kisses. "This might be a mistake."

He pulls back to look at me, eyes dark and steady. "Then it's mine too."

And that's it. That's all I need.

TWENTY-FIVE

CADEN

Theo's breath catches like he's been bracing for permission he didn't realize he needed. He pulls me down again, and the kiss changes. It's not frantic so much as decisive, the kind of hunger that knows exactly where it's going to be fed and still refuses to rush. Theo's hand finds the back of my neck. He holds me there, not tight, just sure, like he's not going to risk me drifting even an inch away.

I'm not afraid of kissing him. I'm not afraid of being wanted by him. What makes my pulse spike is the knowledge that if we keep moving, we'll step past the last barrier I've kept up between us, the one that has nothing to do with distance or time. I've done this—undressed in front of men and women I didn't love. I've learned how to be matter-of-fact, how to answer questions before they're asked. But this is Theo. He knew the boy, the young, naïve man I was before there was anything missing. He loved a version of me that had both feet planted, both knees careless, both hands cocky around a basketball and a future. He hasn't seen me like this.

He kisses me again and again, breath hot, hands fierce, and the thought flickers up anyway: If he looks away—even for a second—I will shatter.

"Theo," I say into his mouth.

He goes still at once. He's always done that—stopped when I speak, like my voice is an instruction he trained himself to follow. He rests his forehead on mine and waits. We're both breathing hard. The room smells like his pine polish and clean laundry and the citrus press of his cologne. My pulse is a drumline.

"I want to go slow," I say. "I need to."

"Okay." His answer is immediate, steady. "We go slow."

He holds my face, thumbs along my cheekbones as if he's memorizing the shape of me now, not the shape he holds in his head. The knot between my ribs eases a fraction. I nod and swallow.

"Undress me," I say. "But let me show you how to help with my leg."

His eyes flare, not with alarm but with focus. He nods again, the movement small and deliberate, like we're spotting each other at the rack.

"Tell me what you need," he says.

I sit back beside him and start with the easy things. He reaches for my tie first, fingers sliding under the knot like he's untied a thousand of them for me. Maybe he has, in rooms that smelled like aftershave and locker room funk and the sharp sting of nerves before a banquet. He works the silk loose without jerking. When he pulls it free, he doesn't toss it; he lays it on the chair by the window. His hands come back to my collar. The brush of his knuckles against my chest sets off small fires as he undoes each button at my throat with a patient care that unsettles me more than if he'd ripped the shirt open.

He leans in to kiss me as he reaches the middle buttons, and I feel his breath catch when his palm flattens against my sternum. I'm not a different species now, I don't think, but I'm not the myth he carried either. He breaks the kiss and watches his hand rise and fall with my breathing for a beat, like he has to prove to himself that I'm here and real. Then he slides the shirt off my shoulders. He takes the time to lay it down with the tie. I realize my hands are clenched.

He notices the tension and covers one fist with his warm palm until it eases. "Good?" he asks.

"Yeah." I mean it.

He goes for my belt, and I stop him with a touch to his wrist. "Before my pants come off," I say, and let the rest of the sentence sit between us. He understands instantly. His expression sobers into something even more attentive.

"Teach me," he says.

I shift back, drawing my left pant leg up to show the edge of the black liner peeking beneath the hem. I've dressed for an event, not for convenience, so there's no quick zip hidden in the seam. He'll have to undress me for real; I'll have to let him. The thought turns my mouth dry and my chest warm at the same time.

"We're going to take the pants off first," I say, voice even. "Then the liner. Then the lock. I'll tell you when to press, and I'll lift. You don't pull. You hold steady."

He nods as if he's taking mental notes. He kisses my jaw softly once, like a seal on a contract. "Okay."

We stand, and I steady myself with one palm on his shoulder. It's automatic, not because I can't balance, but because his shoulder is there and it's mine to use. He exhales like the contact relieves him. He undoes my belt with careful fingers and unbuttons my waistband, then slides the zipper down. I step out of the pants a fraction at a time, weight shifting. He follows my lead, moving with me rather than trying to move me. When the fabric clears my liner, I see him take me in. He doesn't flinch. He looks at the gel hugging my residual limb the way he looks at everything that matters—as if information is intimacy and care is an action, not a feeling.

I sit on the edge of the bed. He kneels in front of me without ceremony, the way he used to drop to tie my shoe before a game if I was running late and Coach was screaming. He sets my pants aside and rests his hands lightly on my thighs, not grabbing, not gawking. He waits.

"It's a pin lock," I say, tapping the side of the socket just below my knee where the release button sits. "There's a silicone liner under the sleeve. We'll roll that down last. First you press here when I tell you. I'll lift and let the air in. It slides."

"Okay," he says. His voice has gone low. I can't tell if it's nerves or reverence. Maybe both.

I breathe once, twice. The world narrows to the points where he touches me and the small silver button that's never meant anything but function until now. "Press."

He does. There's a soft click. I shift my weight, lift slightly, and the seal sighs. He looks up at my face, checking for pain, for regret, for anything that would tell him to stop. I give him a small nod. He keeps his thumb on the release until I say, "Got it." Then he moves his hand away but stays close.

I wrap both palms around the socket just below the lip and ease it down. His hands hover, ready to catch the weight if I need him to. When the socket clears the liner, gravity does the rest. He takes the prosthesis as I lower it and sets it carefully on the rug without me asking, aligning it so the foot points neatly toward the chair. He places it the way he placed my tie, with intention, as if it's not just a tool but part of me that deserves respect even when it's not attached.

"Next?" he asks.

The word steadies me more than he could know. He's not in a rush to get past this to the part that looks more like the movies. He's here for this, the unglamorous mechanics of my body.

"Next is the sleeve," I say, touching the edge of the black neoprene that seals the top of the socket when I wear that setup. Tonight, there's only the liner because of the pin lock. "But the liner first. It's snug. Roll, don't tug."

He nods and slides his palms to the top of the liner, fingers warm against the silicone. He looks up again, waiting. I lift my knee a little and brace a hand behind me on the bed. He feels the shift and adjusts without me asking, one hand stabilizing, the other catching the roll as it moves. The gel gives slowly under his hands, not wanting to let go. That's the way it always is, only tonight, it feels like shedding a layer of armor.

He carefully works the liner down an inch, then

another, evenly each time so he doesn't pull the skin. He keeps watching my face. When I wince at a spot that always gets tender, he eases his pressure and uses his thumbs to soften the edge. He couldn't have known to do that. He does it anyway, instinctively gentle.

"You okay?" he asks, the question shaped by breath I can feel against my thigh.

"Yeah." My throat is tight. "You're good."

He smiles at that. It's a quick, bright thing that vanishes as he concentrates again. When the roll reaches the end of my stump, he slides the liner free. He doesn't stare. He looks and then looks at me, at my mouth, at my eyes, like that's where the truth is. He sets the liner down, careful again, placing it parallel alongside the socket.

The room feels enormous and very small at the same time. I had thought this would feel clinical, the way it sometimes does when a tech is measuring a fit or a trainer is asking if the alignment is still good. It doesn't. It feels like the first time Theo and I ever fumbled our way into each other's bodies as teenagers, nervous and clumsy, neither of us having a clue what we were doing. Back then, it wasn't about knowing how—it was about wanting to know *him*. Wanting to understand, to explore, to learn every inch because it mattered that it was *us*.

Tonight feels like that again, only heavier, sharper, threaded through with all the years we lost and everything we're finally daring to reclaim.

Theo rests his palm just above my knee. He doesn't press. He spreads his fingers a little, as if to say, *I see all of it*. His eyes are wet at the corners. He blinks them clear before a tear can fall. He leans in and presses his mouth to the inside of my knee, to skin that's sensitive for reasons that have nothing to do with sex. It undoes me.

I put both hands on his shoulders, not to push him away and not to drag him closer, but just to anchor myself to the moment. My breathing is fast again. I tip forward until our foreheads almost touch.

"Thank you," I say. The words feel inadequate.

"For what?" he asks, and his voice breaks on the last word.

"For making this feel like… not less."

He swallows. "It could never be less to me."

I close my eyes against the sudden heat behind them. When I open them, he's watching me the way he's always watched the things he cares about, with a focus that is a kind of safety. He reaches my waistband, then pauses.

"Tell me where you want me," he says. "Tell me what feels good."

He's asked versions of that before—back when we were young and inseparable, before the accident, before fifteen years of silence. *"Do you need me to help with your assignment?" "Do you want me to run the last drill again with you after everyone else is gone?"* Back then, I still had both legs, and he didn't have to think about what my body could or couldn't do. Now it's different. Now he asks because he knows I've changed, because he wants to learn me as I am. Hearing him say it—out loud, steady, deliberate—feels like proof that he isn't just chasing the boy I was. He's choosing the man I am. And I've never loved him more than I do in this moment.

"Up here," I say, and I draw him against me by the front of his shirt. He stands, and I stand with him. He slides his hands down my spine, careful not to rush. He kisses me and keeps kissing me until my body uncoils from its guarded stance.

When he goes for the waistband of my briefs, I let him. He takes his time. When the fabric sloughs from me, I don't think about how I look, only about how he looks at me. He steps back for half a breath, not to assess but to honor. He drags his gaze up my body as if reacquainting himself with a skyline he's loved since he was a teenager and noticing every new building with delight rather than resentment. I can almost hear the way his mind narrates it: *"Here's the shoulder I leaned on when I convinced him to climb the water tower; here's the scar he got the summer we thought we were invincible; here's the place where his body ends and his stubbornness keeps going."*

"Can I touch?" he asks, because tonight, consent is not a formality; it's the language we're choosing to speak.

"Yes," I say. "Everywhere."

He steps back into me, and the undressing turns tender again rather than ceremonial. He peels off his own shirt under my palms. He lets me unbutton his cuffs, slide the fabric from his shoulders, skate my hands down the inside of his forearms like I'm reading braille.

He laughs once, shakily, when my fingers find the old scar on his wrist from that time with the broken backboard. He says, "You always remember," and I say, "Always," and it's as much a vow as anything we'll ever say.

He kisses me between every small task like he's stitching the moments together with his mouth. When he lowers his head to my chest and breathes there, I hold the back of his neck and don't pretend I'm not trembling. I let him feel it. I *want* him to feel it.

We climb onto the bed with care. He moves first, and I follow, easing myself onto the mattress with a practiced shift that leaves me balanced and comfortable. He watches, not anxious, just present. He slides in beside me and props himself up on one elbow, his other hand skimming along my waist. He hasn't asked for the facts of my body—measurements, scars, what's missing—because he knows those answers don't matter here. He's asked for guidance instead, and that's what I give him.

"Here," I say, guiding his hand to the place above my knee where the skin is always tender when the day has been long. "Gentle." He is. "Here," I say, drawing his fingers to the edge of my hip where sensation hums brighter than it used to. "More pressure." He listens. He learns me the way he learns poetry—by repetition for the joy of it, not by rote.

At some point, we stop speaking in full sentences. It's not a retreat into silence but a shared language of breath and small sounds. When he shifts lower to kiss the curve of my thigh, he does it slowly, never making my body a spectacle or a problem to solve. He lifts his head to check my face, and I smile to tell him I'm not leaving this moment, not drifting away. He smiles back, big and unguarded, the way he used to right after he hit a shot he had no business taking. It undoes me again, softer this time.

"Climb on top of me," I say. It's not a command. It's a request to share the same line of heat.

He does. We've always fit, and after our breaking

point, we still do. He tucks his face into the angle of my neck and inhales like he's been underwater for years and only just remembered how to breathe. I stroke the back of his head, the line of his spine, the place at the base of his skull that makes his whole body loosen. He drifts there, muscles letting go in increments, until what's left between us is steadiness.

"Tomorrow," he says quietly.

"I know," I answer.

"I don't want this to be just tonight," he says. He doesn't make it a question.

"It isn't," I say. "It won't be."

He nods against my shoulder. I feel him believe me. Maybe that's the miracle tonight, more than the undressing, more than the removal, more than the careful choreography of hands and breath. The miracle is the parts of us that trusted each other as boys finding each other again as men and choosing to trust deeper, with more to lose.

"Teach me the rest," he says after a long while, and the way he says it makes it clear he's not talking about mechanics anymore. He's talking about a life.

"We have time," I say. I mean it, even if the clock on my flight will contradict me in the morning. We have time because we'll make it. We have time because tonight stretched it like gold leaf and laid it over everything we lost for fifteen years.

He kisses my mouth again, and the heat builds in a way that needs no description to be understood. It's in the tremble of his hands against my ribs when I work my fingers inside his tight channel, the catch of his breath when I draw him closer, the way his weight settles over me like it belongs here when he stretches around me and sinks down on my cock.

We move together, slower and then not slow at all, guided by all the yeses we've already said—some aloud, some only in the way our bodies lean and give. I trace the long line of his back, committing each dip and curve to memory as if I haven't been carrying the ghost of him in my hands for fifteen years.

"Theo," I whisper, the name breaking on my lips like a prayer I've been holding too long.

He pulls back to peer down at me, then rests his forehead against mine, and our noses bump, clumsy and perfect. His voice is ragged when he answers. "I'm here. I've got you."

My chest aches with everything that spills into that promise. Twenty years ago, he was the first. My first kiss that meant something, my first confession, my first time feeling what it meant to give myself over completely. And God, lying beneath him now, I want him to be my last.

"I—" My throat closes around the words, but I force them out in fragments. "Don't... don't let go. Not this time."

His mouth finds mine again before I can choke on the plea. The kiss is steady, grounding, like an oath sealed in breath. He enlaces his hand with mine, pinning it to the mattress, and I feel his pulse hammering in his grip.

As he moves, careful and sure, I guide him with small touches, with broken words as he rides me, hips moving, thighs working. "Yes... slower, that's—Theo—God, yes." Each sound is half moan, half confession.

He shudders above me, muttering against my skin.

"You feel… you feel like home. Like—like I've been waiting for this… for you. Always you."

The intensity swells between us, tenderness sharpened by years of hunger neither of us could feed. Every shift, every press, every gasp carries an edge of desperation—like we're trying to make up for every night we spent apart, all the time we should've been here and weren't.

My back arches, dragging him deeper against me, and I stammer through the sensation. "Theo, I—oh, God—I can't—"

"Yes, you can," he breathes, pressing his forehead harder to mine, his voice breaking with need. "We can. Together."

The rhythm builds, faster, fiercer, but never careless. His hands map me like he's relearning a country he once called his own. My nails scrape down his shoulders, not to hurt but to hold, to anchor. The air is thick with the sounds of us—our ragged breathing, the helpless sounds caught between groans and gasps, the near-sobs of *finally, finally.*

"I love you" slips from me in a rush I can't stop. It bursts out raw, desperate, undeniable.

He falters for half a beat, a shiver running through him, then whispers back like it's the only truth he's ever known. "Always. Always have."

That does it. The urgency tips over, all the careful control breaking apart. The world narrows to his weight above me, his breath against my mouth, the heat and pressure that coils tight, too tight, until release rips through me with a cry I don't recognize as mine. His name leaves me again and again, my voice cracking on it like I'm twenty-two all over.

Theo follows me, his body shaking with the force of it, his face buried against my neck as if he needs to hide as he comes undone. I feel him everywhere—his trembling, his broken moans, the way his grip on my hand never loosens, not even for a second.

And when the shudders fade and the frantic rhythm softens into stillness, he doesn't roll away. He stays pressed against me, breathing hard, whispering my name like it's the anchor that will keep him here.

I close my eyes, my heart still pounding, and think, *Twenty years ago, he was my first. Please, God, let him be my last.*

Later, when the room is quiet, he reaches down without thinking and straightens the sock I pulled on for comfort after we had sex. It's such a small thing that it almost undoes me again. I catch his hand before it leaves and keep it there, covering the place he's just tended. He looks at me like I've handed him something. Perhaps I have.

"Stay," he whispers.

"I am," I say, and I'm surprised to hear how certain I sound.

He smiles into my shoulder.

The wind chimes knock softly outside. I close my eyes. For the first time in a very long time, I feel like the story I'm telling myself about my body and the story he's telling himself about me are the same one. It feels like relief.

It feels like home.

TWENTY-SIX
THEO

Morning presses soft light through the curtains in thin stripes that reach across the bed and catch on the crumpled sheets tangled at our feet. I surface gradually, and for a long moment, I don't move at all. The weight in my chest is foreign—not the ache I've lived with for fifteen years, but something fuller, sweeter. Happiness, heavy enough to anchor me.

But beneath it, dread lingers sharp and quiet. Because happiness isn't simple. Happiness has a cost. The reality is thousands of miles between us, a lifetime of separate routines, separate beds, separate cities. Last night felt impossible, a dream transformed into flesh, but now the question hangs between us like morning fog: What does it mean, the morning after?

The sex was phenomenal. There's no point pretending otherwise. Every second of it ripped me open and stitched me together again. But it wasn't just sex. It was the way he said he loved me—simple, unshaken—and the way I believed him with my whole heart. I love him too. God, I do. But do we still know each other? Or did we just fall into old grooves that are too easy, too familiar to resist?

I'm halfway down that spiral when his voice cuts through, rough and low from sleep.

"You're thinking too hard again."

I start, glance over. He's awake, head tipped back on the pillow, eyes heavy but knowing. He looks unfairly good like that—hair mussed, lips swollen from all the kissing we did, gaze steady like he's already caught me in the act.

"I wasn't—" I begin, weak denial at best.

His full lips tilt into the smallest smirk, and then he leans across the rumpled space to kiss me. Soft, unhurried, like he's pressing the truth into me. The protest dies on my tongue.

When he pulls back, he exhales and mutters, "I need to pee."

The glamour of the moment cracks, but it makes me laugh. "Do you... do you need your prosthesis? Or... support? Or are you good to just—" I gesture vaguely, words tangling. "I mean, I don't know—"

The discomfort crawls up my throat. I hate that I don't know, hate that I can't read the rhythms of his body anymore the way I used to. Fifteen years gone, and suddenly we're strangers to the most practical parts of each other.

He notices—of course he does. He lifts his hand and brushes my frown away with his thumb. He kisses me again, firmer this time, until my chest unclenches. "Help to the en suite would be great," he says lightly. "Save me putting my leg on. And with my bladder this full, best not risk bouncing around too much." His grin is sharp, teasing, meant to make it easier.

"Okay," I murmur, relief and affection tangling in my chest.

I slip out of bed and brace his side as we cross the few steps to the bathroom. He moves easily with me, not fragile, not breakable—just mine to steady. When he disappears inside, shutting the door with a click, I stand there for a second like a fool.

Do I get dressed? Cook breakfast? Pretend I know how to be normal the morning after my entire world turned inside out? None of it feels right.

In the end, I head down the hall to the other bathroom, relieve myself, then splash cold water over my face. My reflection stares back at me, raw-eyed, hair a mess. I look exactly like someone who didn't sleep much because he was busy rediscovering the love of his life.

After padding back to the bedroom, I fish my phone from the pocket of my pants. When I stand straight, he's already there, leaning against the doorframe like he owns the place, even naked, something he apparently has no hang-ups about. And he smiles at me.

God. That smile. It's not the practiced one he used to give cameras or teammates, not the sharp one that cut across a room and drew every eye. It's softer, slyer, private. The corners curl up like he's remembering exactly what we did last night, and his eyes gleam with it. He looks hot as sin, casual and devastating, like desire wrapped in familiarity. My chest clenches hard at the sight.

"You're still naked," he drawls as we climb back into bed. "Glad to see some things haven't changed."

Heat floods my face. I flop back onto the pillows, muttering, "You're an ass."

His smirk widens as he pushes into my side, every line of his body promising trouble. And God help me, I want it. For a moment, I just look at him, memorizing the curve of his mouth, the steadiness of his eyes.

The words tumble out before I can stop them. "When's your flight?"

He blinks at me, surprised, then shrugs a shoulder. "Not sure. Early afternoon, I think. I should check." He tilts his chin toward the chair where his jacket hangs. "Hand me my phone?"

I lean over, fish it from the pocket, and pass it to him. The screen flickers dimly to life, the red sliver of battery already threatening.

"Not much juice left," I warn.

"There's a charger in the drawer?" His tone is casual, like he already knows it'll be there because I've always kept spares.

"Yeah. Top drawer, left side."

He shifts, still draped against me, and reaches back without looking. He fumbles through cords and pens until he goes very still.

"What?" I murmur, tilting up on one elbow.

Slowly, he pulls something out. Not the charger.

The firefighter LEGO sits in his palm, tiny and unchanged—helmet red, a drawn-on mustache, a crooked smile stamped on his blocky face.

My chest seizes. Words clog my throat.

Caden stares down at it for a long beat. Then, without accusation, without a trace of mockery, his mouth curves. Soft, aching. "You kept him."

I swallow hard. "Yeah. I—I couldn't not."

He brushes his fingers over the little plastic figure, almost trembling. "Almost twenty years," he whispers. "And you still—" His voice cracks, and he doesn't finish.

I cover his hand with mine, pressing the LEGO between our palms like the fragile thing it is. "I kept him safe. Even when I couldn't keep you." The admission tastes like rust on my tongue.

His eyes rise to meet mine, and there's no anger there. Just something rawer. A brightness that undoes me. He leans in and slowly kisses me, grounding me in the present instead of drowning me in the past.

When we pull apart, he rests his forehead against mine. His voice is quiet, deliberate. "Come with me today."

I blink, pulse stuttering. "What?"

"Come with me. Same flight. To San Francisco." He strokes my jaw, coaxing me to believe him. "Spend time with me. Not just last night, not just this morning. Longer. More."

The words hit my brain like a live current. I want to say yes so badly, it terrifies me. Thousands of miles. A life I've built here. A life he's built there. And yet—here he is, asking. Offering.

"Caden...." My voice shakes.

His eyes search mine, steady and fierce. "Don't over-think it, Theo. Just... say you'll come."

"Yes," I blurt, before my brain can gag me with caution tape. "Yes. I'll come."

Relief breaks over his face like sunlight, quick and unguarded. He laughs—a startled, breathless sound—and kisses me so hard, I forget where my hands are supposed to go. I end up clutching his jaw like I'm afraid he'll disappear if I don't hold him in place.

"Okay," he says against my lips, smiling around the word. "Okay."

We pull apart an inch, and I can feel my pulse skittering everywhere—in my throat, my wrists, my ribs. I said it. I meant it. The part of me that hoards practicalities immediately starts writing on a whiteboard: money, clothes, toothbrush, how long, what if—but the rest of me is louder for once. *Go. Be with him. Figure it out later.*

"Flight," I manage. "What time?"

He lifts the phone I just handed him. The low-battery icon blinks red like it's scolding us. "Let me check."

"Charger's in the drawer," I remind him.

He kisses my cheek and feels for the cable again. When he finally finds it, he plugs his phone in and squints at the screen. "Early afternoon," he says, thumbs sliding. "Two-ish. Enough time to pack if you don't decide to bring your entire library."

"I was considering it," I deadpan.

"We'll buy you a book in the airport. Or ten."

"Dangerous promise," I warn, even as something inside me unclenches. It's ridiculous that looking at flight details could soothe me, but it does. Plans. A path. The next right thing.

He scrolls, then glances up. "I'll put you on the same flight. If not, same connection and I'll wait."

"Same flight," I say, too fast. "I want the same everything."

A spark lights behind his eyes at that. "God, Theo." He exhales, leans in, kisses the corner of my mouth like he doesn't trust himself with more. "Okay. We're doing it."

He props the phone on the bedside table to charge and tugs me closer by the wrist until I'm half sprawled over him. The sheets are cool, his skin warm, the morning light a thin gold drape across his shoulder. We breathe there for a while, noses brushing, the quiet turning thick and sweet.

Then reality taps again. "I should… pack?" I say, the word absurd in my mouth, like I've never done it before.

"Mm. Essentials," he says, counting them off with kisses to my temple. "Wallet. ID. Toothbrush." Another kiss. "A shirt you'll pretend isn't mine that absolutely is."

"I have no idea what you're talking about."

"I literally saw one of my old basketball jerseys draped over your laundry basket in your en suite," he says and trawls a grin across my mouth when I glance down at my very naked chest and cough.

"Details," I mutter, only slightly mortified that I have a shirt that's sixteen years old and that I still wear the damn thing.

He laughs and then sobers, thumb tracing under my eye. "You okay?"

I want to say yes without hesitation, but he deserves truth, not autopilot reassurance. "I'm… scared," I admit. "Not of you. Of the whiplash. Last night, this morning, now a plane. It feels like jumping into the deep end and realizing I forgot to learn how to swim."

He nods, eyes steady. "Then I'll jump in with you and keep a hand on you the whole time."

My throat tightens. "That's not how swimming works."

"It is now," he says. "New technique. Approved by me."

I huff and hide my face against his shoulder for a second. When I lift it again, he's still there, still grounded, still Caden.

"Okay," I whisper. "Then we jump."

He nods once, decisive. "We jump."

I peel myself away before I lose the thread entirely and snag a duffel from the closet. I toss in jeans, underwear, socks, two T-shirts, a hoodie, and toiletries. The firefighter goes last, tucked in a side pocket. I tell myself it's temporary. That I'll set him on Caden's dresser in San Francisco and let him look out a window we haven't seen yet.

Behind me, the bed rustles. "I should put my leg on," he says, practical as breath.

"Want help?"

He looks over like he's cataloging the question. "Yeah," he says finally, quietly. "Thanks."

We move through it together—familiar now after last night's careful unlearning and relearning—our rhythm already smoother. He tells me where to steady and where to wait, when to hold and when not to. The routine is different from undressing; this is the day version, the going-out-into-the-world version. It feels just as intimate. Maybe more so. When everything's aligned and secure, he tests his weight, looks up, and gives me a small nod that lands like a warm hand between my shoulder blades.

"Good?" I ask.

"Good," he echoes. "Really good."

He stretches, grimaces at his phone's battery percentage, and slips it off the cord. "I'll charge it more in the car."

"I'm driving," I say, and the words hang there for a split second, both of us remembering the last time the world tilted behind a steering wheel. I wait for the flinch, despite his quiet acceptance yesterday. He gives me a soft, sure nod instead.

"Okay," he says. "You're driving."

The knot in my chest loosens another degree. We're not pretending the past didn't happen. We're choosing to walk past it—together.

"Text me the itinerary," I add, grabbing my own dead phone and grimacing.

He lifts his. "I'll AirDrop it when we have more than 5 percent life support."

"Romance in the twenty-first century," I say.

"Don't knock it," he murmurs, tugging me by the belt loop back onto the bed. "It also allows for this—two more minutes of me kissing you before we ruin everything with socks and airports."

"Socks can be romantic," I protest weakly, already climbing back over him.

His mouth finds mine, slow at first, then deeper until the decision we've just made hums between our teeth. It isn't last night's urgency. It's something steadier, a promise sealed not with grand speeches but with the press of lips and the easy slide of hands over familiar geography. He tastes like mint and the kind of hope that makes my ribs ache in a way that doesn't hurt.

When we break away, he rests his forehead against mine. "Thank you," he whispers.

"For what?"

"For choosing this. Choosing me." A beat. "Again."

I swallow. "Always."

His smile is small and devastating. He kisses me once more and then sits up like a man remembering he has a plane to catch and a life to disrupt with joy. "Okay. Logistics. You grab your wallet and ID. I'll pull up the app and see if there's a seat next to me. Worst case, we're a row apart and I annoy you from across the aisle."

"You mean like you did through all of sophomore English when our classes had to join because of Mrs. Perry's illness?" I ask, standing to dig in my dresser for a clean tee.

"That was educational enrichment," he says.

"You put googly eyes on my copy of *Gatsby*."

He points at me. "And you never forgot the eyes of Doctor T. J. Eckleburg again."

I can't help it. I grin. It's stupid and wide, because somehow we're talking about googly eyes and also maybe moving our lives around each other again, and the whiplash isn't as scary when he's making me laugh.

I grab my wallet and ID from the tray on my dresser and slide them into my pocket. He checks the app while his phone gasps along on its last drips of battery. "Two seats left in economy," he says. "I can…. Oh. I can upgrade one of us to the bulkhead." He glances at me, reading my face for a group decision. "Or we stay together and both fold up like paper cranes."

"Together," I say instantly. "We can unfold at the other end."

He makes a pleased sound and taps. "Done." He looks up. "You bringing the LEGO?"

I pat the duffel, saying, "Obviously," which earns me a sweet smile.

I pause with my hand still on my bag. "And—I just remembered, I promised Amelia I'd spend more time with Connor this summer. He's eleven now, and I don't want him thinking I disappeared on him."

Caden's expression softens immediately. "Then we'll work it out," he says. "We can even fly him out to San Francisco for a week. Give Amelia a break, give Connor some quality time. Show him the Bay, take him to a Warriors game."

The thought lands in my chest like a light I didn't know I'd been holding my breath for. Not just us, but space for the people I love. Space for my family too.

"Thank you," I say as tuck my phone charger into the bag, zip it shut, and just... stop. The room is still the same. Bed unmade, curtains stirring in the vent's sigh, my life stacked in neat piles on the bookshelf. And yet the air feels different—charged yet elastic, like it's stretching to accommodate a new shape.

"Hey," he says softly, catching my pause. "We don't have to solve the next ten steps. Just this one. You and me. Airport. Plane. A few days. That's it."

"That's it," I echo, and the words settle, surprisingly light.

He takes my hand again, our fingers fitting like they've regained their muscle memory. He lifts our joined hands and kisses the back of mine, still watching my face like he's waiting for panic to return. It doesn't. Or if it does, it politely sits farther away, letting joy take the front seat.

"Do you need to tell anyone you're leaving?" he asks.

"Nope." I shake my head. "I'm not expecting my parents for a visit." I do need to think about what I'm going to about spending time with my nephew, though. But that's tomorrow's problem.

He stands and hooks a finger into my waistband to reel me in for one last kiss in this room before everything is about to tilt again. When he lets me go, his smile is pure trouble. "Just one stop at the B&B to pick up my bag. That'll set the tongues wagging, no doubt."

"Get your phone," I tell him, fighting a laugh. "You're about to lose the last 2 percent of your dignity."

"Impossible," he says. "I lost that the second I asked you to be my prom date."

I grab the duffel and sling it over my shoulder. He reaches for it automatically, like he's ready to take the weight if I want him to. I keep hold. Not because I need to, but because I want to carry this part, at least. He nods once, understanding something I didn't say.

At the doorway, I look back. The bed is a mess. The morning is bright. The space we just remade together looks ordinary again, the way miracles do once you close your eyes after witnessing them and then open them again.

"Ready?" he asks.

"No," I say honestly. Then I squeeze his hand. "Yes. Let's go."

TWENTY-SEVEN

CADEN

THE MORNING LIGHT IN BERNAL HEIGHTS ALWAYS FEELS different—like it softens just enough to forgive the sharp edges of the city. It pours through my bedroom windows, painting the hardwood, spilling across the rug, turning Theo into something holy where he lies beside me.

My bed hasn't looked like this in fifteen years—lived in, warm, shared. I could stay here all morning just to memorize the rise and fall of his chest, the curve of his mouth slack with sleep. My life has had its good turns, its hard-won wins, but nothing prepared me for the quiet miracle of opening my eyes and finding him here.

He stirs when I shift onto my side, lashes fluttering before he blinks awake. His voice is low, rough-edged. "You're staring."

"Yeah," I admit. "Figured I've earned it."

His mouth tips into that crooked half smile that used to undo me when we were teenagers. "Not creepy at all."

"Extremely creepy," I agree, leaning in until I can kiss the corner of his mouth. He hums, catches me in a fuller kiss, and for a second, it's too easy to forget I'm supposed to go to work today.

The last couple of nights come back in flashes—the way we fumbled across each other's bodies, mouths hungry and greedy, the taste of him hot and dizzying on my tongue. Fifteen years of imagining, and then it was real. Him, coming apart under me. Me, losing my breath when he gasped my name. I'd thought that door was closed forever, locked behind guilt and time. I'd been wrong.

Now, tangled in sheets that still smell like us, I want more. I could drag him under the covers, keep us here until the day burns out. But I've never been able to ignore morning, not when the city's waking up, and not when my work waits.

I pull back to see his eyes open fully, still soft from sleep. "I've got appointments starting at nine," I say gently. "But I like to train first."

He stretches onto his back, groaning into his hand. "Of course you do."

"You're coming with me," I remind him, grinning when he gives me a mock glare.

"Right," he says, and then quieter, "Kinda nervous."

"Don't be." My hand finds his, our fingers threading together. "I want you to see it. Everything I've built. You've only ever seen me in jerseys or in pieces. Never this."

His thumb brushes my knuckle, and he holds me like he hears more than I'm saying.

I let out a breath, the confession slipping before I can stop it. "I want you to be proud."

Theo's hand tightens around mine. His voice is steady when he says, "I already am."

That cracks something open in me I didn't know I'd been bracing against. I kiss him again—slow, grateful—and then roll onto my back before I forget the clock entirely.

The truth is, I've done okay for myself. Not perfect, not easy, but okay. I had money from my two years pro, and thank God I invested when I did. It carried me far enough: paid for qualifications, physio training, specialization. My parents tried to cover it, but I couldn't let them. I needed it to be mine.

By the time I finished, I had enough collateral to buy a small studio and an apartment. Five years ago, I expanded into a bigger space and bought this house. A risk, sure, but it worked. I knew people. I knew what I was doing. AJ and Cam told the right stories, and some of my old contacts from the league passed my name around, and suddenly I was the guy you saw when you wanted to train harder, heal faster, keep your body alive for the game.

It's not glamorous. But it's mine.

And today, Theo gets to see it.

I throw the covers back and stand, stretching until my shoulders pop. Theo watches me, his gaze unguarded, and for a second, it feels like it did when we were twenty, except now we're stronger, older, built out of fire instead of just sparks.

"C'mon," I say, grinning at his reluctance to leave the bed. "If you're going to survive San Francisco, you're going to need coffee first."

"Coffee," he repeats, hauling himself up. "That I can get behind."

My chest feels too full as I head for the shower, knowing he'll follow me into this day, into my city, into the life I carved out of ruin. Nervous, yeah. But eager. Because if last night had been another night of reclaiming us, today is about showing him the man I became.

The drive to the Mission District is short. Early enough that the traffic hasn't stacked yet, the streets still quiet, shops pulling up their security rollers. Theo sits in the passenger seat, watching the city with that wide-eyed attention that makes me remember he hasn't ever been here. His hand rests on his thigh, which is so close to mine, I can feel the warmth radiating.

When we pull up in front of the studio, I see him take it in. Three stories, glass front, the name stenciled cleanly across the door: North Performance & Rehabilitation. Five years in, and the sign still makes my chest thrum with pride.

"You own this whole building?" Theo asks, voice caught somewhere between impressed and skeptical.

"Not the whole thing," I admit, cutting the engine. "Top floor's apartments. First two are mine."

"That's still...." He shakes his head, a smile tugging at his mouth. "Jesus, Caden."

"Come on."

Inside, the air smells like eucalyptus oil and the faint tang of disinfectant. Early-morning light streams through wide windows, falling across polished floors, racks of equipment, treatment tables. It's quiet now, before clients arrive, and I love it like this. The calm before the grind.

Theo turns in a slow circle, taking it all in. I can't stop watching his face.

"You built this," he says finally, soft with awe.

"Brick by brick," I answer.

Before he can reply, a voice calls from the reception desk, "Morning, boss."

Lacey stands, tablet in hand, her dark curls piled on top of her head. Tall, poised, with warm brown skin and a presence that keeps this whole place running, she's been with me since I opened this location. She's organized, unflappable, and the reason the studio doesn't burn down when I'm juggling too much. Her eyes flick to Theo, and for once, I see her actually startled.

"Oh." She blinks, then recovers fast, offering a polite smile. "And you must be…?"

Theo steps forward, hand out, grin easy. "Theo."

Lacey takes it, then shoots me a look that's equal parts curious and amused. She's never seen me bring anyone here. Never had reason to. I've only ever talked about him with my parents.

I clear my throat. "Old… friend. Visiting."

Her brow quirks, but she doesn't press. "Well, welcome. If you need anything—coffee, tea, an escape route—let me know."

Theo chuckles. "Good to know."

We move past the desk and into the gym space. I head for the mats, start stretching out, and to my surprise, Theo kicks off his shoes and drops down beside me. He mirrors my movements. He's a little stiffer, but game. The sight makes something sharp and warm twist in my chest.

Soon we're side by side—push-ups, squats, resistance

drills—my morning ritual expanded to include him. His form isn't perfect, but his determination is, and his gaze keeps catching mine between sets, daring me to push harder. Sweat drips from me, strength humming in my limbs, but this time I'm not just showing him I can thrive. I'm moving with him, the rhythm of us syncing like it hasn't in years.

By the time I towel off, I hear the door open, followed by "Well, well, if it isn't our fearless leader actually on time for once."

I turn to see Peppa breezing in. Dark hair in a high ponytail, leggings in some outrageous pattern, grin wide enough to blind. She's been with me three years and is irreverent and competent in equal measure. She flirts with me constantly, but it's never serious. Just part of who she is.

Today, though, her attention snags immediately on Theo.

"And who is this snack?" she demands, striding over and extending a hand. "I'm Peppa. Don't worry, the name's real. You can imagine the jokes I've heard."

Theo laughs, shaking her hand. "Theo. And, uh, noted."

She gives him an exaggerated once-over, then glances at me. "You've been holding out on us, boss."

"Pepp—" I warn, but she waves me off.

"Oh, relax. I never flirt with the clients. Clearly I've been saving it all up for this moment." She winks at Theo, leaning in conspiratorially. "You're safe, though. My taste runs toward bad decisions, not men who look like they've actually got their life together."

Theo grins, eyes bright with amusement. "Then I guess I'm flattered?"

"You should be," she fires back before turning on her heel and sauntering toward the treatment rooms. "Welcome to the madhouse."

Theo bursts out laughing, and even I can't help shaking my head, a smile tugging at my lips despite myself. "She's harmless," I assure him.

"She's fantastic," Theo counters.

"Trust me," I mutter, grabbing my water bottle, "Peppa takes no one seriously. Except maybe her dog."

"Perfect priorities," Theo says, still grinning.

We settle into the flow of the morning. Lacey comes by with my schedule and runs through the day's appointments. My first client, a former basketball player rehabbing his shoulder, will arrive at nine sharp. Peppa's already prepping a treatment table, and Theo follows me around like he's cataloging every detail—the equipment, the staff, the way my name's on the door.

And beneath all of it, I can feel the buzz under my skin. Nervousness. Pride. I want him to see this life, this work, this version of me that isn't defined by what I lost, but by what I built after.

By the time nine o'clock hits, I'm showered, dressed in the studio polo with my name stitched on the chest, and setting up in the treatment space. Theo hovers nearby, running his fingers along the edge of a rack of bands, watching me like he's memorizing every detail. My chest tightens at the thought that this is the part of me he's never seen before.

The door opens, and in walks Ollie Marshall. Even

retired, the man carries himself with the same presence he had on the court. Broad shoulders, clean stride, voice warm as he calls out, "Morning, Caden."

He was captain of the Minnesota Eagles for six, maybe seven years and played until last season before retiring. He's not that much younger than me, which makes it sting a little that he managed to go the distance when I burned out before I really began. I shove the envy down where it belongs and hide it behind the steadiness of my voice.

"Ollie," I greet him, clasping his hand. "Ready to get to it?"

"Always," he says, grin sharp. Then his eyes land on Theo, curiosity sparking. "And who's this?"

I shift slightly toward Theo, pride sneaking into my voice before I can tamp it down. "Theo Brooks. Old friend."

Theo blinks, then lets out a shaky laugh. "Uh, hi. Wow. I—I watched you play at The Garden."

Ollie's chuckle is easy and unassuming. "That so? Guess I've been around long enough to rack up a few fans."

Theo shakes his head like he still can't quite believe who's in front of him. "Captain of the Eagles. Jesus, Caden, you didn't mention—"

"Not my style," I cut in, though the corner of my mouth twitches.

Theo lets out another breathless laugh, still in awe. "I had your jersey when you used to play for the Panthers. Number 12."

Ollie chuckles, settling onto the bench. "Good number, that one."

We move into the warm-ups once I've asked Ollie if he minds if Theo sticks around. I guide Ollie's shoulder through slow rotations, steadying with a hand on his scapula, cueing him through mobility work. Theo hovers close, eager, almost reverent.

"You're working with retired players too?" Theo asks after a set.

I shrug. "We don't usually. But it's Ollie Marshall."

"Yeah, fair," Theo mutters, still grinning like a kid.

Ollie gives him a look, amused. "You play?"

"Used to way back when in high school. Now I coach varsity back home," Theo replies.

My chest swells, hearing him say it like that. No hesitation. No downplaying. Just truth.

"Assistant coach," I clarify, tossing Theo a look.

Theo rolls his eyes. "Details."

Ollie laughs. "Sounds like you two go way back."

"Court was our second home," I say.

Theo leans in, grin tugging his lips. "Yep. He never let me off easy. I can still hear him yelling about rebounds when I close my eyes."

"Somebody had to keep you honest," I shoot back automatically, the words falling into the groove of old rhythms.

Ollie smirks at me, shifting into his next exercise. "Explains why your accent's thicker now. Thought I was hearing things when I walked in."

Theo bursts out laughing, and I shake my head. He's right, though. The drawl always bleeds harder around Theo. My body remembers before my brain does.

We cycle through the exercises—rotator work, wall

slides, stability drills. Theo jumps in, handing Ollie bands, spotting him when he presses, listening with rapt attention when I explain cues. He's not just humoring me. He's genuinely interested. And it shows in the way Ollie warms to him immediately, trading banter with Theo like they've known each other longer than an hour.

And under it all, my thoughts snag where they shouldn't. Watching Theo joke with Ollie, watching him fold so seamlessly into this space, I wonder, could he really fit here? Could he build something with me in this city?

Then the flip side hits. Could I ever give this up, move back to Gomillion, start over again just to be with him?

The envy I feel for Ollie gnaws harder now. Not just because of his career—the years, the games, the glory, the fact that he walked away on his own terms—but because for so long, I thought he had everything I wanted. Only later did I—as well as the rest of the world—learn he was living a lie to keep it. While I crashed and rebuilt in the open, he stayed hidden until retirement gave him permission to breathe. I used to tell myself I'd do the same—come out once I was done, unless someone else in the league beat me to it. Now there's a whole wave of out players changing the landscape. And me? I never even got the chance.

But Theo's bright and easy laugh cuts through the noise, and for a second, it feels possible again—that he might fit, that we might figure this out.

Ollie groans through his last set, sweat beading on his temple. I clap his good shoulder, hand him a towel, and mark down his next plan.

"Good work," I tell him.

"Coming from you, I'll take it," Ollie says, then nods at Theo. "Nice meeting you, man. Don't let him undersell himself. He's the best there is."

Theo meets my eyes, something soft and proud in his expression, and my chest knots all over again.

When Ollie leaves, the silence that follows isn't empty. It's thick with everything I can't quite say yet.

Theo sidles closer, bumps his shoulder into mine. "You're good at this," he says simply.

The words burn through me in the best way. I want to believe them. I want him to see me the way he used to, as well as the way he seems to now.

I smile, the knot in my chest loosening just a little. But the questions linger, heavier than any weight I lifted this morning.

WE STEP out into the San Francisco night hand in hand. Not walking close, not brushing shoulders like we might've done when we were younger, but really holding hands. Palm pressed to palm, fingers threaded together, the kind of grip that makes no room for second-guessing. It's the first time we've ever done this in public—not counting our entrance into my reunion prom.

I half expect to feel eyes burning into us, to hear whispers sharpen behind our backs. Instead, all I feel is Theo's warm and steady hand and the easy cool of the evening air. People pass by, caught up in their own lives. No one gives us more than a glance, not here in San Francisco. The city hums around us, a living, breathing thing.

We find a small restaurant tucked into a corner street, a cozy space with flickering candles on each table and wood beams crossing low ceilings. The host doesn't glance at our hands, and not for the first time, I'm thankful that I moved here. We're seated in a booth near the back, with mostly empty tables around us. It's private enough to feel safe, intimate enough to feel like the world has shrunk to just the two of us.

Theo slides into the booth opposite me, and for a long moment, neither of us says anything. The silence isn't sharp like it was in the car a couple of days ago, or heavy like it sometimes is when my thoughts drift too close to what we lost. It's full and expectant. Like both of us know this is the moment we've been circling all night.

Our menus sit unopened between us. His eyes flick over mine, unsteady and then not. He draws a breath, then lets it out slowly. "We should talk."

"Yeah," I say, my voice low. I toy with the edge of the menu, though I don't look away from him. "We should."

For a second, I think he's going to dodge, to circle around what he means. But Theo's never been one to dance forever around the truth. Not when it matters.

"The accident," he says finally, his voice rough.

My chest tightens. The word still feels like a blade sometimes, even now.

He swallows, eyes dropping to the table, then finding mine again. "I know you said it was an accident. That you don't blame me. But I blame me. Every day." His voice catches. "I was driving. I closed my eyes. I—"

"Theo." I lean forward, closing my hand over his where it rests on the table. His skin is warm, trembling under my touch. "Stop."

"I can't," he says, voice breaking. "I wrecked us. I wrecked you. You trusted me, and I—"

"You think I don't know what it was like for you?" I cut in, sharper than I mean, but I don't let go of his hand. My throat feels raw. "I lost my leg. But you lost us. You lost me. And you carried that alone for fifteen years."

His mouth opens, then shuts, his eyes shining in the low light.

I press on, softer now. "Theo, I forgave you a long time ago, and I want you to forgive yourself too. You don't need to keep bleeding for me. I don't want that."

Heavy, fragile silence holds between us. His thumb shifts under mine, the smallest brush of a movement. "I'm sorry," he whispers. "For everything. For every year I didn't call. For hiding and not fighting. For not being strong enough."

My throat closes around a lump. "Me too. I should've reached out. Should've told you I still needed you, even when I didn't know how to trust myself."

The words burn in me, too long unsaid, and I finally let them out. "And I should've told you why I stayed away. I told myself I was protecting you. That if I cut you off, you'd move on, build a life without me dragging you back into the wreckage. I thought leaving you behind was the only way you'd be okay." I swallow hard, voice low. "But the truth is, I was protecting myself too. I was a coward. And I'm sorry for that. You didn't deserve it."

Theo's gaze sharpens, wet and fierce. His voice is

rough when it comes: "You don't get to decide for me. You don't get to choose what I can or can't carry."

I nod, the weight of it crashing over me. "I know. And I'll spend however long it takes proving I know that now."

The air feels electric now, charged with everything we're finally letting loose. I let the words sit, sink, and then I take a breath. "We can't undo what happened. But we can decide what comes next."

Theo swallows hard. "Yeah. That's the question, isn't it? What comes next?"

The waiter drifts by, leaving two glasses of water, but neither of us touches them.

Theo leans forward, elbows on the table, eyes dark and intense. "You're here. Your life's here. And mine's in Gomillion. My team. My kids. My… everything except for you." He laughs, low and bitter, shaking his head. "And all I can think is, how the hell does this work?"

I let out a heavy breath. "It works if we make it work. That's the only answer I've got."

His mouth pulls tight. "Long-distance."

"For now," I say.

He studies me for a long moment. Then he leans back, dragging both hands over his face. "I don't want to lose you again."

"You won't." My voice is steady, though my chest feels like it might crack open.

The silence stretches. He's staring at me like he's trying to memorize every line of my face. Then, slowly, he says, "I'd give up Gomillion for you."

The words punch through me like a live current.

He doesn't stop there, though. "I would. I will. But I

think we should give it a year. Let me see this through. The team, the kids. They need me. And we—we need time. Time to figure out the men we are now. To learn each other again. Not just what we want in bed or at a reunion dance. All of it."

My throat is too tight to speak. I nod once, hard, clutching his hand tighter.

He exhales, shakily but sure. "I'll spend every school break here. And if you can spare the time, you come out too. We make the distance work until it's not distance anymore. And then—we decide. Together."

I let out a laugh that's half a sob. "God, Theo."

"What?" His smile is crooked, pained and hopeful at once.

"I'm already in love with you," I say. "I've been in love with you. The idea that I get to fall even harder for you? That's more than okay with me."

His eyes soften, unguarded and wide open. He grasps my hand firmly back.

Around us, the restaurant hums quietly as we eat our meal together. Empty tables, low music, the occasional clink of silverware. But in our booth, the world has narrowed to this moment, to the fragile, fierce hope that maybe—just maybe—we can rewrite the story we thought was finished.

When we step back into the night, Theo takes my hand again without hesitation. And this time, I don't just hold it back—I squeeze, hard enough to say, *Yes, we're doing this, all of it.* The city moves around us, a blur of cars and people and streetlights, and every step we take feels like a vow.

By the time we reach my house, my chest is tight with everything I can't say yet. With the relief of his words. With the terror of wanting so much. I fumble the key at the lock because he's right there, heat at my side, eyes on me like I'm something worth looking at.

Inside, the quiet wraps around us. My house has never felt lonely, but tonight it feels alive. It feels like *ours.*

Theo presses me gently against the door before I can even set the keys down. His kiss is soft at first, like he knows the weight of the words we left at the table. Then his groans turn low and rough, and the sound deepens. His tongue slides against mine, his hand gripping my jaw, and suddenly there's nothing gentle about it.

We stumble together through the hallway, knocking shoulders against walls, mouths never parting. He's already tugging at my shirt, desperate fingers finding skin, and I let him strip me out of it. I want to be bare for him. I want there to be nothing between us but heat and hunger and history.

In the bedroom, we fall onto the bed, and it feels like the past two nights and completely new at the same time. Because this isn't reunion-sex anymore. It isn't fueled just by nostalgia or the ache of missing. This is us, knowing what we said over dinner, knowing what we promised.

Theo hovers over me, breath ragged. He drops his forehead to mine. "You terrify me," he whispers. "Because I want this so bad."

I slide my hands up his back, pulling him closer. "Then don't be scared. Wanting it is enough."

He kisses me again, and the heat builds fast. Clothes scatter—his shirt tossed, my pants shoved aside. It's frantic and tender all at once, like we're trying to memorize each other in the dark, the slow unraveling of everything we thought we had to hold on to.

We take our time and we don't. We relearn every sound, every gasp, every shiver, until the world narrows again to the sharp edge of release and the soft collapse after.

When it's over, we lie tangled, sweat cooling on our skin, his chest heaving against mine. The city hums outside the window, but inside this room, there's only his breath and the thud of my heart.

Theo's hand drifts to my chest, settling right over it. "Still scared," he murmurs.

I cover his hand with mine, eyes closing. "Good. Means it's real."

And for the first time in fifteen years, I let myself believe it.

EPILOGUE
THEO

ONE YEAR LATER

MOVING DAY ARRIVES BEFORE I'M READY, BUT THEN AGAIN, I don't think I ever could be.

I stand in the middle of what used to be my living room. The walls are bare. The shelves are empty. No hum of the old fridge down the hall, no smell of coffee brewing in the kitchen. Just dust in the corners and light falling through the windows. It feels wrong and right at the same time—like I'm abandoning something, but also finally setting it free.

The house is sold. The car too. Even the beat-up couch I fell asleep on so many times when the nights felt too long and too lonely. I said goodbye to all of it. Packed what mattered into boxes and sent them ahead—clothes, books, the pieces of a life I can't bear to part with. Everything else? Gone.

What I'm left with is two suitcases. One with the essentials, one with the things I couldn't leave behind.

And the firefighter LEGO is tucked safely in my pocket. That's it. My whole life distilled down to baggage I can wheel behind me through an airport.

I should feel unmoored. Instead, I feel light.

Still, I don't leave without a knot in my chest. Gomillion is the place that sheltered me when everything fell apart. It's where I rebuilt my life, where I found steadiness again. My friends here—they saved me in ways they'll never fully know. And saying goodbye to them over beers last night was harder than I expected. They hugged me and told me I was doing the right thing, even if their eyes betrayed how much they'd miss me.

But there's no doubt in me. This is the right move.

Because waiting for me on the other end is Caden.

The flight is long, but my nerves make it shorter. I doze once or twice, jolt awake with my chest thudding, then remind myself where I'm going. What I'm doing. Every time I picture his face at the arrival gate, the anxiety softens.

When the wheels touch down, my pulse quickens like I'm eighteen again, waiting outside the college locker room to see him after a game. I grip the handles of my suitcases too tightly, my palms damp.

And then—I see him.

Caden stands just beyond the crowd, tall and steady and grinning like he's been holding his breath for a year and can finally exhale. His eyes catch mine, bright as they've ever been, and everything else blurs.

I don't think. I don't pause. I drop the handles of my bags and stride forward.

The moment we collide, his arms close around me, strong and sure, his mouth pressing to mine right here in the middle of the airport. No hesitation. No hiding. Just us. People stream around, voices echo through the terminal, but none of it touches me. All I feel is his lips on mine, his smile breaking against my mouth, the relief of finally being here.

We pull back only far enough to breathe, foreheads pressed together, grinning like fools. My eyes sting. His must too.

"You're here," he whispers.

"I'm here," I rasp, my voice shaking.

I want to stay in this moment forever, but then he glances past me, and his smile shifts—softens. "Theo."

I turn. And freeze.

His parents are standing a few feet away.

For a heartbeat, I can't move. It's been sixteen years since I last saw them. Sixteen years since the accident, since the fallout, since everything fractured. My breath stutters. My chest clenches.

But then his mom steps forward, tears already in her eyes, and before I can say a word, she wraps me up in a hug. The kind of hug that swallows you whole, that doesn't let you go even when you think you don't deserve it.

My eyes burn hot. The years between us dissolve. "I'm sorry," I choke out against her shoulder. "I'm so—"

She shushes me, fierce. "No. Enough of that. You're here. That's what matters."

When she finally lets me go, his dad is there, pulling me into an embrace that's just as tight. His hand claps my back, steady and strong. "Took you long enough," he mutters, though his voice wavers.

My tears spill freely now, but for once I don't care. I look at both of them, their faces lined with years but their eyes just as kind, and all I see is welcome.

Behind me, Caden squeezes my shoulder. I glance at him, and his eyes shine too.

The thing is, I know this reunion matters as much to him as it does to me. He broke when we broke. And his parents lost me, too, in their way. They were like second parents once—until the silence swallowed us all.

And now, here we are.

I manage a watery laugh. "Guess I wasn't the only one who got ambushed at an airport."

Caden grins, wiping at his cheek with the heel of his hand. "Fair. You saw me when I reunited with your parents in Gomillion."

"You cried harder than Mom," I murmur, nodding, remembering the time four months ago fondly.

"Lies," he says, but his smile gives him away.

The four of us stand there, tangled in laughter and tears, and there's another shift—it feels like we're no longer carrying the weight of what happened. We're not trapped in the past anymore. We're here, all of us, and the future is wide open.

Caden's mom touches my cheek, her thumb brushing at the tear tracks. "You look good, Theo. Happy."

I glance at Caden, at the man I've loved for more than half my life. "I am," I whisper. "I really am."

His dad nods, his hand firm on my shoulder. "That's all we ever wanted. For both of you."

We gather my bags, and as we walk toward the car, I can't stop glancing at Caden, at his parents, at the way this all feels so impossibly right. The dread that gnawed at me for months—the fear of how this reunion would go when I eventually saw them—melts away with every step. In the last year, every time I came out to see Caden over school breaks, it just never worked out. Once they were traveling, another time Caden and I slipped away to Hawaii together instead, greedy for the kind of time we'd lost. Each trip passed without crossing paths, and part of me wondered if fate was giving me more time to prepare. Turns out I didn't need it.

This isn't about the past anymore. It's about what comes next.

At the car, we pack the bags into the trunk, then pile in —his dad driving, his mom up front, Caden and me squeezed together in the back seat like no time has passed. His thigh presses against mine, and his hand covers mine on the seat between us.

The city lights slide past the windows as we merge into traffic. For a while, it's quiet, everyone breathing the same air, the weight of reunion still settling. Then his mom turns slightly in her seat.

"So," she says lightly, "where to first?"

I glance at Caden. He's watching me already, his smile small but certain.

"Our house," he says.

My chest tightens at the word. Not *his*. *Ours*.

I try to swallow past the lump in my throat. "I was going to say maybe dinner together? Or at least—you could come by for a bit."

Before they can respond, Caden lets out a groan and drops his head back against the seat. "Theo." The word is half warning, half plea.

I raise my eyebrows, pretending innocence. "What?"

"You've been on a plane all day. I've been waiting for this day. And you want to invite my parents over the second we walk in the door?"

His mom laughs softly, shaking her head. "You two haven't changed at all."

"Unbelievable," his dad mutters, though there's humor in his voice.

I grin, leaning closer to Caden. "Maybe I just wanted to have a celebratory drink at *our* house."

His eyes narrow, but he can't fight the way his mouth tips up at the corner. "You just like making me suffer."

"Always have," I whisper, and the way his breath catches makes heat lick up my spine.

From the front seat, his mom clears her throat pointedly. "We'll take a rain check. You two clearly have… catching up to do."

I flush, but Caden's grin turns wicked, like he's proud of the way she phrased it. His dad chuckles low, steering us off the highway toward our neighborhood.

"Don't keep him up too late," his dad says dryly.

Caden groans again. "Dad."

The laughter that spills through the car is easy, unforced. Sixteen years have gone by, but the rhythm is still here, alive between us all.

When we pull up outside Caden's house—the house he's owned for six years but which, starting tonight, will be ours—his mom just twists around in her seat, eyes shining as she looks at me.

"It's so wonderful to have you home," she says softly. "With him. That's what we hoped for."

Something in me cracks open at her words, and I nod, swallowing hard. "Thank you."

They hug me quickly across the console, his dad giving Caden a pointed look that makes him groan for the third time. We climb out and haul my suitcases out of the trunk. His parents wave as they drive off toward their own place, headlights sweeping across the street until they're gone.

And then it's just us.

Caden leans in before I can grab the bags, kissing me slow and deep, one hand cupping the back of my neck. When he pulls away, his smile is pure trouble. "Finally."

"Finally," I echo, and it tastes like forever.

He grabs my hand again, squeezing tightly as we face the front door together. And as I look up at the place that is now our home, I agree. *Finally*. I'm not just stepping into his life. I'm stepping into ours.

GOMILLION HIGH REUNION

Cooper & Jake by Ashley Rayne

Brad & Finn by D.C. Emerson

Sam & Justin by Essie Sloane

Kellan & Emmett by Denver Shaw

Brett & Rowdy by BA Tortuga

Reece & Holden by Jem Wendel

Atlas & Miles by Lincoln Mercer

Dane & Logan by Michaela Cole

Cam & AJ by Hinsel Meyer

Caden & Theo by Becca Seymour

Rhett & Moses by C.N. Marie / Sophia Nixs

Julian & Shane by Katy Manz

BONUS SCENE 1: FIRST CHRISTMAS

THEO

The first thing I smell when I step through the door is cinnamon. The second is roasted turkey, and I laugh because Caden swore up and down his parents weren't going to "go overboard."

"Overboard?" I mutter, hanging my coat on the crowded rack. The hallway is lined with boots, purses, and a suspiciously large pile of wrapped presents stacked like a fort. "This looks like the North Pole threw up."

Behind me, Caden snorts, setting the wine bottles we brought on a side table. "You don't even know the half of it. Wait until you see the living room."

I follow him in, tugging at my sweater like it might shield me from the tidal wave of family energy waiting ahead. I've been bracing for this all week. Not because I don't want it, but because it's been more than sixteen years since the Brooks and North families sat around the same table. That kind of history doesn't vanish overnight.

But when I step into the living room, all my tension breaks.

Both families are here—my parents on the couch, my mom already chatting with Caden's mom like no time has passed, my dad gesturing animatedly as he argues about football with Caden's dad. My sister, Amelia, is perched on the arm of the chair, sipping cider and watching the chaos like she's at the theater, while my nephew, Connor, is eating snacks and focused on whatever game he's playing on his phone.

And in the middle of it all, the Christmas tree stands tall, lights blinking in an uneven rhythm, ornaments clumped wherever eager hands placed them. At least three separate strands of popcorn garland hang crooked, evidence that the decorating committee had more enthusiasm than skill.

Caden leans close, murmuring, "Told you. North Pole."

I grin, and before I can respond, my mom spots me. "Theo!" She's on her feet in an instant, arms wide, pulling me into a hug that smells like pine needles and her vanilla lotion. "You made it."

"Pretty sure I live here now," I tease.

She swats me lightly, but her eyes shine, and when she looks over my shoulder at Caden, the warmth in her gaze only grows. "And you. Come here."

Caden obeys, and she hugs him just as tightly. Watching it makes my throat ache. A year ago, I wasn't sure I'd ever see this—my mom treating him like the son she once considered him, like all those lost years never happened.

Dad claps him on the shoulder next, then goes right back to arguing with Raymond, Caden's dad, about whether the Eagles' defense is actually worth anything this season.

I glance at Caden, who just smirks. "They've been at it since tip-off. Don't bother stepping in unless you want a headache."

Amelia raises her cider in salute. "I've got five bucks on your dad, Caden. He's ruthless."

The chaos swirls around us—laughter, clinking glasses, the smell of food drifting in from the kitchen—and I let myself sink into it. It's noisy, messy, imperfect. And it's everything I didn't realize I'd been missing.

Dinner is a spectacle. Both moms insist on serving enough food to feed a small army. The table groans under the weight of turkey, ham, collard greens, macaroni and cheese, corn bread, mashed potatoes, and a sweet potato pie I know I'll regret eating two slices of but won't resist.

We squeeze around the table, shoulders brushing, knees bumping. Conversation overlaps, bursts of laughter erupt, and for once, no one seems to care that nearly two whole decades of silence used to separate us.

"Remember when you boys tried to ride those trash can lids down the ditch bank?" Caden's mom says, eyes dancing as she passes the rolls.

My dad nearly chokes on his wine laughing. "They hit the mailbox at the bottom, and Theo cried like he'd broken his leg."

"I did not," I protest, cheeks heating. "I scraped my knee. There was blood."

"Barely," Caden mutters, smirking into his mashed potatoes.

"You cried too," I shoot back.

"Because you cried first." He grins wider, and the table bursts into laughter.

The stories keep coming—basketball games, school dances, summer barbecues. Every memory stitched together like a quilt, patching over the years we lost.

After dinner, we migrate back to the living room for presents. Paper flies, bows end up stuck to foreheads, and Connor starts a contest to see who can stack the tallest pile of discarded wrapping without it toppling over.

Caden and I end up on the rug, leaning against the couch, half watching, half whispering to each other. His knee presses into mine, his fingers sneaking over to tangle with mine under a blanket someone tossed aside.

"This is better than I thought it would be," I admit softly.

He glances at me, eyes warm. "What, you thought our parents would brawl in the kitchen?"

"I don't know what I thought. Just… not this." I gesture to the chaos around us, the laughter spilling loud, the sight of my mom and his mom elbow to elbow in the kitchen doorway. "It feels like we never lost all those years."

His hand tightens on mine. "Maybe we didn't. Maybe we just… paused."

The words settle in my chest like a promise.

As the night winds down, people drift into smaller conversations, yawns sneaking in, pie plates abandoned. I find myself standing in the kitchen, washing dishes with my mom while Caden loads the dishwasher. She bumps her shoulder against mine.

"You're happy," she says softly.

I glance at Caden, who's balancing three plates at once, his grin wide when he catches me watching him. "Yeah," I whisper. "I am."

She nods, satisfied. "That's all that matters."

When it's finally time to leave, hugs make the rounds again. Promises of brunch tomorrow, leftovers to share, more time together. No one wants to say goodbye just yet.

Outside, the air is cold and sharp, stars scattered overhead. Caden slides his arm around my shoulders, pulling me close as we walk to the car. Behind us, our families linger on the porch, waving, voices still carrying in the night.

I lean into him, heart full. "This was a good Christmas."

He presses a kiss to my temple. "The best."

BONUS SCENE 2: THE FIRST BIG FIGHT

CADEN

The fight doesn't start with shouting. It starts with a buzz.

My phone rattles against the counter while we're plating dinner—ginger chicken Theo marinated and rice I somehow didn't burn. The screen lights my palm: Ollie. He's rehabbing a stubborn hip, and if he texts at 7:00 p.m., it's not for fun. I glance at Theo. He's carrying the skillet like it's a trophy he earned. He *did* earn it. He cooked. I promised no phones for the rest of the night.

The buzz comes again.

"Go ahead," he says lightly, without looking at me. The tone is featherlight and somehow still heavy.

"I'll be quick." I step away to the kitchen doorway, answer, and wedge the phone against my ear. "Hey. You okay?"

It's not a crisis. It's tightness and nerves about tomorrow's televised panel, and he wants to run through his post-workout routine one more time. I talk him down, adjust his sequences, promise to text the cues. It takes six minutes. Maybe seven. When I slide the phone face down onto the counter and turn back, dinner's plated, chopsticks set, water glasses filled.

Theo's smile is easy and not easy at all. "Everything okay?"

"Yeah," I say, and I can hear the apology already clinging to the word. "Sorry. He's anxious."

"It's good you picked up." He taps the rim of his glass with a fingernail. "I know he counts on you."

I sit. The food smells like ginger and garlic and something piney from the little herb plant Theo's coaxing to life on the kitchen sill. We eat together as the day slides off our shoulders in steam.

Halfway through, he says, "I had the scrimmage today."

I look up. "How'd it go?"

"We won. The kids executed the press and didn't fall apart in the third. Malik hit a corner three he had no business taking. I yelled. He grinned. I pretended to be mad. It was great."

I smile. "You're good at this."

He shrugs and stares at the table. "You said you'd come."

It lands like a subtle body shot; I feel it two seconds later. He's right. I'd planned to sneak out early from the studio, promised I'd be the loudest voice in a gym full of parents. I'd texted at four that I was running behind; at five that I might not make it; at five forty-five that I was sorry.

"I'm sorry," I say again, because it's true. "A session overran, and one of the machines broke. It ate the whole afternoon."

"I get it." He pushes rice around. "I do."

"What's wrong, then?"

He laughs once, a small, tired sound. "I don't know. Maybe I just wanted to look up and see you there. It's my first season as assistant coach, you know? I've been teaching at the school for two years, but this—this is different. It feels like something I've been working toward finally matters in a new way. And I just... wanted you in the bleachers." He lifts his eyes. "It's stupid."

"It isn't stupid." I reach across the table and lay my hand over his wrist. He's warm. He always runs warm. "I should've been there."

He nods like he's filing the apology in a drawer he's not sure he'll open later.

We finish dinner. We wash dishes together, easy choreography we've learned—I scrub and rack; he rinses and dries. The firefighter and hot dog guy LEGOs on the shelf watch like crooked guardians.

It would end there if the universe were kinder. But I'm a fixer, and the text I promised to send to Ollie is still unsent. When Theo goes to put leftovers in the fridge, I sneak the phone, thumbs moving.

> Me: Band order: green, yellow, red. Two sets, not three. Breathe on the eccentric. Don't hold your breath on camera.

"Really?"

I freeze. Look up. Theo's at the fridge with a container in his hands, brows up, mouth more disappointed than mad. Somehow that's worse.

"It's thirty seconds," I say, and then I hear it—defensive, small.

"Mm." He slides the container onto the shelf with the kind of careful he uses when he wants to slam something and won't. The door closes softly. "I thought tonight was no phones."

"It was—"

"It's fine," he says, palms up.

It isn't fine. The word sits between us like a thin crack in glass, and every exchange to follow is a tap.

"I'm not trying to be an ass," I say. "He needed—"

"You *always* need to send one more text, take one more call, fix one more thing." There's no heat in his voice yet, just exhaustion. "I moved here. I'm trying to build a life that isn't just *your* life. Sometimes I want to feel like I'm not competing with your clients for you."

It's clean, and it hits.

I set the phone down and take a breath that doesn't get all the way in. "I hear you."

"Do you?" His eyelids flutter like he's bracing himself. "Because two hours ago, I wanted to turn and see you at the baseline, and I didn't. And now, after we finally got home and made dinner and sat down, I still can't get more than forty-five minutes without you disappearing into someone else's problems."

I open my mouth with the wrong sentence perched on my tongue—*I never asked you to move here.* I swallow it so fast it hurts. I'm not going to throw that knife.

"I'm sorry," I say instead, and I mean it. "I am. I want to be there. For the scrimmage. For dinner. For this." I gesture to the room, to the stupid plant, to the little LEGO. "Sometimes I don't know how to stop being responsible for people."

"I don't need you to stop. I need you to choose." He meets my eyes. "Sometimes choose *me* first."

Something hot and helpless darts up in me. "I *do* choose you."

"Tonight, you didn't."

It's simple and it's true, and I hate that it is.

"I choose you most of the time," I say, which is not the right answer.

He huffs, jaw set, and looks away. "Okay."

We have rules, the two of us: no walking out, no cruel words, no raising our voices through the walls we share. Ask for a time-out instead of slamming a door. We made those rules in a soft morning when love felt easy. Rules are hard to remember when your chest feels like it's full of bees.

"I'm going for a walk," he says, not unkindly.

"I'll come."

He shakes his head. "I need ten minutes without an audience."

He slips on his shoes, picks up his keys, and is gone.

The door closes quietly. The house exhales. I stand in the kitchen with my apology in my chest and realize how old this ache is for me. Being the one who fixes. Being the one who fails when fixing looks like attention instead of action.

I go to the sink and brace my hands on the edge until the wood creaks. On the shelf, the firefighter LEGO looks like he might be shrugging. *Well?*

"Yeah, yeah," I tell him. "I know."

I don't text. I don't call. I clean the counters. I put away the dishes he left to air dry. I take the phone, put it in the drawer by the microwave, and close the drawer on it like a tiny casket. Then I sit on the bottom stair and count my breaths until ten minutes have passed, and then five more because pride is a loud bird, and I don't want it to fly from my mouth when he walks back in.

The door opens. Theo's cheeks are pink from the wind. He looks tired. He also looks like he came back on purpose, which is what love is, most days: coming back on purpose.

"Hey," I say.

"Hey."

We stay a few steps apart like we're both radioactive. He rubs a hand over his face, sighs, and leans a shoulder to the wall.

"I'm sorry," he says first, and it startles me. "I shouldn't have said *always*. That wasn't fair. It's not true."

"I'm sorry," I say, almost stepping on his words. "I shouldn't have checked my phone. I said I wouldn't. I broke my promise."

We stare at each other—two men balancing on a wire we strung together.

He nods at the stairs. "Sit with me?"

We sit side by side, knees touching. The silence is different now. Not brittle. Expectant.

"Can I try again?" he asks.

"Yeah."

He inhales. "When you didn't show up to the scrimmage, what I *felt*—not what I *thought*—was that I didn't matter. Which is unfair because I know I do. But the little kid part of me that never quite stopped waiting for someone to choose me first? He had a day." His mouth moves like he wants to smile and can't find the right muscle. "And then dinner—when you checked the phone —I felt like… I was in second place again. And I hate that feeling, because I chose you. I moved, I left my life, I'm starting over. I don't regret it. But sometimes I need proof that I'm not the only one leaping."

I turn his hand over and press my thumb to the hollow of his palm. "Thank you," I say quietly. "For telling me what it felt like instead of making me guess." I clear my throat. "Can I try to explain my side?"

He nods.

"When you said I always choose work, the part of me that's been keeping us afloat—me, the studio, the staff, the clients—he got loud and mean. He said, *See? You're failing even when you're doing your best.* And the part of me that's still eighteen and scared of disappointing you said, *He'll leave.* Neither is true, but both are noisy." I laugh a little hollowly. "Also… when you drive at dusk, my skin crawls, and I comment on your speed like a back-seat old man, and it annoys you, and then we're both mad, and that's also the accident talking, and I'm trying to be less of a mess about it."

He huffs a laugh that shakes at the end. "You're not a mess. You're a human being with scars. Same."

"Same," I echo.

We breathe. My heart creeps down from my throat to my chest where it belongs.

"I'll do better about boundaries," I say. "No phones at dinner. If I say I'll be somewhere, I'll be there. If something blows up, I'll tell you *before* it blows up so we can decide together, not after."

He nods slowly. "I'll... be kinder about the scrimmages. Text you sooner. Ask instead of expect. And I'll stop using *always* and *never*. I know better."

We sit with our little treaty. It feels like a real thing, not just words. It feels like we saved something.

"Hey," he says after a beat, and there's sunlight in it. "I'm sorry about the 'competing with your clients' line. I don't want to compete. I want to... be the place where you don't have to compete."

I rest my head against his shoulder. "You are."

He kisses the top of my head, then catches my jaw and tips my face. The kiss he gives me is not apology and not hunger. It's a seal. It's how we sign our names.

Still, hunger shows up anyway. It always does when relief lets your body remember it's alive. His hand slides to the back of my neck, and my breath stutters like a missed step and then finds the beat again. I shift closer on the stair. We knit our knees and shoulders and mouths together. His fingers curl in my shirt, not to pull, just to anchor.

"I hate fighting with you," he murmurs against my lips.

"Me too." I nose his cheek. "But I like making up."

He huffs, and the laugh warms my mouth. "Yeah?"

"Yeah."

We stand and fall into each other in the loose way of people who know where the furniture is even in the dark. The house seems to understand and gives us room. We cross the living room, and the hot dog guy watches over our truce. In the bedroom, the city hums outside, and rain starts gently tapping the window like a soft metronome.

We take our time. Not to prove anything, not to erase

the fight, but to remind ourselves of the reason we bother arguing carefully: because this matters. Because *we* do. Kisses deepen, slow as turning pages. Hands map familiar routes until they feel new. There's laughter when my elbow gets caught in the throw and his sock tries to escape under the dresser, and then there's quiet when everything narrows to breath and skin and the long, patient press of closeness.

I whisper his name like a question, and he answers with mine like a promise. We move together the way we learned—checking in with a glance, a breath, a word. When we crest, it isn't fireworks. It's tide. Full and sure and pulled by a gravity we stopped pretending to fight.

After, we sprawl messily across the bed, legs tangled, his head on my chest. The room smells like rain and ginger and us. He marks lazy circles over my ribs with a fingertip. My phone is still in the kitchen drawer, and I feel better for not caring it exists.

"Hey," he says, voice soft and sleepy.

"Mm?"

"Date nights. Thursdays. No phones. Nonnegotiable."

"Yes, Coach," I say, and he snorts. "Also—game nights. If your kids play, I'm there."

He blinks up at me. "Thank you."

A few minutes later, he adds, "And if you need to take a call because a client is in pain? Take the call. Just... tell me. Let me be on your side, not your obstacle."

"I will."

He yawns, the kind that starts in your toes, and settles heavier on me, warm as a quilt. I stare at the ceiling and think about the boy I was once, the man I am now, the accident that could have ended us, the studio I built out of grief and grit, the place Theo is building for himself here —kids running drills under his voice, a new team calling him Coach.

We will fight again. Love isn't a spell that keeps you from being human. But we have rules. We have this bed. We have the firefighter and hot dog guy on the shelf and a plant on the kitchen sill and a drawer where the phone goes to sleep at night.

He mumbles something I don't catch.

I kiss his hair. "What?"

He lifts his head and says, "You choose me," like he's testing the words.

"Every day," I say back.

He smiles into my skin and drifts. The rain keeps time. I keep watch long enough to feel the truth of it settle: We didn't break. We bent—alone at first, and then we learned the shape of bending together.

Tomorrow, I'll text Ollie during business hours. Thursday, I'll make a dinner reservation and leave my phone at home. Next week, there's a home game, and I'll be at the baseline in a shirt emblazoned with the school's name like I've belonged there all my life.

Tonight, I wrap my arm around the man I almost lost and didn't, and I let sleep take me like a tide.

ABOUT THE AUTHOR

Becca Seymour is a British/Aussie author and the #1 gay romance best seller of the True-Blue series. Known for "steamy and endearing" and "emotionally profound love stories" (InD'tale Magazine) her books have been nominated for multiple RONE Awards.

Becca has a sweet tooth for marshmallow-hearted monsters, swoon-worthy supernatural studs, and everyday guys and basketball players with hearts of gold. If you like your MM romance sweet, spicy, and occasionally action-packed, slip into stalker mode and fall hard for her True-Blue and Minnesota Eagles men—and maybe a shifter or monster two.

To check for updates head to my website:
HTTPS://BECCASEYMOUR.COM
HTTPS://LANDING.MAILERLITE.COM/WEBFORMS/LANDING/
R9F0I4
Plus, join my Facebook group:
HTTPS://WWW.FACEBOOK.COM/GROUPS/ROMMANCEWITH
BECCALOUISA/
Join me on Patreon for early chapters, special edition books, reveals, & more: patreon.com/
BeccaSeymour

facebook.com/beccaseymourauthor
instagram.com/authorbeccaseymour
bookbub.com/authors/becca-seymour
tiktok.com/@beccaseymourwrites